THE QUEEN'S DEVICE

THE QUEEN'S DEVICE

Copyright © 2024 by Brittany Mack.

This book is a work of fiction. Names, characters, businesses, organizations, places, events and incidents either are the product of the author's imagination or are used fictitiously. Any resemblance to actual persons, living or dead, events, or locales is entirely coincidental.

Contact info: writerbrittanymack@gmail.com

Cover Design by Maria Spada Designs

Map by Cartographybird Maps

Formatting Template by Derek Murphy

Chapter headers and dividers made with Canva Pro

ISBN : 979-8-9900737-1-5

First Edition : May 2024
10 9 8 7 6 5 4 3 2 1

THE QUEEN'S DEVICE

Fortitude Press LLC
Copyright 2024 by Brittany Mack

For the ones who wonder if they're good enough—
Here's to knowing that you're worthy, exactly as you are.

And for Nathan, who was the first to push me back to writing.
Thank you for not letting me give up on this dream.

CASTLE GROUNDS
THE HOLD
BARRACKS
CASTLE CIRCLE
POINTE
SALFORD
THE GROVES
THE ISLAND
OF
MIOTA
THE MONORAIL LINES
YORKINSON
KENDALL
CAPE
OUTER ROADWAY
THE FORT

PART ONE

"The king or queen of Delldova blood holds the sole duty of making decisions to ensure MIOTA's preservation. Therefore, anyone who acts, speaks, or thinks against the monarchy is a threat to MIOTA's prosperity and future."

—Introduction to the Treaty of Miota

CHAPTER 1

I never stood a chance against the thick sheet of rain plummeting from the sky. The droplets slapped against my face and weighed my ashen hair into heavy ropes. Even the marrow in my bones seemed soggy as I ran through the streets, but the upward curve of my lips remained unspoiled. I'd waited seven years for Commencement; it would take more than a thunderstorm to dampen my mood today.

Rain rolled off me in droves as I approached Council Hall, the metallic structure in the exact center of our city, Pointe. I peeled my white uniform dress from where it clung to my legs and wrung out its skirt before entering the domed building.

I expected solace from inside Council Hall's lobby. Instead, I found the space congested with other eighteen-year-olds, also here for Commencement. Voices bounced off the tiled ground and collected high in the air, near the dark ceiling.

I lowered a shoulder and weaved through the crowd before a stray umbrella expanded, slamming into my side. I groaned, ready to confront someone my age. But I craned my neck and found a looming middle-aged man brushing rainwater off his umbrella. I recognized him immediately, and my stomach dropped to the floor.

Great. Merick Northe. Not only was he Top-Tiered, but he held one of the ten coveted spots on Pointe's executive council, making him one of the most powerful people in the city.

"I, uh . . . Sorry, Mr. Northe." I lowered my gaze to the puddles of water on the ground.

Mr. Northe's dark eyes glinted as he noted my appearance. "I forgot Lows don't get umbrellas," he mumbled to his long-legged wife, not bothering to mask his sneer.

A burning bite rose in my throat at the sound of Mrs. Northe's responding laughter. "There are *lots* of commodities they don't get, Merick."

"I'll be in the Middle Tier soon," I blurted.

Mr. Northe's lips split under his full mustache. "Keep telling yourself that. Whatever gets you to sleep at night, right?"

I opened my mouth but promptly shut it and let frustration steadily pool in my chest. There was no sense arguing with an executive council member; besides, he would see for himself once Commencement started.

I would make it out of the Low Tier and into the Middle Tier. I *needed* to. I couldn't live another moment tethered to the bottom of society.

Brycon Northe, Mr. Northe's son and my peer, rolled his eyes at our interaction, though I wasn't sure whom he was targeting. "Come on, Dad. You want a good seat, don't you?"

I lifted my eyebrows at Brycon and offered a grateful flash of teeth, though he didn't look my way. The Northes disappeared down the curved hallway.

The crowd thinned as citizens trickled toward the auditorium. Those from the Middle and Top Tiers were given umbrellas as a basic commodity, so they didn't have to dry off as meticulously as those in Pointe's Low Tier—those like *me.* I focused my energy into wringing out the ends of my hair.

Why did I think surviving the rain would be the most difficult part of today? Weather was fleeting; Tiers were enduring. I was unlucky enough to be born into Pointe's Low Tier, and if my Tier didn't change during Commencement, it never would.

On our island nation of Miota, the only structure in the world, it was essential that every citizen played their role in helping the country thrive and persist into the future. Part of that duty required all eleven-year-olds to complete a week-long endeavor of aptitude, knowledge, and personality tests to match each child with their optimal job.

I should've matched with a career as destitute as my place in society—something like farming, which was our city's assigned task from the monarchy, carried out by Pointe's Low Tier.

Even if I hadn't followed in the footsteps of most Lows by matching with farming, the odds weighed heavily toward matching with another Low-Tiered career, something like sanitation or produce packing.

But I'd managed to match with *medicine,* a career reserved for those in upper Tiers. I'd had secret help to make it happen, sure, but I hadn't expected the training to truly come to fruition. After all, it was a known fact that Lows didn't match with careers meant for other Tiers.

Yet, here I was. An abnormality.

I tried not to get ahead of myself, but I didn't know how I *wouldn't* increase my Tier today. I'd already done the hard part of matching with medicine seven years ago. All Mayor Peabody needed to do now was authorize moving me into a Tier that aligned with my job, because no one in their right mind would trust a doctor from the Low Tier.

It meant that only the hour-long Commencement ceremony stood between me and my escape.

I peered out the front door at the crack of more thunder, and my mouth twitched at the lanky figure dashing toward Council Hall. He yanked the door open, and rainwater tumbled off his fingers and mop of dirty-blond hair.

I snorted. "Should've known you'd show up late."

My best friend glared at me before ripping off his fogged glasses, which revealed his blue-green irises swirling with amusement. "You know, Corinn, it takes *work* to look this good—"

"Yeah. For *you*, it does."

Salem shot me a sloppy grin. He and I assessed the rain's damage, taking in his pressed black suit, now heavy with rainwater, and hair that might've been coiffured before, though I'd never know from its current limp state. Salem's next words echoed my thoughts. "By the moon, I think my mom is going to kill me."

Salem's mother, an executive council member like Mr. Northe, would undoubtedly boil with anger upon seeing her only child show up to his Commencement sopping wet.

"You're doomed," I agreed. "Where's your umbrella?"

"Didn't have time to grab it."

I wrinkled my nose. "Think of a better excuse during the ceremony, or your mom might *actually* kill you."

Salem nodded and shrugged his suit jacket off, wringing out the sleeves. We both winced at the puddle of water now pooling beneath him. "Okay, I give up. Time to head in, right?"

I dug my panel out of my dress's pocket to check the time displayed on the handheld device's glowing screen.

"Yep." I nodded. "Let's go become doctors."

Nerves bit at my insides. If my Tier didn't change now, it never would. In Pointe, and probably across Miota's four other cities, Tiers defined citizens—they dictated every aspect of life. My specific job placement within Pointe's hospital wouldn't matter if I stayed a Low.

I padded after Salem into the auditorium, dodging his trail of water. My eyes adjusted to the dull lighting. Most people already sat in their assigned seats and whispered with those near them.

I spied Salem's parents, silent and stiff, in their seats behind the graduates. Mrs. Redding was easy to find with tendrils of fiery red hair framing her face. I ripped my gaze from her before she saw me. She didn't keep it a secret that she despised her son befriending a Low—even though I *had* attended medical classes with Salem for the past seven years.

We weaved through the auditorium's rows of chairs, eventually splitting up because of the assigned seats' alphabetical nature.

It was odd, seeing every eighteen-year-old in Pointe sitting and speaking together, as if we were all friendly with each other. As if this wasn't the first time we'd *all* congregated. Though there weren't physical barriers between those of different Tiers, the strong social stigmas did the trick of keeping us relatively confined.

As I slunk through chairs, I gave friendly nods toward others dressed in white, signifying their place in the Low Tier alongside me. Meanwhile, the Middles in gray and the Tops in black saw my white clothing and averted their gazes on instinct alone.

From what I could tell, about one-third of the graduates wore gray, and only a few handfuls wore black, naturally commanding attention in the inky color. The rest of us—just over half the graduating class—were Low-Tiered. The stratification reflected Pointe's general population.

I found my seat between Gianna Hyte and Brentin Keins. Gianna, in her gray dress, offered me a neutral smile. We ran into each other often in the medical hallway of Pointe's Top-Tiered school. There was always a certain solace with Gianna; though a few Middles usually matched with medicine, the occupation was ruled by the Top Tier, leaving us both out of place.

"I can't believe we're *finally* here!" she squealed. Her afro, adorned with sparkling clips, bounced as she bobbed her head. "You think we're the lucky ones to change Tiers?"

"Hopefully," I answered, forcing a friendly grin to mask my trepidation. Of course she wanted to change Tiers. Who *wouldn't* want to upgrade their Tier, given the chance? Would Gianna rise to a Top over me rising to a Middle?

To my right, Brentin Keins huffed and adjusted his stark black suit. I'd never talked to the Top-Tiered boy before; he'd gone to school for either engineering or mechanics, I couldn't remember which.

Before long, Pointe's frail mayor, Tanith Peabody, took the stage and commanded all attention. I sucked in a breath. It was time to leave the Low Tier.

"Welcome, graduates," Peabody started, his voice as thin and wavering as a leaf on a pruning plant. The microphone's amplifier couldn't even help his meek sound. His old age was nothing new, though it was accentuated with each of his public appearances.

"You're all gathered here at today's Commencement to be given your rightful and deserved places in society. Seven years ago, you were all matched with an optimal career track, and you've spent the time since then training to succeed within your match. Today, you will cement your place in the workforce—these decisions are not only for the good of our city, but for our nation and the royal monarchy."

He cleared his throat, sending a shrill noise through his microphone. Numerous people shuddered in their seats.

"Speaking of the royal monarchy, it is custom for a member of the royal family to present each graduate with their assigned job."

Yes. The *other* reason I was erupting with nerves: I knew exactly which royal was here today. I set my shoulders back and focused on Peabody's words. I didn't need *that* distraction yet.

"Your schooling and workforce mentors have decided your

placements. They've taken your skills and talents into account, so each of you will be placed where you are best fit and most useful in Pointe. Now, with that said"—the mayor pivoted to face one of the stage's wings—"it is my *honor* to present His Most Royal Highness, heir to the throne of Miota, Prince Kierran Cassius Delldova."

The room collectively straightened and held their breath as the Prince of Miota emerged into the spotlight.

His uncropped hair, a regal mix of brown and blond streaks, managed to appear graceful under his gold crown. He held his chin high and pulled his shoulders back, walking with poise.

I suppressed a grin. It was so unlike the Cass I knew in secret, always teasing his uncle or sauntering around the greenhouse we met in.

I'd started going to the industrial greenhouse, deep in Pointe's farming sector and fully abandoned, when I was eight, alongside Bernard Bartholomus, a Top-Tiered doctor. I was young enough that the gravity of the situation didn't fully sink in: Bernard's brother just so happened to be Miota's king. Before King Abner married our current queen and was whisked away to the castle, he'd lived and grown up in Pointe's Top Tier.

Bernard had met with me multiple times a week in that abandoned greenhouse to teach me how to match with medicine, come my career screening at eleven years old. Even after I'd matched with medicine, our lessons in the dilapidated building didn't end.

I didn't know why Bernard cared about me, but his motives became even *more* diluted once Prince Kierran—who I just knew as *Cass* now—began showing up four years ago. The day the prince first arrived, I thought Bernard and I were going to be arrested by Pointe's sentinels. After all, breaking into the industrial building wasn't exactly legal. But Miota's future king had joined our antics instead.

He was begrudging toward me at first. Once, I'd told him no one was forcing him to spend time with me, and he'd simply paled.

I'd bitten my tongue after that, wondering why I dared to speak to the prince so bluntly. But, over time, Cass and I had warmed up to each other. Now, I'd even dare to consider him a friend—a secret and powerful one.

Cass cleared his throat on stage and began his practiced speech I'd heard a dozen times within the mossy walls of the greenhouse, where his voice had absorbed into the rotting wood and tangled vines. It was the same message Mayor Peabody just gave: our assignments today would reflect our abilities, to best serve Pointe and Miota. Cass then acknowledged the graduates and executive council, followed by the mentors and teaching teams present from Pointe's three schools.

Each school, ideally, would encompass one Tier, since almost everyone matched with a career track that aligned with the Tier they were born into. But there were sporadic citizens, like Gianna and me, who hiked across Pointe daily to attend another Tier's school. Medicine was only taught at the Top-Tiered school, which meant I'd walked across our city too many times to count—and I had the calluses on my feet to prove it.

Cass's eyes drifted along the crowd of graduates, and upon finding me, he held my gaze until my face turned hot. I swallowed audibly once he looked away, but a few moments later, his sights settled back on me. Soon, we were caught in a delicate game of sharing and avoiding eye contact.

"By the moon," Gianna whispered, leaning toward me. "I think His Highness keeps *looking at me!*"

I didn't know how to respond.

Cass then arrived at the longest part of Commencement: presenting jobs and Tiers. Most found Commencement to be a redundancy. We'd worked for seven years on a specified track; general careers wouldn't change now. But with Tiers also on the line, this ceremony was everything to me. If I didn't gain freedom from the Low Tier today, I never would.

"Jethro Ambers," Cass started, reciting from the alphabetical list of names. "Job assignment: electrical engineer. Tier: Top." A stale applause followed.

Next was Grey Avalon, Low-Tiered like me. He was assigned to farming unit twelve, which was led by none other than my mother, Cindra Januski. Grey would be gifted the opportunity to leave Pointe's sturdy, heavily surveilled brick wall every day to till the earth and harvest the crops grown in the fields outside our city.

Over a dozen names passed.

"Gianna Hyte. Job assignment: hospital pharmaceuticals. Tier: Middle."

Her Tier hadn't changed, which hopefully meant mine would . . .

I held my breath, bracing for Cass to give my assignment.

"Corinn Januski." His voice softened as my name glided off his tongue. I met his hazel eyes, and his mouth twitched upward.

This was it. I didn't need to be given a Top-Tiered position; something Middle-Tiered would be enough. *Anything* would be enough, as long as it wasn't—

"Job assignment: asympton research. Tier: Low."

CHAPTER 2

My heartbeat bounded through my ears as the world blurred into violent shapes amid the auditorium's gloomy lighting.

I was . . . still in the Low Tier. How? This was a *joke*.

But Cass continued to the next name—Brentin Kines, monorail engineering—without revoking my assignment.

Asympton research.

Low Tier!

The job wasn't the worst. The disease, asympton, claimed lives of countless citizens each year—my grandfather, aunt, and uncle were among the numbers. Though creating an antidote for the relentless pathogen was crucial, every effort had proven pointless so far. Even with the number of autopsies and decades of research conducted, asympton's presentation appeared different in each victim and still puzzled scientists. The only commonality was the tiny microbe that appeared in bodies *after* they'd dropped dead without warning. Scientifically speaking, it was baffling. I was happy to help try to find a cure.

But my Tier! It was a slap in the face. I was still stuck as a

Low. For the rest of my life, I would gasp for air and fight to keep from getting buried.

My Top-Tiered mentor, Dr. Alaric Harrison, had sent his message clearly with my assignment. He wanted me separated from living patients and practicing doctors; he wanted me to rot in Pointe's lowest Tier. I was supposed to rise today. And now . . .

"Salem Redding," Cass said. I tuned back in to the prince's lulling voice. "Job assignment: surgery apprenticeship. Tier: Top."

It was the placement Salem wanted. His success was a single ray of sun piercing through my mind's brooding clouds. Thunder clapped outside, startling a few, but I welcomed the rage as I ruminated on my subpar placement.

The final applause signaled the end of the ceremony. All formation broke loose once a gaggle of castle staff escorted Cass off the stage. Most Pointeans bombarded the prince, and every Top claimed their high status as reason enough to speak to him. I, however, stayed glued to my seat, weighed down by my future.

Salem found me, claiming Brentin's now-empty chair, and looked at me the same way he did sick patients. He offered pity and consolation, and I wanted neither.

I just wanted to be *worth* something.

"Congratulations," I said, mustering my best version of a smile. But my lips felt stretched across my teeth, and the corners of my lips wouldn't rise.

"Same to you," Salem said. "Asympton research is important. And with your personal connection to it . . ." But he knew the job assignment wasn't the problem.

I slumped back in my seat, looking at Cass and his entourage: two Queen's Guard members and his courtier from the castle. "Too bad *he* had to deliver the blow." I sighed.

Salem knew who I meant. He was the only other person on

the island who knew about Cass, Bernard, and me meeting in Pointe's abandoned greenhouse. One day at twelve years old, Salem followed me to the greenhouse, eager to learn from the renowned doctor Bernard Bartholomus himself. Though Bernard was hesitant to have another citizen partake in our covert meetings, the doctor grew to love Salem—like most who crossed his path did. When Cass began showing up at the greenhouse two years after that, Salem was let in on the secret.

"Speaking of the prince . . ." Salem said with an amused glint. "I hope you don't think you just got away with all *that*." He waved a hand toward Cass and the trailing crowd.

My cheeks warmed. "What do you mean?"

"The way he said your name? The way he looked at you during the ceremony? I can't believe I never noticed. *Someone* has a crush."

"I do not!" I whispered harshly, crossing my arms. That was a line I couldn't even *think* of crossing. Cass would marry a Top—he wasn't given an option in the matter.

"I didn't mean *you*, Corinn."

Before I could dissect Salem's implication, Cass approached us with his staff. The prince stopped at the aisle in front of us, and Salem and I sprang to our feet, doubling over in a bow.

"Bowing?" A smile rang through Cass's voice. "By the moon, I thought we were friends!"

A chill ran through me. We were only friends because of our illegal meetings.

"We are," Salem said. "But that doesn't mean we're rude."

Cass broke his formal stature and embraced us one by one. I basked in his delicate touch. The pressure of his fingertips left little sparks on my back, and a chill surged down my spine. Tops watched with shrewd, prying eyes.

"This isn't very secretive of you," I whispered into his neck, trying to keep a level voice.

Cass had somehow evaded detection while traveling to and from the greenhouse for four years, a mystery I'd tried solving to no avail, with Bernard and Cass refusing to answer my prodding questions. If Cass wasn't careful now, though, he'd reveal his secrets. To any onlooker, there would be no logical reason for our next king to embrace a *Low*.

"Couldn't help it," Cass said as he pulled away. "I can go hug the other graduates, maybe plant a kiss on Brycon Northe's forehead—"

"Stop." I rolled my eyes at him.

Something about Cass's statement thickened the air, and Salem must've sensed it, because he adjusted his glasses on the bridge of his nose and left to find his parents.

My peripheral faded to black as I blocked out the eyes glued to Cass and me. The *Prince of Miota*. My ears buzzed with the onlookers' probable thoughts.

Frizzed hair, damp white *dress, Low Tier* . . .

"I wanted to ask you something," Cass said. He must've taken what I said to heart because he now stood stiff with a few healthy feet of distance between us. "It's about my Courtship."

My stomach twisted into too many knots, but I nodded.

Cass's Courtship. His search for a wife. It was the most anticipated event of the decade, scheduled to start in just over a month. Each of Miota's five cities were stratified into three Tiers, and the young women from every city's Top Tier would gather so Cass could choose a wife from the bunch.

I couldn't dwell on it. The thought of him dating a herd of Miota's Top-Tiered women and falling in love with one of them made my lungs compress.

Cass cleared his throat. "I wanted to ask if you'll be in my Courtship."

The ground tilted beneath me. I took a small step forward to keep my balance. Was he serious? Cass's eyes didn't indicate this being one of his usual jokes, like the innocent kind he'd play on his uncle. And if this *was* a joke, it was a cruel one.

I opened my mouth to speak, but my tongue turned to stone. Me? In Cass's Courtship? It was illegal; I wasn't in the Top Tier.

The prince shifted on his feet, taking a more reserved stance. "You're allowed to decline, you know. I won't take it personally, and I hope we can still be friends . . ."

"That isn't it," I said, finding my voice. "Of *course* I want to." But my words hardly eased the tension wound tightly around us. "I'm just . . ." My eyes darted around the auditorium as I dropped my voice. "I'm a *Low*."

Cass's plastered smile didn't budge. "You humble me, Corinn. I'm the only heir to the throne—I think I can bend my mother's rules."

His mother. Her Most Royal Majesty, Queen of Miota. I schooled my breathing to stay even. "I . . . I'll think about it. Your Highness."

Cass blinked at his title coming from my mouth before he turned to his courtier, dressed in the monarchy's color, navy blue. "Max, will you pull up my panel's tag?"

The staff member, whose blond curls rivaled the paleness of my own, produced a panel from his pocket and navigated to a screen showing a unique combination of circles and squares: a panel tag.

I knew the drill. I dug my device from my dress pocket to scan the tag, which would link this panel to mine and allow us to send messages between devices. But when I scanned the tag, a message flashed on my screen.

Link Detected: Kierran Delldova
Link Failed. Try Again Later.

I frowned, revealing my screen to Cass.

He huffed. "Mom has strict settings on my panel. I'll try to convince her to change some of them."

Cass referring to the queen as *Mom* never failed to make me queasy.

"Speaking of Her Majesty . . ." Max started. "We need to go. Best not to keep her waiting, you know."

"Already?" Cass said, wrinkling his brow. He concentrated back on me. "I'll figure out the panel link. I also hope you'll consider my offer." He raised the corner of his mouth. "You'd make it far, Corinn."

My cheeks warmed. I bowed so Cass didn't notice.

Once Cass left in a limo, the crowd followed.

Commencement was over, and I had nothing to show for it.

I didn't bother running home; I was already wet. I took my time, each step slower than the last. Getting home meant encountering my family, and I didn't have the energy to tell them I was staying a Low.

Warm raindrops pelted my skin as I left Pointe's epicenter and headed toward the farming sector, which claimed the northeast part of our circular city.

Pointe was laid out in a series of geometrical, ring-shaped streets, each one encircling the last, with Council Hall at the very center. I walked along a straight pathway that cut through each ringed street, like the spoke of a wheel, toward the farming sector.

If I'd risen to the Middle Tier, I'd get to move out over the weekend. I'd leave the stuffy farming sector, trading it for one of the communal homes of unmarried adults, usually shared by three or four roommates. But I'd stay in the farming sector with my family for the foreseeable future.

I'd memorized the farming sector by now. Clotheslines spun tightly beneath the oppressive wind, and water collected in the stone road's gaping holes. Stenches of damp fertilizer floated through the air, making me scrunch my nose.

My dress, heavy with water, weighed me down as our shack seeped into view. The two front steps groaned as I climbed to the front door.

The living room, immediately to the right of the entryway, was full, catching me by surprise. My parents sat on our worn couch with Grandma Yvette, and my brother Theo stood with his arms crossed. My younger cousin Tellie lay on the floor, using her palms as a pillow behind her head.

My parents knitted their brows at the sight of me. Theo, older than me by one year, bit his lip.

Ice crawled down my spine. "What? What is it?"

Everything remained silent, except for the sound produced from our projector mounted on the wall.

The flatscreen technology clashed with the shack's obsolete and minimal furnishings, but each household in Miota had a projector to deliver news. For the first time since Queen Julia's mother died three years ago, our projector shone. Footage showed a limo swallowed by plumes of gray smoke billowing from the vehicle before simmering out under the rain.

Theo's eyes, the same icy shade as mine, landed on me from across the room. "Where've you been?" my brother asked. "The prince, His Highness . . . he was just . . . how can it *be*?"

I gnawed the inside of my cheek. Had someone taken pictures of Cass and me speaking? If so, they'd leaked quickly, even for *Pointean Gazette*'s standards.

I finally opened my mouth. "Is this about his Courtship?"

My family's trepidation morphed into confusion.

"There won't be one *now*," Theo uttered. "Their limo crashed going back to the castle. Only one person survived it, and it wasn't . . . we don't . . . Miota doesn't have an *heir*."

"*What?*" My brother's words left me sucking for air. "What are you *talking* about?"

Theo blinked. "The prince is dead."

CHAPTER 3

"Dead?" I choked as the world around me froze. "But . . . he was just here!"

My brother was lying. He *had* to be lying, because I didn't know what I'd do if it were the truth.

If Cass was really . . .

"Dead," a faraway voice infiltrated my brain. It belonged to the queen, Her Most Royal Majesty. Cass's mother grimaced, evident even through our grainy screen, as she spoke on the projector.

"Today, on May 22, 26 JD . . ." Her Majesty paused every few words to regain her composure. "My son, the Prince of Miota . . . has died."

The feed cut back to the scene of the crash, just as Queen Julia's face crumpled, the precursor to a sob. Our projector once again showed the thick rolls of smoke and charred car. My stomach roiled as I wondered if Cass had died on impact with the bulky stone wall surrounding the castle grounds or if he'd been forced to endure the scorching flames as he burned to death. They'd barely missed the open gate, the breach in the castle's wall beckoning them inside.

My vision swam. I must've staggered out of the living room and into our house's single bathroom because I was at the toilet's basin when I vomited. After spilling what little sat in my stomach, I slumped against the wall.

Today was supposed to be the best day of my life, the day worth waiting seven years for. But Commencement had come and gone, and now Cass had, too. And here I was, a hollow shell on the bathroom floor.

This was the rest of my life. Low-Tiered, alone, and unworthy of anything better.

I didn't know how long I stayed keeled over on the cool linoleum floor, but long enough to expunge all my tears, and long enough to dry heave into the toilet a few more times. When I stood, I stepped to the sink and splashed water onto my face. I drank out of my cupped hands, nursing my acidic throat.

Though a rectangular piece of reflective glass hung above the running water, I avoided my visage. I didn't want to see myself for what I truly was. I couldn't face this fate yet.

When I opened the door, my young cousin jumped from her seated spot in the hallway and ran into the bathroom, frantically slamming the door behind her.

Someone huffed from down the hall. I pinpointed Theo, and more tears welled in my eyes.

I'd never known life without my brother. My earliest memories contained Theo telling me cautionary tales in the dark, long after we'd been tucked into bed. He'd always protected me.

Or, rather, he did what he *thought* protected me. While Theo believed happiness could be secured by settling oneself into a padded and locked cage, I'd always thought life was a lot more intriguing outside the confines we were bound to.

"Doing all right?" Theo's voice bounced off the hallway's hardwood.

I glared at my brother and crossed my arms. "No." I wasn't sure what else to say, where to begin. "How'd they manage to crash, anyway?"

"They're saying the limo driver had a cardiac episode—I figured you'd know more about that than I do."

I nodded numbly.

"Congratulations on your placement," Theo said, changing the subject. He walked toward me with his hands jammed into his pockets. "I had to scroll through *Gazette* articles about the prince, but I finally found news of Commencement. Asympton research is important. If anyone can find a cure, it'll be you."

I mustered a smile. "Thanks. I'm not sure how far I'll get with it, still being Low-Tiered, but . . . I'll do my best."

Theo tilted his head, and I braced myself for what he'd consider to be good advice. "You're still a researcher, no matter your Tier. You'll do your job the same."

"If that were true, there'd be other Low-Tiered doctors," I countered. Everyone in Pointe knew *Tiers* dictated our way of life. People could only make it as far as their Tier would let them, and as a Low, there wasn't much breathing room.

Theo pursed his lips. "Corinn, you have the best job in the entire Tier. No other Low works in the hospital, unless it's as janitorial staff. If I were you, I'd take the good fortune graciously."

Tellie emerged from the bathroom, humming and stalking down the hallway. I *was* given the opportunity to do research on the disease that killed her parents. But Theo was wrong; this wasn't good fortune. If it were, I would've left the Tier. But there was no escaping who I was.

I was still sentenced to life as a Low, which meant never

having enough food or freedom. And my ephemeral chance of escaping through joining Cass's Courtship had died alongside him.

I traipsed down the hall, though Theo trailed, nearly stepping on my heels as he waited for my response. "Corinn," he prompted.

I whirled on him. "I don't want to talk about it!"

He furrowed his brow, his panel hovering in front of his face. "It's not that. *Pointean Gazette* released photos from Commencement. And you're speaking to Prince Kierran."

It took every ounce of strength to keep my face from contorting. I couldn't give any implication of how personal the prince's death was.

Bernard and Cass constantly warned Salem and me not to tell anyone of our meetings, no matter what. I assumed the rule still stood, even now, which meant I had to bear the weight of my friend's death nearly alone. Only Salem and Bernard could share this pain with me.

"What did he say to you?" my brother asked. He jutted his panel toward me, the screen lit with Cass smiling down at me.

My heart snapped further. *I can't do this right now.*

"It was nothing," I grumbled, turning to hurry down the rest of the hallway. I stopped in front of the second of our shack's two bedrooms, which belonged to Theo, Tellie, and me; Mom, Dad, and Grandma claimed the other bedroom. "I . . . need a second, Theo." Warm stomach acid rose into my throat.

"Sure." But Theo lingered outside, even after I closed the door. As he shifted his weight, the hall's floorboards grunted underneath him.

I crawled onto my cot, the only thing that was truly *mine*. The worn quilt atop my cot always brought me comfort—it had been made in the city of Yorkinson, where all of Miota's consumer goods were produced, and had belonged to Grandma for decades. She gave it to me when I was young, after I'd fallen in love with its deep blue color.

The first time Grandma let me sleep with this quilt, I'd just started training with Bernard to match with medicine at my career screening. I trusted Bernard, since he was the king's brother and a Top-Tiered doctor himself. It was the first time I'd been gifted with hope. The first time I thought I stood a chance at leaving the Low Tier.

This quilt had always contained that same light. But now, its musty smell brought visions of death and decay instead. That was what Cass had become, and it was all my life would amount to.

I buried my face within the folds of the quilt to smother my sobs.

CHAPTER 4

Their Majesties held a ceremony for Cass on Saturday morning. Though it was televised on our projector, I didn't watch. I stayed on my cot and tried not to listen to the fuzzy sounds bleeding into the bedroom. But the harder I tried *not* to listen to the livestream, the more I heard.

By the sound of it, Their Majesties also acknowledged the limo crash's singular survivor. I blocked my ears, refusing to hear about the lucky courtier who'd avoided succumbing to the brick wall's impact *and* persistent battery fire.

As a mourning day, citizens were only permitted to leave their homes to go to the Common, Pointe's dining hall, at their Tier's scheduled mealtimes. It left my mind painfully empty, forced to dwell on the thoughts that gnawed my brain raw.

Cass is dead. I'm in the Low Tier.

At Commencement, Mayor Peabody said our placement was the spot we fit best in society, to help keep Pointe thriving. Clearly, my skillset and worth weren't equal to that of a doctor, the job I'd worked the past seven years to acquire.

I was *best fit* in the hospital's basement, among the corpses. I was best fit for the Low Tier, to starve and stay shoved in the farming sector.

Over the next day, my thoughts grew to eat me alive. It was Sunday, and all those who'd gone through Commencement started work tomorrow morning. It would be my first day in a lifetime of stagnant nightmares and dejected promises.

As my family and I walked to the Common for Sunday night's dinner, I still ruminated on the upcoming week as nerves braided together inside me.

I would conduct research that was so far unsolvable, which was fitting, really. Why shouldn't I partake in something useless? It matched the meaningless hollow of the rest of my life.

But guilt found me as I looked at my widowed grandmother and orphaned cousin. How could I resent the possibility of curing the disease that wounded them so badly?

It was a short walk to the Common, which was the single perk of living in the farming sector among the Low Tier. Those from the upper two Tiers had a much longer walk to the cement dining hall, the sole provider of food in Pointe.

I learned at a young age, as all Pointeans did, that you either show up to the Common at your Tier's assigned mealtime or you starve—*especially* as a member of the Low Tier. We couldn't afford to skip a meal when we hardly received enough food to sustain us.

At the door, my family and I pulled out our panels to verify our allotted number of rations per meal as Low-Tiered citizens. Tellie's rations were programmed into Mom's panel since my cousin wouldn't receive a panel until after her career screening.

Because the island's food was finite, it was the most strictly regulated commodity in Miota. Top Tiers were gifted with three rations per meal, an amount Salem said filled him entirely. Some Tops even purposefully puffed out their bellies, showing off their well-fed statures.

Middle Tiers ate two rations per meal. I'd heard it was enough to satisfy hunger until the next meal. And Lows were only given one ration, the minimum amount necessary to keep a person alive. If the Low Tier didn't house the laborers who supplied Miota with food, I was convinced the monarchy would simply let us wither away. The circumstance taunted me if I thought about it enough—our Tier provided the food, yet we starved.

My stomach growled as we worked through the line to receive our ration. Eddison Ross, a Middle-Tiered server, scraped the bottom of a large metal dish, once filled to the brim with chicken and potatoes. I flinched at the shrill noise.

Mr. Ross glanced at us. "Januski family," he called off. "Three vitamin puree, three regular rations."

We nodded. While Theo, Tellie, and I received one ration of whatever meal was made by Pointe's cooks, my parents and Grandma received a nutrient-packed brown paste instead. *Vitamin puree.*

Their Majesties recognized that Pointe's assigned task of farming was physically demanding. One ration wasn't always enough for the farmers, who toiled in the fields six days a week. If farmers showed clinical signs of malnutrition, they could apply to receive *two* rations per meal. The catch was these rations weren't served in the limited amount of normal food, but rather in a synthetic mush pumped with essential calories and nutrients.

I'd always thought the farmers forced to ingest the mush were being treated like plants being fertilized, kept alive only to carry out jobs for the good of the island.

We waited for Mr. Ross to obtain our family's food. He filled ramekins to the one-ration mark and jutted his hand out, serving us without further acknowledgment.

Common treatments toward me, as a member of the Low Tier, included either being ignored or jeered at. I usually preferred the latter, as painful as it was—at least, if I was scorned, I knew I was worthy of acknowledging.

I reached the six-foot monitor at the front of the line, where I scanned my panel. Upon pulling up my name and allotted ration, the monitor completed my body scan. After verifying I only held one ration of food and no more, its technology unlocked the metal door to the dining hall's main cavity.

I put my weight into pushing the door open, and the chatter of voices washed over me, reverberating off the dark walls. I weaved through the maze of tables occupied by the rest of Pointe's sunburnt and sweaty Low Tier. Virtually every farmer was on a mush diet—sorry, *vitamin puree*—and some still dropped dead while out in the fields.

The Top and Middle Tiers would've eaten at least an hour ago by now; they'd already eaten their multiple allotted rations and cleared out.

I drew in a ragged breath and trudged to our assigned table in the back of the Common. Grandma and Tellie followed while the rest of the family completed their body scans in the locked serving area.

Next to me, Tellie chattered away to Grandma. Those two were especially close, having lived together under my aunt and uncle's roof until three years ago. Tellie's parents died of asympton only weeks apart, forcing Grandma and Tellie to move in with us.

And just like that, my thoughts were back on asympton. My career placement. Commencement, then Cass. And *that*— remembering Cass was dead—was a perpetual scalpel blade carving through my heart.

When I was busy, I could almost pretend it wasn't real. He was still in the castle, and we'd still meet in secret with Bernard and Salem.

But then the lie would falter, and reality would sink into my skin with biting teeth.

Two days ago, Cass told me I'd get far in his Courtship, and that same day, he died. I never deserved a prince, and fate knew that.

We finished the trek to our table. Grandma offered me a smile as I sat across from her, next to Tellie. "That hunk of chicken looks good, Corinn."

"Are you patronizing me?" I half-joked before shoveling a bite of mashed potatoes into my mouth.

Grandma's gray eyes softened. "You? Never."

As far as my family knew, my grief wasn't for Cass, but for my placement of staying among the Low Tier. They didn't know the cacophony replaying within me, forever seared in my memory.

You'd make it far, Corinn. Cass's words were now a piercing mock to what could've been if I'd been allowed to escape my fate.

"What's patronizing?" Tellie asked. "That's when you go frozen, right?"

I crumpled my brow, amused. *"Paralyzing?* That's way different, Tel."

Tellie's career screening was next year, and if she studied hard, I believed she could match with something better than farming. I made a mental note to work on vocabulary with her, even though I knew career screening results comprised of much more than knowledge learned in school.

I recalled ten years ago, when Bernard started teaching me how to properly align with medicine. It was the first time we met in secret, in the abandoned greenhouse.

"You're going to teach me the doctor stuff?" I asked.

"No. You don't need to learn the doctor stuff," he replied. "You need to learn how to learn. *Rationality and decisiveness; those are qualities they want in doctors."*

I didn't know what those words meant, and I didn't know who 'they' were. "Shouldn't I learn how to save lives?"

"No. You learn medical content only after you match with it." Bernard sighed. "Look, kid, you'll either do what I say, or I'll leave, and you'll match with farming—"

"No," I gasped. "I hate the Low Tier."

"Then you'll listen to me."

Theo, Mom, and Dad arrived at our family's table, one by one. My parents' mush sloshed around as they set their ramekins on the table.

"Excited for your first day of work?" Dad asked me, fixing his graying eyes on my face. He didn't mean harm, but the question sent my throat bobbing without warning as I dug for an answer.

"Yeah." My voice cracked. "I guess."

"Bennet would be so proud of you," Grandma said, referencing her late husband.

"Is *that* patronizing?" whispered Tellie at a decibel heard by the whole table. Theo threw her a confused glance.

"Kind of," I admitted, smirking at my cousin. "But thanks, Grandma."

I got away without speaking much after that. I took small bites of chicken to savor the bit of protein as best I could.

Grandma grunted at the table's first opportune silence. "The potatoes in our greenhouse are ready. Anyone care to help me prep them? Executive operatives are coming in the morning to collect. They're sure to be . . . *thorough*, with their new employees."

I repressed a sneer at the mention of executive operatives. It was a job solely for Middle-Tiered citizens, just as farming was wholly for the Low Tier. Pointe's ten-member executive council had operatives whose entire job involved searching citizens' greenhouses to meticulously tally the food we grew, ensuring we never kept any for ourselves and we maintained our quotas.

If families didn't meet weekly quotas, they didn't get the next week's rations, essentially sealing their deaths. I'd seen it only a small number of times, but it was enough of a cautionary tale.

"Can't," Mom answered. "Turns out, I'll have *three* new members in my farming unit tomorrow."

Praises swelled around the table, and Mom beamed, wrinkles appearing alongside the joy on her face.

"Why didn't you say anything sooner?" I smiled at my mother. "That's probably the most of any farming unit."

"It's not a competition," Theo mumbled.

I parted my mouth at my brother across the table. Now wasn't the time for one of his stupid lessons. "I *know that*, Theo. But three new recruits means Mom runs a tight group. That's a huge compliment."

"Thank you, Corinn," Mom hummed, reaching her hand across Tellie to squeeze my own.

Theo slurped his fluff of potatoes, and though he no longer spoke, I saw his mind churn as his eyes feasted upon me.

"Stop looking at me like that," I grumbled.

"Like what?" Theo blinked the scheming look off his face.

"Like . . . like you're about to give me one of your little speeches!" My voice soared in pitch while my emotions coiled even tighter within me. With my troubles piled up too thickly, I knew it was only a matter of time before I snapped and my composed façade unraveled completely.

"About how competitive you are?" Theo asked innocently.

"By the moon." I seethed, propping my elbows on the table to rest my chin atop my knuckles.

"Stop, you two." Dad waved an aimless hand. "Just be happy for your mother."

That's what I was doing. Before I voiced the thought, my panel chimed concurrently with Theo's, their low, dull tones signifying a message from the monarchy.

From Cass's mourning parents.

Theo and I shared a delicate look before looking at our devices, our bickering already forgotten.

I glanced at the message, complete with an image of the royal insignia.

WHILE THE ENTIRE NATION WEEPS FOR THE TRAGIC LOSS OF HIS ROYAL HIGHNESS KIERRAN CASSIUS DELLDOVA, CROWN PRINCE OF MIOTA, MEASURES ARE IN PLACE TO SECURE THE FUTURE OF MIOTA.

ALL CITIZENS OF MIOTA BETWEEN THE AGES OF EIGHTEEN AND TWENTY-FIVE ARE RECEIVING THIS MESSAGE. YOU ARE INVITED TO VIE FOR THE CROWN IN THE TOURNAMENT CALLED ACCOLADE, WHERE YOU WILL BE GIVEN THE CHANCE TO BECOME MIOTA'S NEXT PROSPEROUS HEIR.

IF YOU APPLY TO ACCOLADE AND ARE SELECTED TO COMPETE, YOU WILL BE TAKEN TO CASTLE CIRCLE FOR THE OPPORTUNITY TO SHOWCASE YOUR SKILLS AND VIRTUES TO THEIR MOST ROYAL MAJESTIES. THE QUEEN AND KING WILL DEEM WHO IS WORTHY OF THE CROWN.

ALL APPLICATIONS ARE DUE BEFORE FRIDAY, MAY TWENTY-NINTH.

My jaw slackened. "We'll go to Castle Circle?"

Theo's eyelids peeled back. "There's . . . no way. We're Lows."

"*Castle Circle?*" Dad hissed, leaning toward Theo to peer at the panel message.

Grandma cocked her head, and I slid my screen across the table.

"Who's going to Castle Circle?" Tellie scrunched her face.

"And why?"

I swallowed, turning to my cousin as my mind whirled. Their Majesties had moved on from Cass. They'd devised a competition for the crown, and they were inviting *every* young adult—no matter their Tier—to *Castle Circle*.

Castle Circle existed exclusively for Miota's Top Tier. It was a glittering location outside of any cities' limits, on the northern part of Miota, near the castle itself. Salem had described it as a long street of buildings, fountains, and glass windows. *Where food never runs low, and spirits always run high!* he'd add in insincere delight, mocking his mother's coined phrase.

"Theo and I can go," I answered Tellie.

"Maybe." Theo laughed. "*If* we apply."

I blinked at my brother. Sometimes, I wondered how we were related. I didn't know it was possible for anyone to turn down a chance to visit Castle Circle, especially someone from the Low Tier, who was otherwise sentenced to never experience anything more indulgent than monthly dessert.

"Of course," I agreed. *If we apply*. And I would.

"And get accepted," Theo added.

Yes. That was necessary, too. But nothing could deter me from this elation, the first spark of happiness since Cass died.

The Common's lights seemed brighter. The rest of my chicken seemed to fill me up. After we washed our dishes and cleared out of the Common to walk home, the crickets chirping outside Pointe's brick perimeter wall were more lyrical.

And I was happier. Because, despite Cass and my placement and my Tier, *this* was my silver lining, the glowing moon against the lightless sky.

This competition, Accolade, could save me yet.

CHAPTER 5

In the morning, I met Salem outside the Common, following the Top Tier's breakfast time. Tops reported for breakfast last each morning, which granted them the luxury of sleeping late.

I'd eaten with the Low Tier over an hour ago. By now, all the farmers would be toiling away in the fields outside Pointe's robust wall. Our Tier always ate first so farmers made it to the fields before the sun rose past the Fort, the forty-foot wall sheathing Miota's entire perimeter, protecting our island from the surrounding ocean.

The Fort was built by Cass's ancestors to keep out the harsh forces of nature, like turbulent winds and relentless waves. I should've been thankful for the Fort and the haven it created, yet I constantly cursed the stone wall, wishing to see the ocean just *once*. Stories of monsters dwelling outside the Fort, like Donna Dragon and Gilmore Goblin, rampaged through the heads of young children, but I never bought into the tales. The Fort was just another wall to smother me.

Salem approached, shooting me a grin and wrapping an arm around my shoulders. We walked in step away from the Common, toward the city's center rings. Council Hall lay in the heart of Pointe, in its exact middle. Around it, buildings of executive operative, mechanical, and engineering offices curved so they formed one ring-shaped structure that captured Council Hall. The hospital, a perfect O-shape, contained the offices inside *it*.

The hospital's size and location were a blessing and a curse. While its shape allowed access from anywhere in Pointe, it took ages to walk the circumference, and it split into too many specialty wards to be considered one cohesive building.

Even with all the room, I'd be stuffed in the basement, out of sight.

"You nervous?" I asked Salem, just to hear his voice. It would counteract my nerves as always. Well, not *always,* but at least since we stopped hating each other and chose to become friends after spending our first year of medical classes in an academic rivalry.

I still recalled Salem, after a full year of trying to get me kicked out of medical classes, admitting I was one of the only ones with real intelligence—the rest of our class was smart enough to absorb a textbook, but too dense to truly *think.* We decided to work together after that.

Looking back on our studying sessions, I didn't know when I started considering him my best friend; it came as gradually as the changing seasons. But here we were, eighteen years old and graduated, and my life was nothing without this Top-Tiered boy.

"Never," Salem declared. "It'll go how it goes, and that's how it goes."

I snorted. "That makes no sense."

"It does—good morning, Ms. Dillins!" Salem picked up his arm draped around me to wave at Neena Dillins, an engineer, as she clomped past us. "Think, Corinn. There's nothing I can do between now and starting work in five minutes, so why worry about it?"

"To prepare yourself for the horrendous possibilities," I answered, only half joking.

"Waste of time." He adjusted his glasses on the bridge of his slim nose. "Only *one* of the possibilities will happen, and what if I don't think of the right ones?"

I thought I rolled my eyes, though it was too instinctive to know for sure. "Point made. Either way, *I'm* nervous."

"No need to be," Salem said with such confidence, I almost believed him. We reached the hospital and stopped under one of its bridges crossing over the stone road. "I already know you're going to crack the code to asympton in . . . hmm, less than a year." I gawked. "Seriously, Cor. You've got the brain for it."

I made a face at the awful nickname. "I think I'll be happy if there's an antidote in my *lifetime*." My words deflated me. "See you later, then?" It was time for our first day.

"Yep. Go change the world, Dr. Januski." Salem slapped my shoulder before walking to find his correct entrance.

I chewed on the inside of my cheek and entered the hospital's main door. I scanned my panel, logging my time here to ensure my food rations, before making my way toward the basement.

The cement stairwell seemed to shrink in front of me, and each step downward was a hammer to my chest.

This was my sentence . . .

For now, I reminded myself. I'd apply to Accolade, and with Salem's help, I'd be accepted. From there, I'd compete for a few weeks, until Pointe's executive council saw I was worth something. Maybe they could still raise my Tier after all.

The basement was a long hallway adorned with sporadic metal doors, most of them indicating storage closets. But one of the doors led to a stale, white room, complete with worn slate tables and faded wooden benches.

The city of Cape manufactured furniture. Clearly, our supplier executive—one of Pointe's executive council positions—hadn't prioritized acquiring new lab equipment in a *long* while.

A blonde woman with a birdlike frame, Sigrid Ova, tapped a stick of graphite on one of the tables. Her eyes floated toward me, and she gave a warm smile.

"Corinn Januski?" she hummed. "I'm Dr. Sigrid Ova, head of asympton research. I'm glad you're here."

Warmth filled me. "Thank you, Dr. Ova—"

"No time to waste. I was shocked to walk down here this morning and find the lab empty. You're a Low; you'd already eaten breakfast. Why weren't you here?"

I opened my mouth, but no noise came out. Medical classes ran on the Top Tier's timeline; which meant that, for the past seven years, I had extra hours in the morning after breakfast and at night before dinner, given the mealtime disparity between Tops and Lows.

Dr. Ova waved a dismissive hand. "Never mind. Tomorrow morning, you go to breakfast and come straight here afterward. Same goes for the end of the day. You don't leave until the Low Tier's dinner time." Before I could react, she compiled carbon paper and tapped the stack with a skeletal finger. "I *am* glad to have a Low, though. Run these notes up to the compost receptacle, and we'll talk about your duties once you're back." Her olive eyes narrowed toward me.

I inhaled to speak, but Dr. Ova held up her index finger. "No time to waste! Get on it."

I crumpled my brow, ensuring I flashed my confusion toward the task. Dr. Ova only gave a smug expression as I intercepted the carbon paper.

I glanced at the pages on my way up the staircase, hoping to glean insights on asympton. *Microbes, replication, lytic cycle* . . . I crumpled the notes before tossing them into a receptacle.

A ball of dread tangled within me as I returned to the basement. Dr. Ova said she wanted a Low, and something told me her reasoning didn't involve having me help conduct research.

When I returned to the lab, two men whispered with Dr. Ova in hisses that capered across the floor. Dr. Ova's eyes flicked upward, and she hushed the others. "These are the other members of the asympton team," Ova sang, her dulcet tone seeping into me slowly, like that of poison. "Dr. Ekhart and Dr. Fuge." She pointed to the former, a round man with a thin sweep of gray hair atop his head, and the latter, a stocky man with a cropped afro.

"Nice to meet you." I nodded. "I'm Dr. Corinn Januski."

Dr. Ova's lips thinned into a fake smile. I recognized staged expressions too well after eighteen years in the Low Tier. "Well, not *doctor*. But, yes, this is Corinn Januski."

I felt my face and neck bloom with heat. "What do you mean, not a doctor? I completed the track in school, and I was assigned to research at Commencement, same as you all."

Dr. Ova tapped the table, letting her nails *clack* against the hard material. I tried not to balk. "My dear, we're Middles, and you're a *Low*. If your mentor wanted you to help us conduct research as a fellow doctor, he would've had Mayor Peabody raise your Tier."

"I matched with medicine!" My voice rose. "Seven years ago!" If I'd matched with something like the janitorial track, as Theo had, I would've expected to come here and clean after them. But I'd been sent as a fellow researcher.

Or so I'd thought. Clearly, Dr. Ova had different plans. The worst part was, as much as I hated her mentality, she wasn't wrong. I was a Low, and Tiers dictated everything.

"That, you did," Dr. Ova agreed. "Which is why I'm keeping you around—as long as you're useful. You know where compost is now, which is good. But one wrong move or refusal to listen, and I'll have a wonderful time demoting you."

I let out an amused noise at her threat. My nerves, once aimless with anxiety, were now steeled with rage at the mention of a demotion. While Pointeans had seven years—from career screening to Commencement—to practice each facet within a career track, some still weren't able to meet their job's demands upon their official assignment. These people were demoted to farmers, Pointe's default job, which guaranteed them a life in the Low Tier. To live in a shack and eat one ration, regardless of who they were beforehand.

If Dr. Ova demoted me, my job would finally match my Tier. There'd be no hope of ever escaping Pointe's bottom.

While I wasn't sure if Ova held such a power, I didn't want to find out if she was bluffing. I *couldn't* get demoted; the thought suffocated me.

"So, you want me to . . . what?" I said after composing myself. "Clean after you? Do the work of a Low? And if I don't, you'll demote me?" I let my ice-colored eyes glow in unforgiving flames.

"You're finally catching on." Dr. Ova motioned toward the shelves of clear bottles. "Our chemicals need to be organized. You can start with that."

My throat worked shut. I was convicted to *live like this* for the rest of my working life. As I walked past my superior, the words tumbled from me without thought. "I *hope* they accept me into Accolade. Anything to get out of here—"

"You applied?" Ova snipped, grabbing my wrist. I wriggled in her grasp, but her slim digits held me with surprising force.

"Not yet, but I will—" I shook my arm. "Let go of me!"

Ova released me and cackled. The other two joined. Anyone in the basement would've heard them. "Why would they . . . ever accept a . . . a *Low* into Accolade?" Ova wiped under her eyes between laughs.

My vision went red, and I crossed my arms, hoping my angry tears didn't escape. Why did Cass have to die? If he were here, I'd join his Courtship, and he could've hopefully chosen me as Miota's next queen. But he was gone, and I was left to fend for myself.

"They could," I blurted.

"If they accept any Low," said Ova, "it won't be *you*. Because I won't let you apply."

My mouth gaped. "You can't do that. I'll apply if I want."

Dr. Ova shrugged, lifting her brow, unamused. "Fine. Get demoted, then, for going against my wishes. It's all the same to *me*."

My anger stilled, staying suspended in my chest before dropping into my stomach. I grew nauseous. "You'll get me demoted for applying? You can't do that."

Ova sighed. "Like I've already said, Corinn, you'll be demoted as soon as you stop following orders. I'm in charge down here, so what I say is what goes—whether it's about running carbon paper to the compost or not applying to Accolade."

I took advantage of her pause. "And *why* don't you want me applying?"

"Because you're a Low," she gritted out. The men nodded in agreement, refusing to meet my gaze. "It's unnatural, delusional. No Low in their right mind would think they have a shot."

The pang in my chest was undiluted grief. If Ova knew about my friendship with Cass, she never would've spoken such words. The prince had once been a means of escaping this life.

I clenched my hands into fists. "For someone who seems to want me around to do your dirty work, you seem awfully eager to demote me. How does that make sense?"

Dr. Ova sneered, her temper bubbling beneath her skin. The lab was otherwise silent. Had I been too blunt? Finally, she spewed her poison. "You don't belong here, Corinn. I'm not sure how you matched with medicine seven years ago, but such an anomaly hasn't happened before or after you, so I have to assume it was a fluke, and this is all a mistake. While you're here, we'll use you. But the second you try getting *smart* with me, you'll be more trouble than you're worth, and you'll be a farmer . . . where you belong."

While a thousand retorts grew on my tongue, I didn't dare open my lips to speak them. Anything I said now would undoubtedly get me demoted.

Dr. Fuge cleared his throat amid the painful silence. "Corinn? I'll show you how we organize the chemicals." Though he sounded annoyed, I appreciated his attempt to help.

I followed him to a slate table housing dozens of colorful substances. Even from across the room, we were still well within Dr. Ova's wrath.

"Don't apply," Fuge muttered while rifling through bottles. "No matter how rough your life is now, it *will* be worse if you apply for that tournament." The fear in his dark eyes pressed into my mind, molding my expression into one of concern. "You won't have a job here anymore. She's serious about demoting you. You understand that, right? I'm trying to look out for you."

I nodded once. "Thank you," I whispered. Except, I knew he wasn't truly regarding my well-being. He only wanted me here, same as Ova, to complete the work deemed worthy of a Low.

My one chance of leaving the Low Tier flitted out of my reach—just as it had three days ago. And this time, Cass wasn't here to save me.

Fate mocked me. *Again.* I was stuck here with Dr. Ova, and if I tried escaping by applying to Accolade, I'd end up in a spot much worse.

I knew the Low Tier was merely an ember compared to the inferno that came with a life of power in a better Tier. I could try stoking my flame, but with one wrong move, I'd extinguish it entirely.

CHAPTER 6

As the week continued and Accolade's application deadline approached, unrest settled into the crevices of Pointe until our city steeped in chaos. Flocks of screaming Top-Tiered girls flooded the streets, and throngs of backlash from older employers jammed *Pointean Gazette* articles. I wondered if Miota's four other cities were also in an uproar over the competition.

Miota's five total cities were cut off from each other, each civilization tucked within its own set of walls, which bred superiority complexes. Though Pointe needed the other cities' commodities, hence our weekly trading, we believed we were the best—and identical paths of thinking likely transpired in the other cities.

"I just don't understand why *anyone* can apply to Accolade," Dr. Ova groaned to Dr. Ekhart, knowing her bleating voice carried to my ears across the lab. "Why not only Tops? That's how His Royal Highness's Courtship would've been."

Tears pricked my eyes at the mention of the doomed Courtship. Theoretically, it would've been Top Tiers and *me*.

I spent my hours completing monotonous tasks that made me want to gouge out my eyes with a spare scalpel. I learned my way around the chemicals, taking care regarding the poisons and noting their appropriate antidotes. I organized carbon paper in pristine stacks; I sharpened graphite into perfect points. How would I survive a lifetime of being throttled like this?

Wednesday promised a rare autopsy day. Only a few bodies were set aside for research each month, and the remaining deceased were floated out into the ocean. I was instructed not to touch any of the corpses, naturally, and was ordered to instead sanitize goggles and surgical tools for the three researchers. I grimaced at Dr. Ova's incisions as she tore into one of the bodies—she never would've made it on a surgical floor upstairs. Pride swelled within me when I remembered that was where Salem was.

The three researchers clocked out before me to make it to the Common for the Middle Tier's assigned dinner time. It left me to deal with the aftermath of the autopsies alone, which included mopping flesh off the floor and incinerating the cadavers' remains. I was thankful everyone else had left; I barely contained myself as I erased all traces of these poor Pointeans I knew by name.

I couldn't go on like this, as Sigrid Ova's personal minion. I hadn't gone to school for seven years just to ultimately do the work of a Low. I'd spent so *long* outrunning myself and my Tier, and once on the cusp of freedom, I'd fallen back to the bottom.

An angry grunt escaped me. Though I'd heard of Dr. Ova in my years—as I'd heard everyone's name in Pointe at least *once* before—I never imagined she'd be so insufferable. She was still relatively young, maybe thirty at best, so she had a long working life ahead of her. I wondered why she was in charge here instead of her senior, Dr. Ekhart.

For the next few decades, *this* would be my life. Scrubbing tables and floors. Incinerating the guts of people I'd seen walk the streets of Pointe only weeks before. Being hushed whenever I gave input. Leaving work to eat my single ration in the Common. Going home to my family's shack to sleep and do it all again in the morning. Repeat. And repeat, and repeat.

I wanted to *scream*. None of this was supposed to happen. I wasn't supposed to stay in the Low Tier, and Cass *wasn't supposed to die*.

I collapsed to the floor, which sent a shock through my knees as they thudded against the cold ground. I stayed there, joints vibrating, unable to rise. Unable to hold myself.

It fit the mold of my life well.

In times of complete despair, I went back to the small pocket of time when the prince had wanted me. When he'd asked me to join his Courtship, even though I was in the Low Tier.

It hardly helped once I remembered Cass was nothing but a memory now. But being stung by the past seemed better than thinking of my shredded future.

I met my family in the Common for dinner, where we recounted our days. Dad, a supply packer, stored a record number of broccoli stems into crates to be traded with Miota's other cities. Tellie prepped for her career screening at school. If she matched with farming next year, she'd begin her rotations through the different farming units and packing centers, so by the time her Commencement came, she'd receive an optimal placement. Theo, a janitor at the *Pointean Gazette* studio, relayed the gossip he heard while mopping the floors in a production room. My brother said two employees theorized who'd likely get accepted into Accolade.

"Any insider news on the competition?" Dad asked Theo.

My brother shook his head, which displaced strands of his hair. "It's all just speculation. They're predicting who'll be accepted, who could win, that sort of thing."

"And let me guess," I chimed, "they're all Top-Tiered?"

Theo gave a cheeky smile. "Pretty much."

I stirred my pea soup. "What are the odds *I'd* get accepted?"

The table went still as my family narrowed their gazes on me, effectively strangling me.

"You're thinking of applying?" Grandma asked coolly. Her words delivered like the pinprick of a needle as I heard their undertone: *You think you have a chance of being accepted?*

"I don't know." All explanation died in my mouth. Would my family listen to a word I had to say about it? They didn't understand how much I longed for freedom.

Though applying to Accolade meant a chance to go to Castle Circle, the ardent mockery and reprimands that came from higher Tiers dissuaded a good number of Lows from applying. Apparently, we only muddied the applicant pool.

I, especially, shouldn't have entertained the idea of applying. It meant only having a miniscule chance of acceptance, while my rejection would get me demoted. Even if I was accepted, I was still in danger of demotion. *Maybe* Dr. Ova would show mercy if I made it far in the competition, but I wouldn't count on it. Something told me if I performed well in Accolade, she'd have even *more* fun demoting me upon my return to Pointe.

If I applied, the only way I wouldn't become a farmer would be to win the entire competition and become the next queen.

"Don't you like being a doctor?" Mom asked, ever the encourager in our family.

Why don't you want to be like your mother? everyone always asked me. *She's a farming unit leader. She provides Miota with food!*

My silent answer was always the same. My mother was a great woman, prominent in the Low Tier. But I didn't want to stay contained in this Tier; I wanted to leave the Lows, leave Pointe. And the only citizens who did that *freely* were Tops, when they went to Castle Circle, outside all city walls and jurisdiction.

"I'm not *really* a doctor," I answered, my voice barely above a whisper. I hated admitting my failure.

"You are," Grandma pressed. "Your research is important."

I looked at my grandmother through my glassy filter of welling tears, and she was nothing more than a blurred shape.

As far as everyone outside the asympton lab knew, I was doing research. I was included in autopsies, and I was giving my talents toward finding an asympton cure. No one knew the work I was *actually* doing in the lab.

"Corinn," Theo prompted, his voice gentle for once. "I know the *Gazette* is only talking about rumors right now, but I think there's truth to some of it. I doubt Their Majesties are accepting many Lows, no matter who you are."

Theo didn't view his statement as a personal attack, but I did. I could have *more* than this gray life, if only the chances of escaping myself stopped dwindling away.

"Are you applying?" I asked Theo, shifting the table's focus to him.

He studied me, searching my expression for something. "No, Corinn, there's no point."

"You won't *try* going to Castle Circle? Even if it's just for a few weeks?" I had Dr. Ova to discourage me, but if I were Theo, nothing would stop me from applying.

"No!" Theo laughed. "Why would Their Majesties accept *me* into their competition to rule the damn country?"

"Language." Tellie clucked her tongue and pointed her spoon at Theo. "Don't say 'damn' at the table."

Theo smirked at our cousin, who now sat amused as ever that *she* got away with breaking Mom's rule of no cursing during meals, instilled years ago because of my brother.

"The point," Theo started, returning his attention to me, "is that we won't make it. No offense."

The burn before crying worked through my throat, and I clamped my jaw shut to keep my mouth from quivering.

This was so wrong. If I was truly destined to be Low-Tiered for the rest of my life—to live in that basement with the horrid Dr. Ova—I hoped to fade away entirely. Asympton could claim me for all I cared. And then Dr. Ova could sneer over my body, split me open with uneven scalpel cuts, and burn my remains *herself* since I wouldn't be alive to do it for her.

I didn't speak for the rest of dinner. We left the Common, and thanks to the May sun setting later than usual, the sky still shone a vibrant blue. Crickets hummed beyond Pointe's perimeter wall. Theo found the bugs' singing to be a dissonance, while I latched to the existence of life beyond Pointe's borders.

The crickets were masked for a few moments as a boxcar whirred by on the monorail outside the city wall. It was likely on one of its last rounds before the system shut down for the night. The monorail, programmed remotely by engineers and controlled physically by monitor systems, staked claim to the space between Miota's five cities to transport commodities across the island.

Its tracks slashed through fertile farmlands, sentencing Pointe's farming units to cross the railway. In my lifetime alone, there'd been dozens of lives lost due to the monorail rattling by as units crossed its path. Mom witnessed it once, claiming the unit was dead before they could even scream.

"This'll all be behind us soon enough," Theo said, patting my shoulder as we approached our shack of rotting wood. "The deadline to apply is in two days, right? Then things can go back to the way they should be."

The way they should be. Yes. The bitter reminder that I was nothing more than a worthless Low, as it was *supposed* to be.

I didn't know how long I could suffocate like this.

Instead of going to the living room, as I usually did after dinner, I staggered down the main hallway to the swinging door at its end, which opened into our greenhouse. I scarcely visited the humid room, stuffed with thick plants and lush foods—a great temptation. Executive operatives methodically monitored our greenhouse's supplies, and if *anything* went missing, the monarchy would grant our family a death sentence.

Though, in Grandma's long life, she'd mastered sneaking food out when one of us fell ill from hunger. It was more difficult in this late spring season, since new employees had joined the operatives' forces. But as winters came, with operatives growing lazier and temperatures plummeting, Grandma knew how to creep around the law.

I didn't linger in the greenhouse for long. Its damp atmosphere stripped my lungs of much-needed fresh air. I stalked through the room to the door that let out at our back patio, which was nothing more than a square slab of cement littered with potted herbs.

The greenhouse's exterior polycarbonate wall had a chip halfway up it, making the perfect foot hole. I jammed my shoe into it and extended my legs, driving myself up and onto the roof. I scooted along the greenhouse's plastic covering, toward the shingled portion of our shack.

I lay on my back, savoring the heat rolling off the slates as the moon rose. The roof was a place of tranquility, as close to the moon and stars as I could get. When I was little, I regarded the moon as a friend. It was like me in so many ways: sometimes visible and sometimes not, but always secluded, alone and unreachable.

Tonight, the moon was succumbing to shadows, just as I was. In two days, once Accolade's deadline passed, I'd be stuck in the Low Tier for the rest of time.

Was there any chance of escaping who I was?

My whirlwind of thoughts all led back to Cass; none of this would've happened if he hadn't died. The half-moon smiled down at me in a leer. *You were never good enough for him,* it seemed to taunt me. *It was too good to be true.*

Tears caked my cheekbones, making my face itch. After the stars seeped into view, footsteps approached our house from below. I sucked in a swift breath, willing myself to appear invisible against the shingles. Though I didn't think being up here broke any explicit laws, a city patrol member on duty would undoubtedly question me. And if there was any reason to suspect I was watching the stars, or anything outside the Fort, I would get arrested. Theo had always warned me to be careful on the roof.

But warmth filled my stomach as the footsteps drew nearer. I recognized the visitor's gait. Salem muttered a curse louder than he'd probably intended before climbing to the roof. I wiped my eyes and sat up, watching him struggle to scale the greenhouse's wall.

"As great as the view is," Salem grunted as he shimmied closer, "I still think you're stupid for climbing roofs."

I tried to smile, but it faltered. "Shouldn't you be at home?"

"I told my parents I was reviewing patient charts late."

A fleeting twinge of jealousy traveled through my veins. He was a *real* doctor with living patients. I picked at my nails to keep my hands busy. "Do you want me to guess why you're here this late, or do you plan on telling me?"

Salem eyed me before lying on the shingles, now cool against the night air. He drew in a breath. "You're applying for Accolade, right?"

My eyes fluttered shut. "No. I mean . . . I don't know. I can't." When I opened my eyes, they lost focus, and the stars blurred together.

"But you've always wanted to go to Castle Circle."

Yes. But I'd also wanted to see the fields outside Pointe and the world beyond the Fort. I'd always wanted to bask in the ocean's presence, drink in the starry sky, and fly with the moon.

But I couldn't say *that* out loud—it broke multiple laws. Besides, wanting to witness the torrential oceans and violent storms beyond the Fort would only lead to my ridicule.

"I can live without applying," I murmured, even as the words sliced my throat in betrayal.

"Liar," Salem shot. "What's the harm?"

I pounded my fist against the roof. The shingles' texture stung the thin skin of my knuckles. "Ova is demoting me if I apply." There. I admitted it. With the words now materialized, their weight hung heavier. "If I apply and don't make it, I'll be a farmer. Low-Tiered for life."

"She can't demote you if you're living large in Castle Circle."

I froze, shielding myself from Salem's false hope and sickly sunrays. "Not possible. Theo said so himself—Lows won't be accepted."

"Theo works for the *media*. He doesn't know what's true and what's not."

I cracked a grin that matched the moon's. "I want to apply, I just . . . I can't risk it. I can't stay Low-Tiered forever."

"Corinn, you're so much more than your Tier, so stop pretending you're nothing more than the soil on the ground. *I know* you shouldn't be in the Low Tier; Accolade is a chance to show others where you belong." He nudged my shoulder. "Your *last* chance."

"Are you applying?" I watched Salem's silhouette next to me.

He scoffed. "And *voluntarily* go to the street of chaos? I'll pass."

"You're sure?"

"You *do* realize the thing I looked forward to about my job placement was finally being able to get out of going to Castle Circle? My one weekend every month in that place is already two days too many, so I'm good." He paused, and his tone transformed into something much lighter. "It's really fun, though. You'd love it."

I cackled. "You're *so* full of fertilizer." He'd never liked visiting Castle Circle, though his mother forced him to go each month growing up. Now that he had his own career, he was deemed old enough to opt out of his monthly trips across the island, as some Tops inevitably chose.

Castle Circle was a luxury for each city's Top Tier, not a necessity. While our city was built to survive two days a month without pompous Tops, a fraction of them stayed behind during Pointe's assigned weekends.

Who would look after the Lows if we all left? I'd heard in my time at the Top-Tiered school, as if it wasn't the Middle Tier primarily overseeing the Lows, keeping us in line. I knew the truth: some Tops feared that regularly vacating the city for one weekend a month would slowly dissolve their rich imprints in Pointe.

"So . . ." Salem gulped, and the light moment passed. "Ova said she'd demote you? Just for applying?"

"Yeah. Whether I'm accepted or not, as soon as I don't win the entire thing, I'm a farmer. The only way out would be—"

"To win Accolade," Salem finished. "Damn, Corinn."

"Maybe she'd make an exception if I made it far." We were silent for a moment, chewing on the possibility of Sigrid Ova's leniency.

"If you stayed at research," Salem started, "could you move up? Take her job someday? Work your way into another ward?"

"No chance. She *wants* me demoted; she's only using me right now to do the lab's dirty work. I'm ... taking out the trash, sharpening graphite, mopping the floors, and ... and burning the bodies once they're done with them."

Even in the dim light, Salem's visage twisted, morphing into rage. "She's treating you like a Low."

"Well, yeah. That's what I *am*."

"You *have* to apply," he decided. "Please. Get as far away from Ova as you can."

"It's not that simple," I bit out, meaner than intended.

Irritation flashed through Salem's eyes. Before I could apologize, his panel sounded with a message, and he glanced at it. "I've got to go. Almost curfew. You have less than two days to toughen up and apply. Your whole life is *sort of* dependent on this."

"Salem," I pleaded, wishing the city-wide curfew wasn't driving him away. "I can't—"

"By the moon. Just believe in yourself, Corinn." He squeezed my hand before leaving.

CHAPTER 7

Sleep was impossible after that. I'd gone straight to bed once Salem left, but drowsiness never found me. Instead, I lay on my cot and stared at the slice of sky visible through the crack in the bedroom's curtains. Tellie and Theo both slept soundlessly while I remained awake, driven toward madness regarding Accolade. Salem was right; I needed to make my choice *soon*. I had less than two full days to decide my life's trajectory.

I wished I didn't ache to go to Castle Circle. I wished I didn't care about Accolade, and I *especially* wished I didn't care about living in the Low Tier; it would've made this decision much easier. But the longer I stared at the small sliver of the star-speckled sky, the more I knew where my heart resided. I wanted to escape more than *anything*.

But my one chance of leaving would also result in my guaranteed demotion. As a farmer, I'd never amount to anything worthy. The only way to avoid that fate was to not only thrive in Accolade, but *win*. And how could I do *that* as a Low?

I couldn't apply. It would be social suicide at first, and it would eventually kill me entirely, but it was my only option.

My palms became slick from the mere thought of being stuck in the Low Tier for eternity; I was made for *more than this*.

Maybe Dr. Ova would eventually see my merit. *Doubtful.* Maybe she'd treat me like a real doctor. I recalled Salem's words: *take Ova's job someday.* As in, take her job in thirty years when she retired. When that time came, I'd be around fifty years old. *If* I was named Ova's replacement—already a far reach—the executive council wouldn't do anything to change my Tier. I'd still be a Low.

I turned onto my side, and my thin bedsheet twisted around my ankles. Sweat coated me, making me even more restless.

There was no way I'd leave the Low Tier. *Ever.*

Unless . . .

Unless I applied to Accolade and was accepted, which was a feat out of my control. And, upon my acceptance, I'd have to win. After all, how could anyone from the Top Tier tell me I wasn't worthy if I was the queen?

I laughed at the thought, then slapped a hand over my mouth to keep from waking Theo or Tellie. My cousin rolled over in her cot but stayed asleep.

Yes. This would be my only chance of leaving my Tier once and for all. An event like this wouldn't happen again. This tournament, Accolade, was the *only* way to escape myself.

I slipped off my cot. The shack's air was stuffy, but it still provided solace from the layer of sweat plastered to my limbs. I tiptoed to the window and grabbed my panel.

The time shone brightly, making me wince. 03:26. Only decisions of the heart, not the mind, happened at this hour.

And this decision was completely of the heart. As much as I knew I shouldn't challenge the odds and should instead curl back up in bed, a shard deep in my chest begged me to *try* escaping the Low Tier.

Despite everything. I needed to try. I couldn't let this *last chance* slip through my fingers.

"I better not regret this," I mumbled.

My thumb trembled as I opened the application.

Nausea was my only constant feeling for the next two days. I didn't mention Accolade around the lab, and Dr. Ova never asked about it. She probably assumed she'd scared me out of applying. I smiled each time I thought about her finding out I'd applied. Of course, it would only be funny if I *made* the competition.

As soon as I'd applied for Accolade in the middle of the night, I'd known it was a mistake. I was stupid, self-sabotaging, delusional . . .

I spent Thursday and Friday cherishing my walk to the hospital, accepting that they'd be my last days of doing so before I was demoted. Though farmers *did* leave Pointe's walls, I'd gathered from Mom that it might as well be a prison itself, with armed guards breathing down your neck, reminding you of the lethal consequence of straying from your unit. If a bullet to your brain wasn't threat enough, countless farmers were claimed by sunstroke, dehydration, exhaustion, and, evidently, asympton.

It was the one thing Dr. Ova and the rest of us knew about the disease: it preferred farmers. And starting next week, that would be my life.

On Friday, I couldn't calm my limbs, couldn't coerce my body into stillness. I left the lab multiple times to vomit, though, with a near-empty stomach from my single ration, I primarily dry heaved.

"Are you pregnant?" Dr. Ova had the guts to ask from behind a monitor screen.

I rolled my eyes, mopping the floor for the second time today to keep my hands busy. It was either this or rearranging the chemicals and poisons for the umpteenth time this week. I lapped water across the floor in chaos, thanks to my buzzing arms.

"No," I moaned. I might've bitten something worse toward her if this wasn't my last day under her supervision. As soon as *Pointean Gazette* released the list of names of everyone who'd applied to Accolade, I'd become a farmer. I nearly crumpled to the floor. Maybe I should've asked Theo if there was a way to keep my name off the list of rejected applicants—or a way to withdraw my application completely.

Dr. Ova pointed her eyes at me. "Corinn, what is *wrong* with you? Are you drunk? I *know* alcohol isn't a commodity Lows get."

"I'm not drunk," I managed to get out before excusing myself to the toilet. The day continued in such a fashion.

When I ascended the basement staircase to go to dinner, after every other staff member had cleared out—save the rotational overnight staff—I collapsed onto a step and cried into my knees. It was my last time in this hospital as an employee.

For seven years, I'd dreamed about being a doctor alongside Salem. Helping people. Proving myself to be worth something— *anything*. But none of it had come true.

"Corinn?" an aged voice uttered.

I looked up and found my tutor, Cass's uncle, at the top of the stairs. He must've been on overnight duty. I choked on a sob before running into his arms. Tears streamed down my cheeks until I was nothing but salt and wet lips and dead memories. The last time I saw Bernard, Cass had still been alive.

Bernard pulled away and gave a hollow smile. "What're you doing here? You'll miss dinner."

"Who cares?" I grumbled, avoiding his eyes. "Nothing matters anymore. I'm done here."

"Done?" He searched my eyes. "Done with *what*, exactly?"

"Being a researcher. Ova's demoting me. Except, I never *was* a researcher, really. I was doing janitorial work."

Bernard knitted his gray brow together, creating extra creases on his face. "You should've told me. I could've helped."

"Not worth your time," I whispered.

Bernard gave me an expression I'd seen from doctors who knew their patients' bloodwork results before anyone else. It was the same elusive look he'd share with Cass in the greenhouse.

Bernard was keeping a secret.

"You're worth my time," he finally said, grinning to himself. "More than you know. How . . . how are you doing? Haven't seen you since—" His lip quivered. "Well, you know."

I sniffed. "As well as I can be, I guess." I looked at my feet. "I . . . appreciate all the time you spent with me. I'll keep the knowledge, even as a farmer."

"Tutoring you was a joy," Bernard said. "Hard to believe it all started because your brother came in needing to be stitched up."

"Who knew," I mused, "Theo busting open his hand would spark my match with medicine?"

"Yeah, well, you wouldn't stop talking about how badly you wanted to help." While Bernard wasn't wrong, I often wondered if I'd only wanted to help people to increase my worth. "And you were only eight . . . I knew you were the right person for the job. And you still are, so don't worry about Accolade. Hopefully, it'll all end up working out."

I didn't remember telling him anything about Accolade specifically, only that I was being demoted. I'd likely blubbered about it without realizing, though.

"Besides, remember what I always tell you?" Bernard continued.

"Don't tell the queen?" I joked. Salem's and my biggest instruction about meeting Bernard and Cass in the greenhouse was to *never* let Her Majesty know about any of it. *Because I run into the queen all the time,* I'd always thought, wondering why Bernard and Cass gave such a useless commandment. As a Low, I'd never seen Queen Julia in the flesh.

I expected Bernard to laugh at the phrase now, but his face hardened. "*Yes.* Still hold true to that. But, right now, I meant the *other* phrase. I don't see you for a week, and suddenly, you drop into despair, hmm?"

"I remember it," I assured him, suppressing an eye roll. "Dig deep and find strength."

"And you can do that for me, right?"

No, I'm not sure I can. But I couldn't say that. So I lied. "Of course."

"Good." Bernard patted my shoulder and helped me stand. "Now, don't miss dinner because of me. Good to see you, Corinn."

"Always a treat," I agreed. He'd at least given me the strength to leave the hospital. Each step away from the building felt like two hands writhing around my neck, growing tighter with the more distance I put between myself and the hospital.

I could hardly breathe once I reached the Common. Though dinner was one of the better meals in the rotation—chicken and flatbread—I could hardly stomach the gristly meat. I didn't speak, except to answer Dad when he asked how my first week of work was.

During our walk home, I paced myself with Grandma, whose hip had been bothering her lately.

"You don't need to stay with me," Grandma insisted. "Run up there with Tellie and Theo. I'll be all right."

"Just . . . let me stay."

"Corinn, I'm fine. Thanks for your concern, though."

"Grandma!" It was more of a whine than I'd wanted, and I cringed at the tone. "Please," I whispered.

Her face softened. "Hey. Sure."

My panel chimed delicately in the tone signifying a message from Their Majesties.

My stomach lurched into my throat. Had they already accepted citizens into Accolade? Applications were due today at noon . . . Had they truly sifted through everyone so quickly?

My muscles became jelly. I couldn't grab my panel or read its news; it was all I could do to keep *walking*. If this message entailed what I thought it would, my rejection from Accolade would seal my fate as a Low-Tiered farmer. As soon as *Pointean Gazette* published a compiled list of Pointe's applicants, I'd be a goner.

Grandma nudged me with her elbow, pulling me out of my trance. "Well?" she grunted. "What are you dawdling for?"

My hands shook as I dug my panel from my pocket. The previewed headline was enough to make my heart heave against my rib cage.

CONGRATULATIONS!
YOU HAVE BEEN ACCEPTED INTO ACCOLADE.

I squealed and shoved my panel toward Grandma. "*I made it!*" I cried. "I applied, and I made it!"

Her eyes grew wide before crinkling, and a grin of yellowed teeth overtook her. She squeezed me in a tight hug. "Good for you, Corinn!" The rest of the family, a dozen paces ahead, turned around at our outburst.

"How?" I scratched my head. "Why would they choose *me*?"

I scanned the rest of the message. The family would get to

keep my allotted rations as payment for my service to the crown. It wasn't much—one ration to split between five people.

Accolade candidates were permitted one bag of belongings. And we'd go to Castle Circle on Sunday afternoon, less than two days from now.

I gasped. "We move in on Sunday!"

A laugh escaped Grandma. "Well, don't stand back here with me! Shoo, go pack!" She swatted at my side.

"Congratulations," Theo said as I jogged past him. He patted my back, and I flashed him a grateful smile.

Tellie ran home with me, asking endless questions between quick breaths. "Are you going to ride in a limo there? Will you see the castle? Will you be the only Low? Will you meet anyone from outside of Pointe? How fancy do you have to dress?"

Nothing could ruin this elation. Nervous energy rolled off my shoulders in waves. I was accepted. I was *chosen.* Why Their Majesties chose *me,* I couldn't say. The application for Accolade had requested information about my Tier, occupation, family lineage . . . none of my answers made me worthy of competing to be one of the country's next rulers.

But I wouldn't waste this single opportunity. From here on out, it was up to *me* to stay in the competition—to stay out of Dr. Ova's grasp, to keep from getting demoted.

Pointe was in a trance on Saturday morning, full of gossip and theories and tears. Even from our house, deep in the farming sector where Accolade was hardly mentioned, excitement clung to the air. Theo worked weekend mornings at *Pointean Gazette,* and when he came home, he boasted the paper list of applicants he'd managed to smuggle. Stealing *paper*—a rare commodity—was an impressive feat, no matter the circumstance.

The list encompassed the name of every Pointean who'd

applied for Accolade, and whether they'd been accepted. Once this list of names was published later today, the city's buzzing rumors would morph into concrete facts. I could only imagine the shock on Dr. Ova's face upon realizing I'd applied and been accepted.

I scanned the list. Nearly every Top I could think of had been accepted: Izzy Eddison, Brentin Keins, Halee Morris, Brycon Northe and his sister Blaire, Salem Redding—

Salem Redding! I messaged him, wondering how he made Accolade if he didn't apply. His answer came quickly: his mother filled out an application in his name. Mrs. Redding was nothing if not headstrong.

Despite Salem's sulking, obvious even through our thread of panel messages, I smiled to myself. *Thank the moon.* I was going to Castle Circle with my best friend. Maybe I could do this after all.

I couldn't sleep that night thanks to the gleaming visions dancing behind my eyelids. Salem, Castle Circle, leaving Pointe, escaping Low-Tiered life . . .

But as the hours trickled by, fear crept in. I needed to make it *far* to escape Dr. Ova and the Low Tier. And I was already at a huge disadvantage. How could I fight for a crown I didn't deserve? Blind hope didn't weigh well against the facts. I'd have to find some advantage to help my odds in Accolade, and quickly. But I scoured my brain, unable to produce any idea. I was no one; I had nothing to my name.

Night bled into morning, and for once, I didn't mind the early call time to the Common for breakfast. I rose from my cot, restless as ever.

Later that morning, everyone gathered in the living room to tell me goodbye. I carried a large straw sack, which was usually used for transporting produce from our greenhouse to Council Hall. The sack now carried my belongings, though I couldn't shake the onion stench from it, so my clothes were doomed to be soiled. Hopefully, I could wash them in Castle Circle.

Mom spoke first, crushing me into a hug. "You're going to do great. Don't worry about us while you're gone; just enjoy yourself."

Dad came next in a juxtaposition of clapping my back and kissing my forehead. Tellie cried as she and Grandma folded their arms around me. Theo came last, squeezing me tightly as he whispered, "Be careful, okay? But have fun, too."

I grinned. Of *course* his parting message came laced with a warning.

I waved as Grandma closed the front door, leaving me alone on the shack's front steps. The looming reality sank in, chilling my bones. I was going to *Castle Circle*. To compete against others for the chance to rule Miota.

Because Cass died, I reminded myself, as I did every time my excitement grew. *I'm here because Cass is dead.*

My feet grew heavy as I trudged toward Pointe's center, especially once I noticed sporadic citizens looming in side alleys with camera lenses fixed on me. I assumed these citizens were recruited by *Pointean Gazette* to stream live footage of Accolade.

I wanted to cower at the attention. I swore I could read their thoughts: *How did* she *make it into the tournament?* As one of the three Low-Tiered Pointeans to be accepted into Accolade, I was wondering the same thing.

Projectors in Miota sat inactive unless they played a mandatory royal broadcast. This morning, however, a stream called *Accolade Times* began, where screen time would be split equally between each city's news studio: two hours per city, per day, giving all of Miota ten hours' worth of daily footage to watch.

A crowd formed as I drew nearer to Council Hall, where candidates would fill out forms before being whisked away to Castle Circle. Citizens clogged the streets, forcing everyone to a standstill.

I quickly realized how underdressed I was. I'd worn the richest-looking outfit I owned: my only dress, the white one from Commencement, whose color unfortunately pegged me as a Low. My skin crawled as I studied the other girls' outfits of frillier, dark-colored dresses. I pulled out my panel with my acceptance message to prove I was, in fact, supposed to be here. Despite the warm weather, a chill burrowed into my bones as eyes feasted on me.

The line inside Council Hall extended beyond the building, so I joined the messy queue spilling onto the road. My face baked and vision swam as the crowd thickened.

"Corinn," a voice called over the hum of conversations.

I whipped my head around and exhaled. Salem materialized in the conglomeration of bodies. He carried a navy-blue bag—his monarchy-issued suitcase for traveling between Pointe and Castle Circle. His freckled skin shone against his black shirt and slacks.

"And you actually showed up," I crooned.

Salem rolled his eyes. "If I didn't come, the jokes about my mom killing me wouldn't be much of an exaggeration."

"Think of the scandal," I said cynically. "Well, *I'm* glad you're here."

Salem nudged my shoulder. "And I'm glad *you're* here."

We finally made it inside Council Hall. Next to us, a group of Top-Tiered girls shrieked, claiming their makeup was melting in the jam-packed room. I lifted my brow, unaware it was possible for makeup to melt. Not that I would know; makeup wasn't a Low-Tiered commodity, so I'd never worn any before.

Members of the Queen's Guard—the prestigious Top-Tiered militia tasked with protecting the castle grounds and royal family—sat at a row of tables, sending documents to each candidate's panel. The forms asked for our hobbies, dating history, favorite foods, and more.

Upon submitting the documents, a foreign folder downloaded onto my panel's dashboard labeled *ACCOLADE*. I fought every urge to click on it.

A number of sleek limos appeared outside Council Hall from the northeast street leading to Pointe's farming sector, the same street I'd just used to walk here. I shook my arms to release nervous energy as candidates piled into the vehicle. I'd never been in a limo before since the small fleet was reserved for transporting Tops to and from Castle Circle.

Salem and I exited Council Hall and climbed into one of the glossy limos. A potent whiff of leather hit me, bringing on a swift headache. Seats lined the spacious interior, and I settled next to Salem. Once the vehicle burst at the seams with candidates and luggage, the doors were sealed shut, and we started toward Pointe's perimeter wall.

CHAPTER 8

A small laugh escaped me as the limo lurched away from Council Hall, driving toward Pointe's singular gate, a guarded chink in our city's exterior wall. It was located in the farming sector, convenient for the Lows who traveled out to the fields.

Anticipation bubbled in my stomach. I'd *finally* witness the world outside Pointe! I craned my neck to peer out the window as we exited the city. The paved stone turned into nothing more than a dirt path, and the limo churned a thin layer of dust into the air.

Lush greens and browns and blues exploded. Vast fields stretched in every direction. My heart sang. I didn't realize Miota was so *vast*. Flourishing lines of crops stretched toward the sky in neat rows. Strings of vineyards and orchards and shrubs alike occupied the entire green space outside Pointe. The view wasn't blocked by buildings or a brick wall. Everything was free— untethered and thriving.

Though the fields currently sat empty, I imagined speckles of farmers dotting the land, usually harvesting this earth. If I left Accolade, I'd join the slew of laborers out here. It wouldn't be like *this*, though, winding through unoccupied land. I thought of Mom and her leathery, sunburnt neck; the permanent bow in her back; her chapped hands and cracked lips; and her weariness around Pointe's law enforcement because of their strict rules in the fields.

I tried masking my awe once I noticed the Tops' amused glances trained on me. They completed this drive on a monthly basis, so my excitement at the novelty was clearly some form of entertainment for them. I wanted to melt away.

I didn't know how much time had passed since we left Pointe. Although our city and Castle Circle were both on the northern half of the island, Pointe lay near Miota's western shore while Castle Circle resided on the eastern shore. By the end of our ride, my joints had grown sore from being crushed in the crammed limo. I was thankful when we approached the black iron gate ornamented with swirling gold patterns surrounding Castle Circle.

We piled out of the limo, tugging our luggage behind us. My insides pitched at the sight of my straw sack against the vast number of Tops' monarchy-issued suitcases.

The limo had stopped in a gravel lot on the west end of Castle Circle's long, singular street. The main road was made of a black material as smooth as tile. I now understood why Salem often complained about the loose stone roads back home.

Beyond Castle Circle, on the northernmost tip of the island, rested the castle grounds. A sturdy wall, much like Pointe's brick perimeter encasing, concealed the royal grounds from view. A wave of nausea swept over me as I realized *that* was the wall Cass's limo had crashed into. The wall Cass grew up within ultimately betrayed him.

I blinked back tears and clenched my jaw, focusing on Castle Circle. Its glittering road extended eastward in a straight line, with buildings of smooth glass and sharp angles occupying both sides.

I couldn't help but scan the road for other Miotans. While

most Pointeans were glad to navigate this place without running into those from the other cities, I'd always wanted to meet people from outside Pointe. I'd never understood why we bothered slandering the other cities. We all traded commodities with each other; no city could survive on its own, and there was no superior.

A thin, raven-haired woman in a navy dress intercepted us. "Welcome, Pointe, to Castle Circle! Who's been here before?" Hands flew up around me, and I chewed the inside of my cheek, wanting to chuck my onion-scented bag far away. "Perfect. I'll show you to your apartment buildings!" The cheery woman led us down the road.

My mouth parted at the grandiosity. Though Salem had described Castle Circle before, this was bigger and better than anything my imagination could've fabricated. It truly was the Top Tier's play place. The lane boasted lustrous waterfalls running off buildings, sparkling stones embedded in sidewalks, and glistening buildings reflecting the vibrant sky.

We never saw other Miotans, which dampened my spirits. Still, I summoned the names of the four other cities to my brain's forefront, knowing we were bound to eventually meet their citizens. *Kendall, Cape, Yorkinson, and Salford.*

The woman stopped us at a line of charcoal-gray buildings. While these structures didn't feature crystalline exteriors or dazzling water displays, their simplicity nodded toward a unique beauty. She called names in front of the first building.

"Izzy Eddison, Corinn Januski, Halee Morris, and Pollie Wienst. You're here in First Residence."

I squeezed Salem's hand before walking alongside the three girls. I smiled at Pollie, a Low-Tiered farmer a couple of years older than me. She offered a timid grin in return. I wondered why *she'd* been accepted, and she was probably wondering the same about me.

I was familiar with Pollie because of her brother. Though he was only one year younger than me, his cognitive level had never progressed beyond the age of a young child. Since he also presented with physical deficits, he spent most of the day with Pointe's disability services located in one of the hospital's wards.

Halee and Izzy were both Tops, and they made a point to dissociate from Pollie and me. Halee even scowled at the white dresses Pollie and I wore.

We entered the gray building to find a golden lobby hidden inside. Two gilded staircases rose from either side of the room, meeting on the first floor.

A middle-aged lady with a sharp face welcomed us. "You must be the candidates from Pointe. Welcome, all of you." The lady beamed, showing a mouthful of straight, sparkling teeth. "My name is Clarissa; I'm the overseer of First Residence. You'll stay here for the duration of your time in Accolade, no matter how long *or short* it may be." Her gaze snagged on Pollie and me, noting our white dresses. "If you have questions, you may ask either your floor's maids or myself. Ready to see your rooms?"

I shot Pollie an incredulous look. *Maids?* Even Izzy and Halee raised eyebrows at the announcement.

We climbed the stairs after Clarissa, and I watched her navy dress sweep the stairs as we went. I'd never owned a dress outside of the one I wore now and couldn't imagine wearing a garment of Clarissa's length. We stopped on the second floor and turned onto a cool tile hallway.

"Ms. Halee Morris, your suite awaits," Clarissa announced. Halee offered Izzy good luck before scanning her panel at the bedroom door. I tried giving Halee an encouraging smile, but she ignored Pollie and me entirely.

The stairs to the subsequent floors resided in a side stairwell, not as glamorous as the lobby's gold-plated steps. Izzy's room was on the third floor, and Pollie's room was on the fifth floor, leaving only me to follow Clarissa to the sixth floor—the top floor.

I suppressed my giddiness as I anticipated the view from the window. Pointe's hospital was the tallest building I'd been in, though it was only three stories tall and didn't have windows. The highest view I'd ever encountered was the rooftop back home.

Clarissa led me to the last door on the left. "Corinn Januski, your suite awaits." I noted how neither Pollie nor I had received the title of *Ms.* like Izzy and Halee had.

"Thank you." I tapped my panel on the doorknob, which fortunately unlocked. I really was supposed to be here.

I sucked in a breath and opened the door. My lower extremities turned to lead, and I froze. The bedroom seemed about half the size of my family's entire shack. Sunlight, pale and blinding, poured through the windows lining the back wall. Adorning the white furniture, fresh daisies released a sweet aroma into the crisp, filtered air. I eyed the fluffy bed that could easily fit four people. Back home, my feet hung off my cot. If I wasn't paralyzed right now, I'd leap onto the mattress.

A delicate chandelier hung above the bed, its stems of lights glowing a dull rose color, mimicking a sunrise. My hazy reflection glimmered back at me as I peered toward the waxed floor. Bronze hues brushed the edges of my vision, and I noted the room's gold embellishments.

A woman who hardly looked older than me emerged from a door I hadn't seen until now. I jumped but played it off by bending to pick my sack off the ground.

The brunette woman, wearing a floor-length, sky-blue dress, smiled at the sight of me before setting one hand under her chin.

"Er, I'm Corinn Januski," I said, feeling like a science project. "From Pointe."

"I know who you are." The woman chuckled as she dropped her hands to her side. "I'm Lily, the maid you'll contact if you need anything. I'm overseeing the fifth and sixth floors of First Residence. Congratulations on making Accolade! How does it feel?"

"Amazing," I admitted, taken aback by her kindness. Was it artificial? It must've been, if she knew who I was. "This whole place doesn't seem real. I've only been here for ten minutes, and I never want to leave."

"Maybe you won't have to." When Lily grinned, her eyes shone a much darker shade of blue than mine. "I just put fresh towels in your bathroom, which was the finishing touch on the room, so you're all set."

"My . . . bathroom?"

Lily pointed at the door she originally emerged from as I pressed my lips into a line. "Through there. Since Pointe arrived first, you'll have more time than others to get ready. I have a dress for you, and I don't think it'll need altered . . ."

"Get ready for what?" I asked.

Lily stopped short, leaning heavily on one leg and resting her hand on her jutted hip. "Did anyone tell you what's happening tonight?"

"No."

Lily threw her hands in the air. "Leave it to Their Majesties to keep things as vague as possible! Oh—don't let that leave this room. Um . . ." Lily waltzed toward the bathroom. "There's a masquerade ball at the castle tonight! Everyone in Accolade will be there. Follow me."

Lily showed me to the bright room boasting a shining white bathtub, sleek shower, and two copper sink basins set in black-veined countertops. My jaw slackened at the raw beauty. If this was only Castle Circle, I couldn't imagine what the actual *castle* looked like. Though, apparently, I'd see its regal glory tonight. My head spun.

"I have to go welcome other candidates, but I'll be back to help you get ready for the ball." Lily paused. "*Breathe*, Corinn. You look ghastly. Trust me, this is all nothing. Today hasn't even begun yet."

CHAPTER 9

A few hours passed before Lily breathlessly returned to the bedroom. "We don't have as much time as I thought we would," she slurred. As she darted in and out of the bathroom, a pale pink shimmer of fabric wafted behind her. "Here's the dress I made you!" She splayed it on the bed, and I gasped.

This dress, the same dusty pink as a muted sunset, shimmered under the chandelier's lights. It slinked off the bed in arcs of ruffles and silk.

"Let's get you into this thing," Lily said.

I eyed her. "Did *you* make this? For me?"

Lily's eyes crinkled. "I hope you like it."

"I love it," I assured her, using every ounce of self-control to keep from flailing across the room in excitement and wrapping her in a suffocating hug.

Lily helped me step into the dress. Its thin straps wrapped around my shoulders, and the cold material hugged my trunk before pooling in sweeping layers of satin, sparkling jewels, and something Lily called tulle. The dress left my back exposed, and I only hoped my ribs—prominent, thanks to a life of one-rationed meals— weren't too obvious.

I didn't feel worthy of the gown.

"Test it out," Lily encouraged me.

I blinked, too enthralled with the gown to have heard her correctly.

"Give it a spin," she elaborated, twirling her index finger in the air.

I knew my face glowed at the idea. I spun in a number of circles, and the dress's skirts fanned out around my legs before I stopped to steady myself.

"Gorgeous," Lily gushed. "Now. Makeup or hair first?"

I licked my lips. "I've . . . never worn makeup before."

Lily shrieked and sat me in front of the room's vanity, a lacquered piece of white furniture holding a sparkling mirror. I watched my face transform as Lily worked.

A light dusting of eyeshadow, drying out my eyelids. A swipe of gel eyeliner and mascara, making my eyelashes reach outward. A pink cream on my cheeks, giving my pallid skin an artificial breath of color. Golden powder across my forehead and near my mouth, which made me look like Mom after a summer day in the fields. A nude-colored lipstick, coating my lips in a velvety layer. When Lily moved to my hair, my face was unrecognizable.

Nerves flapped inside me, carrying too many emotions at once. The excitement of meeting *others* churned against the dread of remembering this was a competition and I was a Low. Would this ball be the time to make friends and allies? And, if so, would anyone want *me*?

Time slipped away. Lily curled my hair and pinned half of it to the crown of my head in an interwoven braid. To complete the outfit, Lily gave me sparkling heels—I stood no chance of keeping my balance in them—and a glittering pink mask that would cover the upper half of my face.

"Head downstairs," Lily started, "and the limo fleet outside the apartments will take you to the castle. Have so much fun!"

"Thank you, Lily. For everything."

Lily grinned. "It's only day one, Corinn. This is nothing." She pulled her panel out of her pocket and frowned. "A Kendallian needs me. Are you good from here? You can make it down to the lobby?"

I didn't want Lily to leave. I didn't know why she was being so kind, but I knew she'd be one of the only people to treat me with such decency while knowing my Tier. If only she could come to the ball with me.

"Yes," I answered, accepting my fate. I was going to the castle. I'd find Salem or Pollie. "Thanks again."

"Get out of here." She beamed before we parted ways.

I descended First Residence, finding the lobby illuminated in gold against the outdoor twilight. I didn't recognize anyone, especially in our masquerade attire, but my heart raced as I realized I was among citizens of different cities.

Each city had an assigned fleet of limos waiting outside the residence buildings. I found Pointe's limos and proved my identity with my panel.

Pollie, wearing a sequined dress that almost matched the shade of her mousy brown hair, was in the same limo as me. We sat together, silent but comfortable. In one wide-eyed exchange, I knew our thoughts mirrored each other's: *Did you see the size of the bedrooms? How does it feel to have your* own *bathroom? What do you think of these dresses?*

Our limo hitched before rolling off into the empty lawn between Castle Circle and the castle. When we entered the castle grounds, our vehicle's windows tinted, blocking our view outside.

When the limo halted, the windows cleared, revealing two

lines of Queen's Guard members spanning from the limos to the castle's front door. Goosebumps erupted on my arms at the sight of them.

Only the best Top-Tiered city patrol members became members of the Queen's Guard, and the unit wore their malice like it was chained to their existence. Their faces, clad in neutral shadows, were summed up with clenched jaws and empty eyes.

There was something *off* about them. I supposed that was what made them members of the Queen's Guard—they'd do anything to maintain their spot in the elite group.

The castle, a structure of cream-colored stone, soared high above us, an intimidating building I couldn't believe Cass had called *home*. The charcoal roof was made of sharp angles and swirling spires, and glossy windows spilled oily light into the growing darkness outside.

Pollie and I stayed glued to each other as maids and butlers escorted us to the ballroom. I swayed in my heels, unable to walk steadily in the pointed shoes.

As suspected, the line of guards extended into the castle, occupying the main hallway finished with scarlet carpet. Guards watched us with pinpointed eyes, and their hands settled behind their backs where they probably held weapons in case anyone stepped out of line. Fear kept us all silent as we traipsed through the hallway. I only chanced glancing upward once and found warm stone gently molded into geometric shapes across the ceiling.

The ballroom, one of the first rooms on the left, was nothing short of spectacular. Delicate gilt lined the cream walls and pooled together on the ceiling, creating a shimmering roof. Floor-to-ceiling windows cast moonlight into the aureate space.

A handful of tables clumped together, adorned with every food and drink imaginable. The cuisine boasted vibrant colors and perfumed the air with a sweet decadence. Candidates from other cities already claimed sections of the room, and I schooled my breathing to stay even.

Stringed instruments played in a corner, producing sounds that wrapped around me in a soft caress. In Pointe, we had field songs, which I knew because of Mom. The tunes were passed down between farmers, and they infiltrated the rest of the city. But *instruments* were rarities, mythical things I didn't think existed outside this ballroom and Castle Circle. I only knew of their existence because of Cass.

With our costumes and masks, it would've been difficult to tell who was from which city, if not for the distinct groups forming. My pulse was erratic, being surrounded by Miotans from other cities, yet I seemed to be the only one enthralled by the idea of meeting others. While I wanted to flit around the ballroom and meet as many people as possible, I refrained, noting the air tense enough to slice through.

Next to me, Pollie groaned as we wedged through Pointe's crowd. "We better not have to talk to anyone from another city."

"Do you think we'll be forced to interact?" I asked as harmlessly as possible.

Pollie gave a shrug. "Hope not."

I shoved my curiosity deeper within me. There would be no interacting with anyone outside of Pointe tonight. It would only make for suspicions, and I'd become a target.

Jubilee Rivera, the third and final Pointean Low accepted into Accolade, found us and squealed in relief. But Jubilee ran up to Pollie and grabbed her arm. They chattered at a rate my ears couldn't decipher, and I knew there was no point in trying to follow their conversation. I left to look for Salem.

I hated intermingling with Pointeans. The pattern was cyclical: someone would meet my eyes with polite joy, only for recognition to flash behind their mask, and they'd promptly turn away. It was hard to believe I'd be more of an outcast among a cluster from another city.

Before I found Salem, butlers in navy suits ushered us to the dance floor to deconcentrate each city's group. Candidates gathered in the ballroom's center, though everyone remained careful with their interactions. The harder I studied the candidates, the more subtleties I found between Pointeans and the others, even amid everyone's formal costumes. Anyone from outside Pointe possessed some odd quality, whether it was their hairstyle, stance, or the way they talked—some used elaborate hand gestures, while others remained too reserved.

My dress swished around my ankles as I weaved through the crowded dance floor. I moved gingerly to avoid stepping on the fabric, tripping over the gown.

Not that it mattered. Because a few heartbeats later, a man carrying two flutes of wine crashed into me, spilling the drinks on both of us as the glassware clattered to the ground.

# CHAPTER 10

I froze. My dress was spoiled, the pink fabric now tainted with dark splotches of wine.

The man bared wide eyes at me from behind his stark black mask. "I'm . . . I'm so sorry." His rich voice left me blinking. His inflections didn't indicate him being from Pointe.

Which meant he was an outsider. The first Miotan to speak with me, besides Cass, who wasn't from Pointe.

"I . . . it's . . ." *It's all right.* Except, it wasn't. I didn't know what to say, so I bent to the floor to collect the shards of glass at our feet.

"Stop," the man said, also crouching. "Please, let me do that. This was my fault."

I looked at him. When our gazes collided, he studied me, mentally stripping my mask from my face. My skin burned under his scrutiny.

A few sneers bled through the mass of candidates. I tried tuning them out, but they surrounded us in a vortex of whispers.

"She's finally doing the work of a Low."

"Howard? Cleaning?"

"Get up, you two," a large butler ordered. I straightened alongside the stranger, holding bits of glass. "Set that down. We'll clean it up."

"Where's a good place to wipe off?" the man asked, handing glass shavings to the butler.

With the attention off me, I safely stole a real glance at the culprit who'd ruined my dress. Dark brown hair, slightly overgrown, kissed the shells of his ears. His skin, a deep olive tone, seemed to glow against his black suit and mask, which were tailored closely to his body, hinting at swells of muscles in his arms and legs. I wondered what job he held to get a body like *that*.

The butler scratched his head of thinning hair. "Wipe off?"

"I'm soaked, and so is Co—ah, my friend."

My stomach dropped to the floor, among the broken glass. Was he . . . going to say my name? No. That was impossible.

The butler sighed. "Follow me. *Quickly*."

The broad-shouldered man flashed me a victorious expression, though I didn't return it. I only followed for the promise of a towel and maybe a spare second to compose myself.

The butler opened a door along the ballroom's wall, carved in gold luster. If he hadn't opened the entrance, I might not have ever realized it was there. It revealed a quaint parlor covered in baby-blue wallpaper. Sharp perfumes of lavender and mint left me blinking.

"I'm not supposed to open this door," the butler said. "So come *right out* once you're cleaned up."

"You can stay here with us," the man offered. "There were plenty of other butlers there to handle the mess."

"Plenty?" the butler muttered. Something fearful flashed in his eyes before he spun and left the room, slamming the door behind him.

It left me alone with this strange man, who now eyed me like he'd won some prize.

I swallowed hard, probably loud enough for him to hear, and crossed my arms. "Can you give me a towel?"

He rummaged through a cupboard and produced a towel, tossing it to me from behind his back.

I set my jaw as I caught it.

"Sorry for crashing into you," he said, though remorse didn't reach his tone. His words tumbled together, each one quicker than the last. "But I needed a minute alone with you. You're Corinn Januski, right?"

My heart hammered against my ribs. This man *knew my name*. Did he know I was a Low? Had word of my status circulated already? I chewed on my lip, refusing to look at him. "Does it matter?" I barely got out.

The man huffed. "Yeah, I think it's *pretty* important." I waited for him to elaborate, but he didn't.

Who was this? Why did he need me alone? "What city are you from?" I asked, deciding it was a safe enough question. I turned toward him and fought to hold his relentless stare.

"Salford," he answered.

That confirmed it. He was from somewhere else. It should've felt freeing, except somehow, he knew my identity.

"Salford," I echoed, breaking eye contact to dab the towel on my dress. I hoped Lily wouldn't hate me for dirtying the gown. I recalled Salford's role assigned by the monarchy, carried out by *their* Low Tier. "Lumber and livestock," I recited.

Pointe and Salford complemented each other; Pointe provided fresh produce to Miota, and Salford provided meat and animal byproducts. Our cities kept the island from starving.

"That's the one," he sang. "You're welcome for all the *good* foods. Bacon, eggs, burgers . . ." He threw his towel in the air—a pointless trick—and caught it flawlessly. "And you're from . . ."

I ignored his stunt. "Pointe. You're welcome for all the healthy foods." A heartbeat. And then, "You know, the stuff you can't live without."

A muscle jumped in Salford's cheek. "If only that made it *taste* better."

I set my jaw to stifle the grin forming on my lips.

The man eyed me for a few breaths too long, which had a palpable effect on my heart rate. "Corinn Januski is also from Pointe." His accusation sucked all amusement from the room.

"Why do you know Corinn?" I asked.

He opened his mouth, then shut it. "You wouldn't believe me if I told you."

"Try me."

Salford tilted his head. Underneath his mask, his dark eyes roamed my face. "I *really* can't say, lovely. Not in the castle."

"You crashed into me on purpose, got me alone, and now you refuse to talk? That's effective."

Salford was . . . entertained, studying me as he leaned against the wall. "This must be going worse than I thought, if you won't tell me who you are." His relentless eye contact scattered my thoughts.

"You ruined my dress," I shot, "so I'm not sure why you thought this was going well."

His hypnotic eyes glinted. "I'm sorry about your dress. Really. It was beautiful. Though I think the crash did *me* a favor . . . my suit has a nice *splash* of color now." The corner of his mouth twitched as he waited for a reaction.

My ears burned. "You know, if you were half as careful as you are funny, I don't think we would've crashed."

He shot me a lopsided grin—the kind I thought most girls

would swoon over, which only upset me more. "You think I'm funny?"

"I didn't say that."

"You implied it."

"Did *not.*" His annoying arrogance prodded at me, tiny hooks clawing my skin, digging deeper with every word he spoke. I ripped my gaze away from him. "I'm heading back out there. My dress is pretty much done for. Thanks for the interrogation, though—"

The parlor doors whipped open. I turned, bracing myself to see the same rotund butler who escorted us in here.

My stomach lurched, however, at the figure in the doorway. I bowed deeply, letting my curled hair fall around my face.

"Your Most Royal Majesty," Salford said from behind me in a tone as smooth as the silk of my dress.

"Stand." The queen's command rang cold and stoic. I rose, looking at the monarch. Behind her, a small corps of guard members kept keen eyes narrowed on Salford and me.

My throat quivered. There was so much of Cass in her. The point of her chin, the arch of her brow, her perched posture. The paralysis broke, however, as I noticed her smoldering eyes.

This wasn't how I intended to meet Cass's mother. I'd imagined a kind, compassionate woman who raised Cass to be like her. But this woman was marked with glowing fury.

"Your Majesty," Salford repeated. "There was a wine spill, so we were sent in here for towels—"

"Yes, Mr. Howard, I'm aware." The queen's gaze skirted behind us, deeper into the room, and her posture relaxed slightly.

I held onto the surname. *Mr. Howard. Salford.* How did she recognize him on the first night of Accolade? Did she already know candidates by name?

The queen composed herself with each passing second,

smothering her anger into silence. "And are you two cleaned up now?"

"Yes, Your Majesty," I answered alongside Mr. Howard.

Cass's mother turned to me. Blood roared through my temples, rushed through my ears. "Ms. Januski, I was awaiting our meeting. The photographs I saw of you and my son at Pointe's Commencement were . . . *touching*." Her tone suggested otherwise.

My throat squeezed shut. I hadn't realized those photos circulated outside of Pointe. Although, this *was* the Queen of Miota—she could access anything she wanted on the island.

"Thank you, Your Most Royal Majesty," I choked out.

Queen Julia sneered slowly, and I read her malevolent thoughts toward me from behind her green eyes. I'd never felt smaller in my life.

Her Majesty turned to face the ballroom from the parlor's doorway. As she did, Mr. Howard stole a sideways glance at me. My heart sank; he knew I'd lied about my identity.

"Let this be a reminder," she announced to the room. "My husband and I see everything on Miota and in Accolade, and we will judge accordingly. For those here to play games, you will not burden us with your presence for long." She turned back to pay me a warning stare. "Enjoy your night." She departed from the ballroom with her skirts flowing behind her.

CHAPTER 11

JULIA

I kept my head high and ignored the quiver in my throat. I would not break my countenance now.

All of it was so wrong—this competition, the chasm in my chest, the empty seat next to me. Cass should have been here, preparing for his Courtship. He should have been gathering the cities' Top-Tiered women to select a wife.

But he was damned by fate. Just as my brother had been—the crown atop my head served me *that* bitter reminder daily. Josiah was always supposed to rule, yet here *I* was.

"My sweet." The sound of Abner's voice made me jump, pulling me from the vicious thoughts preying on my mind. If I had slipped any further, Father's resurrected ghost would have grabbed hold of me, as he tended to do these days. "Are you all right?"

I searched my husband's concerned visage and only found his typical clueless grin, brightened by the fresh morning sunlight spilling into the dining room.

"I am fine," I insisted, keeping my lips drawn tight. "Just thinking of all we have to do today."

Abner reached across the lacquered table to collect my hands. I froze, wanting to pull away, but I could not in the presence of our personal staff. They sat behind me at their own table: Abner's courtier, my lady-in-waiting, and—

No one else. Cass's courtier no longer held a place in our dining room. I missed Max, my friend since early childhood.

My eyes fluttered shut in a prolonged blink. I could not cry here. I channeled the sun's radiance as I smiled back at my husband and slid my hands out from under his.

"Can I do anything to help?" Abner voiced, resuming picking at his oatmeal.

He had always been this way, since my own Courtship over twenty years ago. Back when his blond hair was not peppered with gray, and his smiling eyes were not set in wrinkles. He had always asked what he could help with. As if he could ever help *me* and my life.

He could not take away the burden of carrying a dynasty. And he could not turn back time to save Josiah, to let my brother rule instead. And Abner could not raise our son from the dead.

You're all alone, Jules, Father mocked me, slinking into the corners of my thoughts. *But you'll always have me.*

No. Not him. My stomach lurched, and I answered Abner to chase Father away. "No," I started. "There is nothing you can do. Unless you already have a replacement in mind for head butler of faction three."

"Faction three?" My husband cocked his head, his gray beard moving with his face. "Paulos?"

"Yes," I snarled. "Learn your staff, Abner." He only blinked like a fool. "Well? What is it?"

"Why are we replacing Paulos?" he asked, his voice low.

"Because he is dead." I narrowed my eyes, sharpening my gaze on my husband, channeling the steel of a butcher's knife. Abner only stared back like his tongue was too dense to function properly. "Is he not dead yet?" I pointed my spoon at Abner, and I practically heard my late mother scolding me for such table manners.

"I don't think so, sweet."

"Why not?" I pounded a fist on the table, causing a dissonant clanking of silverware against porcelain dishes. Ruffles of movement breathed to life behind me as our personal staff scrambled. "He broke the law last night!" I shouted. "I do not ask much from you, Abner, but I expect you to keep the butlers in line."

Abner dipped his head. "Yes, Your Majesty."

I could not bear to look at him. I pinpointed Gwynn, my lady-in-waiting. She approached swiftly, her navy dress rustling around her ankles.

"Call for Paulos Everton. *Immediately.*" My voice embodied stone and metal, and I hoped my emerald eyes burned.

Gwynn bowed deeply, letting her thick curtain of dark hair fall around her shoulders and into her face. "Yes, Your Most Royal Majesty." She departed from the dining room.

"Jules," Abner growled, a low warning. "What did he do worthy of death? Shouldn't he go to the Hold first? Have a trial?"

"There is too much going on in this castle already," I spat, reminding myself of the three hundred adults currently running around Castle Circle. The reminder always brought on a swift rush of dread. "If Paulos did not want this fate, he should never have let Griffith Howard and Corinn Januski leave the ballroom!"

Abner peered into his lap and pushed his oatmeal away. "No. He shouldn't have."

"Why those two?" I croaked, flinching at the weakness in my voice. "Why *Griffith*?"

Abner knew I was not so distraught over the boy, but his father. Abner's eyes flashed with pain, a window to his broken heart. I did not care; if he was jealous of a dead man, that was his own fault.

Luckily, I did not have to endure Abner's coercion for pity much longer. Gwynn entered with Paulos, who wore fear across his shoulders, weighing him down.

I mustered a grin and interlaced my fingers to keep them from shaking.

For Miota. For Father. For the dynasty. I would *not* be the weakest Delldova, the one to ruin our island. I had already kissed the edge of that fate when Cass nearly died at birth. Fortunately, he'd survived, because he was the only child I ever brought to nearly full-term; every other pregnancy ended in death.

Death and I possessed too many mutual acquaintances. And I was about to add another to the list. I was tainted, a walking curse.

"Good morning, Paulos," I cooed. "How did you enjoy the ball last night?"

His throat bobbed; he must have already guessed his fate. "It was w-wonderful, Your Most Royal M-majesty."

I copied what Abner had done earlier and pushed my food away. This part was always a bit gruesome—the light leaving their eyes, their fingers curling into half-fists, their abdomens stilling.

"Paulos, would you care to admit your faults, or should I do it for you?"

He gulped. "Your Majesty, I brought two candidates to a parlor." His words tumbled from his mouth. "They spilled wine, and there was glass on the floor, and they suggested towels, so I thought of those from—"

"You should have denied their request!" I spoke over Paulos's blubbering. Adrenaline pooled in my stomach. "You should *not* have let anyone leave the ballroom, and you *especially* should not have closed the door on them!"

I was no longer afraid. *He deserves this*, Father cackled.

I slipped my hand into the folds of my skirts to produce a small vial filled with a foul-smelling purple liquid. I had learned, through using it many times, that a little went a long way. I released two drops into a chalice of apple cider.

"Do you understand your crimes?" I asked, my tone as smooth as the poison now curling in the cider.

"Yes," Paulos breathed. "*Yes*, Your Most Royal Majesty."

I stood from my seat and presented the goblet to the butler. "Then you know I am not serving you malice, but justice. There are laws for a reason, Paulos."

With shaking hands, he took the goblet. A tear rolled down his cheek as he eyed the muddled drink. "*Please*, Your Majesty. Please, *please—*"

"Drink, Paulos."

The butler was a mess of tears and snot and shaking arms. From within my skirts, I gripped the hilt of my knife made of iron and ruby. Some refused to drink, therefore choosing a slower, more painful death. A foolish alternative.

He brought the goblet to his mouth, but upon smelling the liquid, he gagged and dropped the cup to the ground. The cider, dyed purple, ran on the hardwood. "Please! Your Majes—"

In a rapid swing, I embedded my knife into his lower left abdomen, wielding my weapon just as Father had taught me. Paulos's sticky blood gushed onto my hands before I could retreat, though I withdrew in time to save my dress.

Paulos wheezed, writhing and dropping to his knees. I navigated behind him and raked a hand through his wilting hair, grabbing a fistful to force his face toward the ceiling. While gritting my teeth, I released two droplets of poison down his throat. The pungent stench of death infiltrated the air.

Once the life left Paulos, I dropped his body. His head slammed against the floor with a dull *thud*. I turned to Gwynn as my stomach roiled. "Send staff to clean the dining room and apologize for the mess. I will order guards to dispose of the body."

Gwynn curtsied and nearly sprinted out of the dining room, causing Father to permeate my mind. *She can't wait to get away from the monster,* he chuckled.

Abner stared. Through the years, his horror had become muted, though it was always present.

"What are you looking at?" I charged. "Breakfast is over. We have candidates to go meet."

PART TWO

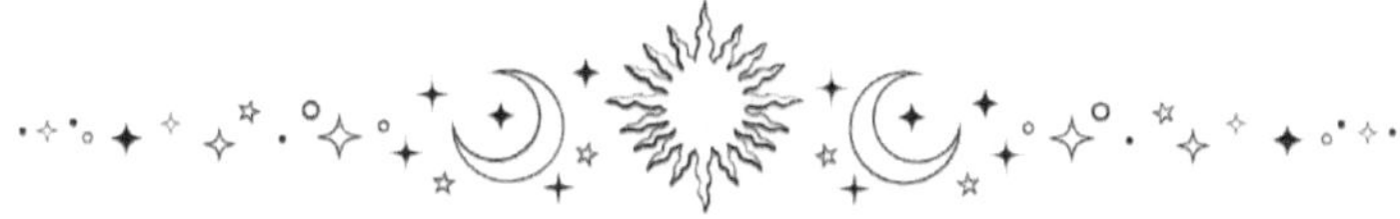

"A wall will be built around the island's perimeter to keep out the oceanic swells that ravage MIOTA. This structure will provide sanctuary from the unforgiving wilderness. Forces outside of this wall will be deemed deadly; therefore, any citizen who dwells on what is outside the Fort will be deemed deadly in turn."

—*Treaty of Miota, Amend. III*

CHAPTER 12

Soft sunlight seeped into the bedroom. *The sun!* I stretched across the feathery mattress, basking in the golden light. Back in the Low Tier, we stirred before dawn to eat breakfast in the Common. To sleep in with the sun was to miss a vital ration of food. But here in Castle Circle, in a room of finery and lavish commodities, daylight coaxed me awake. I grinned to myself.

My light mood dampened, however, once I recalled last night's events. The orchestrated wine spill . . . the man who knew my name, yet wouldn't reveal his secrets . . . the queen barking at us.

I groaned and rolled over in bed. I hadn't been here even a full day, and Cass's mother probably hated me.

The earthy aroma of coffee hit my nose, and I shot up. The beverage was a scarce commodity—grown in Pointe's temperature-regulated greenhouses—offered only on weekends. Which was unfortunate, since it was my favorite drink Miota had to offer.

Lily stood near the door with a platter of crumbling muffins, fluffy eggs, and colorful fruit. It must've been four or five rations. I licked my lips to keep drool from leaving my mouth.

"Good morning!" Lily chimed, setting the plate on the bed

next to me. "It's a big day. You're due at The Gathering Hall in less than an hour."

Though I heard her words, I couldn't comprehend them with all this food in front of me. "Do I just . . . pick one thing?" I asked, eyeing the tendrils of steam swirling from the eggs.

Lily paused from her spot near the desk. "No, that's all yours. Eat up!"

I nodded, hesitant to take a muffin, waiting for a catch. I might've been in Castle Circle, but why wouldn't I still be treated like a Low?

All inhibitions melted once the warm muffin passed my lips. There was a hint of . . . cinnamon? Nutmeg? I knew my spices, a consequence of living in Pointe, though I wasn't sure how to differentiate their tastes when the cooks hardly used them in rations back home. After inhaling the pastry, I went for the eggs, which also tasted better than the rubbery kind in Pointe.

Eggs came from Salford, just like Mr. Howard. My grip tightened on the mug as I sipped my coffee, willing my thoughts away from the man who made my skin bristle.

Lily bent to the floor to pick up my wine-stained dress from last night. "Oh, poor thing."

"It was an accident," I bumbled. "Not my fault. There was a man—"

"Stop." Lily smirked. "It's okay. You weren't going to wear this again, and you'll have more dresses in no time."

"I . . . will?" I blinked from around my mug.

"Yes. For starters . . ." She stepped into the hallway and came back with a sundress the color of green olives.

Lily helped me dress, apply makeup, and style my hair until it looked like I actually belonged here. By the time I needed to leave, I was a state of grace—a *caffeinated* state of grace, after three cups of coffee. Though I'd learned about this effect in school, I hadn't expected my limbs to rattle so much.

"The Gathering Hall is the huge building at the end of the lane," Lily verbally guided me. "You *can't* miss it. Just follow the crowd. You're going for orientation, where Their Majesties will explain all the rules of the competition. Don't be nervous, okay?"

That was an impossible command. Nerves bounced through my entire body—partially because of the caffeine, but mostly because of my anticipation.

Lily sent me out, and I descended to First Residence's lobby with a foreign candidate whose room was across the hall from mine. I debated introducing myself to the curly-haired redhead, but she didn't acknowledge me, so I did the same. I saw the conversation so clearly in my head: I'd tell her my name and Tier, and she'd mock me to no end. I wanted to stay as anonymous as possible in my time here.

The heat bogged down on my head as I walked the long street of Castle Circle. Sunlight ricocheted off buildings, making me squint more than usual. Curls slipped out of my hairstyle, going limp in the oppressive heat. I avoided my reflection in buildings' glassy exteriors; even the weather wanted to expose me. I didn't belong here. But I *needed* to stay here to avoid becoming a farmer.

The Gathering Hall loomed in the distance, settled at the lane's end like the dot of an exclamation mark. A crowd formed as I neared it, and the silent tension in the air was palpable. We were all competing for the same crown.

I had to beat *everyone* here to survive outside the dreaded life of a farmer. Could I somehow beat the odds? Or was I a fool, walking to my demise?

Butlers and maids ushered us into the hall, and the large, sparkling façade was hiding exposed wooden beams and earthy tones. Windows soared to the ceiling, bathing the open room in warm sunlight.

Hundreds of labeled seats packed the large internal cavity in prearranged lines. I found my chair at the end of a row, in a section made solely of Pointeans. My spot neighbored the aisle and Remi Hushe, a Middle-Tiered cook.

"Morning." I smiled at the girl with wiry brown hair chopped just below her ears.

Remi grinned back, though she said nothing. I couldn't blame her; she had no reason to want to talk to me. We were competitors, and I was below her.

I was below *everyone*. Sure, I had equals like Pollie and Jubilee, but I was above no one.

As seats filled, the gravity of the situation sank in, and I slumped in my seat. I'd have to fight my way from last place to first place . . . with hundreds standing in my way, competing for the same spot.

Their Majesties mounted the quaint, raised stage at the front of the hall, and everyone fell silent. The only movement came from the shadowed corners where different city's cameramen were perched like birds ready to record us.

They'd document every detail since Accolade was receiving ten hours of daily coverage. After projectors spent years on end sitting idly, flickering on only to give crucial announcements from the monarchy, I couldn't imagine the nonsense filmed to fill a daily *ten* hours.

Queen Julia wore a deep green gown matching the color of her eyes—a hue I was familiar with, thanks to our proximity last night when she'd scolded Mr. Howard and me. I wondered where *he* was now. Hopefully, I'd never get tangled in his antics again.

"Good morning, candidates," Her Majesty spoke into a

microphone, her voice carrying through the hall. "And thank you to everyone watching at home as we begin this unprecedented journey into the future. On our island, self-preservation is paramount. We will take this competition *very* seriously.

"Today, we will go over the logistics and timeline for Accolade. We will only introduce this information once, so make sure you are listening carefully. In fact, it would be best if you took notes."

She barely paused before continuing. I scrambled to retrieve my panel from my pocket, and others around me did the same. I jabbed my thumbs on the touchscreen, furiously trying to keep up with the queen's cadence.

"As you are aware, our son, Prince Kierran Cassius Delldova, His Royal Highness of Miota, has died. As a result, my husband and I are burdened with the task of setting aside our grief as we look to Miota's future with hope. His Highness, Prince Kierran, was supposed to have his Courtship this summer. Then, on his twenty-first birthday, he would have been crowned sovereign ruler of Miota alongside his bride."

My vision blurred. If Cass were alive, I'd have a real chance at becoming something *more*. But here I was, determined, poised, and ready to fight for a glimpse of life outside the Low Tier. It was time to escape.

" . . .Accolade will take place over seven weeks."

My stomach dropped. What had I missed? The topic was no longer of Cass, but of Accolade.

"There are three hundred of you to start. We will narrow you down until two remain—these two will, in due time, be crowned the next king and queen of Miota. We will select rulers who will best ensure peace, equality, and prosperity."

I wasn't sure anyone in Miota would use those three adjectives to describe their lives. In Pointe, everyone knew death too intimately, whether it was a Low-Tiered family who'd lost a father to malnutrition or a Top-Tiered family who lost a sister to asympton. And I knew better than anyone there was no equality on Miota, not when my family faced impending starvation while Tops possessed heavy bodies of stockpiled calories.

"Our two winners will not be coronated soon; they will be given time to learn the . . . *demands* of ruling this island. Now, enough about the winners, because that hardly applies to any of you."

Beside me, Remi shifted in her seat. She tucked her hair behind her ear, but at its cropped length, it immediately fell back into her face.

"Candidates will accrue points each week by competing in activities that showcase necessary traits to rule Miota. These points will be totaled to determine your overall ranking among all candidates, and at the end of every week, those ranked in the bottom fifty will be eliminated from Accolade."

The hall fell still as Her Majesty's words robbed the room of its air.

The queen pushed on. "This will be the method for eliminations until the last two weeks, which will be further explained once that time comes. If you happen to make it that far, you will have earned your place of respect among Miota. But you still must earn *my* approval."

I did the quick math. If I made it that far, to the final one hundred candidates, I'd have earned the respect of Miota. Would that be enough to keep Dr. Ova from demoting me?

Disgust bit through my rising spirits. Even if I stayed in the lab, I'd be nothing more than the girl who cleaned trash and catalogued poisonous chemicals and incinerated flesh. That wasn't a life, either.

I needed more. I needed to *win*.

King Abner spoke next. He sounded so much like Bernard; I could look to my feet and pretend my old tutor was here, standing on stage.

"Three competitions will happen each week," the king started. "The first is a group contest where each city will work together as a team. You'll be rewarded points based on your city's placement in the competition.

"The second is a head-to-head competition. You'll each be assigned a head-to-head partner for the week, and you'll compete against this person in history quizzes, lecture exams, and a candidate-wide vote. At the end of the week, the winner of each pairing will gain *more* points, and the other will *lose* points.

"Lastly, a solo competition will take place, where a large number of points will be rewarded to *some*, not all."

I stuck out my tongue, typing furiously on my panel to keep up. But it was too much. It was just as mind-spinning as the math classes I'd taken in school among the engineers and mechanics. Why doctors required years of complex math, I still didn't know.

Julia reclaimed the microphone. "These three competitions will all make more sense as they are conducted. Along with competitions, there will be mandatory daily hours spent here in The Gathering Hall—whether you use the time to strategize, make alliances, or make enemies is up to you. Each city will also attend weekly lectures.

"I will also mention the obvious: *two* candidates will win, a future king and queen. This will require you to *pair up*. After four weeks of competing, the remaining candidates will partner up, and your fates will be tied for the remainder of Accolade. You will either win, or be eliminated, as one."

Candidates rustled in their seats at this announcement. *Pairing?*

In four weeks, we'd pick who we'd potentially *marry*?

I hadn't put much thought into the fact this wasn't a solo competition. If I was going to win Accolade . . . I'd need to win with someone else.

The only man I knew here was Salem, and he didn't want to be here. He belonged back home, learning surgery and brightening Pointe. *This* put a wrinkle in my plan.

"Silence!" the queen hissed, her cold voice echoing among the wooden rafters. She regained her composure as the hall went still. "Do not think about partnering yet; half of you will not make it to that point."

Her statistic burned like acid in my brain. As one of the few Lows present, what made me think *I* could make it to the partnerships in four weeks? And what made me think I could win?

I couldn't. Yet, somehow, *I had to.*

Queen Julia moved on. "Today, you will meet your head-to-head partners. This is the person you will compete against for the next six days. If you open the Accolade folder on your panels, your partner assignments have been sent to you."

My heart raced. The caffeine wasn't helping *anything* this morning. I opened the folder, unsure of what to expect. Would I be competing against someone Top-Tiered? Would it be a Pointean or someone foreign?

I found the head-to-head assignment and tapped on it. A man's face appeared on my screen. Familiar brown hair and eyes the color of rich chocolate occupied my panel's screen.

No. Was this . . .?

I pressed my lips into a thin line as I read the man's demographic information. This assignment was *not* a coincidence.

Griffith Howard. From Salford. Top-Tiered.

My partner was the man from the parlor.

CHAPTER 13

I couldn't pry my eyes from my panel. His photo gave me a wicked, taunting smirk. Griffith Howard. Salford. Top Tier.

Top Tier! He'd beat me this week. I couldn't compete against a Top and stand a chance.

"Everyone, please find your partners now," Queen Julia prompted.

The Gathering Hall exploded into chaos. Everyone sprang from their seats and called out their partner's name. Remi muttered a curse and raked a hand through her hair before storming off in a mad search.

I didn't know where to begin, considering I didn't know which section of the hall held Salford's candidates. Aside from scanning the crowd, I didn't do much. Besides, I wasn't in a *rush* to find Griffith Howard, the man who somehow knew me.

I'd just stepped into the aisle when he materialized in front of me, weaving through the throngs of candidates. He had the same glimmer in his eye as last night, and his lip curled upward in a snarky grin. I suppressed an exaggerated eye roll.

Griffith Howard inhaled to speak when Her Majesty shouted

at everyone to freeze. The bodies stuffing the hall stilled. "If you are with your head-to-head partner," the queen said, "tap your panels together."

I shifted my attention from Cass's mother to Griffith. He jutted his panel out, and I tapped my device to his. This was *odd*.

"All right, carry on. Please find your partners *quickly*."

Disorder ensued. I looked at my panel as it buzzed, and I realized Griffith and I received *points* for finding each other.

Fifty points. Eightieth place. My eyes bulged.

Griffith hummed. "Fifty points. Well, this makes our reunion a *little* better."

I gave a contrived grin. "Maybe if we're going to see a lot of each other this week, you'll tell me why you know who I am."

"Only if you'll tell me why you lied about your identity." His eyes roamed my face, making me forget we were in a crowd of people.

"You're a stranger, from another city and Tier, who somehow knew my name. You expected me to just *trust* you, Griffith?"

"Just call me Griff," he said, strained. "Please."

My breath snagged in my lungs before I released it. "Fine. Griff." My accusation evaporated.

He beheld me with such intent care, like he was either studying me or pitying me, and I hated that I didn't know which.

Was he plotting how to beat me? Or was he, like everyone else, wondering how I got here at all?

"I didn't expect your trust," Griff said. I had to backtrack to remember what was last said. "But I expected the truth."

"Why?" I snapped. "You don't know me." *Except,* I indignantly reminded myself, *he thinks he does.*

"Not personally." A muscle in his jaw ticked. "But I'm hoping to change that."

"Is it like the expression?" I breathed. "'Keep your friends close and your enemies closer?'"

He furrowed his brow and shoved his hands into his pockets. "Who said we're enemies?"

"We're competing against each other *as we speak*," I said, the sentence laced with a nervous laugh. Why was he so persistent? And annoying? And why didn't he seem to hate me, as everyone else did upon learning my Tier? He'd seen my profile; he knew I was a Low. It even took Salem a year before warming up to me.

"We're only competitors *this* week," said Griff.

Their Majesties called for our attention once we were all paired off. A tense current filled the air as Griff and I turned to the stage. Our shoulders brushed as we spun, and I sidestepped away from him.

"Miota's history is something we hold dear," Queen Julia started over the strained crowd. "We can only secure our futures by learning lessons from the past, so every week's head-to-head challenge will include taking an exam on Miotan history. The exam's answer choices will appear on your panels. Of your pairing, whoever answers questions more accurately and swiftly will win this first phase of your head-to-head competition. May the best candidate win."

Everyone navigated to the correct screen on their panel. In my periphery, Griff glanced at me, playing it off as he swept his hair off his forehead. He was sizing me up.

I stood, poised. *An exam.* I could do this. I was relatively good at tests; I'd taken too many to count in my schooling years. Unfortunately, I was sure Top-Tiered Griff had, too.

Her Majesty gave the first question. "Who is my great-great-great-grandfather?"

I bit back a scoff. Did anyone know such a random fact?

"It's alphabetical," Griff whispered to me.

I tuned out his nonsense as six answers appeared on my panel. My mind whirled. I had to be quick, but precise. Her Majesty's father was Iven Delldova, who'd died before I was born. His mother was ... Harriette Delldova ... whose father ... and his parent ... I didn't know. I guessed a name, Blanden Delldova, and hoped to the stars.

After some time, my answer shone red. *Incorrect.* A few candidates shouted, claiming they didn't know it was timed; they hadn't answered and didn't receive points.

"Did you get it?" Griff asked.

I rolled my eyes and focused on my panel.

The queen gave our next question. "Who was the first ruler to create the career screening, and therefore greatly increasing productivity across all five cities?"

I guessed again. Erick Delldova. Why not? I almost laughed. Griff was going to *destroy* me this week. Question after question came, each one burrowing its way underneath my skin. This wasn't Miotan history, as promised; it was Delldova trivia.

"Last one," the queen announced on our tenth question. I'd so far answered *nothing* right, and I could've screamed. "Who was the first ruler to claim asympton an island-wide emergency?"

I sighed. Thank the stars. This was Aris Delldova, the first king of the modern era. All records from before Aris's rule were destroyed in an oceanic flood.

I tapped Aris's name on my screen, and my heartbeat roared in my ears. It was right! My excitement vanished, though, once reality set it. I'd gotten one question correct. *One* out of ten. Griff would've laughed if he saw my score.

On cue, Griff's score became visible. He'd answered every question incorrectly.

My partner offered me a sheepish grin as my gaze snapped to his face. "Good game, Corinn." He jutted out his hand for me to shake. I only stared, and Griff dropped his arm to his side. "Right. Er, I guess I'll have to do better on our other exams."

"You'll win the candidate-wide vote against me for sure," I said, glancing at my rank. *Thirtieth.* How long would it take for my status to catch up with me?

I wasn't sure why disappointment, of all emotions, flashed in Griff's dark eyes. "Well, you never know. You could pull it off."

"I don't want your pity," I shot. "I know my Tier; I *know* you're better than me. You don't have to act like I stand a chance."

Griff lightly recoiled and searched my face. For what, I wasn't sure. "Corinn, you don't think—"

"Please go back to your seats," the queen commanded. "You have all completed your first competition."

The rest of the morning simultaneously dragged on and blurred by until my mind was mush. Being talked at by Their Majesties managed to feel like a full lecture day at school—only this stuff seemed superfluous to my brain, and I fought hard to retain it. My only hope was in the jumbled notes on my panel.

When lunchtime came, we were given an hour in our residences before returning for the afternoon. I found Salem, and we walked toward our buildings in step. I hadn't seen him since last night's ball. After the parlor incident, Salem had pressed for details, and I'd refused to give any. Since we were equally stubborn, the argument had lasted the entire night.

"Do you think they'd notice if I didn't go back after lunch?" Salem muttered.

"Maybe not," I mused. "You have big plans?"

Salem shrugged and pushed his glasses higher up his nose. "I'm convinced I'd have more fun watching flowers bloom." He sighed. "Hopefully, I'm not here for *too* long. Our head-to-head exam earlier? I answered those questions wrong on purpose to let my partner win. She's a mechanic from Cape and kept rambling about how she hoped to climb the Fort. Is that idiotic or what?"

I squinted as we passed a particularly reflective building and digested Salem's morning update. Somehow, the mention of his partner wanting to *climb the Fort* wasn't the most jarring part. "You . . . knew those answers?" I asked. "You let her win?"

"Yeah, it was pretty rudimentary. I mean—didn't you get history lessons in your primary school?"

My primary school. The Low-Tiered one I'd attended before matching with medicine. "No," I scoffed. Anger coated my veins— because of my unjust primary education *and* because of Griffith Howard. "By the moon. I'm a *moron*."

"No, you're not." Salem nudged me with his shoulder. "So you didn't know the queen's great-grandmother's favorite color was periwinkle? No big deal—"

"Not *that*," I said, nudging him back and letting my smile run its course. "That would've been a great question, though."

"I know."

I huffed through my nose. "Anyway, my partner's a Top. He must've let me win, too. He scored zero."

"Wow." Salem lifted his brow. "Who is it?"

"Salford. Griff Howard."

"Oh, Howard," Salem said, sympathy etched on his face. "Yeah."

Each city's Top Tier spent one weekend per month in Castle Circle. Salem said cities had to share the lavish lane every so often due to there not usually being five weekends in a month. During times when cities overlapped, the Top-Tiered families of the two cities would learn each other's names, though apparently, they never spoke outright to each other.

"He must not want to be here, either," Salem ventured.

I wasn't sure that was it, though. I thought back to some of the things Griff said during our head-to-head exam . . . my senses told me rather than wanting himself to lose, he'd wanted me to *win*.

What game was he playing?

I parted with Salem at Sixth Residence, his building. I walked the rest of the way to First Residence with quaking legs. I didn't want to meet the people in my building; they'd inevitably learn where I came from.

A fuchsia hallway extended from the left side of the golden lobby. I followed it to the room at the end, where daylight flooded the hallway.

I clasped my hands together upon entering the room consisting of bright windows and a long, varnished table. Six girls sat at one end, and the redhead who'd ignored me this morning was among them. The clique held themselves with so much confidence I figured they must've belonged to the Top Tier.

My ears rang and vision darkened as I sat next to a honey-blonde girl on the edge of the group. Hopefully, Pollie would arrive soon; I needed her company.

The girl at the head of the table spoke, twirling her limp maroon hair in coils around her index finger. "There are too many people who shouldn't be here. Middles, even some *Lows*. How'd they swindle their way into Castle Circle, of all places?"

Swindle? My mind snagged on the foreign word, inferring its meaning. I stared into my lap, hoping to remain unacknowledged. Any Top would spit in my face upon learning where I came from.

Well, any Top except for Griff Howard, apparently. He was

the exception, a puzzling anomaly I simultaneously wanted to solve and throw far away.

"I don't recognize you," someone said. A chord of dread sang through me as I dared to look at the maroon-haired girl. Her dark eyes hardened on me. "City and Tier?"

I parted my lips at her bluntness. She didn't care about my name; she wanted to know my status and if I was competition. "Pointe," I answered, leaving it there. "I'm Corinn."

The girl leered. "And your Tier, Corinn?"

The six ladies looked at me, the weight of their eyes like a heap of bricks sitting on my chest. I struggled to inhale. "Low," I finally mumbled.

The group cackled.

"She'll be gone by next week," Maroon Hair said as if I wasn't sitting *right here*. My blood boiled.

"I knew it," the redhead chimed. "I saw her this morning, and I knew she wasn't one of us."

"Doesn't belong here," another agreed. I clenched my fists, letting my nails bite into my palms. I wanted to defend myself, but I couldn't afford to make Top-Tiered enemies.

Were they right? How far could I make it in Accolade? I was a clock ticking to my destruction. This road would end in me farming in the fields, drowning in the Low Tier, starving with my single ration per meal, and hopefully, just collapsing one day to put me out of my misery.

The girl next to me, whose hair tumbled to her waist, smiled at me. "I'm Pandora. How'd you *get* here? As a Low?" Her tone indicated genuine curiosity.

I gulped. I had no idea why I was here. Neither one of Their Majesties knew of Cass's and my secret friendship, so I must've gotten here for some other reason. "I don't know," I admitted.

"Keeping secrets, are we?" Maroon Hair taunted.

"Oh, hush, Nelly," Pandora said. "We're all from Kendall, by the way." Kendall. Their city powered Miota's electric grid, solar panels, and energy reserve.

The maroon-haired girl, Nelly, groaned. "You don't need to talk to Lows just because you feel *bad* for them," she told Pandora. "She'll be back to farming soon enough. That's what they do in Pointe, right?"

Nelly's words sliced me, hitting a nerve. "I'm a doctor, you know," I blurted without thought. What was I saying? But it was only *half* a lie, really. "I matched with medicine. It wasn't my fault I was born into the Low Tier."

The group looked at me with fiery stares.

Nelly chuckled, shattering the stillness. "A Low-Tiered *doctor*? I wouldn't believe it if you swore it on the Fort. If you're in the hospital, you're there to clean after everyone else."

I swallowed, and my throat turned to stone. My silence was confirmation enough for Nelly.

She gave a smug smile. "As I thought, *Low*."

Tears burned my eyes. I debated arguing, but it would likely only cause more harm. What was her problem? I tried pretending Nelly's vicious stares rolled off me after that, but it was impossible.

I shifted in my seat, turning my back on the Kendallians. When Pollie eventually showed up, I latched onto her. For all of lunch, my mind spun as I wondered how I'd make it through the week, surrounded by Tops everywhere I looked.

And I started to wonder if applying for Accolade had been a *terrible* idea after all.

CHAPTER 14

Wednesday held our first group competition. Every candidate stood outside The Gathering Hall, underneath the harsh sun now dipping in the sky. I stood cross-armed next to Salem as the queen's words washed over us.

"Welcome to the first group competition." Queen Julia's voice fell flat in the humidity. "Candidates from each city will compete as a team to win this evening's contest. Citizens of the first-place city will receive one hundred points; for the following cities, seventy-five, fifty, twenty-five, and zero points."

I dug my nails into my arms and surveyed the surrounding candidates. If Pointe came in last place, my rank would drop dramatically. The rankings had already started fluctuating; two cities, Salford and Yorkinson, already had their lectures and associated exams, which meant those candidates ruled the top spots.

Though I sat in 130th place in the rankings, I needed Pointe to do well in the group competition. Since Monday, I'd only fallen in rank, which was a trend that would get me sent home.

"I will be on a microphone in The Gathering Hall," Queen Julia said. "Follow me inside."

All three hundred of us slowly squeezed into the hall. Five heaping piles of chairs created obstacles in the otherwise empty space. Salem and I exchanged confused glances.

"There are certain qualities we expect in a ruler," Her Majesty boomed into her microphone. I couldn't pinpoint her location, now somewhere among the swarms of bodies. "Teamwork. Creativity. Decisiveness. And being prepared for the worst."

The lights flickered off, submerging us in darkness. A few shrieks bounced through the hall, followed by shushing. The yawning windows of The Gathering Hall must have been covered, because no light came to save my sight. I grabbed Salem's hand.

The queen continued. "You and your city must work together to find your key out of here. You will be rewarded points based on the order that cities exit the hall—and everyone alive from the city needs to make it out to count, so do not leave anyone behind. Best of luck."

I jolted. Did she say . . . everyone *alive?*

Whirling strobe lights turned on, too dim to do more than help me make out hordes of anonymous bodies roaming about. Hissing filled the room, and I realized *gas* was being pumped into the hall. Everything turned hazy, and my eyes watered.

"We probably need to gather Pointe," Salem said.

"Or should we find the way out and *then* congregate?" I offered.

Nearby candidates turned on their panel's flashlights. I mimicked them, though the light only revealed how foggy the room truly was. As time ticked by, the room's energy spiraled. No one knew where to begin.

"Should we check the doors?" I asked, knowing it was a dumb question. But I wasn't sure where else to start. Other candidates moved with purpose, now scanning the hall's perimeter. I couldn't afford for Pointe to lose this. "Let's go." I dragged Salem toward the entrance we came from, using my panel to light our path. Plenty of others were at the doors, though I didn't recognize any of them.

The heavy doors were locked, as suspected, but at least I wouldn't have to wonder now.

"I should have mentioned," Her Majesty said through her mic. "The Queen's Guard is in the building with us. They are . . . taking people out at random. These people will not be able to leave the premises with you, so leave them be. Again, good luck."

A chill swept through my bones. "What do you think *that* means?" I whispered, turning off my panel's light. Others hissed and squealed, eager to leave.

"Taking people out at random?" Salem echoed the queen's words. "It has to be metaphorical for *something*."

Bodies scuffled around us, skimming my arms and nearly knocking me to my feet. As Salem and I bumbled aimlessly, my fear grew. I didn't mean to jump to conclusions, but the Queen's Guard was only good for one thing: executing. The queen had first mentioned something about everyone *alive*, and now guards would take people out . . .

No. That was impossible. Their Majesties wouldn't round us up in the dark to kill us. Right? There were too many prominent young adults here—Tops, doctors, engineers, family members of those on the executive council . . .

All of which *I* was not. Would I be targeted?

Salem and I maneuvered through the piles of chairs that did nothing but slow down the crowds of candidates. A fraction of my brain prompted me to look *in* the mounds, but I wasn't sure how we'd find a way out underneath a pile of chairs. Plus, we couldn't—

Bang.

Bang.

I shrieked before clapping my hands over my mouth. *"What was that?"* I hissed to Salem, reaching out to grip his inky figure beside me. My eyes couldn't adjust to the darkness. "Do you think the Guard is . . ."

"No way," Salem whispered. He tugged my arm, and we cowered behind a pile of chairs. "This wouldn't go over well in the cities. Think of the families. They can't be killing."

He was right. The guards weren't killing people; they *couldn't* be. But we'd all heard the distinct firing of a weapon. Maybe they were only paralyzing candidates?

"You were right," I breathed to Salem. "About Castle Circle. This place is *crazy.*"

Salem huffed a laugh. I looked at my best friend, and my stomach didn't even have time to drop. It all happened so fast: the blurry red dot on his chest, the weapon firing, Salem's body crumbling backward.

"Salem?" I studied him, hoping to the moon my paralysis theory was correct. But he was motionless and unresponsive.

I shrieked. "Salem!" In the back of my mind, my self-preservation told me to run. Surely, I was the next target. I fell forward, and my palms hit the floor, reverberating my bones and sending an ache through my wrists. My stomach clenched—

Bang.

I waited for the sharp blossom of pain, but I only felt steady pressure around my shoulders as I was hauled away from Salem.

"Rise and shine, lovely," a deep voice hummed in my ear.

This wasn't real. I didn't know what was happening, but *this was not real.*

I twisted myself out of the pair of arms ensnaring me and collapsed on the cold floor.

"Get up, Corinn. We're close."

"Griff?" I croaked, squinting to make out the voice's owner.

"Yes." *Great.* My head-to-head partner could easily sabotage me right now. "Did you two figure out the key, too?" Despite the scene, his voice held a reserved quality. Candidates tripped over my legs and screamed at each other to hurry. Anxiety laced the air like it was bottled in the thick rolls of fog around us.

"Griff," I breathed again. *Get back to Salem. We need to check on him.* But I couldn't get past my first syllable. "Griff."

He hovered over me. "As much as I love my name in your mouth, we have important things to do. Let's go." He pulled me up and led me farther along the pile of chairs.

"We need to find Salem," I protested.

"No, we need to find the *key*. And this'll all be over."

Right. Escape. We needed to escape the hall while evading the Queen's Guard blasting weapons at their own will. Salem had already failed the competition. Would he lose points for it? Was he all right?

"Corinn, your friend is fine." Could he read my thoughts so easily? "You said his name is Salem? As in, Salem Redding?"

"Yes."

"His mom is on Pointe's executive council, right? Julia would have a revolution on her hands if she ordered her guards to truly *hurt* everyone right now."

In the darkness, my mind worked. Their Majesties would never risk Genevieve Redding's son. Slowly, I nodded, choosing to ignore how casually Griff had referred to the queen. "So, where's this key?"

Griff's eyes pinned me into stillness. "You know where. Think about it. What's the common theme throughout Miota?"

"Throughout Miota?" I didn't know anything about *all* of Miota; I only knew Pointe and what was within our walls. And I supposed I somewhat knew Castle Circle now, tucked within its *own* steel gate, but I knew nothing about the other cities. We were all sealed off from each other.

That was it. Adrenaline coursed through me. Our cities, Castle Circle, the royal grounds, our entire island . . . "Everything is trapped within a wall." *Including me.*

Griff nodded. "Lead the way."

A muted sense of victory flared in my chest. I'd thought of this initially, and it had been *right.* The key—whatever it was—was within the chair barricades.

I wound into the nearest pile of chairs by locating a chink in its perimeter. I held my breath, navigating the pile of chair limbs with caution. One wrong move would send the pile crashing down on me. I blindly probed the floor and . . . *there!* I gripped the small metallic object. It was an actual *key,* an outdated object that had since been replaced with the technology of panels.

"How'd you know there'd be a key?" I called to Griff as I reversed out of the mound. No answer.

I turned around and flashed the key to show Griff—who smiled at me as I noticed the hazy dot centered on his chest. "Go win this," Griff mumbled. "Remember what I said—"

I flinched at the weapon sounding, and I ran, refusing to watch him fall to the ground. Even if it wasn't real, *something* about it wasn't completely fake.

Holding the key, I ran for the nearest Pointean. I didn't have time to dwell on Griff's motives for helping *me,* a Low and his competition.

I found Mathilda Levvyn, a Top-Tiered article director at *Pointean Gazette.* In another situation, I might've wondered what the news station was doing without her, but this wasn't the time to dwell on it.

"Mathilda," I breathed, running into her with full force.

The tall woman shrieked. "Who are you?"

I stopped short. Was I so forgettable? She should've recognized me—everyone in Pointe knew everyone, and her job revolved around pinning names to faces. Maybe she couldn't see me well enough in the dark.

"Corinn Januski," I answered, burying my only shred of pride. "I have the key, so we just need to gather the Pointeans—"

"Key?" She ripped the object from my hand and waved it in the air. "Pointe! Gather around! Pointe! Gather—"

"*Stop!*" I hissed. "You'll get—"

Bang.

Shot. Yep.

I fumbled for the key and pried it from Mathilda's hand. As soon as I secured it, I ran again, slinking into one of the shadowed corners.

My stomach dropped when I dared to turn on my panel's flashlight and study the key. *Key for Kendall.*

This wasn't for Pointe.

I gathered my strength, leftover from what Griff had given me. I *needed* to win this; I couldn't waste away in fear now.

I threw Kendall's key into the darkness, smiling as I thought of Nelly and her city stuck in here. I ran to the barricades of chairs and wiggled through one of the piles. At its center, I found another cold key. *Key for Salford.*

A surprising pang shuddered through my chest. I wished I could give it to Griff.

I left their key and scooted out of the chairs. Someone grabbed me, and I froze in their arms. If it was a Guard . . .

"Pointe?" they whispered. "Follow us."

I noted the trail of figures snaking through The Gathering

Hall, inconspicuous enough to look like candidates fleeing in a general direction. But a sense of relief washed over me when I realized these were Pointeans. Someone else must've found our key. We made it to the front door, scanning our panels as we exited a few at a time.

The street was empty, save for King Abner and a blond guard. I must've remembered the guard from Sunday night at the castle—the only other time I'd seen the Queen's Guard—because he was oddly familiar. He and the king bowed their heads, whispering together.

Pollie found me, squealing and wrapping her arms around me. "We did it! Thank the stars! I was ranked 260th, but now, maybe I'll be okay . . ."

"We will be," I said, reassuring us both.

We watched the rest of the conscious Pointeans file out of the building. Once everyone had shuffled out, our panels buzzed, rewarding us one hundred points.

Sixty-seventh place.

I gasped, unable to hide my smile, and hugged Pollie again. Pointe had won.

We stood on the street as we waited for the rest of the cities to emerge. The sun bore down, absorbing into the paved black street and reflecting onto our faces. Sweat beaded at my temples, and my hair stuck to my arms.

Fifteen minutes later, Cape streamed out of the building, followed by Salford, and then Yorkinson.

Kendall didn't emerge for so long, I began to regret moving their key simply because of how sweaty I was. When the sun dipped entirely below the Fort, Their Majesties grew as impatient as the rest of us, and they called the competition. Kendall was in last place anyway.

They'd spent hours locked in a foggy, dark hall, and they had no points to show for it.

"Your peers who were shot are fine," the queen announced after gathering all the candidates. "They were tranquilized, temporarily sedated. This symbolizes the deadly disease running rampant throughout Miota, taking lives from every city. Asympton is random, as were the targets just now.

"If you rule this country, you must be able to work metaphorically in the dark *and* keep your brains about you, all while evading a deadly disease with no cure that threatens to take your friends and family. Do you all think you can do that? Because I can ensure that my husband's and my lives are much worse than anything you just experienced in that building."

Silence loomed, with only the whirr of bugs in the distant fields as an answer.

Her Majesty sighed. "You are all dismissed for the night."

And that was the first group competition.

While I'd been excited for Pointe's lecture day, ready to outscore Griff on the associated exam, the day wasn't what I'd imagined.

All Pointeans gathered in an office building, which was a plain room made of transparent walls and filled with nothing but rows of desks. Salem said Tops sometimes needed to fill their weekly work quotas over their assigned weekends in Castle Circle, so they'd conduct them in here.

Our lecturer was Sharlee Winnet, a stout woman on Yorkinson's executive council, and she happened to be one of the most pretentious people I'd ever met. Every few minutes, she'd sneak a bit of hair gel into her palm and smooth her inky hair back. Her head glistened in the natural light flooding the room, and I could hardly keep a straight face.

The whole day consisted of describing each city's role in *painful* detail. I'd never forget a city's monarchy-assigned task again, even if I tried. Some candidates snuck out after lunch, which would've tempted me more if I wasn't in the front row with Salem, right in Sharlee's line of sight. Plus, there was the obvious: I needed to ace this exam and beat Griff.

The test, administered to our panels, was simple; I could've taken it without the lecture. I missed one of fifty questions, and the ninety-eight percent translated to an added ninety-eight points to my week's total score. Griff's score from a few days ago now flashed next to mine. He'd gotten eighteen points, answering only *nine* questions correctly. What sort of game was he playing?

Regardless, my rank left me beaming. *Forty-second place.* It was almost safe to say I'd survive this first week. Still, I wouldn't rest easily until after the first elimination on Sunday.

The week crept forward. We had required hours in The Gathering Hall each day, which ate up every morning and some afternoons. Griff always managed to find me during those hours. I thanked him for his help in the group competition, but outside of that, we resorted to dodging each other's stares. I hated the attention Griff Howard gave me. How did he know who I was? And why did he care?

I noted his usual crowd, though. He most often spoke with a man who had russet skin and dark hair that fell past his shoulders. The two usually kept their heads dipped together, clearly scheming. A black-haired girl, who always wore sheer dresses, often lingered near Griff, too, which put a knot in my stomach, though I couldn't pinpoint why.

Every Friday night, Their Majesties met with Miota's full executive council in The Gathering Hall, and Accolade clearly wouldn't halt those meetings. Council members from all five cities arrived on Friday evening, and with the way I was treated, my Tier might as well have been branded on my forehead.

Mrs. Redding gushed on Salem's success so far, which did nothing but disgruntle him. Other Top-Tiered candidates greeted council members—their family and friends, no doubt—while I barely mustered a polite smile to anyone who accidentally met my gaze on their search for others.

Others more important than a Low.

At least, because Castle Circle was jam-packed with Accolade candidates, no city's Top Tier would stay here for the weekend.

Our rankings disappeared that same night. Last I knew, I was ranked seventy-first. I didn't foresee dropping almost two hundred places by Sunday, so I almost relaxed. We wouldn't see our rankings again until after eliminations, when fifty people would leave Accolade.

The solo competition took place Saturday, which consisted of solving riddles. I'd always proved too impulsive and impatient for logic games, so I didn't fare too well. I'd probably drop a few places in the rankings, though it was unnerving not to know for certain. Hopefully, others weren't good with riddles, either.

The weekly polls opened on Saturday, where we'd vote on our panels for one person in each head-to-head pairing. There wasn't a standard of measurement for how we'd choose candidates, and we were only given everyone's name, city, Tier, and portrait. I voted for all the Pointeans, and in the pairings where I didn't know either person, I chose the lower Tier. In partnerships of the same Tier, I went off who looked more pleasant to be around.

I hadn't understood this vote correctly before. Yes, the winner between Griff and me would receive points, but each vote also counted as a point. If one person in a pairing received a vote from every candidate, they could receive upward of three hundred points today.

This candidate vote had the potential to hold more weight than any other competition of the week.

I wasn't anywhere *near* as safe as I'd thought. After all, in a partnership between a Low and Top Tier, the Top would win almost every time.

At house dinner Saturday night, Nelly gloated about how she'd placed in the top ten before our rankings disappeared. "I was right behind Addison Maybee," she said, like that was some feat in itself. Though *I* didn't recognize the name, everyone else certainly did. Regardless, it seemed safe to assume Nelly would be back next week. Meanwhile, Pollie had hovered around 270th place before the rankings disappeared, so I wasn't sure of her fate.

After dinner, I was too anxious to go to my room for the night, knowing sleep was the only thing between now and tomorrow morning's eliminations. I didn't want to leave, but it also exhausted me to think about doing this all again next week when the points reset.

I strayed outside and sat on First Residence's curb. The setting sun painted the sky a vibrant pink in its final statement before night sank in. Candidates congregated on outdoor patios for drinks and desserts served by residence maids and butlers. A stone building down the street produced muted music, and I assumed the culprit was Club Castle, a bar often featured on *Accolade Times,* known for hosting parties. Sporadically, the club's door opened, and a drum's beat trickled outside.

With everything happening around me, I still found my spot on the sidewalk to be a perfect pocket of serenity. The sky, slowly being leached of wispy daylight, begged for something bigger and better. Something unknown, waiting to be found. I tried to forget about everything—the candidate vote, my head-to-head partner, eliminations—even if it only lasted a few minutes.

"Can I crash your party?"

I craned my neck toward the intruder and found Griff Howard interrupting my tranquility. My emotions always knotted around him. We were competing against each other this week, yet he seemed to want me to beat him. Did it have anything to do with how he knew me?

"This isn't a party, first off," I said with a huff. As if anyone in Castle Circle would invite *me*, a Low, to a party. "And you can only join if you promise to answer some questions."

"Deal." Griff plopped onto the curb, sitting so close that our knees almost knocked together. I held my breath, unsure if I could scoot away without him realizing. He set his elbows on his knees and clasped his hands together. "It's beautiful, isn't it? When day becomes night?"

I glared at him. "Poetic."

"You think? I have plenty more where that came from." He grinned before tipping his head upward. "You know, I was hoping that, when I saw you were my head-to-head, we'd have more time together. Maybe we'd have a chance at becoming friends."

"I'm not here to make friends," I shot without thinking. "At least, not yet. I'm just focused on surviving right now."

"Don't think you can do both at once?" he asked. "Become my friend, and I promise to help you."

"Why?" I scrutinized him, unsure of where to start with my questions. But they all started with *why*. Why did he know my name? Why was he helping me? Why did he want to be friends? "At least tell me how you know me. Please." I added the last word, remembering I *was* talking to someone Top-Tiered.

Griff now studied the street, which was succumbing to darkness. Buttery light from buildings' interiors fell onto the sidewalk, bathing us in a warm glow and kissing the tips of Griff's dark hair. When his gaze found my eyes once again, I realized how *close* our faces were.

"What do you know about the world outside of Miota?" Griff asked, barely audible. His mouth hardly moved as he spoke.

I knew why he was being covert. Dwelling on the world beyond Miota—unless it was to tell some cautionary tale about the monsters looming outside the Fort—was illegal. Theorizing and conversing about the world beyond the island broke explicit laws. It was treason, which was why Theo had always worried when I climbed our family's shack to watch the stars.

"That has nothing to do with my question," I said.

"It all relates. I swear on the moon."

I swallowed and looked at a spot of sidewalk. "Nothing. I mean, I've watched the stars, and I like the moon, but . . . all I *know* is we shouldn't be talking about this."

Would he report me for admitting that much? The moon was an entity used for cursing at and swearing tenuous promises on; it wasn't an object meant for affection.

"Corinn, *I* know about the outside world."

My eyes flew to him. His irises held an intensity they hadn't moments ago.

"You can't," I said matter-of-factly. His claim was impossible.

"But I do." Griff grinned wildly. "I learned about the stars and moon from my dad. And *he* . . . told me about *you.*"

"Your dad?" I confirmed. "Why would your *dad* know me?"

Griff shifted, extending his legs onto the street and leaning back on his palms. "He . . . had a friend who knows you. I can't say more yet."

I wrinkled my brow. "You're being very cryptic, you know."

Griff's laugh was as warm as the summer breeze. "With this subject, I have to be, if I want to keep my head."

"*On that note,*" I said, peering for any signs of cameramen. I was pretty sure they'd left for the night, back to their cities, but their threat still loomed. They often hid in shadows, hoping to catch drama between candidates, and this wasn't a conversation they needed to hear. "Are you letting me win competitions?"

The words hung in the air, suspended in front of Griff as he fought for a response. He opened his mouth before promptly closing it. *Twice.*

"You are," I decided. "Why?"

"Like I said. I can help you win."

"By jeopardizing yourself?"

"*I'm* not the one in danger. The other Tops are targeting Lows and Middles, trying to chop you down and get you out of here." *Chop you down.* I gleaned it to be equivalent to the Pointean expression *weed you out.*

"Well, I can keep myself here," I said, crossing my arms. I didn't want to stay here at the mercy of a Top-Tiered stranger. If I was going to remain in Accolade, it would be because *I deserved* to, not because some Top played the system. "I never asked for your help in the first place, and I don't want it now."

Griff eyed me like he wanted to say more, but he kept his mouth shut and scanned the street.

I tore at my nail beds. Tomorrow, when Lily would inevitably panic at their state, I'd blame Griff Howard. The man who claimed to know about the turbulent domain outside our island. The same man who knew my name for some unknown reason.

He'd said it all related somehow—his treasonous knowledge and me—but it didn't make sense. How could Griff's father, a man from Salford, know *my* name? And how was it connected to the world of ocean and skies beyond Miota?

I wanted to groan, but instead chanced peeking at the stars winking against the swell of black sky. I could only imagine how untroubled they must've been up there, outside of walls and conversations with strange men and competitions to rule the country. I craved their freedom.

"You know about the stars, then?" I blurted. Ice lathered my stomach. "Uh—*no.* Never mind."

Griff shot up, once again invading my personal space. "I knew you cared—"

"I said *never mind*, Griff."

"You want to know about the stars?"

I buried my face in my hands. "No, I don't."

"At the group competition, when I asked about Miota's common theme, you said it was the *walls*. You wouldn't have said that if you didn't want to escape them, too."

I chewed on his last word. *Too*. Was Griff like me? Did he long for freedom? He couldn't. He was Top-Tiered; he knew about all Miota had to offer. He left Salford's walls one weekend a month. Did he need more?

I lifted my head, bested by my curiosity. "Fine. But keep your voice down." In eighteen years, this was the *first* I'd heard someone talk about what was outside Miota.

Griff swallowed hard, his eyes roving across my face. "You're sure?"

I met his challenge, nodding once. "Tell me what you know."

I'd surely regret this. But my kindling interest in the stars and moon left me with no choice.

Griff's face lit up, brighter than any star in the sky. He leaned in, keeping his voice low. "Is there anything specific you'd *like* to know?"

I mulled over the question. "Do you know why they're . . . so far?"

"Just the way it is," Griff murmured, keeping close. We caved our shoulders and leaned our heads close enough for me to occasionally feel his hair on mine. I almost twitched away entirely. "The sun is a star, too, you know. The only difference is it's close to us."

I blinked. "One giant star during the day . . . and a bunch of tiny stars at night."

Griff glanced upward. "Exactly. The night stars make pictures called constellations. Here, I'll show you one . . ." He squinted before pressing his temple to mine. Soft sweeps of his hair grazed my face, making my skin buzz. "Quick. This one is called the big dipper. Do you see it?" He pointed upward for only a second before dropping his arm, playing it off by scratching his head. If anyone saw us conspiring over stars . . . I didn't want to know the consequences. "It starts at that bright star, which is a handle . . ."

"You're full of fertilizer," I said, pulling away from Griff with a nervous chuckle.

He returned the laugh, a low roll in his throat. "Full of *fertilizer*? In Salford, we just say someone is full of—"

"We say that, too." I flashed an amused grin. "You're making this up about . . ." I whispered the rest, *"constellations."*

"Have some faith in me, lovely." A smile played in his voice. "I'm not making this up."

I clucked my tongue. "Whatever you say—"

"Hmm. And what do we have here?" a silky voice snickered from behind us. I jolted, distancing myself from Griff.

My head-to-head partner leaned forward, burying his face in his knees.

A woman stared down at us, and I recognized her as the bronzed girl who spoke to Griff in our required social hours at The Gathering Hall. She narrowed her eyes at us and threw her waterfall of sleek hair behind her shoulders.

"This should be good," she hummed. "Who's this, Griff?"

"Corinn," he mumbled from his lap. "Januski. Pointe."

"Ah." Her emerald eyes targeted me, and she flashed a wicked smile. "So *you're* the girl my boyfriend keeps talking about."

CHAPTER 16

"I'm Addison Maybee. The oldest daughter of Mayor Tulane Maybee of Salford. It's so *nice* to finally meet you." Her teeth glinted in the moonlight.

What was *happening?*

Griff had a girlfriend, and it was *Addison Maybee.* It was the name Nelly mentioned at dinner that had rattled the table. No wonder, either. This was the daughter of Salford's mayor. She was in the most affluent Salfordian family.

And Griff was sitting on the curb with *me,* a Low from another city.

"You're not my girlfriend, Ads, and you know it," Griff said, sitting up and shooting Addison a look sharper than one of Dr. Ova's scalpels.

Ads. The nickname curdled my blood and sat like a rock in my stomach.

Griff tried meeting my gaze, but I wouldn't let him. "Corinn, she's not my girlfriend."

What was I supposed to say? I shouldn't have cared if Griff had a girlfriend. I *didn't* care—

"Does she talk much?" Addison asked, lifting her brow at me.

"Of course I *talk*," I spat.

"What do you want?" Griff asked his potential girlfriend as he stood to her level.

Addison shrugged and ruffled her dress of layered sheer fabric, alluding to her curves underneath. "I could ask you the same. A *Low*, Griff? What do you want with that?"

I stood, ready to head into First Residence. I'd rather wait for tomorrow's elimination sleepless in bed than with an arguing couple.

"Corinn," Griff said, pivoting on his foot to face me.

"I needed to go to bed anyway." I offered my most polite smile. Why *wouldn't* Griff have a beautiful, Top-Tiered, powerful girlfriend? I was such an idiot.

"Corinn," Griff tried again. Had he been playing me for a fool this week? I ignored him and left the lamplit street, stalking into my building for the night.

When Lily woke me, I had more pent-up nerves than I'd imagined. While I'd been nervous about my rank since Griff told me the Middles and Lows were being weeded out, I'd also been restless upon learning about Addison Maybee.

She was the daughter of Salford's mayor. Why had Griff prioritized *me* over *her*? I'd turned in bed for hours last night trying to figure it out. I'd concluded that Griff Howard wanted something from me, and it had to do with his father knowing my name. I didn't actually *mean* anything to my partner.

I prepared myself to never speak with Griff about the stars and moon and sun again. Even if I miraculously *wasn't* eliminated today, I'd have a new head-to-head partner this week, and so would Griff. He'd have someone new to bother.

Lily readied me in a blood-red dress with a ruffled skirt that swiped just above my knees. By the time I left for The Gathering Hall for the final ranking reveal, I shook fiercely. My core was rigid, but my extremities were made of acid.

"You'll do great." Lily beamed. "I'll see you this afternoon, okay?"

I gave my best smile, but it wasn't genuine. I just wanted to get this over with. I wished our panel links hadn't been severed from everyone back home. I'd give anything to receive a message from Theo or Mom right now.

The Gathering Hall was set up as it had been for orientation, into five sections of chairs. I averted my eyes from the dark corners as memories of the group competition arose: Salem and Griff collapsing, candidates' screams, the thick fog . . .

I found my seat next to Remi, who offered a small smile this morning. Nerves ate away at her as she slumped in her seat and wildly bounced her crossed legs.

Their Majesties appeared on the dais, regal with their gold crowns and matching blue velvet garments. Queen Julia possessed a microphone.

"Good morning, candidates of Accolade. And good morning to everyone watching from home."

Right. This was broadcasting to every projector in Miota, so anyone who left would do so in front of the entire country. I imagined my family gathered in the living room, watching this livestream on our fuzzy projector screen. I saw it too clearly: Theo standing in the corner with his arms crossed, Tellie laying on the floor, Mom and Dad sitting on the sofa's front edge, and Grandma listening in from the greenhouse.

"It has been our honor to learn more about the candidates sitting in front of us right now. While we appreciate all of you taking the time to fight for the opportunity to rule Miota with strength, valor, and justice, we are also tasked with the difficult decision to decide two winners. As stated previously, the fifty candidates with the least points this week will leave. We will now reveal the rankings, starting at the bottom. If your name is called, please leave the hall, where staff will be waiting to escort you to your room to pack."

I inhaled deeply, slowly, willing my body to calm down. Her Majesty began calling candidates.

Most names didn't mean much to me since they were from another city. But the Pointean names pierced me—they were all Middles and Lows.

Griff was right: Tops were hunting us.

Forty names were called. And then, "Pollie Wienst of Pointe."

I dared to turn around as my friend left. Either I'd be called right behind her, or I'd survive the week and fend for myself at every meal we had in our residence building.

The remaining names were called, and mine wasn't among them. Relief rolled off my shoulders, and The Gathering Hall swelled with timid celebration.

"Good job," I said to Remi, basking in the brighter air.

"Congratulations," Her Majesty sang from the stage. "You have all survived the first week. Your rankings will now show on your panel, and all points will reset tomorrow morning. You will receive your new head-to-head assignments tonight, along with your weekly schedules."

I looked at my panel for my final ranking, and my stomach dropped.

231st. I likely would've left today, had Pointe not won the group competition or if Griff hadn't tried to let me win our head-to-head. Even with all the points I'd racked up, I'd dropped 160 places in the rankings in just over one day.

One day. The solo competition and head-to-head voting didn't take place until our rankings had disappeared, and they'd completely changed the standings. And now, as one of the few Lows who'd survived the first week, I'd be a huge target. Dr. Ova's wicked smile poisoned my mind. I was sure she couldn't wait to watch me get eliminated. While I survived this week, it wouldn't matter if I was ultimately eliminated and demoted. The second I stepped foot in Pointe, I'd be nothing but a Low who was stupid enough to try becoming something greater.

The thought was like breathing in a mouthful of water. I *had* to stay here. *Somehow.*

Griff had said if I became his friend, he could help me win . . .

Absolutely not. I couldn't dwell on that option. There had to be another way. A friendship with Griff would also mean being burdened with forbidden knowledge about the things outside Miota. I needed to find a different way to get through Accolade, and *quick*, or else it would cost me everything.

Sunday was for rejuvenating for the week to come, our reward for surviving eliminations. I spent the rest of the day with Salem, and we paced Castle Circle.

A group from Cape played a game made of catching and running with a wicker basket. Patios, strewn with small tables and adorned with florals, were packed with flocks of candidates chatting about the past week. Butlers and maids bustled to provide drinks and rations of food.

I'd read a *Pointean Gazette* article criticizing Accolade's logistics; apparently, food was being prioritized to us here, and rations were being shorted back home. While I doubted my parents were affected with their meals of vitamin puree—a slew of Top-Tiered nutritionists mass produced the stuff for Lows on the two-rationed diet—I figured Theo and Tellie were receiving less food, even with my ration there to help them. The thought made me sick.

Thick clouds danced through the sky above us, quickly whisking across vibrant blue. I kept my face tipped to the sky until mine and Salem's panels chimed with a new message. Our new head-to-head partners and weekly schedules had been sent.

My new partner was Natalya Lil from Cape. I didn't recognize her picture—a woman with dark skin and hair, and a dazzling smile—but she was Top-Tiered, so I showed the image to Salem.

He sighed. "I don't think I know her. Her family probably isn't on the executive council, then."

It didn't matter *what* she did in the Top Tier; the fact that she wasn't a Low just about sealed her victory over me on the spot. "Who's your partner?"

"Jubilee." Pollie's friend, the Low-Tiered farmer. She'd made it another week, too. Knowing she was a Low pinned to compete against a Top made her situation seem bleak. Then, like an icicle through my veins, I realized she and I were in the same situation. Lows against Tops.

My mood hadn't improved by morning. While shadowing Salem during our hours in The Gathering Hall, I couldn't help but watch Griff across the room. He kept his hands stuffed in his pockets, speaking to his usual dark-haired friend.

"Do you know who Griff is talking to?" I asked Salem, purely out of curiosity.

Salem grinned upon finding them. "Oh, yeah. Lorenzo So. His dad *and* aunt are on Salford's executive council."

Griff's friends, Addison and Lorenzo, were both so *powerful,* it was hard to believe Griff acknowledged me at all last week, even if we were assigned as partners. I swallowed, eyeing the two men with their heads dipped toward the floor. At once, their eyes flitted toward me.

My face heated upon the sudden eye contact, and I faced Salem, who wore a stupid smile on his lips.

"What did Griff Howard *do* to you last week?" he mused.

"*Shut your mouth,* Salem." If Griff somehow read Salem's lips . . .

Salem, amused as ever, stroked a finger across his chin, miming deep thought. "They're still looking at you. What do you think they're talking about?"

"I don't care," I said with a sigh. "Since we're on the topic of Salfordians . . . what do you know about Addison Maybee?"

Salem quirked an eyebrow and adjusted his glasses. "Don't think I don't know what game you're playing."

"What do you mean?" I faked innocence.

I watched Salem's expression turn pensive as he dug into his memories, into past times Pointe and Salford had overlapped in Castle Circle. "Griff and Addison. Friends, if not more, for as long as *I* can remember. I think she's broken off from him and Lorenzo in the past few years, but . . . growing up, it was always those three."

I nodded, wishing I felt numbness instead of a deep, dull chill. *Childhood friends.*

I cursed myself—once, then twice for good measure. *Why* did I care about Griff's history with Addison? I didn't. I couldn't.

Salem bit his lip. "They're definitely talking about you."

"*Okay,* thanks!" I peeled my eyelids back. "Stop talking about it."

He shrugged. "You brought it up first."

132

When I glanced back at Griff, a giddy smile crept onto his face. We were in a subtle match of trying not to overlap gazes for the rest of our required hours. I didn't know what his goal was, but I wouldn't get caught up in his game.

Our head-to-head competition was the following day, which again consisted of a history quiz about the queen's bloodline. Natalya scored a perfect ten out of ten, while I was lucky to answer three correctly.

Natalya found me in The Gathering Hall on Wednesday to comfort me about the loss. "Don't take it personally." Her candor was believable with her straight smile and soft brown eyes. "I hope you have it in you to stick around this week, even with a head-to-head loss. I admire what you're doing. I hear you're an asympton researcher?"

My throat burned like acid at the topic. "I . . . I am." *Though only until the second I leave Castle Circle.* Besides, I had never truly done any of the research.

"Very neat," she purred. "My aunt died of it a few months ago. Miota appreciates your work."

"Thank you." I spoke in a whisper to keep my voice from cracking. Now I couldn't hold a bitter grudge against Natalya for our rankings. She was too sweet.

I was ranked 174th on Wednesday evening, the night of the second group competition. I hoped this week's contest didn't include tranquilizing candidates, but when the Queen's Guard showed up, I knew it was only wishful thinking.

This group competition encompassed a slew of team-building events while random candidates were tranquilized. The lights stayed on this week, so as candidates were shot, their crumpled bodies remained visible to all. As we continued, we had to step over the unconscious. Every candidate shouted over the next to make sure they were heard, so in the massive hall, the voices reverberated off the hard floor in an abrasive cacophony.

Jubilee tripped over an arm sprawled on the ground, and as she landed on another body, I heard the resounding *crack* of bones breaking.

I let go of our thin twine rope—our current and last task involved untying a hundred-foot string of knots—to assess the damage. Jubilee had broken the arm of Elliot Stanton, a Middle-Tiered sentinel who'd been tranquilized.

Mathilda, the *Pointean Gazette* editor, screamed something in my face. I couldn't interpret her words as I focused on Elliot's bowed forearm. Even under the sedative, his face bunched in pain.

I hovered over Elliot's broken body as Jubilee screamed over what she'd done.

"*Get up*, Corinn!" shrieked Mathilda. "Grab your rope. *Now!*"

"Elliot's arm is broken—"

"I don't care!"

"I'll stay with him," Jubilee called over the swell of voices.

"I'm the doctor," I shouted back.

"You're not!" Mathilda said in sync with my internal voice.

Tears burned in my eyes until the bodies cluttering the ground were blobs. Cheering came from across the hall. A city—Kendall, based on their vivid outfits and artificial hair hues—had untangled their rope. One hundred points for them.

Instinctively, I looked for Salem, though he couldn't do much for Elliot, either. My best friend was nowhere to be found. Was he a body on the ground again?

I couldn't leave Elliot; he needed help.

But we also needed to untangle this rope. Bile rose in my throat. *I* needed our city's points.

I ripped myself from Elliot, leaving a piece of my humanity

with my choice. But I *had* to abandon him—for Pointe's sake, and for my *own*.

I held my section of rope with trembling fingers. My mind drifted to Elliot until we untangled our rope, finishing in third place. *Fifty points.* It wasn't enough, and I hadn't fixed Elliot.

On Thursday, our assigned lecture day, Elliot came wearing a sling. It made it impossible for me to focus on the topic of city trade. I didn't know what I could've done to help Elliot, but I'd chosen to abandon him, and that thought was like a knife swishing inside me.

I received a perfect score on the lecture's test, though it didn't feel deserved, and my rank rose to 132nd. It only left me with about seventy buffer slots in the rankings as we went into the weekend.

Our solo competition was announced on Saturday as an interview with our residence's staff. I didn't bother worrying since Lily was one of the few people in Castle Circle who actually liked me.

Lily rapped on my door once, a solid knock. I stifled a laugh, waiting for her to come in.

But she knocked again, and I figured this might be part of the interview. I crawled off my bed and staggered to the door. "You know, Lily, I didn't expect you to—"

When I opened the door, I froze. And then bowed. "Your Most Royal Majesty."

Queen Julia grinned at me. "Hello, Corinn. May I come in?"

CHAPTER 17

I stepped back, letting Her Majesty into the room as I tried to keep my thoughts from unraveling. Panic seized my limbs, and I fought to stay upright.

I summoned everything I knew about Queen Julia to the forefront of my mind. Cass always said she was stern and deeply set in her ways. As she swept into the room, I saw the weight of the island on her shoulders.

I wished this was anyone else from the castle. *Anyone.* I wasn't sure how to navigate through an interview with the queen when Cass and Bernard's fundamental command replayed in my head. I could never let her know about Cass showing up in Pointe. Although, I wasn't sure why it still mattered—how would the queen punish Cass for sneaking out *now?*

"This is an honor, Your Majesty," I breathed. My voice died in the air in front of me.

Queen Julia sat at my desk and studied me. My arms hung limply at my sides, and I wasn't sure what to do with them. I straightened my spine and set my shoulders back. Was I supposed to maintain eye contact? Probably not. I dropped my gaze to the floor, then wondered if *not* looking at her was rude.

When the queen cleared her throat, habit won. I ultimately met her green eyes, as pointed as the emeralds embedded in her crown.

"How is Castle Circle treating you?" she asked. "You have miraculously survived the first week."

I laced my fingers together behind my back. "It's amazing, Your Majesty. I . . . appreciate you letting me into Accolade. I know I'm in the Low Tier, so your kindness can't be understated."

Her face softened at the flattery. "You are likely wondering why you were accepted at all," she offered. "It is because I am curious about you, Corinn."

My intestines knotted, not unlike the rope from the group competition. I chewed my cheek as the image of Elliot's warped forearm surfaced.

"Of course, Your Majesty." I hoped the goosebumps on my arms weren't obvious with the ten feet of distance between us. She eyed me lethally, the way Pointean farmers described the look of field snakes before they struck. She fumbled in her skirts, though for what, I wasn't sure. "I'm happy to answer any questions you may have." *Don't you dare ask about your son, though.* "It's the least I can do."

"I saw the photographs of Prince Kierran speaking to you at your Commencement," the queen started. I held my breath. "He was . . . rather endearing toward you, was he not?"

"He was," I said quickly; hopefully, not *too* quickly. "He was very nice. My time with him was invaluable." I was going to have to lie my way through this interview with the most powerful person on the island.

Queen Julia perked. "Yes. Precisely. And exactly how *much* time did you have with him?"

I stuck my tongue out, giving my best pensive expression, as my core slowly turned to ice. Scalding, burning *ice*. What a contradiction.

Did she suspect I knew her son? How much trouble would I be in if I just confessed?

But Bernard's warning protruded from my thoughts. The queen could *never* know about Cass coming to Pointe, at any cost. The uncle and nephew had only reminded Salem and me of that instruction *every time* we met in the greenhouse.

Queen Julia could never know about our meetings. *Explicitly* her. Everyone, but *especially* her.

"Likely five minutes or less, Your Majesty," I finally answered. My vision darkened around her figure.

She stroked her polished index finger along her chin. "I *see*. I only found it odd that he embraced you and Salem Redding as if you were, say . . . old friends."

By the moon. Did she already know? Was she only leading me on, trying to catch me in a lie? Why was I choosing to listen to Bernard over the Queen of Miota?

That was it. Bernard. I faked nonchalance, though I doubted it met Julia's standards. "Oh, that was because Salem Redding and I know his uncle, Bernard Bartholomus. We often crossed him during our clinical rotations in Pointe's hospital."

Julia's face sharpened again, all taut muscle and hostile angles, as she gritted out her next words. "Bernard Bartholomus has never met my son. That man was my son's uncle by blood alone."

I bowed my head, hoping it disarmed the queen. *I'm innocent, I'm innocent.* But I wasn't. And something told me she *knew* that, deep down. "Yes, Your Most Royal Majesty."

"Good. Then, my only other question for you is about Griffith Howard. He was your head-to-head partner last week, and as I am sure you can assume, it was because of your illegal location in my home. I hope you understand why that was so wrong?"

I nodded, biting back an excuse about how I never wanted to venture outside of the ballroom that first night of Accolade.

The queen's face twitched at my silence. "Well. He scored very low last week but is doing *much* better this week. Some might wonder if he was acting in a way to help you. Have you formed an alliance with Griffith Howard?"

First Cass; now Griff. I'd be lucky to make it out of this interview without being sentenced to the Hold. Cass had snuck out of the castle for four years, and Griff held information about the world outside the Fort.

"No, Your Majesty. I . . . didn't know he did that." Adrenaline jolted through me. Why was I still lying? I had reason to lie about Cass, but Griff was different. I was now tying my own noose. "Frankly, we aren't even friends." At least that much was true.

"How reassuring," she said, rising from her chair to walk toward me. My stomach hitched. "I reward you one hundred points for your honesty," she started. My *honesty*. My blood thickened. "And I demote you one hundred points for leaving the ballroom last week, for a net gain of zero points. Best of luck at eliminations tomorrow." Her merciless eyes bored into me.

I bowed deeply, eyeing my toes, which had gone blue underneath my stiff posture. I shook out my legs as the queen left the room.

"How was your solo interview?" Salem asked on our walk to The Gathering Hall. Sunday morning came with low-hanging clouds, matching my mood since the queen's visit yesterday.

I licked my lips. "Fine."

Salem glanced at me before offering his elbow. I took it,

grounding myself in his touch. "What's wrong? I thought you and your maid were friends—what's her name? Rose? Petunia? Daisy?"

"*Lily.*"

Salem laughed to himself. Over the names of flowers. What a *Pointean.* "Did it not go well?" he finished.

I scanned the street for nearby eavesdroppers, but there were none. Other candidates were dressed-up figures dotting the street from afar. Still, I leaned in and whispered, "The queen did my interview."

Salem sucked in a breath, which made my heart beat so wildly, I thought it would erupt from my rib cage. "Sorry," he whispered. "That was just . . . unexpected. What did you *do?* Well, aside from the whole parlor situation with Griff."

"She asked about that." My next words were so low, they might as well not have been spoken at all. "But she also suspects about Cass. I'm surprised she didn't conduct your interview, too."

Salem's throat worked, but he kept his eyes straight ahead, refusing to lean in and make it look like we were conspiring—as Griff and Lorenzo so often did. "Yeah, that's odd. She asked about him, then? Cass?"

"Yes. I played it off, using Bernard as our connection, but . . . I don't know. Something's not right about it all. She asked if I was in an alliance with Griff right after talking about Cass, and . . ." My tongue went limp. "It sounded like she thought . . . the matters of Cass and Griff were connected."

Salem gave a slow, measured nod. "That's impossible, right?"

"Right." But now that I'd spoken it into existence, the idea clung to my brain, claiming my conscious thoughts. Did Griff and his father somehow know my name through *Cass?*

Don't tell the queen. Don't tell her about Cass; don't tell her about Griff's knowledge. Griff's father, a Top, had a friend who knew me. I hoped it wasn't all interwoven.

I staggered into The Gathering Hall, inhaling the crisp air. We arrived early enough that candidates swarmed in groups, gossiping and offering last-minute encouragements.

Griff, Lorenzo, and Addison stood in a circle, the boys with their arms crossed and Addison with her hands on her hips. Her dress hugged her curves and was strategically bedazzled with only enough sparkling stones to be deemed socially acceptable.

I tightened my grip on Salem.

Griff's dark gaze floated toward me, like he was somehow trained to pick me out of a crowd. I ripped my eyes from Salford's section of chairs.

I parted with Salem when we made it to Pointe's portion of The Gathering Hall, and I took my seat next to Remi. Her dark hair was curled, springing around her ears.

"Good luck," I offered.

She only wrinkled her forehead, barely brushing her eyes past me. "You need it more than *I* do."

I focused on mastering my nerves as the start time crept closer. I didn't receive any points in the solo competition yesterday—no thanks to the queen—and I couldn't have received many votes against Top-Tiered Natalya Lil.

It was torture, sitting here useless, knowing I hadn't done enough to secure my spot this week. I couldn't stay in Accolade based on sheer hope. I needed to train; I needed to learn to play this game the *right* way. Hopefully, I hadn't come to this realization too late. The pit in my stomach grew.

Their Majesties took the stage, and the hall immediately hushed. I was too nervous to comprehend their words of welcome and praise for completing the second week of Accolade. Remi was right; I needed every spare ounce of luck I could get.

I only knew the moment Her Majesty began calling names,

because everything grew eerily still. Except for one unlucky person at a time.

Ten names passed, and I wasn't one of them. Twenty. Then Jubilee, the Low-Tiered farmer, was called. Top-Tiered Brycon Northe followed her. If *Tops* were leaving now, I was definitely in trouble.

Thirty candidates exited. Then forty. With each name called, tensions both grew and diminished in a baffling paradox. A merciless spike of fear entered every sliver of silence, and it dissipated as the queen called a name that wasn't my own.

Forty-nine names called.

One more. It *couldn't* be me.

But my heart fractured as Queen Julia spoke the final name all too clearly. "Corinn Januski of Pointe."

CHAPTER 18

I went rigid. But I knew my legs would be jelly if I tried to stand, and I would fall to the floor.

Remi gave a sigh of relief next to me.

I was leaving. Going back to the Low Tier. I'd be a farmer. After two weeks here, it amounted to nothing. Everyone else in the Low Tier seemed to know their place, content with staying where they were. But I'd tried to leave, and I'd failed, and it made me a bigger fool than if I'd never tried at all.

A tear rolled down my cheek. Why couldn't I just be *complacent?*

Remi elbowed me, baring wide eyes. "Get *out*, Corinn, before a guard forces you."

My eyes skittered to the Queen's Guard members planted throughout The Gathering Hall. Their blank faces indicated boredom, though I knew they'd jump into action at any moment.

Remi was right. I needed to leave.

I stood, holding out my hands for balance.

I couldn't do this. I was walking toward my doom. Toward my *ruin.*

Make it stop. Please, make this stop, make it stop—

"Unfortunately," King Abner's voice drifted, "this week involved a scandal between two candidates, and they were attempting to keep it undercover. Corinn Januski, please sit down."

I parted my lips. What was happening? When I sat back in my chair, I plopped, unable to control the descent.

"Calvin Velez of Cape, and Brenn Rollins of Cape," King Abner announced. "You two were caught cheating on your lecture exams *and* messaging answers during the head-to-head competition." He looked at his wife, who wore her tension like a gown. They had a silent conversation in front of us and everyone watching on their projectors back home.

"Yes," Queen Julia answered after a beat. "The punishment for cheating is elimination. We cannot have an unjust or unfair ruler. You two may leave."

The two men from Cape left, glaring at each other. One of them kicked the ground, making a few candidates wince.

King Abner reclaimed the microphone. "Since we promised only fifty candidates would leave each week, this means Corinn Januski of Pointe and Plentie Grandison of Yorkinson may stay."

The queen gave her husband a fiery grin. "Yes. *Thank you* for bringing light to the subject of cheating. May it serve as a reminder for candidates that it will not be tolerated, and it will cost you your spot in this competition."

Her stony voice sustained, telling us we'd have the rest of Sunday off again, and our new assignments would be sent soon.

As we were ushered out of The Gathering Hall, a few Pointeans sneered, claiming I should've left.

I couldn't disagree with them; I was *supposed* to leave. I knew the king's fortunate timing wouldn't happen again. From now on, if I was to make it to the next week, *I'd* have to make it happen myself. I'd have to fight with everything I had to give.

To make it further in Accolade, I'd need to make friends.

Pointe had our lecture day on Monday, so we didn't have social hours until Tuesday. It only gave me more time to second-guess what I needed to do. I was going to ask Griff to teach me Delldova history.

It would potentially help me win the head-to-head history exam, and I needed every point I could get this week, since my partner for week three was Addison Maybee. Plus, it was time to branch out and make new friends who'd choose me in the head-to-head vote to earn me more points. As one of the *two* remaining Lows in all of Accolade, I didn't have a long list of potential friends, but Griff Howard's name was at the top, however I felt about it.

Even with the benefits of befriending Griff, my trek across The Gathering Hall during Tuesday's social hours was torturous. My core buzzed and heart thrashed as I moved toward Griff, who stood with Lorenzo. I hadn't spoken directly to Griff, outside of a few passing words, in over a week. And now I was going to ask him to tutor me. Would it seem too self-serving?

But he'd said he could help me win if I befriended him. So I forced my feet onward until I reached the mass of Salfordians.

Griff watched me approach, a muscle working in his jaw as he chewed on a smirk. Lorenzo's eyes glowed with amusement, like I was the punchline of some inside joke between them. My nerves nearly undid me.

"Corinn." Griff spoke my name with a probing lilt. "I knew it was only a matter of time."

Until what? I bit my lip. Crossed my arms. Tried to keep my eyes from flitting to Griff's tailored black shirt gliding across his shoulders as he moved. "Don't worry, I'm not here by choice. I . . . have a favor to ask. My head-to-head this week is Addison Maybee, and I know she's your friend—"

Griff's face darkened, and Lorenzo scoffed. "*Not* our friend," Griff's companion insisted.

Griff gave him a neutral look. "By the way, Corinn, this is Lorenzo."

I feigned surprise. "I'm Corinn—"

"No need." Lorenzo laughed, looking down at me from his towering height. "You're Griff's favorite subject these days."

I knew my ears reddened, if not my entire face. "All good things?"

"Yes, lovely," Griff answered, the corner of his mouth flicking upward. "I'm not rude. What's your favor?"

I swallowed and gathered my strength. "I need to win a head-to-head competition. Addison will win our head-to-head vote, but I need to learn Delldova history and beat her there." *And Pointe needs to do well in the group competition.* And *I'll preferably win the solo competition.* But none of that had to do with Griff.

His eyes roamed my face. "You didn't ask Redding?"

"He has a first name." The familiar, dull sting of annoyance surrounding Griff returned, coiling in my chest. "I would've rather asked Salem to teach me, but you made me an offer the first week that I'm hoping still stands."

Something dark flashed in Griff's eyes before he regained his composure. Lorenzo glanced at Griff, assessing him. What did I say wrong?

"It does," Griff finally answered. "If we're going to be *friends*, though, I get to ask you favors, too."

At that, I laughed. "In case you forgot, I'm a Low. I can't help you."

A muscle jumped in Lorenzo's face as he smothered a grin. It was meant for me, no doubt; he must not have realized I was Low-Tiered. But I kept my spine like steel, refusing to cower in front of these two. Griff was one of my only options to surviving Accolade right now. My days here were numbered, and I was growing desperate.

"You'll help me more than you know," Griff said.

I wanted to grunt; Griff Howard was nothing if not vague. But I had to agree. I'd help him, and he'd help me, and we'd both use the other for selfish reasons.

My blood vessels turned to lead as I recalled my interview with Queen Julia. Did this count as an alliance with Griff Howard? And if it did, why did she care so much?

I swallowed hard. Maybe I didn't know what I was getting myself into. Then again, I didn't have much of a choice. Right now, staying in Accolade was synonymous with learning from Griff.

"Fine," I agreed.

"Good." Griff's eyes flickered to Lorenzo's so fast, I almost wondered if I imagined it. "Then . . . it's a deal." He held out his hand, ready to seal this with a handshake.

I set my jaw, hesitant to accept it. What if Her Majesty was watching? What would happen to me? But when I saw the queen's back turned to us, beyond a thick slew of candidates, I grabbed Griff's calloused hand. He stopped breathing at my touch, and I withdrew quickly. Were my hands clammy? Too warm? Or did he realize he was shaking the hand of a *Low* in public?

Griff's throat worked before he spoke. "The head-to-head won't be until later this week, so we'll have plenty of time to study. Come to my room after dinner tonight."

I challenged his stare and glued my arms behind my back. "We can meet somewhere more *public*. And how do you know when the head-to-head will be?"

Griff's tongue slid across his teeth inside his closed mouth. "I have my ways. Let's meet on the outdoor patios, then? We'll have dessert."

"That's better."

"Dessert?" Lorenzo frowned. "I want in."

"Do you know Miotan history?" I wondered.

"He doesn't," Griff said. "He's awful with history. *Fertilizer*, as your people might say."

I laughed once, an ugly sound, before I could stifle it. I tried clearing my throat to play it off, but heat still traveled up my neck. "Okay. Then . . . I'll see you tonight."

Griff's face softened as we worked out a time to meet.

I traipsed back to Salem, whose irises danced behind his glasses.

"I don't want to hear it," I muttered preemptively. "That wasn't what it looked like, I promise."

"Oh? Because it *looked like* Howard has a little obsession."

I rolled my eyes. "Griff's going to teach me history and help me win competitions, and I'll help him with . . . I don't know what. But I assume it has something to do with his dad." *And maybe Cass.*

Salem's face grew somber. "Right. Poor guy."

I blinked at Salem's off-kilter reaction. Had I mentioned Cass aloud without realizing? Before I dwelled on the dead prince for too long, I changed the subject.

When our required hours in the hall were finished, I went to First Residence for lunch, just in time to avoid the evident afternoon storm. Without Pollie in the building, each meal felt like navigating Pointe's emergency wing of the hospital. I never knew exactly what was happening, but it always involved people screaming, bleeding, or crying—we'd had all three happen, thanks to a Salfordian whose knife slipped at dinner a few days ago.

Pandora and I exchanged rare pleasantries, though she was often glued to Nelly's side, and Nelly was still the same pretentious Top.

The drizzly afternoon was slow, filled with meal etiquette lessons in our residence building, which we'd utilize that evening. Those from Cape, who had lectures all day, were clueless at dinner when we were presented with four types of each utensil and three drinking cups.

I returned to my room after dinner, having downtime because of how late Griff wanted to meet. Lily occupied my desk as she laced beads onto a satiny maroon dress. I couldn't help but wonder if the gown was for me.

The maid's eyes briefly flickered to me when I entered. "Want me to draw up a bath? You look exhausted."

A whisper of a smile claimed my face. "That sounds great, but I can't. I'm studying later."

Lily's face creased; I wasn't sure if it was in concentration or confusion. Our silence left only the sound of rain slapping at the windows. Would Griff want to cancel our plans if the weather endured? I debated messaging him, since we'd linked our panels earlier, but decided against it.

"I need to win a head-to-head for once," I told Lily, elaborating. "So I'm starting by learning history. I guess Tops learn that sort of thing in primary school, which I didn't realize."

"Mmmpheefer," she said, holding her sewing needle between her teeth. Once she retrieved the needle, she repeated herself. "*Me neither*, I mean. Being born and raised in servitude . . ."

I wondered what it was like to be born into a specific *job*, as children of maids and butlers were, destined to follow their parents' roles. Would such a life feel as restrictive as being born into a predetermined Tier?

"Are you teaching yourself?" Lily asked, drawing me from my trance. "Or is someone helping you?"

The chicken from dinner churned in my stomach. "Griff Howard is teaching me. He's from Salford."

Lily gave a closed-lip smile. "Salford, hm? Are you two studying in here? I can leave for the night—"

"No. We're going to the patios across the street. They're covered, right? From the rain?"

Lily only stared at me for a heartbeat. "The *patios*? So . . . you're studying over drinks and dessert?"

I threw my arms in the air. "You're just like Salem, you know that?" I glanced at my panel to avoid Lily's eyes.

"We love you," Lily sang as a light rap on my door saved me from the conversation. I padded across the bedroom, only hoping I wasn't about to come face-to-face with Her Majesty again. But I opened the door and found Griff, glistening with rainwater, leaning against the frame.

I crumpled my brow. "How'd you get here?"

A muscle jumped in Griff's cheek as his mouth curled into a smile. "Don't sound too happy to see me," he drawled, producing a bouquet from behind his back. I gawked at the spray of pink buds. "For you."

"Begoniums?" I asked, my voice slow and deliberate. "*And* you're an hour early? What's the occasion?"

"No occasion," he said, extending the flowers to me. "I picked these from the greenhouse. Lorenzo told me they were petunias."

"I'm from Pointe," I reminded him. "I know my plants. Besides, my grandma used to cross-pollinate begonia and geranium—" I cut myself off. He was a Top, and I was a Low, and he didn't want to hear about my grandmother pollinating flowers. "I'll spare you the details, though."

Griff's eyes caressed my face. "Corinn, don't *ever* spare me the details."

Lily made a small noise from across the bedroom, and I took the flowers from Griff, hoping he didn't notice Lily's behavior.

"Let me put these away real quick." I closed the door on him. "And thank you!" I called, summoning my manners too late.

"Studying," Lily started, keeping her gaze fixed on her silks and beadwork, though a smile overtook her face. "Just *studying*. Forget the dessert and flowers; you're just studying."

"Yes!" I insisted. "Trust me, Lily, we're both in this for our own selfish reasons." I fluttered across the floor, wondering where to put the bundle of flowers. There wasn't a vase in the room, save an already occupied ceramic piece, so I set the stems on my dresser. If Grandma were here, she'd chide me for not taking proper care of them.

Lily shrugged. "Not sure the selfish reason behind making a bouquet."

"You're impossible!" I grabbed a pair of sandals and strapped them on, leaving the room, though not before Lily laughed.

CHAPTER 19

Outside the haven of First Residence's gold-plated lobby, a gray sheet of rain pummeled the island. Milky fog swirled above the sidewalk, visible under streetlamps.

"I didn't know it was raining this hard," I said.

Griff swiped a hand through his hair and swallowed. "You're not having second thoughts, are you?"

"No." I held my ground. I needed to study and start *winning*.

He nodded. "On the count of three, we run for it?"

"Sure."

Griff counted, and we bolted. I flinched at the droplets, which transported me back to Commencement, the last time it rained this hard. I continued to the patios, but halfway there, Griff slowed his pace to skip around and let the rain hit his face.

"Isn't it nice to *feel* something from the clouds?" he called.

"If I wanted a shower, I wouldn't have left my room."

But Griff only spun in tighter circles. "I didn't realize you were so *boring*, Corinn."

My eyes fluttered shut as a gust of wind blew water into my face. Maybe I'd enjoy the rain if it didn't remind me of Cass. My heart twisted with grief, and the summer raindrops seemed to morph into tiny pinpricks of ice.

I swallowed and left Griff, jogging the remaining distance to the covered patios before I drowned in misery.

"It's just me and *him*," I told the lone butler staffing the patio as I motioned with my head toward the lunatic twirling in the street.

The butler's throat worked as he choked down a laugh. "Any table you want. I don't think others will be joining you tonight."

I chose a table in the middle of the patio to best cover us from the rain. I lit our table's candle with a stray box of matches, and the orange sparks crackled to life as I wondered how long they'd last against the storm.

Griff joined after a few minutes, leaving a puddle in his wake as he sat across from me at the small, circular table. "Are you not a rain person?" he blurted.

I huffed. "A *rain person*? No." Not when being weighed down by rainwater was now mingled with the memory of being placed in the Low Tier for life and Cass dying.

The butler told us he was leaving for the night but could grab quick drinks for us. I asked for coffee, and Griff asked for tea. I grimaced at his choice; I'd only tried tea a few times, since it was just as much a controlled substance as coffee, and I *despised* it.

The butler left into the adjacent building to ready our drinks.

Griff leaned in, resting his forearms flat on the table. "If this is going to be a real friendship, we need to learn things about each other. So, for every fact I give you about Miota, you have to give me one about yourself."

"And what about you?"

Griff's eyes crinkled. "I'll tell you anything you want to know about me."

I didn't believe him. Because if that were true, I'd know more about how his father knew my name. "Why don't we just do Miotan history?" I tried. "Or else we'll be here all night."

"That's kind of what I'm hoping for."

A gust of wind swelled, and I braced myself. The candlelight danced, though the flame nursed itself back to life, refusing to snuff out. After too many seconds of silence, I broke the stiff tension hovering between us. "How do you know the head-to-head competition won't be until later this week? You said you . . . have your ways?"

"Butlers talk."

"Okay . . ." I wasn't sure why Griff tried giving off an open, trustworthy persona when he never volunteered extra information. "Fine. Let's start with Aris Delldova, then. He was the first ruler of the modern era, right? Who comes next?"

Griff widened his eyes. "You're awfully *eager*. No exchange of pleasantries first? No 'how are you' or 'how's your week'?"

I shrugged. "It's late."

Griff blinked before yielding to me. "All right. Learning the order of the modern rulers is simple. Remember when I said it's all alphabetical? Their names are in alphabetical order. Aris, then Blanden Delldova. Charise, Blanden's daughter. Demitris, then Erick. Fugueton, Gemma, Harriette, Iven, Julia. Kierran. That helps keep the years in order, too."

That made sense. While I knew we were currently in the year 26 JD, signifying the twenty-sixth year of Julia Delldova's reign, I'd never thought to dwell on the alphabetical nature of the modern rulers who came before her. How could I have, when I hadn't known their names until now?

"My turn," Griff said. "Where do you spend your free time in Pointe?"

I inhaled to answer, but my throat closed after understanding his question. "Could you *be* more random?"

"Trust me." Griff tried prying me open with his eyes, as if he could read my mind for an answer. "This is *not* a random question." His intensity sent a chill down my arms.

I chewed on my cheek. *My free time?* I didn't have a lot of it during the school year, but I'd usually spend spare moments with Salem, either at my family's shack or in the greenhouse with Bernard and Cass. But I couldn't tell Griff that.

Before I answered, the butler returned with our drinks.

"I'll tell you something." I smiled, eyeing his muddy beverage. "I hate tea. With a passion."

Griff's jaw slackened and visage flashed with betrayal. "Did you just insult the greatest drink known to Miota?"

"No, that would be coffee." I motioned to my mug. "I'm talking about tea, the flavored water that makes me want to gag."

In that moment, I thought Griff was going to walk away. "Lovely. Are you serious?"

I refused to break eye contact as I leaned in closer. The air between us was more electrifying than the storm. "*Completely.*"

"No!" He laughed, throwing his arms in the air. "I knew you were too good to be true."

A fleeting warmth curled in my stomach, and I sipped my coffee to settle it. Griff followed suit, drinking his tea.

"I know Aris dealt with the floods and asympton," I pressed, hoping my dislike for tea counted as an acceptable fact about myself. "Did Blanden do anything notable?"

Griff traced his teacup's stem with a finger. "Blanden . . . He started building the Fort. His daughter, Charise, finished it." It made sense. Blanden would've wanted to prevent the floods that tormented his father's rule.

I nodded, keeping mental tabs on each ruler. *Aris. Blanden. Charise.* So far, so good.

I threw question after question at Griff before he had time to ask me any in return. He intercepted each one, giving a thorough synopsis of each Delldova's rule. After almost an hour of unending questions for Griff, my mind spun as I tried keeping the information straightened out. The butler had long since left for the night, and my coffee had been robbed of its warmth.

"You know," I finally said. "You could be lying through your teeth right now, and I'd have no idea."

Griff smirked. "That would be cruel."

"I wouldn't put it past you." I gave a playful shrug. Something breakable flashed on Griff's face before he artfully buried it within himself. I sighed. "I'm joking, Griff. Sorry. Thank you for helping me. I . . . can't go back to Pointe like this, so it means a lot that I might stay here because of you."

Griff stirred his last bit of tea to keep his hands busy; the beverage had surely gone cold by now. "You deserve to be here, you know."

When I met Griff's eyes, he held my gaze like I was made of the same delicate porcelain as his teacup. I failed to produce a response. Only the rattling sound of rain saved us from true silence.

"I've seen the way you talk about yourself," he continued carefully. "Like . . . like you're *less than* others. Because of your family, your Tier, whatever the case. I hope you know it's not true."

I averted my eyes. "You sound so Top-Tiered." He was *wrong*. So wrong, but he'd never know that from his pretty seat atop Salford's apex.

"You can't *sound* Top-Tiered—"

"Trust me, you can. You *do*. My family starves, the farming sector is overcrowded, we're forced to stay at the bottom of Pointe, and you're telling me that *doesn't define me?*" Rage burned inside me as Dr. Ova's face appeared in my mind's eye. "If I'd been born into a different family, another Tier, I'd be a doctor right now. But I'm not, and . . ." I clenched my jaw.

"And?" Griff prompted gently.

A cord in my chest snapped. Thinking of Dr. Ova, hearing the rain, seeing Cass's spirit in the corners of the patio, Griff's antagonizing.

It was too much.

I propped my elbows on the table and hid my face in my palms. "And I'm *drowning.*"

A warm thumb was on my elbow. I buried my face deeper. I couldn't look at Griff, couldn't bear to see the sympathy and *pity* swirling in his hypnotic irises. He was no solace to me; he was a Top from a different city. I wasn't the type of person he should've been speaking to, and we both knew it.

"You should be with someone like Addison Maybee right now." I couldn't refrain from speaking the rising thought as I lowered my hands from my face and slumped in my chair.

His fists clenched at the mention of her. A cloud grew over his face, a bleaker veil than the tempest surrounding us. "By the moon, Corinn, don't say that."

"You two have history," I pushed. I didn't know why.

"And it's in the past for a reason." The veins on the dorsum of his hand were a prominent lattice crawling up his forearm.

"What happened between you two?"

"It doesn't matter." Griff scowled, rounding his shoulders. "It's over now."

"So much for telling me more about you," I grumbled, crossing my arms. I shut Griff out, unaware of how much I'd taken his kindness for granted. *This* was the Griff I should've received from the beginning: Top-Tiered, broody, and snippy.

"I'm going to bed." I placed my mug on its saucer. "Thanks again for the lesson."

Griff's eyes churned. "If you're upset because I dated Addison years ago—"

"No!" I stammered. His audacity only stoked me. Maybe Griff was a typical Top after all, pretentious and condescending. "Believe it or not, I'm not upset about your *love life*. It's your comments about my Tier, your cryptic reason for knowing my name, and your inability to answer any question I ask you! Just teach me history, help me win competitions, and then I'll be out of your way."

This time, when pain rippled through Griff's face, he didn't hide it. "That's what I am to you? A way to help you win competitions?"

It sounded selfish when he phrased it like *that*. But he didn't know what my life was like, what I had to go through daily. He was a *Top;* he had nothing to complain about.

My brain snagged on the memory of walking away from Elliot and his fractured arm. I didn't know why that memory surfaced, so I shoved it far away.

"We both have our own motives," I defended myself. "Don't we? Though I still don't know what *your* reasons are."

"Answers, Corinn. You're . . ." He grinned, of all things. "Well, you're a key, of sorts."

I opened my mouth, but clenched it shut, gnashing my teeth together. "Is that supposed to make any sense?"

He shrugged. "Probably not."

"Right," I huffed. "Well, find me when you're done speaking in riddles. Good night." I stood, and Griff didn't stop me as I ran into the rain, back toward First Residence.

CHAPTER 20

Griff kept tutoring me, though his attitude was more apt to the Top-Tiered behavior I'd expected from the start. I tried convincing myself his stiff musculature and reserved expressions didn't bother me as much as they did.

We'd greet each other civilly during mandatory social hours, he'd quiz me with history until I was content, and I'd thank him before promptly leaving.

Our head-to-head history exam *was* later in the week, as Griff had foreseen. On Friday night, we congregated in The Gathering Hall, and I was forced to confront Addison Maybee.

"It's nice to see you again, Corinn," she hummed in her slinky, condescending voice. She eyed me with a cunning stare before smoothing her high-slitted, golden dress, which showed off her bronze legs.

I coiled all my emotions into a neat ball and summoned my newfound knowledge from Griff. I could beat Addison. I could, and I would, because I *had* to.

Pointe had placed third in this week's group competition a few days ago, and I'd received a perfect score on this week's lecture exam. I was currently ranked 105th, so I didn't feel anywhere *near* safe. I needed to stay above 150th place, and the only way to make that happen would be to win this head-to-head exam *and* the solo competition. And even that wouldn't be enough, if the candidate-wide vote went badly—which was a real possibility against Addison Maybee.

"I hear Griff's been tutoring you," Addison commented, placing a hand over her heart. "That must feel special, being his charity work. I'm not sure it'll save you this week, though."

My surroundings blurred into fractals among the chandelier's delicate lighting. "Charity work?"

Addison shrugged, wearing a face of nonchalance. "Be honest with yourself, Corinn. What reason would he have for caring about a Low?"

I had no response, not when it took every cell in my body to keep my composure.

"It's nothing personal," Addison continued. "*Any* of this, I mean. Just try to understand my situation. I'm the daughter of Salford's mayor, and I'm trying to become the next queen. But I'm first expected to compete against a Low, as if it's a *legitimate question* of who deserves to rule the country more? It's embarrassing."

She'd killed me without holding a weapon. My chest ached as Their Majesties called for our attention from their place on the raised stage.

"It's not just you," Addison muttered. "It's every Low and Middle. You never should've been allowed here in the first place."

I didn't respond. I couldn't. Because she was *right*. Castle Circle was built for Top-Tiered citizens alone.

I didn't realize Queen Julia asked the first question until after she'd said it, and I nearly burst into tears. I *needed* to win this. I guessed an answer, and it was . . .

Correct!

I sighed and regrouped. I'd dissect Addison's words later; right now, I'd fight. The next question asked about when the Queen's Guard trials became so rigorous.

Arduous training. Order. Restriction. It aligned with Charise Delldova, Aris Delldova's granddaughter. It was correct. I could've cheered, or squealed, or thrown my arms around Griff, had he been near—

The queen read the next question. Right again. Griff had taught me more than I'd thought. By the end, I'd racked up every point but one. Our partners' scores were revealed, and I'd tied with Addison.

I hadn't lost!

Addison flared her nostrils as she looked at me, and her warm skin developed a red hue. "Good game, Corinn."

"Good game," I echoed.

After the exam, our rankings disappeared, not to be revealed until Sunday's elimination. Since it was Friday night, the executive council arrived to meet with Their Majesties—the fifty members filed into the hall as Accolade's candidates shuffled out.

Someone fell in step next to me on the diamond-embedded sidewalk, and I knew it was Griff from the way my core began to buzz. I held my breath as Addison's words resurfaced. Griff *had* been trying to help me since the first week of Accolade. He'd tried letting me beat him in our head-to-head competitions.

I plastered a stale smile onto my lips as I looked toward Griff. His hand brushed mine, and I crossed my arms as a jolt of lightning shot up my hand.

"How'd it go?" asked Griff.

"We tied," I said coolly. "But Addison called your tutoring charity work."

Griff's forehead creased with too many wrinkles. "She has no idea what she's talking about."

I kept my gaze fixed ahead of us, toward First Residence. The clouds above were dipped in rosy hues, compliments of the sunset. The color matched that of the bouquet Griff had given me earlier in the week.

"I just want to know *why* you're tutoring me," I said. "I have so many questions about you, and you've managed to evade all of them. I barely know anything about you."

"I . . . want to tell you everything." Griff picked his words carefully. "And I will. Once I know I can."

I huffed. "You're so difficult."

"I get that a lot," Griff mumbled, shoving his hands into his pockets. He cast his head to the ground, disheveling his hair.

My heart wrenched. I nearly reached out a reassuring hand on his shoulder. "I'm sorry," I said. "I didn't mean that."

Griff's shoulders twitched. "No, it's true. My father, Addison, *her* father, all my teachers in school . . . they all called me *difficult.*"

Shame overtook me. I realized it would've been like hearing him call me worthless. It wouldn't be anything I didn't already know, but it'd still hurt to hear from someone new.

I wanted to console him—just as he'd tried to do for me that night on the covered patio. And instead of hearing him out and accepting his kindness that rainy night, I'd *run away.*

By the moon. There was no salving this feeling. In fact, the bitter humility only grew when I saw Elliot Stanton enter Sixth Residence in his cast.

Griff slowed at Fifth Residence, his building. We peeled off from the thinning crowd and stood at the building's front door. "I know you have questions about me," he said. "And I'm sorry I can't answer them right now. I want to tell you everything—give you everything. I just . . . need some time. For your own sake, as much as mine." His eyes scanned the crowd before he leaned in, lowering his voice to me. "Because this isn't exactly *legal* stuff we're talking about."

Right. His knowledge of the world outside Miota. While nothing should've scared me more than a Top with knowledge of the stars and moon, my soul was drawn to it instead.

He continued. "I need to know that you're not just using me to help you win competitions. The whole favor-for-favor mindset won't help earn each other's trust. But . . . we can retry being friends the *right* way. If you want."

I met Griff's soft eyes. "You still want to be my friend?"

"Yes." A half-smile.

"I thought you hated me," I breathed. He *should've*. We were from different cities and opposite Tiers. And I'd done nothing but push him away.

He worked to keep his grin from filling out. "Corinn, I have a lot of feelings toward you, and none of them are even close to hatred."

I debated befriending Griff, *truly* letting him in and trusting him. Was it possible? "If we become friends," I started, *"real* friends, you'll tell me why you and your dad know my name?"

"Yes, lovely. I'll tell you everything."

I gulped, wondering why Griff called me that. *Lovely.* "Okay, then." Curiosity bested me. I swayed forward, putting my weight onto the balls of my feet. "Let's do this the right way."

Griff lidded his eyes. "This all started wrong from the beginning. So . . . nice to meet you. I'm Griffith Howard, but everyone I like calls me Griff." He reached out his hand.

"Corinn Januski." I returned his handshake and smile. And, suddenly, I didn't feel so alone.

Saturday's solo competition was announced alongside a party in The Gathering Hall on a scale equivalent to a formal ball in the castle. The knowledge of such a party sent Castle Circle into chaos.

Lily arrived Saturday afternoon with a frantic expression and the maroon dress she'd spent the week detailing. She flung the dress at me before charging to the nearest power strip to plug in a curling iron. "You're late!" she cried.

I almost replied that *she* was the late one, but I was too busy clenching my jaw to keep from laughing as she whirled about the room in hysteria.

"You have a date, right?" Lily asked before checking the curling iron's temperature. "That's thirty points on its own."

I dreaded the question, though I'd known it would come up. I needed as many points as I could get, though when I asked Salem to be my date earlier, he'd declined. He said it was for my own good, though I wasn't sure what was *good* about missing thirty free points.

"I'm trying," I answered, shimmying into the dress. I shivered at the silky material. The gown, ornamented with sequins and jewels, clung to my torso before tumbling loosely to the floor in a shimmering pool of ruby. "Lily, it's gorgeous," I said, playing with the straps hanging off my shoulders.

Lily grinned. "Let me curl your hair." But it wasn't a matter of *letting* her as she gripped my shoulders and tossed me into the desk chair. "Now, you better have a good reason for not having a date tonight."

I sighed, shifting in my seat. "I asked my best friend to go with me, and he wouldn't do it."

Lily made a sympathetic noise as she grabbed a section of hair to wrap around the metal wand. "Oh? Who's that?"

"Salem Redding. Pointe."

A line appeared between her eyebrows. She didn't take her eyes off the hair-wrapped wand. "Why don't you go with your study partner? If he'll give you flowers for a study session, I can't imagine how he'd treat you as his *date*."

"Lily!" I wished there was a way to flee this conversation without my scalp getting burnt. "I'm not going with Griff."

She shrugged and grabbed a new section of hair. I should've known her silence wouldn't last long, though. "Who do you think you'll pair with? That'll be here before you know it."

If I make it that long. Accolade would change entirely with the pairing of the remaining candidates. If I miraculously survived past a week from Sunday, I *would* have to partner with someone. But who would I choose? Salem didn't want to win Accolade—he didn't want to be here in the first place. Who else was there? My newest friend?

My throat bobbed to keep from laughing. I smothered the thought of pairing with *Griff Howard* as fast as I could. I needed to find someone from Pointe. Someone strong, who wanted to win as much as I did.

But Griff stayed plastered to the grooves of my brain.

"I . . . don't know," I said. "Haven't thought about it yet."

"You need to." Lily dropped a finished ringlet, and it burned against my back. "I won't tell you what to do, but candidates are pairing in just over a week. You'll need to have someone in mind."

The thought was too daunting. I needed to find a potential husband by *next week*. I couldn't do it and claim sanity.

"Of course." My words sounded artificial. Though Lily noticed and narrowed her eyes at me, she didn't press me further.

After my hair was curled, Lily left to make her rounds with the other girls on my floor. I kept a steady focus on my makeup, and I managed to do a decent job with the creamy mascara and glittering blush. When Lily came back, she completed my look with a sparkling necklace, heavy against my clavicles, before shooing me out the door.

Outside First Residence, on the moonlit street, mayhem ensued as candidates met up with their dates to walk to The Gathering Hall. I prowled through the street for Salem, ready to insist on him being my date. But I sooner ran into a set of eyes that quickened my pulse.

"The Gathering Hall is the other way," I said to Griff. "So you're either terrible with directions, or I'll have to assume you were looking for me." I stifled a wince; the words had tumbled out flirtier than intended.

But warmth swirled within me as Griff flashed a wicked smile. "The latter. My sense of direction is impeccable, *thank you.*" He drank me in. "You look so lovely, Corinn."

I knew I blushed, my cheeks likely nearing the color of my dress. "Thank you." He looked good himself, wearing a dark, tailored suit that rippled against his chest, clinging to his outline. The full moon's light gave the tips of his dark hair a silvery halo.

He didn't take his eyes off me. "I was hoping you'd be my date tonight."

I froze. A thousand bumbling thoughts, incoherent as ever, surfaced in my mind. I should've accepted immediately. *Thirty points!* But I wasn't going to take advantage of Griff anymore. I opened my mouth to speak, but nothing came out.

"You . . . already have a date," Griff said. It was hesitant; both a question and statement.

"No," I blurted. "I mean, I asked Salem, but he refused, so . . . no."

Griff's mouth twitched. "That works well for *me*, doesn't it?

Looks like we're dating tonight."

"Bold of you to assume I'm accepting."

Griff took a step toward me, which effectively sent my heart pounding. "Corinn, will you be my date tonight? Please." His stare, though a delicate caress, threatened to crush me in its wake.

I swallowed. "You want to go with *me*," I confirmed. "A Low." Since Griff had called off our tentative, favor-for-favor type of relationship yesterday, this would mean we'd attend the party as friends. *Real* friends, transcending not only Tiers, but cities.

Griff nodded and gave a quick shrug. "Call me crazy."

I let out a breath through my nose. "You're crazy."

"I'm also your date." He offered an arm, and at a loss for words, I gripped the crook of his elbow. I tensed upon feeling the corded muscle beneath his midnight-blue blazer.

Candidates stared on as we walked Castle Circle's lane with linked arms. It was similar to the feeling of talking to Cass back at Commencement. I practically heard others' thoughts slithering into my ears.

A Low with a Top. . . from different cities . . .

He's too good for her . . .

She looks like a fool with him . . .

Tears pricked at my eyes, though I blinked them away before they fell and ruined my makeup. Griff's arm was my anchor to the physical world; his steadiness kept me from losing my balance or catapulting into the depths of my mind's fears.

At the hall's entrance, Queen's Guard members surveyed each couple to award points accordingly. When my panel chimed with thirty points, my nerves dissipated a little. Maybe this wouldn't be so bad.

My jaw dropped when we entered the hall. Tables adorned with glowing orange lanterns were centered around a blank space—

a dance floor, I realized. Moonlight poured in through the soaring windows above, bathing the space in silver light. Five musicians played sweet melodies, and aromas of cooked meats waved through the air. I located the table stockpiled with colorful foods.

"Solo competitions focus on problem-solving and logic," Griff mumbled, leaning in so close to me, his breath tickled my ear. "Just keep your eyes peeled tonight. It's anyone's game."

"So you're my competition," I teased.

"Yeah, right. I want you to win this. It may be the only way to secure enough points for the week—I'm assuming Addison took most of your head-to-head votes this morning."

"Probably," I agreed, gritting my teeth.

Griff found Lorenzo seated at an outskirt table with a dark-haired girl, who introduced herself as Selleca, a Middle-Tiered butcher from Salford. I couldn't tell if she and Lorenzo were a couple; I'd never seen them together before.

Dinner was delicious, consisting of braised steak, decadent berries, cold salad, and a thick pudding for dessert. The meal was only spoiled by Selleca's gruesome details of how to prepare a cow's meat for eating.

"Are you and Lorenzo together?" I asked Selleca to make her talk about *anything* other than cow meat.

Lorenzo choked on his wine. Tonight, he donned a gold suit that complemented his dark skin, and he'd tied his hair into an elegant knot. "No. By the moon, no. We just . . ."

Selleca, fork in mouth, turned red as she froze, waiting for Lorenzo to finish his sentence.

"They enjoy each other's company," Griff offered.

Selleca and Lorenzo snorted. "Something like that," Selleca said after swallowing her piece of steak.

"Keep quiet about it," Lorenzo told me. "It's not exactly

public knowledge back home, since we're in different Tiers and all."

Griff gave a low laugh as Lorenzo slumped in his seat.

Lorenzo's statement held such gravity; he didn't want to be associated with someone from a lower Tier. Sometimes, I grew desensitized to the fact that my best friend was Top-Tiered. Salem's friendship with me was bold on his part, though he always stood firm in it, even against his mother's threats.

After dinner, maids and butlers forced everyone to the dance floor. I studied our surroundings with prying eyes in case any of this had to do with the solo competition later.

Griff extended his hand to me. I didn't know how to dance, especially with a man. Before I had time to conjure up an excuse, a thick hand patted my shoulder from behind me. Griff's face paled.

I turned and met the king, holding his hand out for a dance.

CHAPTER 21

"Your Majesty," I said, bowing my head.

"Corinn." King Abner's voice was as gruff as his brother's. They shared the same gray eyes, thick heads of hair, and inset lips. King Abner, however, had a bushy beard while Bernard had no such facial hair. "It's so nice to finally speak to you. Would you care for a dance?"

I figured I couldn't reject the King of Miota, especially after he saved me from being eliminated last week, so I nodded.

He took my hands in his rough palms and whisked us into the thick of the crowd. Though, as other candidates realized the king was on the dance floor, they cleared a path and kept their distance.

"I'm not the first royal to visit you," King Abner started with a knowing glint in his pale eyes. "Am I?"

"No. Her Majesty conducted my interview for last week's solo competition."

King Abner's eyes widened. "She . . . did?"

"Yes." Why did he seem surprised? If he hadn't known of his wife's visit, then what royal encounter would he be speaking of?

One of his eyebrows twitched, and he cleared his throat. "Did she . . . like you?"

I contemplated the answer as my hands trembled against the king's palms. Though this was Cass's father, the prince hadn't inherited much from the king, aside from the point of his ears and a playful aura. It was as if Cass's blood had known Queen Julia was the true royal, and his features had molded to fit hers.

"She liked me as much as she could," I answered.

"What did she ask you? Surely, she asked if you knew Cass. She's really held on to that one. The *Gazette* never should've gotten pictures of you two together; the history was clear just in the way he looked at you. That was his fault, though, not yours."

My blood turned to stone as I tensed in the king's arms. "What history? There's no history, Your Majesty—"

"Don't be ridiculous, Corinn." He dropped his voice, even though no one else danced within earshot. "I know about all that. Who do you think sent him to the greenhouse in the first place?"

I parted my mouth, and goosebumps exploded on my arms. The king. *Sent* Cass. "You . . . what?"

"Brought Cass to you and my brother." It couldn't be. And yet . . . it was the only explanation. "Corinn, you didn't think the Prince of Miota just began *showing up,* did you?"

I blinked. Because that was exactly what I'd thought. I'd assumed Cass stumbling into my life was because of Bernard, not the king.

"What else did my wife ask you?"

My eyes wandered, and they landed with Griff, who watched from the edge of the dance floor. Worry knitted his brow. "Um, she asked if I was in an alliance with Griff Howard."

"And *are* you?"

I gulped. "No, Your Majesty." We were trying to be friends, not allies. We weren't working together.

"Why not?" the king challenged.

"Because." The air became too stale. "We're from different cities *and* Tiers."

"Don't be so petty, Corinn." We circled near the musicians, the sounds of their instruments growing. "If you want to survive, then I suggest you listen to him. The boy's father knew what he was talking about."

My eyes widened. "How . . ." I cleared my throat. Fear crackled down my spine. Was Griff's father somehow connected to the royal family after all? I shook my head. Only the music filled the space between us for a few heartbeats, before I opted to change the subject. "I meant to thank you for saving me last week. That was kind."

Abner winced as if I'd conducted a sternal rub on him. "My wife didn't see it as kindness . . . She properly tortured me for it. I'm only here right now thanks to bandages, salves, and too many painkillers."

My mouth went dry. "I'm so sorry, Your Majesty. I didn't mean—"

"Don't be sorry, Corinn. I had to do it for you; you're the key." His eyes skittered across the crowd as my thoughts spun. *You're a key of sorts,* Griff had told me before. "Under the tables. Look under the tables and find the prize."

"What does that—"

King Abner twirled me out of his arms. When my gaze leveled off, he'd disappeared in the thick crowd, leaving me with only my bubbling thoughts and dizzying theories.

So. Four years ago, King Abner sent a prince to me. And last week, the same king saved me during eliminations.

I had to do it for you. But why?

When Griff found me, my head pounded, sending pressure to my eyes. "Lovely." He slipped one hand in mine before I realized what he was doing. His other hand slinked around my waist, and my heart catapulted against my ribs. We swayed slowly while everything inside me *raced*. "What'd he tell you? Is everything all right?" His voice was calm enough to remind me I probably shouldn't have had a dysfunctional heart rate.

I eyed Griff. "Do you know him?"

Griff inhaled. "Who, Abner? Not personally."

I took a ragged breath, and Griff's calloused hands tightened on mine. For not knowing the king, Griff called him by his first name too casually. And the *key* reference was too uncanny.

Griff pulled me closer, increasing his pressure on the small of my back. My heart bellowed in my ears, behind my eyes, and in my neck. My line of sight met his jaw, chiseled and freshly shaven.

The more I begged my hands not to get clammy, the sweatier they became. My eyes darted around the room, looking everywhere but at Griff. I couldn't meet his eyes. Outsiders' thoughts once again grabbed hold of me, like talons to my brain.

Top-Tiered and Low-Tiered . . .

"Corinn?" Griff murmured. As he spoke, I was cursed to watch his lips move in the forefront of my view. "What did he tell you? Did he threaten you?"

"No," I whispered. "He . . . he told me I should align with you. Because of your father."

Griff opened his mouth to speak but closed it and spun me. Upon reconnecting, he pressed his body too close to mine. I tried to stretch the distance between us, but my arms were pudding. I hoped he couldn't feel my heart beating against his chest. Why was every part of Griff Howard taking such a hold on me tonight?

"We need to talk." Griff's mouth moved against my hair, and the quick brush of his bottom lip against the shell of my ear scrambled my every thought. "Not here, of course, but . . . it's time you know what's at stake. Tomorrow, after eliminations, we need to talk. In one of our rooms."

While I was curious to learn about the wild world beyond the Fort, the subject was illegal. By agreeing to speak with Griff about all this, we'd be giving each other the power to kill one another.

But I couldn't shake the feeling that this all connected back to Cass. King Abner sent Cass to me, and Griff's father knew my name . . . Somehow, we were all ensnared in the same web. I just didn't know how or why.

My thoughts spun, the same way many of the girls were swirling around the hall. I spied Salem dancing with Izzy Eddison, a Top-Tiered Pointean from my building. When Salem saw me in Griff's arms, a sloppy smile illuminated his face. I only smirked back.

"And this all relates back to how you and your dad know my name?" I asked.

"Yes. You're supposed to play a role in all this."

Abner's words arose yet again. *I had to do it for you.*

"Okay," I started, succumbing to my storm of thoughts. "You *do* know the king, don't you? Or . . . does your father?"

Griff tensed underneath my hands. "This isn't the time or place—"

"*Please*, Griff." I needed to know what was going on, how we were all interwoven.

His throat worked. "My father and Abner saw a lot of each other growing up, even being from different cities. They interacted in their overlapping weekends in Castle Circle, and they were the final two in Julia's Courtship. Even after that, they saw each other at executive council meetings."

I stuck my tongue out as aureate bodies floating across the dance floor turned to blurs. Executive council meetings? His father was one of Salford's ten executive council members, meaning Griff hailed from one of the most powerful families in his city. And here he was, dancing with a Low.

My stomach roiled. No wonder Griff was close with Addison Maybee, the mayor's daughter. Addison's leer poisoned my mind.

"So . . ." I shook my head as I connected the pieces. "Your dad and Abner talk every weekend." That was surely how Griff had heard of me before. The mental image remained blurry, however, as I gnawed on the biggest question of all.

Why did Abner send Cass to the abandoned greenhouse in the first place?

Griff's hand on my waist clenched, gripping me tighter, as the rest of him went rigid. "Well, they *used to* talk, yeah. My father died. Three years ago." His weighted words dropped to the floor.

"Oh . . . Griff." It took all my self-control to keep from wrapping my arms fully around him. "I can't imagine."

Griff inhaled deeply, consequently pressing our bodies closer together. "The pain comes and goes, though I *always* miss him. He's the one who taught me about the world outside Miota. I hold on to that knowledge because . . . I don't want to forget the sound of his voice, his exact words . . ." His throat closed.

"Of course." Our swaying halted. "I'm so sorry."

Griff leaned his chin against my forehead, and I swore I felt his lips on my hairline. Even once we pulled apart, now done with dancing, my skin burned with his heat.

I recalled Salem telling me a council member had died a few years ago. I knew it was a prominent person on the island, and now that Griff mentioned it, it *had* been a finalist in Julia's Courtship. I'd been apathetic toward the very situation that had shattered Griff.

Salem's words from earlier in the week, *poor guy*, made more sense now; he hadn't been talking about Cass's death, but Griff's father's. I wondered if it was due to asympton, the disease that claimed too many lives. In times like this, guilt ran its stake through me for how bitter I was about my job assignment.

"We can talk about it more tomorrow," Griff said. "Somewhere with privacy."

I pressed my lips together. "What if I get eliminated?"

"Have some faith, Corinn." A smile laced his voice. "We'll both make it. You'll win this solo competition once it starts."

I nodded, remembering the king's parting words to me. "His Majesty said to look under the tables for the prize. Do you think . . . that has to do with the solo competition?"

Griff bit his lip in realization. "Did he say *when?*"

I shook my head. "You don't think . . ." It clicked into place. There wouldn't be a separate competition later; this party *was* the solo competition. "It's happening right now."

Griff drew the same conclusion. "Let's split up. Cover more ground that way."

I weaved through the maze of orange-lit tables, back to our spot from dinner where Lorenzo and Selleca still sat. I crouched under the tablecloth but found nothing.

When I resurfaced, Lorenzo's eyes bulged. "Careful, Corinn, or people will wonder what you're doing under there."

"Shut up," I shot, giving a grin. "It's the solo competition. I'm looking for clues."

Selleca jumped to her feet. Her gauzy gown floated out from her hips. "It *started?*" She scanned the hall and adjusted her coils of hair.

I paused. "It started the second we got here. They're seeing who'll figure that out. I don't know anything else, though."

Look under the tables and find the prize. I conveniently left that part out, and guilt rose in my throat. I suffocated it before dwelling on it too much. The king had gifted *me* with knowledge; surely, *I* was supposed to benefit from it.

I crawled under a number of tables, and others joined in, copying Griff, Selleca, and me. Before long, a slew of candidates crawled around the hall.

My heart quickened. I *needed* to find the prize first.

Someone rammed into me after I'd checked nearly a dozen tables. *Griff.* Relief clamped on my chest. He steadied me, slipping me a piece of paper in the process. He continued walking, and I unfolded the note.

Show this to Her Most Royal Majesty to claim your prize.

"Griff," I called, scurrying after him. "Where'd you find this?"

He whirled, looking back at me. "Taped under a table. Go win this." Then he *winked.*

I chewed the inside of my cheek. "I don't deserve this." *I don't deserve* any *of this.* "You're the one who found it."

"I found it, and I want you to have it. No offense, but you probably need it more than I do. Plus, there are more floating around. Natalya Lil found one already."

I heaved a breath, refolding the paper and pressing the flimsy fibers into my palm. Paper was a rare commodity; I'd hardly touched it outside of my week in the asympton lab, fetching carbon paper for Dr. Ova and the other two.

I combed The Gathering Hall for Her Majesty, practicing breathing evenly as nerves flew through me. I found her on the edge of the hall's main cavity, speaking with Abner inside a circle of Queen's Guard members, whose navy suits absorbed the hall's shadows.

"There's more water, Abner, if that would get you talking," the queen rumbled.

My intestines writhed. She was threatening the king.

Her Majesty's sentence cut off upon eyeing me between two guards. "Oh, *here she is.*"

I bowed as my core shook in her presence. The queen's green eyes had percolated into my nightmares before, and they were no different in reality. "Your Most Royal Majesty." Even my voice quivered. "I found this piece of paper. Under one of the tables."

When I leveled my gaze, Queen Julia pointed her venomous eyes at the king. Did she suspect he'd given me the answer?

"Congratulations," Queen Julia lulled. "Your prize is up to you, though you must speak within points."

My eyes grazed over Abner, but he offered no sign of helping me further.

Points. I had to speak within points. I assumed that meant I could add points to my weekly score, but how many would I need to stay immune from leaving Accolade?

"Is three hundred points enough?" I asked. "Is that too many?"

"I cannot help you."

Would three hundred points be enough? What about *five* hundred? I couldn't guarantee anything; Griff had said there were other papers floating around. Other candidates could ask for thousands of points, or the best rank—

A solution materialized, and I hoped it was allowed. "Can you grant me the minimum number of points needed to stay out of the bottom fifty tomorrow? Whatever that number may be?"

The queen grunted, and from behind her, King Abner beamed. "Yes. Congratulations, Corinn. You will be safe for another week."

CHAPTER 22

Nerves still wound tightly within me during eliminations. Even though I knew I was safe, I kept imagining the queen going back on her word.

My solo competition victory proved useful; I ranked 150th, and though that was last place, I was grateful to survive another week. I'd been saved by Griff Howard yet again.

At the end of eliminations, Julia reminded us we were now in the fourth week, which meant the final one hundred candidates would pair up after the next elimination. Partners' fates would be united, subject to either win or lose Accolade together.

Her Majesty also said pairs hailing from different cities would lose a fixed number of points each week. I couldn't afford to *lose* points, which meant I'd need to partner with someone from Pointe. But who?

I should've considered potential partners after that, but it was difficult to think about such a weighted topic when I needed to first *make* it to next week. My new head-to-head partner was Holland Stanzifer, the mechanic from Cape who'd been Salem's partner during Accolade's first week. She'd spoken of climbing the Fort, which was more treasonous than anything Griff and I had ever conversed about. And that made me feel a little better.

Griff appeared at my door that afternoon, a few hours after house lunch. It was time to test our trust in each other—and learn the truth.

Griff's eyes tracked me across the gilded bedroom, as if I was somehow the most valuable thing here. Though he'd closed my door, he stood across the room with his arms hanging limply at his side.

This was it. Griff would *finally* answer my questions. He'd tell me more about his father and King Abner's relationship, and why they'd talked about *me* before. I'd probably have to tell Griff I knew Cass, but it was a risk worth taking. I could trust the Salfordian.

"Want to sit outside?" Griff strode to the balcony door.

I swallowed. "Is it safe? With the subject?"

He nodded. "Balconies are private. Even from the floor right below, no one could hear us."

"Have you tested it?" I asked. Which only reminded me that Griff came here every month with the rest of Salford's Top Tier. It was a sour note, punching a hole in my mood.

"Yeah. Lorenzo and I have." Griff sensed my apprehension and shoved his hands into his pockets. "Or we can stay in here. It's up to you."

I chose the balcony. The sun—our day star—radiated oppressive heat, cooking the ground. While there were two chairs, Griff elected to lie on the stone balcony, propping his hands behind his head. I ignored the strip of toned abdomen peeking from under his raised shirt. I sat cross-legged next to him, knowing we'd still need to keep our voices down, private balcony or otherwise. The hot stone burned my calves, uncovered in my sundress.

"So," Griff started, squinting hard against the sun bathing his face. "Where should we start? My dad and Abner, or you and Kierran?"

My jaw hung. He *knew*? It disarmed me completely, stripping my lungs of air. "How . . . What . . . How long have you known?"

"Oh . . . four years?"

Four *years*? Dread ran through me like an injection, a potent elixir spoiling the serene sunrays. I'd only *met* Cass four years ago, so Griff had known from the beginning.

I matched Griff's eyes. "Did your dad ever say anything about *why* the king sent Cass—er, Kierran?"

Griff's jaw twitched. "Cass?"

"Kierran Cassius," I clarified, suddenly not wanting to talk about the prince with Griff. "He goes—*went*—by Cass. Do you know why he came to Pointe, then?"

Griff swallowed. "No. I can tell you how everything relates, why everything has happened, but I don't know why it all revolves around *you*." This all revolved around . . . *me*? "I need to go somewhere for more answers, and I think you need to come with me."

"*Go* somewhere?" I blurted. "Can you explain everything you *know* first? Please, Griff."

"Sure. Of course." He stared at the sky from his supine position, and I knew he was a prisoner to his thoughts. "I guess it all starts with Julia's Courtship. Dad, being one of the finalists, had a lot of time with Julia. She gave him information during their time together—Dad said she'd drink too much wine and leak secrets about the monarchy she wouldn't remember by morning." A knot quivered in Griff's throat. "He spent the time after her Courtship trying to find out *more* about what's outside Miota. Julia caught on a few years ago, and the Queen's Guard took him for questioning . . ." He raked a hand through his hair. "He never came home."

The only movement on the balcony was the wafting breeze. Griff eventually sat up, bracing himself with his arms outstretched behind him. He leaned back on clenched fists, where his knuckles were white from bone pressing against skin.

"The queen killed him for the information *she* gave him?" I whispered.

"Yeah."

Even in the sunlight, my skin pebbled. The queen had spilled secrets, then blood. Cass always spoke about his mother with hesitant adoration—he said she was loving, but he held her at the highest regard, scared to speak poorly of her. Did Cass have reason to be afraid of her?

"Dad taught me about the stars and moon in secret. He had a *book* about that sort of thing. With a note—"

"A book?" I gawked. Paper was a rarity; entire *books* were archaic. All information and communication had been traded out with electronic means generations ago, when the floods from Aris Delldova's time had destroyed all physical data stores.

Griff had taught me that.

"Yeah. There's a note in that book, and it talks about a place with more answers about what's beyond the Fort. It's a place in Pointe, so I think we need to go there together."

I blinked. Waited for him to crack a smile, or shrug it off, or . . . do *anything* besides stare at me expectantly.

Griff wanted us to go to Pointe. *During* Accolade.

"We can't do that," I said, smoothing my dress. "You can't be serious, Griff!" My hushed tone rose into the sky.

"You want *more*, just like I do. You want more than what Miota can give."

"Don't tell me what I want." But he wasn't wrong. My soul always felt weightless, untethered, when I thought about the world outside the Fort.

I might as well have handed him my heart. Griff knew I'd been friends with the prince, he knew my identity, and he *knew* how I beheld the stars. I could've screamed. Why could he dissect me so easily?

"Not to mention you're talking about treason," I added. If a soul overheard us, we'd be imprisoned in the Hold, where we'd wait for a royal hearing that would inevitably end in our deaths. "It would get us killed.

"I know," Griff said in a meek voice, momentarily covering his face with his hands. "Trust me, Corinn. *I know.*"

Right. His father. A chill crept into my bones, trumping the sun's scorching rays, as the weight of the situation hit me. One of the most powerful men in Salford sought out *more,* and he'd paid the price.

"But there's a right way to do this," he finished. "We won't die."

I blew out a measured breath and prudently chose my next words, letting them first marinate on my tongue as I weighed Griff's expression. "We don't need to risk our lives to learn about what's beyond the Fort. Maybe what happened to your dad was a warning. It's not worth dying for the stars."

Griff licked his lips. "I know the cost of what I'm asking; I know the damage it could do. But this book . . . Dad spent his life learning more about where it came from. He risked his life again and again for it, and he did it for a *reason.* I think going to Pointe is our only chance at finding the answers we're really looking for."

I threw him a disbelieving look. "What *answers* are we looking for, Griff?"

"Why *your* name is caught up in all this." Griff scanned our surroundings out of habit. But my room was on the top floor, so no one would ever know we were here, sitting below the balcony's top ledge. "I'm going to show you something." He met my eyes with a startling weight. "Don't say a *word*. Just read, okay?"

I swallowed hard, debating my answer. But it was too late. Griff unfolded a piece of paper he'd pulled from his pocket so casually I could've teased him about it in another circumstance. My hands shook as I intercepted the page. Three of the four edges were straight, while one was sheared, clearly ripped.

I let the question show on my face as I read the vaguely familiar handwriting scrawled on the paper. These were . . . directions. In Pointe. Farming Sector, Ring 16. Building 16400—

My heart pinched. "Where'd you get this?" I uttered. "Did you write these directions?"

"No. Keep reading," he prompted with a certain lull.

I wasn't breathing. These were directions to the abandoned greenhouse. How did Griff get these? Who wrote them?

But the instructions didn't stop at the greenhouse. They prompted one to go . . . underground. I skimmed the rest of the page, unable to make sense of the nonsense: *maples, stairs, north, alcoves, tunnels . . .*

I didn't truly freeze until the last line.

charles—show to corinn (key to freeing Miota?)

I shoved the page back toward Griff, not wanting to claim any part in his schemes. My fingerprints on that paper felt like my demise.

"What does that mean?" I dropped each word with a powerful force. My thoughts were jumbled, an indiscernible soup of words. What did any of it mean? Fear settled over me like a blanket.

Key to freeing Miota. Was this the key Griff and Abner had both alluded to?

The icy pinpricks formed on my shoulders as Queen Julia's

primary warning of Accolade resounded in my head. *My husband and I see everything on Miota and in Accolade.* Could they somehow see us now, with omnipresent eyes and ears?

And, if they *could* see us now, how differently would they react? Abner sent Cass to Pointe. Cass's biggest rule was to never tell his mother of his visits. Abner clearly shared knowledge with Griff. It all made my head pound, and the beating sun didn't help.

"This is a page from that book I was talking about. I ripped it out before coming to Accolade."

"You're going to get yourself killed."

"No, I'm not," Griff stated firmly. "You read it yourself: *Show to Corinn.* We need to go to that building in Pointe for answers. And, apparently, for our *freedom.*"

For a fleeting heartbeat, excitement churned in my stomach. But it iced over quickly. "Griff, I know that building. It's an abandoned greenhouse. It's where I met Cass—the prince, I mean." The veins in Griff's hand ran up his arm like a spiderweb. "There aren't answers there. And who's Charles, anyway?"

Griff pressed his lips into a firm line. "My dad."

"Oh."

"What's down there?" Griff asked. "Below the greenhouse?"

I hesitated. "Nothing." I gave my straightest face.

"But the directions say—"

"They're wrong," I said, shrugging.

Griff's brow crumpled. "Lovely, these directions are the answer to *everything.*"

"I'm not going to Pointe during Accolade. That sounds like a good way to get killed."

"We need to know what's down there, and you're clearly supposed to see it. And we need to know whatever this *key to freeing Miota* is."

Admittedly, I was stuck on the phrase, too. It implied Miota was imprisoned. But who were we imprisoned by, if not Their Majesties?

We were *not* going to Pointe. But my curiosity decided to muse Griff and tease out his plan, just to hear how stupid it was. "How would we leave Castle Circle, anyway?" The gate surrounding this place was tall and thin, crafted of smooth iron and completed with sharp points.

"That's the simple part," Griff answered, his face growing cold with shadows. "There isn't security here like in the cities. People aren't so eager to leave the walls they're trapped in when they have everything they want inside them."

His words pierced me as I grappled to absorb them. "And what about Pointe?" I prompted. "How do we make it in and out unseen?"

Delight danced in Griff's eyes. "You don't have faith in us?"

"I just don't want to die."

His eyes fluttered shut. "We won't. The fields are big, and there are only so many guards. We'd go at night, getting in and out of Pointe before anyone realized we'd left Castle Circle."

My decision wavered. My unyielding stone walls nearly turned to fragile glass in Griff's wake. He'd put it so simply, and there was so much to gain from it . . .

But he was asking for madness. To *leave Castle Circle*. Cross the rolling fields. Enter Pointe. Go under the greenhouse. Then retrace our steps back, somehow surviving it all.

It was impossible. And yet, Griff's determination, this page with directions, his talk about the stars and skies . . . Faith coursed through his veins, forging his willpower. He believed we could do this. He believed in *me*. Somehow, I was supposed to do this. Maybe it was all inevitable.

Ultimately, my spirits faltered. The trip was a death sentence.

"I get why you want to do this, Griff. I *do*. And if there weren't laws, and the chance of dying wasn't so high, I'd go."

"Can you trust me on this? Since we're trying to be real friends and all?" He looked at me like his life, his happiness, depended on my answer.

"I trust you," I said. "But friends don't just commit treason together."

"You and Salem don't go frolicking through the fields?" he asked drily, quirking an eyebrow. "Hmm. I can picture it so clearly."

"Now that you mention it, we did once," I responded in kind. "Pretty sure we saw you and Lorenzo out there."

Griff laughed, tipping his head back. The sound of it was warmer than the sun.

After I'd sufficiently soaked in Griff's low voice, I asked my burning question. "That note talks about freeing Miota. Free us from what?"

He didn't answer immediately. "I don't know. But I *do* know you long for freedom, same as me. You want what's beyond the island. And I think the stars put that longing inside you for a reason."

I stilled, and Griff noticed.

It was too much, too quick. A secret book, Queen Julia's malice, the page with my name, the connection to the greenhouse. Though it was all interlinked, there were still vital bits of information missing, things I'd likely only learn by going to Pointe.

The image of my name on that page burned onto the backs of my eyelids, the faded ink stamping a permanent place in my mind. Griff offered a promise of freedom I'd never known before, a vow to a better life. I *wanted* answers, wanted to accept Griff's proposal.

But how could I give into curiosity, no matter how its hooks jabbed and prodded at me? I couldn't take such a risk. Reason *finally* set in. I was here to win Accolade, not to go on daring, treasonous adventures. Griff was only a distraction.

I'd stifled my curiosity before, and I'd do it again. I straightened out my legs and sighed, ready to change topics or leave the balcony altogether. "Griff, I can't do it. I'm sorry. I need to stay focused on winning Accolade."

"I want to win, too," Griff said softly. "Which is why I was thinking we should pair up next week—"

"Not a chance." I laughed, nearly choking. Griff? Pair with *me*? "We'll lose points for pairing with someone from another city. I'm only hanging on by weekly miracles, and my luck *will* run out. I'd be eliminated, and you'd be tied to me, and we'd both leave."

I'd bring us both crashing to the ground.

"I don't care," he murmured. "I just want to pair up with you."

"Why?" I pointed daggered eyes at him.

His mouth twitched once, an upward flick of his lips. "Have I really been so vague?"

I thought about the ballroom last night, how he'd held me close as we danced. All the delicate stares. The way he tracked me across The Gathering Hall during social hours. The times his hand brushed against mine and lingered.

It suffocated me.

"But . . . you're a Top," I choked out. "And I'm a *Low*."

"Have I ever cared about your Tier—"

"This isn't about you," I heaved. "Griff, *please*. It would be the most humiliating thing of my life, being linked with someone that far above me."

The omnipresent jeers would never stop. The backhanded comments, the judgmental stares . . . I'd only be viewed as the pathetic girl Griff carried through Accolade.

Or the culprit who wrecked his shot at the crown.

Griff knelt in front of me, reaching out a hand while bearing a soft look that juxtaposed his chiseled features. I saw it scribbled on his face—the overwhelming pity and sympathy. "Corinn . . ."

"Please leave," I whispered. Angry tears were going to fall onto my cheeks. "I need to think. Please."

Griff's hand froze. His throat worked, but he eventually nodded and left. A fragment of my heart must've latched on to him, because now an aching rift disfigured my chest.

Fury. Curiosity. Misery. But mainly *regret* churned inside me as I went back to my cool room and buried myself in bed, deciding to stay tucked away until I was forced to leave.

CHAPTER 23

The next group competition took place in the dark, and barricades littered the floor, making the environment feel like the first group competition, when fear ran rampant.

We were tasked with placing glowing markers on those from other cities, and the city with the least number of tagged players in half an hour would win the group competition. What this had to do with ruling the country, I couldn't say.

I strode the murky outskirts of The Gathering Hall with Salem as we navigated through the artificial fog, moving quickly to avoid getting tagged. Some candidates ran in sweeping circles, blindly tagging as many as possible, while others waited in the barricades to ambush passersby.

I clung to Salem's hand. We dodged players and reached out with our own tags, sticking any candidate within reach. I—*Pointe*—needed to win this. Holland, my head-to-head, currently had more points than me, but I wasn't far behind. She was my first partner who wasn't Top-Tiered, which gave me extra verve for the week.

The drive to beat her kept me going now, reaching out my glowing tags as far as my arms would let me, racing to stick them on as many people as I could.

Although, as much as I wanted to beat Holland, I understood her. She'd talked about her love for the ocean, her desire to float on the ocean's waves.

"Don't talk about that," I had told her during our history quiz earlier in the week. "You know the law."

She had simply shrugged it off. "If the monarchy is so worried about me just *talking* about floating on water, they have real issues."

I'd only laughed and thought about how I should've extended Griff's offer to *her*—she'd probably go to Pointe in a heartbeat. I hadn't spoken to Griff in three days, ever since he left my balcony. His antics of sneaking off to Pointe were going to get him killed, and I wanted nothing to do with it. I valued my place in Accolade.

Salem veered, though I didn't realize in time. His grip on me held, yanking my body after him. My shoulder shifted in its socket, and I stumbled, narrowly avoiding a glowing marker.

"Thanks," I breathed, rolling my shoulder in small circles.

"Saving you, as always." The impish grin sliced through Salem's voice. "Did you like that dodge?"

"Digging for compliments, are you?" I asked wryly as we quickened our pace.

A Queen's Guard member slinked along the side wall with his tranquilizer in hand. Within another second, he was gone. Ice capped my stomach. I hadn't realized guards were here this week.

Salem gave a low chuckle. "You know I live off them—"

The rest of his sentence was muffled by a weapon firing.

I whipped my head. I guessed it was back to normal now, watching for tranquilizers in addition to the task at hand.

Screams worked their way around the hall—

A prick on my thigh nipped my bare leg, and biting pain radiated through the limb.

The hall spun wildly. Salem let go of me . . . or *I* let go . . .

Salem. I couldn't open my mouth, couldn't *see.*

"Sssss . . ."

The lights flickered back on. My eyes flew open, summoning a headache that pounded rhythmically.

Bodies littered the ground of The Gathering Hall. Were these . . .?

Oh. We were the tranquilized.

But there were so *many.* Usually, the Queen's Guard fired a fraction of candidates, replicating the incidence rate of asympton in Miota's population. I craned my neck through the screaming pain and found limp bodies every few steps. No one else was waking yet.

The queen stood with a guard forty or so feet away. Julia had her back to me, and the blond guard—scrawny, frail, around the queen's age, and oddly familiar—stared at her with gaping eyes, as if he'd lose his head if he missed a word she said. His bleached, coiled hair sprung about his ears each time he nodded frantically.

"Good work, Reno," Julia said. "You have certainly proved your place today."

"Thank you, Your Majesty." By the moon, even his *voice* was small and reedy. "Who would've seen *this* twenty years ago?"

The queen made an amused noise, her version of a laugh. "My father would be speechless. Now, dispose of the body. Before everyone wakes up."

I didn't know what she was talking about, but it was safe to assume I wasn't supposed to be conscious yet. I dropped my head and shut my eyes as my heart sped up. *Dispose of the body.* Which one? What had happened?

"What will you claim?" the guard, Reno, whispered, his voice skittering across the polished floor.

Had I misheard him? Claim what?

"You know the answer. I will check her panel's location history later." She paused. "Thank you for taking care of her."

My eyes, though closed, fluttered as the queen's skirts swept through the crowd of fallen candidates. I stiffened and held my breath, becoming an iron statue, as her footsteps approached.

Did I look unconscious? Was the confusion etched into my face? Had Reno seen me looking at them?

But the queen passed, leaving me alone with my pounding pulse. A few moments later, a dull dragging filled the otherwise silent hall. It was in a pattern—a long heave, followed by two quick footsteps.

The noise was retreating. I chanced glaring upward, craning my neck only the miniscule amount necessary to find the noise's source, and it took every cell in my body not to shriek.

Reno lugged a girl into a closet on the hall's perimeter. Shadows bathed the two until they were gone.

Was she dead? Reno was disposing of the body. He had . . . *taken care* of her.

I didn't move. I *couldn't*. Reno had killed someone under the queen's orders, I was sure of it.

I lay still and wondered what the girl did to deserve death. After an eternity, candidates lulled into consciousness. Gently, slowly, the hall groaned with movement. I let my eyes open. I stretched my fingers, which had gone numb in my paralyzing fear.

I was okay. We were all okay.

Well, except for that girl. She was *dead*.

The queen had killed Griff's father a handful of years ago, and she had ordered a guard to kill this girl today. Her Majesty's demeanor had been so calm, as if this was part of her daily routine. As if murder was as mundane as making one's bed in the morning.

I surveilled the room for others I knew. Of the 150 total candidates left, I estimated at least half of us were here in the hall. Had Reno killed the girl when we were all unconscious?

A hand brushed the outside of my arm, and though the knuckles were warm, I flinched as a small shriek escaped me.

"It's *me*." Griff's honeyed voice washed over me. I bound myself to his cocoa-colored eyes. "Lovely, you look like you've seen a ghost."

Rumor had it ghosts wandered outside the city walls, scavenging on spirits of citizens. I didn't believe the stories, but I knew the expression.

"When did you wake up?" I whispered. I crossed my arms to keep from embracing Griff, craving physical reassurance.

"Just now, with everyone else. Why?"

I blinked hard, scanning for anyone who might be listening. But no one was interested in us as the hall breathed back to life. "Come here," I muttered, not willing to speak any louder.

Griff softened in stature and demeanor, bringing his arms around me and letting me melt into his planed torso. I ignored how sturdy he was, how secure he felt.

I stood on my toes, and he tilted his head so his ear was angled toward me. For the faintest breath of time, my lip touched his earlobe, sending an electric pulse through my face. Griff went rigid around me, and I swore his breath hitched.

I decimated the moment with my words. "The queen killed someone."

Griff pulled only far enough away to look into my eyes. His face promised a storm. "What? *When?*"

"Just now, I think." I kept my voice quiet. "I woke up early. She was talking to this guard about . . . how he needed to dispose of a body. He dragged a candidate away, into a closet."

Griff's visage morphed into one not of terror, but of anger. With one look at his churning eyes, I knew he wasn't next to me; he was with his father. "Did you see who it was?"

I shook my head. "A dark-haired girl . . . it was too far away."

His shoulders slumped, and the air seemed to cool as tension rolled off his shoulders. "Corinn, I know you didn't want to talk about this the other day, but . . ." Butlers materialized, ushering us outside. Some distracted part of me hoped Pointe had won the competition. "There's something bigger going on," Griff whispered against my hair.

He was right, though I wished he wasn't. This was bigger than Accolade—this had to do with Julia killing people like Griff's father. People who spoke of the sky and the ocean outside Miota.

Holland needed to be more careful. Or . . . had my head-to-head partner been Julia's latest victim?

Outside The Gathering Hall, stars winked at us, and the moon gave a red tint—fitting, given tonight's events. Their Majesties waited outside with the candidates who hadn't been tranquilized. I recognized only a few from Pointe.

Her Majesty wore a somber expression, though it appeared practiced. Her brows were arched perfectly, and her mouth gave just enough of a frown to keep her skin from wrinkling.

I stood next to Griff in the mob, and in the close quarters, our shoulders touched.

Julia first congratulated us for surviving another group competition—ironic enough for one person. I missed the next part due to Griff leaning harder against my left arm. That side of my body, brain and all, tingled under his touch.

"A horrific event occurred during this competition," Julia said. "We send our condolences to the Stanzifer family of Cape. Holland Stanzifer, who was initially assumed one of the tranquilized, has passed on. We are sending her body to Cape's hospital for proper investigation, to check for the asympton pathogen, since she appeared to be in good health earlier today."

I shifted. I was going to vomit. Because I knew the truth: Holland was murdered. *She* was the dark-haired girl Reno had dragged away. And Julia was blaming her death on a faultless cause. To keep her trail hidden; to protect herself and Reno.

Around me, those who I assumed were from Cape wailed and let out clipped cries.

"Dead?" a female across the group wept. *"Dead?"*

"Asympton prowls across Miota," Julia continued, ramming through the sporadic sobs. "Nowhere is safe, not even Castle Circle."

I chewed her words like acid, detesting their metallic taste. She was conveniently blaming Holland's death on a disease with a grim outlook.

Griff leaned in. "Holland was your head-to-head, right?"

I nodded. I wasn't sure what would happen to my points this week since my partner was no longer living. It had been murder, falsely pinned as asympton.

All I knew was, if anyone heard the treasonous conversations Griff and I had been having, there wouldn't be a winner between Holland and me because we'd both be dead.

CHAPTER 24

I agreed to meet Griff in Castle Circle's greenhouse, a building I somehow hadn't wandered into yet. By now, at least *Salem* should've dragged me in here.

Glazed crystal walls allowed natural light in, which I knew would heat the space if it wasn't downpouring outside. With the fat raindrops pelting the roof and a thin layer of condensation on the outer walls, this seemed like a private enough place to talk.

Vines curled along the cement path, though navigating the tripping hazard was worth the view from the heart of the building, where pavement pooled together and the glass ceiling bowed into a dome. Vivid florals exploded in colors only seen in the rare rainbow: garlands of lush red roses, sprays of yellow tulips, and clusters of the same pink begoniums Griff had given me.

As if also remembering, he reached out and picked a few stems for me. I held them close.

We settled on a bench on the greenhouse's perimeter, deciding it was as secretive a place as possible. I wiped back the hairs stuck to my sweaty forehead, quickly realizing the humidity was oppressive enough to keep candidates away.

Griff sat with his right shoulder pressed against my left. Even though we were the only two in the greenhouse, and the rain pattering on the ceiling provided white noise, we couldn't take chances, not with this topic of conversation.

I twirled the floral stems in one hand, watching them to avoid looking at Griff. Because I sensed him watching me.

"You said you met Kierran—Cass—in a greenhouse? The one . . ." he trailed off, but I heard the rest. *The one we're supposed to find to free Miota.* "Was it like this at all?"

"No." I smiled. "That one's abandoned. It was a warehouse that closed down before I was born. Pointe restructured the farming jobs or something. My parents would know the details."

"So *this* greenhouse is better, is what I'm hearing." Griff draped an arm around my shoulder.

My face reddened, and I didn't know what to say or where to begin. "Well, this *is* Castle Circle. I'd hope it's better than a neglected building in Pointe." Griff grunted in response. "Why?"

"Just curious," he bumbled, giving a quick shrug. "Dad told me Abner was sending the prince to Pointe to win you over, so . . . I know it's dumb, because he's dead, but I just want to make sure I'm holding my own against him. Because this is all real to me."

Adrenaline shot through me, though it was quickly strangled as my blood went cold. Abner sent Cass to Pointe with the intention of winning me over?

You'd make it far, Corinn.

It was . . . because of Abner? I recalled Cass's initial bitterness toward me; the way he'd pale when I told him no one was forcing him to see me; his mysterious ploy to get me into his Courtship.

It had all been *Abner?* The king had used his son and me, though for what, I didn't know.

Sure, I'd just discovered that Abner was the one who'd sent

Cass to Pointe in the first place. But I'd at least assumed Cass's *feelings* were his own.

I thought Cass had been my friend. Had it been nothing more than a royal orchestration? After all, why would a prince truly befriend a *Low*—

"Lovely."

I forced myself to meet Griff's eyes, hoping my pain didn't show. "You didn't think to mention this the other day? I thought you said you didn't *know* why I'm caught up in all this."

"I don't. My dad told me Abner sent Cass to you. To win you over. He wanted to tell me more, but . . ." Griff sighed. "He didn't do it in time."

In time. Before the queen came for him. And killed him.

I stuffed these fresh emotions, this new information, deeper within me. It didn't matter *now*, I supposed, if Cass's feelings had been genuine or not.

"Holland," I reminded Griff, eagerly changing the subject. My throat wavered. "She was murdered on Julia's command. I think it's because she talked about the ocean."

Griff nodded. He withdrew his arm from around me and placed his elbows on his thighs. "That's *definitely* why. I wonder what she knew of it."

It was terrifying, knowing she died for something so trivial. Wanting to know what the ocean's waves felt like was similar enough to when I wondered what it would feel like to be suspended in the night sky, in the land where stars breathed.

Yet both matters were much less treasonous than sneaking out to Pointe in the middle of the night, following directions on how to find a key to *free Miota.*

"What do you think is in Pointe?" I asked. "Why would you risk everything to go?"

Griff's eyes fluttered. "The book my dad found . . . it referenced others like it. Diaries and textbooks alike. I think the rest of the collection is under the greenhouse, and if we find it, we'll finally learn what's really at play here. Because the monarchy is up to *something,* for killing Holland and claiming asympton."

I exhaled, starting to accept his logic. The royal family had their mess of secrets, and Griff and I were somehow tangled in it all.

If I were to follow this beckon and accept what Griff was telling me, I couldn't inch my way toward it; I'd have to charge at full speed. In school, we were always given simulated patient scenarios and lots of practice. If I went to the greenhouse with Griff, rehearsal wasn't a freedom I'd have. There wasn't a gray area between *legal* and *illegal.* I'd cross the discrete line and commit treason, forced to live—or die—with the consequences.

Griff swallowed after I'd been silent for too long. "I have a hard time figuring out why Her Majesty would kill someone just for wanting to *see* the ocean, unless she was hiding something."

Yes, I'd figured that much. There were secrets with Julia, with Abner, with Cass . . . and secrets helped sustain power.

I bit my lip. "I just don't get why Abner would want Cass to pursue *me* instead of a Top." *Someone like Addison Maybee.* But I didn't say that in front of Griff, whose emotions became erratic whenever I mentioned her. We were finally entering the same headspace, and I couldn't risk it crumbling now.

"I think you'll find your answer underneath that greenhouse. In Pointe." He gulped, searching my eyes. "You and I can make it in and out of Pointe undetected. We can discover the monarchy's secrets, and we might be able to use them to win Accolade."

A creeping chill unfurled inside me, settling into the marrow of my bones. I knew Griff was right. This was what needed to happen.

Cass had evidently spent his days lying to me, befriending me for his father's sake. But here Griff was, telling me we could discover more. *This is all real to me.* To him, I was enough. He beheld me like he did the stars and moon and everything that glowed amid the darkness. We were intertwined, and I couldn't run from it any longer.

"You said getting out of here is the easy part?" I asked.

Griff clapped once and pumped a fist in the air. "Yes!" he exclaimed before rounding his shoulders and scanning the greenery for any wanderers, conscious of his outburst. But it was only us in here. He scooted closer, breathing the same air as me. "You're sure about this? You *want* this?" His voice was a low, ragged mumble, and the sound of it grabbed my heart.

"Yes," I admitted in a shallow breath.

"Thank you." For a fleeting moment, his gaze dipped to my lips. "Yeah, getting out of here won't be hard. There may be a night guard or two, but they'll face the north, protecting the grounds between here and the castle."

"There'll be more guards patrolling Pointe's fields," I said. My thoughts whirred. "We'll have to get around them, too."

"I've been thinking about that. We'll have to leave our panels behind, in case we get a notification—the sound would give us away."

I closed my eyes. Wandering through the fields without panels, all while dodging the Queen's Guard, seemed impossible. We'd be walking corpses living on borrowed time. But I knew he was right. "When Holland was . . ." I waved a hand. "Julia mentioned checking her panel's location history. Is it possible our panels are tracked?"

A muscle jumped in Griff's cheek. "Yes." He said it like he was delivering a harsh verdict. "No panels, then."

"No panels." That was final. "And once we're in Pointe? How will we avoid being seen?" Pointe's city patrol roamed at night, enforcing curfew and detaining any strays. Though they weren't as menacing as the elite Queen's Guard, if they recognized Griff and me—who were supposed to be in Castle Circle—we'd be as good as dead.

"Good thing you know the city like the back of your hand," Griff said, his mouth toying with a half-smile. "Is the city's entrance at least near the farming sector?"

"It's *in* it."

"Then we're fine, lovely. We just need to pick a night."

I bunched my lips, looking at the pink buds in my hand. "Friday is an executive council meeting. That seems as good a night as any." Hopefully, Their Majesties would be too distracted by their council on Friday to worry about two meddlesome Accolade candidates.

"We'll have to go late," Griff said. "Probably around one or so. Get back by six, before the sun comes up."

I didn't balk at his mention of the hours I saw too frequently as a medical student. "Make it five," I said. "Cooks get to the Common early to report for breakfast duty."

Griff nodded. "It's a date."

Solidifying the plan invited a thousand butterflies into my stomach. I tried focusing on anything else—the humid air, the rain slapping on the ceiling, even the floral perfume surrounding us— but it was no use.

I was going to Pointe, to the old greenhouse, with Griff. And we'd either learn everything I'd ever wanted, or we'd die trying. I shook involuntarily and fidgeted to keep Griff from noticing. Thoughts of our lifeless bodies floating off the island—the fate of all the dead—swarmed my brain.

And yet, for some baffling reason, my wild heart fastened itself to Griff's promises and fierce spirit. He had faith in us, in *me*. He believed we'd survive this and be better for it.

Maybe I subconsciously wanted my curiosity to destroy me. It would be a relief to control my ruin for once; it was so often society strangling me, determining my harsh fate, deeming me unworthy without giving me a say in the matter.

Or maybe I trusted Griff more than I cared to admit. He thirsted for freedom, as I did, and he wanted to uncover the monarchy's secrets.

Or maybe I was finally giving in to the terrifying hold Griff Howard had on me.

Whatever the reason, I chose to believe his promise. I internalized it. We'd make it in and out of Pointe.

We *would* attain our inevitable freedom, no matter what happened. Though I hoped to the moon it would be through enlightenment and not death.

CHAPTER 25

On Friday night, I arrived in the shadowed alley beside Club Castle a few minutes early and found Griff already waiting. His hands were crammed inside his pockets, and his neck craned upward toward the sky. Club Castle's multicolored lights bled through the opaque windows, and a subdued drum thumped in sync with my heart.

I cleared my throat when Griff didn't acknowledge me. "Distracted on the job?"

He pulled his gaze back to earth, and his shoulders rolled back. "Showing up late, lovely?"

"I'm still early." I instinctively reached into my pocket for my panel, though my fingers grasped at nothing. *Right.* My stomach acid chewed a hole inside me as I thought about traveling without our panels, without a way to call for help if this took a turn for the worse.

Griff leaned in, and his breath tickled my hairline. "Ready?"

Adrenaline seized me as I nodded.

"We'll climb the southern gate, then either go through my lumberyards or your fields." Griff's face was taut, set in concentration, and his fingers mindlessly moved.

A smile played on my lips at his referral to our cities not as Salford and Pointe, but as his and mine.

Geographically, our cities were closest. They shared land outside the city walls. It was jarring to think I could live so close to someone like Griff and, without Accolade, never meet him.

We slinked along the alley, to the back exterior wall of Club Castle, which faced south.

Castle Circle's metal gate was about a foot or so taller than me, and the iron rods were placed close enough together that no one could fit through them. This only left the option of scaling the fence, a skill I didn't have. I echoed my worry to Griff.

"I'll help if you need it," Griff said as he ran a hand along one of the gate's smooth horizontal rods.

Though buildings concealed us, my shoulders still prickled with a burning sense of someone watching us. Any stray guard in the field would pick up enough evidence to get us thrown into the Hold.

"Reach for this rod first." Griff motioned to the higher of the two rods running parallel to the ground, this one just above my eye level. "I'll push your feet up, and then you'll get over as fast as possible."

It didn't seem like a full plan, considering I had no idea how to get over the gate *as fast as possible*, but we didn't have time to waste. I grabbed the cold iron as Griff squatted to get under my legs.

I ignored the current that surged through me as Griff's slender fingers grazed my ankles. He thrusted me as high into the air as he could, giving me enough leverage to crest the fence. I jumped, hurdling the gold tips.

My stomach flew into my throat once I realized what I'd done. I was higher than I thought; I plummeted to the ground, and for a fleeting moment, I was weightless. I luckily had the sense to crumble upon reaching the ground. I'd seen the effects of falling firsthand: patients braced themselves too hard, displacing their wrists or breaking their clavicles.

A quick pain shot through my ankle, which throbbed for a handful of seconds before subsiding. I held my breath, trying to shunt the medical part of my mind. We had a long road ahead of us, and this wasn't the moment to diagnose myself.

Griff scaled the fence easily, using his upper body strength to pull himself over the fence. Unlike me, he had the forethought to hang with straight arms before dropping to the ground outside Castle Circle. While I'd jumped from nearly seven feet in the air, Griff hadn't even dropped a full foot.

"How was your jump?" he asked before I could compliment him. "Are you hurt?"

I opened my mouth and shut it, taken aback by his concern. "I'm fine."

Griff knitted his brow. "Can you go on? You can use me as a crutch—"

"Who here went to medical school?" I said, attempting a playful demeanor. "Seriously. I'm okay. I don't think it's even a sprain." I paused. "But thank you."

Griff smiled, sheepish at first, before it settled into the lines of his face. His shoulders relaxed, and he scanned the vast space between Castle Circle and Pointe's outer fields, likely searching for signs of the Queen's Guard.

In the moonlight, Griff glowed majestically. His facial musculature eased, and his hair ruffled in the sporadic swells of summer wind. He looked like he belonged out here, unbound by city walls, a child of the night.

A warm feeling blossomed in my chest at the serenity around us. We were *outside* all walls—save the Fort—in the company of only each other and the stars. "It's beautiful out here," I breathed.

"Isn't it?" Griff inhaled deeply. "I want to feel this free every day without fearing for our lives."

I understood. Our hearts ached for the same thing.

"We'll need to stay low to the ground," Griff said, pulling me back to the daunting task in front of us. "I think we can make it to Pointe's outer fields without being seen. No need for the lumberyard."

"The corn should be tall by now," I offered, recalling Mom's conversations last month. The thought of my family wrenched my chest. I hoped I was making them proud.

"Perfect. Let's go."

My biceps and shoulders and abdominals burned as we crawled on our forearms through the grass. I couldn't keep track of the passing minutes, and without our panels, there wasn't a way to know the time for certain—it crept slowly as we trudged on all fours, but when I remembered we only had a handful of hours to go to Pointe and back, each second blurred by. Upon reaching Pointe's outer fields brimming with soybeans, we straightened, and my blazing muscles sighed in relief.

"No guards," I noted, looking to the shrubs while regaining my breath. My limbs trembled, unsure how to handle the now absent load.

"Don't speak too soon," Griff replied. "How're you holding up?"

"Fine." I brought my hands behind my head, gulping in air. "How much time do you think has passed?"

Griff eyed me for a moment too long before digging a small brass object from his pocket, a circular, palm-sized trinket. He squinted before handing it to me. I intercepted the item. "We're doing well," he said. "An hour and twenty minutes? Now that we can stand, we'll be under the greenhouse by the top of the hour."

I ogled the gold object. Was this . . . tracking our time? I dove into old memories, summoning basic skills hardly brushed over in school, but I didn't recall knowing about clocks outside of what panels provided. Still, I did the math, figuring Griff hoped to arrive at the greenhouse by three o'clock.

Griff's hand lingered on mine when I gave the timepiece back. I withdrew, though his soft expression, a moonlit caress, took hold of me in a way his touch couldn't. In Castle Circle, it wasn't uncommon to find him uptight. Out here, he was so *free*. His raw beauty delighted in this independence.

We doubled over as we rushed through the rows of soybeans, ready to crumple to the ground if any guards neared us.

Eventually, soybeans turned to corn, and I stopped at the towering, thready stalks. Thick shoots housed pale silk and twisted stems, groping outward like fingers ready to curl around my shoulders.

I gulped and started into the corn. With Griff behind me, I tried burying my fear, though it was surely written in my posture.

"You don't believe in ghosts, do you?" Griff chuckled. His warm voice didn't belong out here, amid the eerie darkness.

"It's not ghosts I'm worried about," I replied. The Queen's Guard was somewhere in these fields. We hadn't run into them yet, so I figured our odds of crossing them only increased with each forward step.

"We're doing fine," Griff said. His hand found mine, and I let him lace our fingers together. The last time I'd allowed our skin to touch for longer than a moment, we were in The Gathering Hall on the dance floor, enveloped in warm lights and decadent music, wearing silks and lace. Now, we were painted in shadows, surrounded only by the crunching sounds of our shoes in the firm dirt. "We won't get caught."

"We better not," I said. Now I shook not out of fear, but because of Griff's deepening touch and his breath on the back of my neck.

"I won't let *anything* happen to you, Corinn."

I clung to his promise the same way the dried stems snagged on us as we traipsed onward. We'd be okay. Nothing would happen. We'd figure out what was under the greenhouse, learn how it all related to Griff and his father and me, and we'd make it back to Castle Circle. And once this was all behind us, I could go back to focusing on winning Accolade and staying out of the Low Tier.

We reached the opposite edge of the cornfield, and the only thing between us and Pointe's perimeter wall was a yawning grass field.

I sighed. *Thank the moon.* "Come on," I whispered to Griff, turning back to face him. We were so close—

And then the beam of light found us.

CHAPTER 26

My heart jumped into my throat as Griff tugged me backward. We tumbled to the ground, landing just within the curtain of crops.

My chest thudded against Griff's, and I choked on a groan for air. *Breathe, Corinn.* I regained my bearings and tried rolling off Griff's broad chest, but his firm hand stayed on my back, keeping me pressed against him.

"The corn rustles every time we move," he whispered, merely an inch or so from my face.

I peeled my eyelids back. "If we don't leave, they'll find us—"

"They didn't see you." Griff's gaze jumped from my left eye to my right eye, over and over and over . . .

My heartbeat pummeled as every cell in my body trembled. "You saw the light yourself! We can't just *lay* here. They're going to find us—"

"Give it a second."

I couldn't move either way, not with him holding me in an iron grasp against his solid contours. As time passed, I comprehended just how *close* we were. My forearms were braced on the ground, on either side of Griff's head, while my face hovered above his. It would've been too easy to dip my head and kiss him—

Kiss him? By the moon, what was wrong with me? Griff's irritating hold on me had somehow infiltrated this lethal moment.

Did Griff know where my thoughts were? Because he stilled underneath me. "Did you know your eyes glow like moonlight?" he said, his words hushed.

I hoped Griff couldn't feel my heart drumming in my chest. "There's no way you can see my eyes clearly right now."

He tipped his head upward, toward my face, which forced us into sharing the same air. Adrenaline zipped through me as the gravity of the looming Queen's Guard now interacted with whatever this feeling surrounding Griff Howard was.

"Maybe not," he admitted. I swore I *felt* his lips moving, fluttering too close to mine. "But I've thought it ever since I met you, and I figured I might as well tell you now."

I huffed, letting out the breath I'd sucked in earlier. "I'll have to teach you a thing or two about timing."

Griff laughed silently, his core shaking and fingers floating across my back. My heart tumbled. His dark eyes, generously dipped in shadows, traced from my irises down to my lips, where they fixated. Our ragged breaths intermingled, my mouth just over his.

Footsteps approached. I went rigid and squeezed my eyes shut, as if I'd become invisible. At least we didn't have our panels—a single notification would've cost us our lives.

Had the guards seen me? Did they know we were here?

How would they end us? Would we be shot, stabbed, or taken to Their Majesties so they could do their worst?

Griff tensed underneath me as footsteps plodded past where we lay within the corn's border. Griff's nose brushed mine, and paralyzed in fear, I couldn't move away. We stayed there, noses kissing, foreheads brushing, lips lingering.

The guards were eerily silent, which curdled my blood. The

footsteps swelled before retreating, though neither Griff nor I dared to move for a few minutes. Just to be safe.

Finally, I slumped against Griff. His breaths became fuller against me. They hadn't seen me after all.

I slowly rolled off him and kneeled beside him. "They were moving toward Pointe's wall," I whispered. "Right?" I'd noted the trajectory of their footsteps as they'd passed—judging by the volume of footsteps, I guessed there to be three or four guards.

Griff propped an arm behind his head, staying firmly on the ground. Desire danced in his eyes, as if we hadn't almost been caught and killed. "Yes. We'll . . . have to scale the wall from elsewhere. Hopefully, we can navigate within Pointe unseen."

I nodded, accepting the insurmountable task ahead of us. "Okay. Let's go." I waited for Griff to move, but he didn't.

I cleared my throat. "My mom talks about these ugly bugs that crawl around out here. Green and fat and glowing, they burrow . . ." I shuddered. "One could be on you as we speak. Let's go. For your own sake." *Because, apparently, being out here illegally isn't reason enough to* hurry.

Griff, seemingly in a trance, stood while keeping his gaze on me. His face morphed into . . . affection? Curiosity? Was he also thinking about how close we'd just been?

I pushed the thought of Griff Howard's lips *far* away. We skirted the cornfield's southern perimeter, which faced lush vineyards. Somewhere beyond the fields, Yorkinson, Cape, and Kendall sat within their own walls.

I stole a sideways glance at Griff from our concealed spot in the corn. "We just . . . make a run for the wall?"

Griff nodded, still saying nothing.

After ensuring guards weren't nearby, we sprinted at full speed. My stomach lurched as we floated through the grassy field. My feet barely touched the earth before I took the next stride. After a minute or so, my legs burned, bathing in fire. I'd be *so sore* tomorrow . . . assuming we made it to sunrise.

We had to run across the monorail's metal tracks, and though I knew the system wasn't running right now, it still made my pulse hammer.

We reached the southeastern portion of Pointe's perimeter wall. I was *here*, on the opposite side of the stout structure I'd stared at in disgust for eighteen years.

"This'll take teamwork." Griff finally broke his silence as his eyes spanned the wall's height. "Do you trust me?"

I chewed on my cheek, holding back a comment about how I thought this entire endeavor was based on trust. "Yes."

Griff turned to face the wall, planting his feet in the supple dirt and setting his palms on the brick. "Okay. Quick, then, get on my shoulders."

I climbed onto Griff's back, meticulously keeping my weight on his muscle bulk instead of on his nerves and vasculature.

"I'm not hurting you?" I murmured, kneeling atop his shoulders.

"No. You feel fine."

I suffocated on the thick air between us before summoning all my attention to the brick wall in front of me. If guards rounded the wall right now, we'd become corpses.

After taking a measured breath, I slowly stood on Griff's shoulders, propping my arms against the biting brick wall for balance. My center of mass was so high, I could've easily toppled to the ground.

I reached for the top lip of the wall, and pinpricks of rough brick dug into my skin. Griff slid himself out from under my weight, cupping his hands around my feet before pushing my legs upward. I mounted the wall and lay flat against its top edge.

I soaked in the elation offered from this view. To one side, Pointe's streets were neatly laid in geometric, orderly rings. To the other side, vast fields of cultivated land promised freedom.

Griff took a running start and bounded up the wall in two fluid steps, stretching for the top lip. He grabbed it and used his strength to pull himself up and over the edge. We fully hung off the wall with extended arms before dropping to the ground.

I wished we'd brought surgical masks to help keep our anonymity. Pointe's outer streets consisted of logistical offices and food-packing facilities, so we roamed desolate roads, but I still felt the prickling sensation of being watched. A stray Pointean sentinel on night patrol would recognize us, and we'd be goners. We traveled along the wall, on Pointe's outermost street, until the business sector bled into the farming sector.

My breathing stilled as I led Griff deeper into the city, toward the greenhouse. This was my *home*. My family was here, not even five minutes from our location. I'd give anything to relish in Theo's encouragements, or smile at Tellie's jokes, or even listen to Grandma's snarky comments.

But the pleasant memories were only contained within our family's shack. The familiar stone streets, its divots like calluses on my feet, brought back the lowly feeling of not being good enough. These shacks were marked with hunger and disease. Starvation claimed the shacks' dwellers, and fatigue clung to the dilapidated homes the same way that dirt caked the road's fissures.

Though the sector remained unchanged, it seemed so different at this hour, a ghost town holding nothing more than spirits and dead recollections. I swallowed hard when we approached the greenhouse as images of Cass strangled me.

The greenhouse sagged into the ground more than the others around it, a danger that likely contributed to its abandonment. I led

Griff inside through a back door boarded with rotting wood, partially concealed by overgrown ivy slithering up the building's exterior. We shimmied between splintered boards, entering the gaping space. I swore I felt a presence watching us before we disappeared into the building, and my spine turned to ice.

The greenhouse had always made my skin crawl, thanks to the rodents and large bugs that skittered about and nested in soil or decaying wood. But at this hour, and without light, fear coated me *entirely*. I strained to see but couldn't make out anything.

"I've got just the tool," Griff mumbled. The sound of him ruffling through his pockets filled the moldy air.

Then came the light: a creamy yellow beam, produced from a small cylinder Griff held.

He met my gaze. "It was Dad's. Same with the pocket watch keeping our time. His secret stash of stuff is really coming in handy, wouldn't you say?" He nudged me lightly, awaiting a compliment.

I huffed a laugh. "Thank you, Griff's dad," I mused. With these tools—devices to keep time and provide light—we didn't *need* our panels. We couldn't message others, but that didn't matter right now. These tools allowed independence from our panels, the devices that tracked us.

Griff kept his light low to the ground, and though we could only see a fraction of the greenhouse at a time, my past and present were brought together in a painful collision.

The smell of dirt raised Cass's ghost in every corner. I'd met Bernard here since I was little, and though I was thankful for our lessons, this place hadn't been fully animated until Cass stepped foot in it four years ago.

And now I was here with Griff.

"What are we looking for?" I whispered, passing the task off. I navigated Pointe; this part was Griff's realm.

He pulled the stray page from his pocket—the one with my name on it—and squinted to read the directions.

"By the maple . . ." he mumbled, his eyes sweeping the area.

"Maple *tree*?" I wondered aloud. "There's one over here." I led him through the sinkholes of dirt and loose cement to the lone maple, dead from its lack of light.

"Southeast door . . ." Griff whispered. "In the ground." He got to his knees and dug through the dirt. Odd-shaped blobs scattered from Griff's hands, evidence of the bugs residing here.

He hit something hard: a steel door, deeply inset. He grunted as he fiddled to open the trapdoor, ignoring the bits of rust and dirt flying through the air.

My mouth went bone dry as Griff threw open a hatch, which revealed a staircase plunging into darkness. "This is it," Griff murmured. "We'll go down, then close it behind us."

My fear spiked. "Close the door?"

"Yeah, to keep it inconspicuous," Griff replied lightly and offered his hand.

I didn't take it. I stood firmly in the dirt, planting my feet in the earth. Coming here was a *horrible* idea. I knew my inhibitions would eventually catch up to me—too bad it wasn't until now.

"Lovely, what is it?"

"It feels like I grew up here." I crossed my arms, nearly shivering despite the muggy air. "This greenhouse was always a safe spot. But now, it feels like we're endangering our lives, and for what?"

Griff turned to me, letting his flashlight brighten the space between us. "To figure out the monarchy's secrets, and to create a *better* Miota when we win Accolade."

I couldn't help but catch his phrasing. *When* we *win*. Together.

Griff handed me the paper. He'd circled my name, and I

remembered why I was here. *Show to Corinn.* This place was meant for me to find.

I inhaled, and though it was ragged, it filled me with a newfound ember of courage. Interlacing my fingers in Griff's only stoked the flame. "Let's get this over with."

Griff led, taking the first step down the staircase. The wooden step creaked under his weight, and I winced at the echoing noise. My grip on Griff clamped harder as we descended. Once we'd taken enough steps, Griff used his free hand to close the trapdoor, now above us. We were underground. With a dull *thud*, the door landed shut, submerging us in darkness.

CHAPTER 27

GRIFF

I'd nearly kissed her in that cornfield. It would've been too easy.

It was all I could think of as we descended the craggy staircase. Thoughts of her lips, her laugh, those blue eyes, begged for my attention.

And they had it. By the moon, Corinn had *all* of me, even if she didn't know it.

Focus.

I blinked the visions away and rubbed my thumb across Corinn's hand. I drew strength from her touch, strength I hadn't felt since the day Julia took Dad away.

The bottom of the staircase met a dirt path, and my flashlight revealed nothing but rocks and grime. The damp air left my lungs begging for me to turn around, but I wouldn't. We were so close to getting answers.

"There's still a chance for things to get better," Dad said. We lay on our backs in Salford's grassy area deep within the agricultural sector, with our heads together to keep from speaking above a whisper. "I ... well, I spoke to Abner last night."

I jolted, sitting up. "What?" Dad saw Abner last night and didn't tell me sooner? "What'd you talk about?"

Dad gave a mischievous grin. "The usual. His wife is as mentally deranged as ever, and he's still forcing his son to woo Corinn, the Pointean."

"Typical royal shenanigans." I quoted our household's favorite phrase with a small huff.

"Exactly." Dad laughed, shifting in the grass. "Abner also told me his grand plan. I—well, I want to tell you, but . . . not here."

My spirits tanked. "Why tell me anything at all, then?" It was so typical; right when Dad was about to make a breakthrough with me, he shied away. I lived every aspect of my life for him, and he still wouldn't tell me why his orders were necessary.

He was especially this way with Addison. I was dating her for some covert reason Dad refused to give, and I was expected to be fine with the torture *of it.*

"Have some patience, Griff," Dad scolded. "Please. Now's not the time to be difficult." He glimpsed at his pocket watch. "All right, it's almost curfew. Let's get out of here."

I rolled my eyes.

"Hey." Dad was gentler now, as he often was after snapping at me. "I'll tell you soon. Maybe even tomorrow, if I can."

Except, he couldn't tell me the following day, or any day after. Because the Queen's Guard took him that night, and he was dead by morning. The thought made me *sick.*

This tunnel was the only trace left of Dad. If spirits were real, Dad's had left the ocean to deliver Corinn and me here. So, despite the dark air and squelching mud, we couldn't turn around.

"How're you holding up?" I asked Corinn, needing to hear her voice. My question sent her fingers fluttering against mine, making my heart thump loud enough for her to probably hear.

And just like that, my thoughts snapped back to the cornfield. In that moment of impending death, on the edge of being caught, I'd never felt more *alive—*

"Ask me again once we've followed all the directions. What's next?" Her voice wrapped me in its own embrace, though her tone put me back in my place. We were tenuous friends and nothing more.

Our relationship started out complicated from the beginning, when I'd spilled wine on her to get a private moment—which, in hindsight, hadn't been my smartest move. Since then, we'd become closer, though we were far from where I wanted to be. Sometimes, it seemed she was equally enthralled with me, and other times, I wasn't sure of the silent thoughts racing through her head.

I studied the page of Dad's book. When Dad died, our house was turned upside-down since Julia claimed Dad had stolen her possessions. Guards searched every square inch of our house, but they failed to check our backyard's chicken coop—under a loose floorboard, the spot Dad hoarded *everything* illegal.

I'd read the book from cover to cover after Dad died, gathering it had once belonged to Moriah Delldova, originally from Pointe, who'd married Aris Delldova, Miota's first modern king.

The book's words had faded with time, and I hadn't been able to decipher most of them. Still, the hazy, hand-drawn images of charted stars and moon phases held a concrete grip on me, along with the few legible paragraphs about her loveless marriage to Aris and references to other books.

But in the back, on the last page, bold ink slashed the paper with the instructions we followed now, accompanied by the words that held permanent residence in my mind.

Charles. My father. *Show to Corinn.* My moonlight. *Key to freeing Miota?* My greatest mystery. What did it all mean?

"It just says . . . 'in an alcove,'" I replied. "And you know the rest."

"Great," she huffed. "Where are we going to find an *alcove* down here?"

"I don't—"

A deep thud echoed through the dark hall—once, twice—sending a jolt through me. I recognized the noise: the trapdoor opening, then closing.

We were no longer alone.

"Griff," Corinn hissed, jumping to cling to my arms. "What's that?"

"It's all right," I whispered, keeping the flashlight between us and the intruder—not that Corinn and I weren't also trespassing. I vowed to myself I'd protect Corinn, the way I couldn't protect Dad when he'd been taken.

We tensed as a beam of light bounced toward us. This was no panel light, the harsh white type that fanned out like the sun's rays. This was another *flashlight*. My pulse bounded out of control as I stood paralyzed, fixed on the glowing barrel flitting through the tunnel.

Until the gun fired.

I'd only heard of the fight-or-flight phenomenon before, and I hadn't cared to know if it was real or not.

Turned out, it *did* exist. And I was a fighter.

Keeping my body between Corinn and the intruder, I charged toward the assailant, ready to tackle him to the ground. The only citizens with firearms like *these* were in the Queen's Guard.

They had somehow tracked us.

But I stilled after easily trampling the man—gray, fat, and sputtering curses. This was no guard. I knocked the gun from his sausage fingers and wrapped an arm around his neck, forcing him into a chokehold. The man wriggled in my arms, but it was futile for him.

Corinn's movements rustled behind me; she'd evaded the bullet. *Thank the moon.* My throat bobbed, and I nearly succumbed to the red flare deep in my chest at the mere thought of her getting hurt.

"Who are you?" I gritted at the man. "Why were you following us? And how'd you get a gun?"

"My brother," he choked. Whatever *that* meant. Before I could snap back, he rasped another word. A summon. "Corinn."

I glanced back at her. She had picked up my flashlight and watched us with a pained expression, obvious even though the flashlight's glow hardly touched her face. "What are you doing here?" Corinn uttered.

"I c-could ask you . . . the same thing, honey," the gray man hissed from within my grasp.

My insides churned. *Honey.* I didn't want Corinn's name, or any terms of endearment, coming from anyone's mouth but *mine.* Besides, why would this man call her *honey?*

"Wait." My thick command left Corinn and the man flinching simultaneously. It was like watching two friends partake in their own secret. "You two . . . know each other."

It wasn't a question.

It shouldn't have surprised me, considering we *were* in Corinn's home. This was her city, and she knew these people.

"Let him go," Corinn said.

I schooled my face to stay neutral. "Let *him* go?" I confirmed. *The man who just tried to shoot us?*

She groaned in reply. "*Yes,* Griff. Please." I nearly heard the string of words attached to her complaint that I heard too often. *Don't be so difficult.*

"I would listen to her," the man gurgled. "She's stubborn."

"I know that." Who did he think he was, telling *me* about Corinn? As much as I wanted to keep this man throttled, I caved to Corinn's request, dropping my arms. I scrambled to take the man's gun from its abandoned spot on the ground. "Who are you?" I pooled venom into my voice.

"Bernard Bartholomus," Corinn answered for him, keeping the flashlight steady on the man. "The king's brother. Bernard tutored me growing up; he helped me match with medicine." She glided toward us in slow, steady steps.

Abner's brother? I shifted my gaze back to the plump man still on the ground, pinpointing the structures he shared with the king. Gray eyes and hair, stout frames. I now understood the gun; Abner had an arsenal at his disposal. Or, rather, his *wife's* disposal.

Bernard stood and brushed off his pants before looking *through* me to Corinn, which stewed my temper. "How did you get here?" he asked her, red-faced and snarling. "Why would you *come here?* This is beyond reckless! You don't have your panels, do you?"

"We snuck out," Corinn said simply. Pride rushed through me at her sharp, defensive look. She was still on *my* side. I swore she glimpsed at me for a small increment of time, catching the adoration I knew claimed my face. "And, no. No panels. We're here because of Griff's dad. Oh, Bernard, this is Griff Howard. Griff, Bernard."

"Howard?" Bernard's face lost all sign of color. "As in, er . . . related to Charles Howard?"

"My dad."

Bernard nodded, swallowing hard. "Ah, that explains it. Charles Howard was the only other visitor of this tunnel. Well, besides my brother and nephew."

I recoiled. He knew Dad. Dad had *been here.*

I loosened my grip on Bernard's gun.

"You . . . know this place," Corinn accused him. "You followed us down here. I thought I saw someone watching us outside the greenhouse."

Bernard's smile was more of a sneer. "You're in mine and Abner's childhood playground. I always wanted to show you this tunnel, but I was hoping you'd be with Cass when it finally happened."

My blood scalded at the mention of the prince; I couldn't help it. It was so different from how things were with Addison, where I'd *hoped* someone would steal her from me. But now, my heart was making up for its apathetic years wasted on Addison. Because the blooming feelings I felt toward Corinn, the same ones I was trying not to be downright *terrified* of, were not normal.

Then again, we were under a greenhouse in Pointe after temporarily escaping our place in a competition to rule Miota. None of this was normal.

"You don't need to talk about Cass right now," Corinn whispered.

"I do," Bernard insisted. "It's fitting, really. That if it couldn't be Cass, it'd be the son of Charles Howard."

Corinn and I exchanged a look of confusion. The cornfield slid back into my mind's eye *again*.

"Is this about the king forcing Cass to befriend me?" Corinn handed me my flashlight and crossed her arms.

Bernard flinched at the question. "You know about that?"

"Yes, and I don't want to hear your excuses about it. We just want to know what this *key to freeing Miota* is so we can get back to Castle Circle."

I stared on in adoration.

"Ah." Bernard piqued, wringing his wrinkled hands together. "Abner and I wondered about that book. We knew Julia's guards didn't find it in your house"—he jerked his head at me—"after Charles died, so we figured he must've hidden it somewhere well."

I clamped my lips together, hoping I wouldn't regret pulling the page from my pocket and handing it over.

Bernard scanned the paper using his flashlight.

In the silence, my eyes drifted to Corinn on instinct. I still wanted to kiss her. I'd been hesitant in the cornfield, making sure *she* was in control. It had been torture, lying underneath her like that. Perfect, blissful torture . . .

I blinked, realizing she was eyeing me back.

It almost wasn't fair. Why was I still thinking about that almost-kiss now, of all times?

What? I mouthed, giving her the smirk that always made her eyes glow brighter than the moon. The red tint to her cheeks gave me the impression she knew exactly where my thoughts were.

All my thoughts are of you, lovely, I wanted to tell her. But saying such a thing would take more courage than our current undertaking.

Bernard's jaded eyes bounced from me to Corinn. "*I* wrote these directions. In case Julia ever found the diary, it couldn't have Abner's handwriting in it." I piqued at the foreign word. *Diary.* Was that what this book was called? "Since you're here, I can tell you what I know. It isn't much compared to Abner, but . . . I know the important stuff."

"Like what?" I blurted.

"Like how to liberate the damn island," Bernard said, raising his voice. His words hit my chest. He narrowed his eyes at me, then at his gun still in my hand, but he ultimately turned to traipse down the earthy tunnel. "Come on, you two. Might as well make this trip of yours worth it. There's a lot to discuss."

CHAPTER 28

Without explanation, Bernard started down the tunnel of loam and wooden foundation. After Griff and I shared a look, we followed my tutor.

Now that my body was calmer, I studied our surroundings with Griff and Bernard's flashlights. The walls, caked with dirt, housed molded wood beams, keeping the ceiling from caving in on us. Griff and I stayed at an identical pace behind Bernard, and when Griff's hand gravitated toward mine, warmth curled through me.

It almost wasn't fair. I should've focused on deciphering Bernard's cryptic sentences and vague implications instead of daydreaming of Griff.

I supposed, though, it was all equally enthralling. Even with Griff's fingers interlaced with mine, questions about Bernard still catapulted through me.

What was this place? Why would Bernard ask Charles Howard to bring me here? Was *this tunnel* how Cass made it to the greenhouse?

And what did Bernard mean, liberate the island? From whom?

We stopped in front of a flat, wooden board, flush against the muddy wall, which Bernard slid away to reveal an outcropping from the main tunnel—a quaint hole constructed from mulch, not even large enough for me to crouch in. *Ah.* This was our alcove.

It contained a stash of about a dozen books, leaving Griff and me to gawk. It was the most paper I'd ever seen at once.

"Where to begin?" Bernard said as he kneeled on the ground next to the tome-filled cavity. Griff and I sat across from him, and I tried ignoring my reservations about sitting in dirt. The two men propped their flashlights so we could all see each other *and* the outlet demanding Griff's and my attention.

Griff peered around Bernard and set my tutor's firearm on the ground. The two let it sit idly between them, and I took it as their sign of trust. "Those are all . . . *books.*"

"Congratulations," Bernard said flatly. "Your vision is terrific."

My stomach kinked into a tight knot. *"Bernard."*

His gray eyes flicked to me before he brushed dirt off his pants. "Sorry. Just my . . . odd way of mourning, I suppose."

By the moon. "Just tell us what you wanted to tell us," I replied. "Don't bring Cass into this."

Bernard's eyes danced as he debated heeding my request. "Fine," he conceded. "Let me start at the beginning, then, when Abner and I were growing up. We lived in the executive sector— our father was on Pointe's portion of the council—and we hated the Top Tier. When the monarchy closed this industrial greenhouse, we snuck in and explored just to have some *fun.* We never expected to find the trapdoor leading to this tunnel."

Bernard pointed behind him, deeper into the section swathed in shadows we hadn't ventured into.

"Farther down there, this tunnel connects with a branch of Miota's underground tunnel network that's monitored by the monarchy."

"Tunnel network?" I wondered.

"You didn't think Cass traveled *above* ground to come see you, did you?"

I had no response. I'd never thought about *underground* being a means of travel; it was a dangerous world we were warned about from a young age. We'd get electrocuted by a stray live wire, or doom Miota by interfering with the batteries that stored our solar energy. Being here, in this tunnel, was reckless enough; how could one get from here to the castle?

"The underground tunnel network reaches all five cities. Lucky for us, *this* portion we're in right now isn't on the monarchy's radar. Abner checked every map and chart available once he married Julia, and this tunnel doesn't exist in their resources." He swiveled on the ground to better face the stack of books. "Which leads me to this . . ."

Bernard heaved the books, dropping them in the middle of our trio. Dust collected on their covers, emulating a thin layer of frost. Griff snuck a glance at me before looking at the books, and I bit my cheeks to keep from grinning.

Bernard went on. "Once Abner had been king for a few years, he realized how corrupt the Delldova family was. It's nothing you'd know from the outside, but . . . ask Abner to tell you the stories sometime." The look Bernard gave us had my insides curdling. "These books are the few Abner was able to sneak here from the royal collection. They contain stories about how Miota came to be . . . and what's outside our island."

Griff and I exchanged chilled looks.

"What do you mean?" I wondered. "I thought everything was destroyed from before Aris Delldova." An oceanic flood destroyed countless artifacts, materials, and resources during Aris's rule; it was why his successor built the Fort. "How can there be books on . . . how Miota *came to be?*"

I spoke with delicacy, keeping my words slow, bracing myself for Bernard to act like I'd asked a dumb question. It was funny how natural this Bernard in front of me was. The version of Bernard who taught me medicine was kind and encouraging, though it had always seemed like the demeanor was a few sizes too small for him to fit into. *This* Bernard in front of me was the edge of a knife, and it matched his steel eyes and lead personality.

I took one look at Griff and knew he had the same question. Information about anything from before Aris Delldova was nonexistent.

"These books were saved from the floods?" Griff wondered.

Bernard rolled his eyes. "There *were* no floods." He took a labored breath. "Has Abner told you about the supercontinent?"

I met Griff's eyes with hesitancy, and we shook our heads.

Bernard clucked his tongue. "Really? What's he been *doing?* Well, I never thought *I'd* be the one breaking this to you."

I leaned forward. Finally, the promise of *answers.*

Bernard volleyed his gaze between Griff and me. "The supercontinent is a landmass across the ocean. Thousands upon thousands of times larger than Miota, big enough to hold hundreds of *millions* of people."

Though I heard Bernard's words, they washed over me, incomprehensible. There was . . . *more.*

"So . . . there's more land," Griff drawled.

"Not just land," Bernard snipped. "Civilization. *People!* Other countries! Miota would be nothing more than a *city* to them."

Wait.

What?

There were other people. Other *cities* and *countries.*

The damp tunnel spun. My brain reeled with thoughts and questions and confusion. Bernard was lying; he had to be. I needed to stand, or run laps, or scream, or vomit—

"Corinn." Bernard's voice was a warning. He knew I was spiraling into the chasm of my thoughts. "Corinn, hear me out."

I whipped my head, seeing double—two gray heads of hair, two sets of stone-like irises . . .

"We're not alone in the world?" Griff voiced my immediate fear.

There's more.

More people. More land. More nations, more cities, more life, *more, more, more.*

It was a lethal chant, wailing within me, threatening to gut me. And I couldn't outrun it.

More. More. More . . .

"No." Bernard simply dropped the word. "We're not alone. Not. Even. Close."

I clapped my palms over my face. If I thought I was suffocating before, stuck inside walls, I didn't know what I was now. A walking corpse, most likely. I'd died the day I was born on our isolated island.

More, more, more—

"Now, let me explain," Bernard offered. "And then you two can ask your lingering questions. Can you do that?" He spoke to us like we were children, naïve and pathetic, and he wasn't wrong for it.

Somewhere in the crevices of my mind, an endless stream of questions built, each one tumbling over the next. But I couldn't hear them against the swell of unrelenting remorse and rage.

I centered on Bernard as best I could. When Griff's arm draped across my shoulder, I didn't fight it. I couldn't move. What was the point when I no longer knew what was *real?*

Bernard cleared his throat. "Aris lived hundreds of years ago, as you both know, I'm sure. He was *from* the supercontinent; he lived there. His nation was . . . diseased, literally and figuratively.

There were too many people, not enough resources, and the constant threat of war loomed over them."

"War?" Griff asked. With his arm around me, his mouth landed right at my ear, and I shivered at his breath on my skin.

Bernard heaved. "War. It's where people die, land is taken, commodities are destroyed . . . Think of war like a deadly competition, of sorts. Anyway, they needed a solution, or they'd run their nation into the ground and bury everyone with it.

"Along came Aris. He spent nearly twenty years building a man-made island. Very impractical, considering the time and resources poured into it, but he wanted to prove that people could expand into the ocean—the same ocean we're surrounded by now." Bernard's body stilled. "Aris built *one* prototype of his island concept before the whole thing was considered a catastrophic failure. Care to know what he called that prototype?"

My brain turned molten. I didn't let my thoughts walk down that path on their own; I needed Bernard to *tell me.*

"It was the Man-made Island of the Atlantic." Bernard analyzed us as I wondered what the Atlantic was. "You'd better know its acronym, though: MIOTA."

The circuit completed in my brain. Griff blew out a breath.

We were on a *man-made island.*

I ground my teeth, staring at a spot on the muddy floor. My nails pinched into my skin from how tightly I clenched my fists. Every nerve in my body buzzed as I tried not to spill my stomach's contents on the ground.

My body begged me to fall apart, to crumble. I was one slip away from losing all control over myself.

"Aris built it well, admittedly," Bernard continued, "accounting for how long we've lasted. The vibro-compression, geotextile fabric, solar power, underground electric system . . . he wanted this place to be permanent."

I blinked, wondering what most of those words meant.

"Once Aris finished the prototype, he brought hundreds of volunteers to live here for a year to test the island's durability. But in that year, the supercontinent broke into war. You see, there are multiple supercontinents, actually, and the war spread over most of them—"

"Multiple?" I seethed. The musky tunnel swiveled as my head inflated. What were we *doing here*? I'd spent the last few weeks of my life worried about leaving my Tier and winning Accolade . . . why? So I could rule a man-made, miniscule rock while there were *multiple* supercontinents out there?

I stood up, needing to pace. Needing to move, to flee. *More, more, more—*

"Yes, multiple," Bernard answered matter-of-factly. Like it didn't change a thing.

Griff's face had drained, noticeable even in the dull light. He was a statue, jaw clenched shut, chest rising slowly with each breath. The same storm within me churned inside him, only he better regulated it.

"War broke out on every supercontinent, but it never reached Miota. Out here, in the ocean, on our own . . . no one paid it any attention. Most people didn't even know it existed. But Aris rode out the war with his volunteers, and after a few years, it was pretty much settled. Aris kept these people safe, ensured their survival . . . He was exuberant and well-loved, and he made these people believe Miota was a sanctuary from their war-torn home. He convinced them they were safe here, and they should be *happy* to be here. Because this was the only unscathed place in the world."

"And they believed him?" My voice broke, unable to carry the weight of the information.

All those people could've left Miota, but they'd stayed. We were trapped here because of *them*. Because of Aris Delldova.

Bernard cast his gaze to the ground. "Well, these people only knew what Aris told them: their families were dead, their homes were destroyed, and everything they knew was *gone.*"

"Why?" I raked a hand through my hair as I gasped for air, still pacing. Still needing to get away, still wanting *more.* All my life, it was all I'd wanted. "Why would they *stay here?*"

I always thought the Delldovas were kind and noble, like Cass. But between what Julia had done to Griff's father, and what Aris did to the island, the Delldovas seemed worse than I'd imagined.

"I don't know," Bernard admitted, glancing up at me before musing his own questions. "Why didn't those people—*from* the supercontinent—tell stories about where they came from? Why is the supercontinent completely hidden from everyone today? Answers to our questions probably only come from Julia."

Tears rolled down my cheeks.

Bernard grabbed a yellow book from the stack and flipped through it. "But I'm done torturing myself over the past. We need to look to the future. *Our* future, Corinn. Listen to me."

Something about his tone made me heed. I froze mid-step, keeping my fingertips glued to my scalp.

Bernard pulled a metallic dial, much like Griff's, from his pocket before cursing. "You two need to head back to Castle Circle, and *soon.* Quick, I'll tell you the rest of what I know."

I didn't know how there could be more to tell. Bernard had already shattered every perception I knew to be true.

"Aris Delldova wanted a dynasty, and that's what he got. Over time, Miota was no longer a place of peace, but a place to quench the Delldovas' thirst for power. His successors built the Fort. They tortured people who spoke against them. They built walls around the cities, keeping people busy by forcing them to provide for the island. Those loyal to Aris became the Top Tier, and those deemed unruly were placed in heavily surveilled, demanding, high-mortality jobs . . . if they weren't killed first."

The Low Tier. The farmers in Pointe—who sacrificed their lives, who hardly received the rations to survive. Just like, I figured, the Lows in the other four cities.

It was all purposeful.

My heart lurched as I thought of Tellie, my younger cousin destined to match with farming. To become nothing more than a body wasting away, a laborer of the crown.

"Aris wanted a perfect society, and the Delldovas still live by that philosophy. They want to preserve his dynasty, or else they will have failed him, the man who gave them all this *gift*."

Griff, grimacing, finally exploded. He slammed a fist into the dirt. "*That's* why Dad died? For Julia's *dynasty*?" He jumped to his feet alongside me, bobbing his head and pacing in such small laps he could've been spinning in circles. "She's psychotic."

"Yes," Bernard agreed. "It's cruel. And it's why you two need to *listen to me*. Abner has a plan. He has the details, but I know the gist. The supercontinent . . . it's rebuilt from the war." Every bone in my body became metal. "In fact, it's better off than Miota will ever be. The war was so long ago, they have enough food, water, shelter, and jobs for *everyone*. There aren't food rations, shortages, or communal meals. There isn't a curfew or walls. There aren't population controls and career screenings. You're free to live where you want—no need to stay in one city your whole life. The citizens control the government, not the other way around. There are mountains and valleys, rivers and lakes—you don't know what those are yet, but I hope you will one day."

Though Bernard spoke to the very center of my soul, the crux of my existence, the new song in my heart paled next to the *outrage* flowing through my blood.

"Then let's go there!" I shouted. *"Let's leave.* How can you know all this and stand to *stay?"*

I wasn't sure when the tears wetted my cheeks. Or when Griff brought both arms around me, coating me in his earthen scent.

"We'll leave." His mumbling voice reached only my ear. "You and me. We can do it."

"You've pinpointed Abner's plan," Bernard said. *"You're* the key to freeing Miota, Corinn. You were supposed to do so with Cass, but it'll be you and Griff now."

Still wrapped in Griff's arms, I looked at my tutor, ignoring the itchy tears crusting on my jaw and neck. "Me?" I gaped.

"Yes. You've been our plan tentatively since you were eight, but *officially* for the last four years. You were a Low, which was unassuming to Julia, and you wanted more. Cass was going to advocate for you to join his Courtship, and Julia wouldn't refuse because he *was* the only heir. Once you married Cass, you two were going to free the island."

I trembled.

I'd been an instrument from the start. With Bernard, Cass, and Abner. I was being used for others' gains. It shouldn't have bothered me, since their goal was to free Miota, but it stung more than I cared to admit.

Though, honestly, why did it matter which facets of my life were real? Everything on this damned island was a lie.

"What's the plan now that Cass is dead?" I spat poisonously. There would be *no recovering* from learning this information.

Bernard swallowed, and his expression of apprehension told me he *knew* how betrayed I felt. "First, Abner convinced Julia to host Accolade. I made sure you applied, or else I would've done so in your name." I would've been dragged to Castle Circle just like Salem had been. "You've made it this far, and partnerships are happening next week. You two are Miota's best bet at freedom from Julia. You *do* know what this means, correct?"

I gulped. Griff nodded.

I was supposed to stay in Accolade and pair with Griff Howard. And we were supposed to win together.

Bernard's face was the unlit moon, shadowed and bleak where I'd expected light. "You two are going to win this thing. And once you hold the monarchy's power, you're going to expose the Delldovas' secrets. You're going to ruin Julia. And then you're going to get us all off this cursed island."

PART THREE

"Every citizen of MIOTA will stay within the country's boundaries to maintain security and safety. Any citizen with an intent, attempt, or act of leaving the boundaries will be sentenced to death."

—*Treaty of Miota, Art. I, Sec. 1*

CHAPTER 29

Bernard granted us ten minutes to scour the mildewed books and glean what we could. He riffed through texts, finding important bits for us to read, while Griff and I scrawled notes using spare graphite stored in the alcove. We skimmed different books simultaneously, scribbling notes on whatever piqued our brains.

My handwriting had never been neat; the skill wasn't emphasized in school since everything was done digitally, and with my pulse pounding, my hands shook relentlessly.

I soaked up everything I could, though the thought of each second ticking against us made it difficult to focus. As Griff and I traded books and reached for graphite concurrently, we brushed arms and grazed fingertips, sending shock waves up to my shoulders.

Though we didn't have the time or space to acknowledge Bernard's order—to win Accolade *together*—it hung densely between us, making me question my every move around him.

But this wasn't the time to dwell on whether Griff would want to pair with me. Or if I wanted to pair with *him*, a man I hardly knew.

So I shoved it from my thoughts as much as I could. I focused on the maps of the underground tunnel network. I studied the pipeline and electrical systems. Floating vessels called boats, which transported people across the ocean. The castle's original building plans.

My mind caught on a half-ripped page with the letters TRC scrawled across the top. Were they someone's initials? The paper seemed to outline a trade deal . . . between Miota and Red Fox, a city on the supercontinent. The two entities appeared to trade technology and other supplies for . . . *people.*

"What's this?" I asked Bernard, who rummaged through a book.

"What is *what?*" he replied flatly.

Frustration curled in my chest. Right now, I wanted my old tutor, not this man with a secret mission to overthrow the monarchy. "This trade deal." I willed steel into my voice. "Technology for people. The supercontinent knows about Miota?"

Bernard paled, snapping all attentions to me. "Ah. Yes, there's only *one* city that knows about Miota. They trade with the Delldovas: Julia provides Red Fox with people to fill their land, and Red Fox gives Julia surveillance technology and other necessary supplies—machinery, medical equipment, items like that."

I swallowed, digesting the fibrous words. "But . . . I thought you said the supercontinent was bigger and better than Miota."

"It is."

I creased my forehead. "Why would they need *our* people, then? Shouldn't they have plenty?"

Bernard rolled his eyes. "They probably have more land and jobs to fill. I don't know, Corinn. I doubt Julia can question them; she has to do what they say. That place is a much greater force than anything or anyone from Miota."

I shrugged, unable to look at him. "Just seems kind of dumb," I grumbled.

"On *that note*," Bernard shot, "time to go. If you two don't make it back to Castle Circle alive and unseen, I'll bring you back from your inevitable death so I can kill you myself for ruining Abner's plan."

I studied the man in front of me. It was like meeting Bernard again for the first time. His gray eyes were no longer pacified, but brazen. His face, usually soft and molded with smile lines, was now set with a fierce determination.

This was not the man who told me to dig deep and find strength; this Bernard would tell me to rise up and *become* strength itself.

I knew this was Bernard's true personality, as if he'd shed a stifling coat. Had his years of kindness only been a façade to ensnare me in Abner's plan?

I was their tool, a utensil groomed to carry out the task *they* couldn't do themselves. The red-hot thought urged me to spit the words in Bernard's face before we left. He needed to know how unfair that was.

"Get going, now," Bernard droned. "And *don't you ever* come here again, or I'll shoot you for disobeying orders." He stooped to pick up his firearm from the ground, giving the weapon a quick wave above his head to emphasize his threat.

When Griff shouted at Bernard for performing such a careless gesture, my tutor tucked the weapon into his pants with a shrug.

"Oh, and I figure this goes without saying," Bernard said as an afterthought. "But if Julia suspects you two know anything at all, she'll kill you."

Yes. I *did* know that, thanks to Holland. Her dead body being dragged by that pale guard swished across my memory. Had Holland known about the supercontinent?

"Noted," Griff said.

Bernard nodded. "Now get out of here."

Griff and I left the tunnel, leaving Bernard to clean up. We stuffed our handwritten notes deep in our clothes and trekked back through the tunnel the same way we came. It was easier this time, retracing our steps. I sighed with relief when the trapdoor opened for us; the air was lighter above ground, and my ears didn't ring with warning.

"He's not usually so . . . aggressive," I told Griff once we'd closed the trapdoor.

Griff gave a shimmer of a laugh. "My dad was like that sometimes—he'd snap at me, scolding me as if I'd already done something to put my life in jeopardy. I think . . . it was his weird way of protecting me."

I reflected on his words as we crept through Pointe and scaled the outer wall. Once we were in the fields, my nerves settled slightly.

There was a lot to whisper about on this side of the journey, though we kept quiet, too scared to talk about the inevitable fact that we needed to pair up. We'd work with Abner to win Accolade. Surpass Julia in all her power. Tell Miota about the supercontinent without losing our lives.

I glanced at Griff as we passed through the cornfield. Under the silver moonlight, color rose on his neck, his cheeks. His pace slowed, and I might've matched it if my mind wasn't whirling. Even though we continued back toward Castle Circle, my heart stayed planted on the edge of the cornfield, on the cusp of feeling Griff's lips.

The most strenuous part of the journey back was scaling Castle Circle's gate. My arms wilted since we'd just crawled through the gaping grass field, and I required more help from Griff this time.

The glittering lights of Castle Circle seemed dull upon our return. Its luxuries now paled compared to the wonders of the supercontinent. I grew nauseous.

The lane was a ghost town at this inhumane hour. We tried staying swallowed in shadows, but I reminded myself we were *supposed* to be here. This was no longer illegal. We approached Griff's building first, and our pace slowed to a halt.

I clasped my hands together. "So . . ." I breathed. I didn't want to leave Griff, but we needed sleep. Even now, fatigue loomed in the corners of my vision, probing my eyes, ready to pounce.

Griff eyed me like he was memorizing every freckle sprayed across my nose and each blue fleck in my irises. "What do we do now?" he murmured.

My heart cartwheeled at his rough voice. "Sleep now, talk tomorrow?"

Griff leaned toward me and tucked a piece of hair behind my ear. My face tingled at his touch. "What if I'm not ready to leave you yet?"

My cheeks warmed. "You'll survive."

Griff's hand lingered on my neck, and his fingers grazed my jaw. They were quick, hesitant brushes, but the moon shone brighter with every sweep of his skin on mine.

When a hurried breath escaped me, I hoped it passed as being a sigh of fatigue. "Griff," I whispered.

"Tell me." He bowed his head, bringing his face closer to mine. "Tell me all of it."

"All of what?" When I looked into his eyes, mere inches away, they pinned me to my spot on the diamond-embedded sidewalk. In this moment, *we* were like the paved material ourselves: rare, shining, and implanted in something so *dull*.

There's more to life. There's more to the world.

More. There'd always been more.

"Tell me if you want to pair up," he said carefully. "Forget Bernard. Forget everyone else and whatever judgments you think they'll put on you. Do *you* want to pair up with me?" He eyed me, completely and intently, as his thumb brushed my jaw. My pulse jumped in my neck, and it didn't help that I knew Griff felt it under his hand.

My eyes scattered, looking for any way out of this. His question was so direct, answering it would be almost as difficult as finding out life on Miota was a lie.

I swallowed the lump in my throat, ignored my heart recoiling off my rib cage. "I'm a Low, Griff. And we're from different cities, so we'll lose points each week. It won't be easy." I inhaled. *I'd lose Accolade for both of us. For Miota.*

"But what does your heart say?" His eyes were wide, frantic. His hand traveled to cup the base of my skull, and he weaved his fingers into my frizzy hair. Did he know he was undoing me? "Ignore the rankings and competition. When *you* look at the stars, and you think about us, what does your heart say?"

My mouth went bone dry. Because my heart seemed to know the stars placed Griff and me here on purpose, fractions of their celestial cogs.

But the stars wouldn't help us win Accolade. So I stole the phrase he'd once told me. "We're too good to be true."

He pressed his lips together and dropped his hands. The night air ambushed me without Griff's body heat. "I won't pair with you if you don't want it," he said. "I don't care what that grumpy old man had to say about it." He wasn't lying, based on the storm roiling in his eyes.

I nodded. "Thank you."

Griff searched me for a few more breaths before accepting my answer. He blinked and turned to walk into his residence hall.

This was for the best. I already ran too hastily from the Low Tier, from an eternity of farming. I didn't need to bring Griff into this—

But something cleaved deep within my chest.

My Tier didn't *matter* as long as I was stuck on Miota. Even Tops lived blinded and gagged, bound to the walls Julia imprisoned everyone in.

I couldn't run from this. This was bigger than me—this was about freeing every Miotan who suffered because of the crown. This was about liberating a nation.

Griff and I needed to end Julia by winning Accolade. *Together.*

"Wait," I choked out, grabbing Griff's hand, catching him as he turned.

His eyes, deep and turbulent, met mine.

"Griff . . ." My grip on him faltered. "You're right. We need to pair up."

But he didn't smile. "I need to know that *you* want this. On your own. Because what I'm feeling toward you . . ." He raked a hand through his hair, struggling to get the words out. "If I give into it, I don't think it'll ever *stop*. And I'm terrified."

Griff Howard *felt* something toward me? Was I finally outrunning myself after all? My heart rate galloped, seizing hold of my entire body, setting my muscles into motion.

"I want this," I croaked, collecting every spare ounce of bravery from tonight's adventure. "I *do*, Griff. We . . . want the same things, and maybe that's for a reason. Maybe the stars knew what they were doing with us."

Griff's expression turned covetous, like it had in the cornfield. His next words were unhurried. "I think the stars were smiling when they placed us together, Corinn Januski."

"By the moon," I whispered. Though it was a curse, I was glowing.

Had the stars led me to Griff? Was everything unfolding according to their cosmic plan?

Griff drank me in. "Do you remember, on your balcony, when you said it wasn't worth dying to learn about the stars?"

I recalled the day we'd basked in the sun's golden warmth, which had been just as comfortable as the current ebony night. And I couldn't help but wonder if that feeling wasn't because of the weather, but because I was with Griff.

"Yes."

"Well, I've been thinking about it a lot." Griff swallowed hard as he stepped closer, reaching a hand to the nape of my neck. His fingers brushed my earlobe, and my heart tried leaving my body. "The stars hold our unspoken wishes. They're a vessel of light and hope . . . honestly, there's nothing I'd rather risk my life for." His throat worked. "Besides, I have to protect the stars. Because I've told them all about you."

I melted into Griff's touch, letting my eyelids flutter. The cells in my body nearly begged for more from him. More of his hands; more of his breath mingling with mine.

More. More. More. More from this life, more from this world. Griff offered it all.

We stood pressed together, taking up the same pocket of space, savoring the thrill of this *almost*.

We were so close to pairing. So close to acting upon our fate to fight for freedom.

So close to kissing, just as we'd been in the cornfield.

Sharp, high-heeled shoes clacked along the sidewalk from the neighboring residence building, making me jump, snapping the pull between Griff and me. The remaining world outside of *us* ambushed my view. Natalya Lil, my head-to-head from a few weeks ago, scurried down the street. I looked back to Griff, whose face and body teemed with desire, and offered him a sheepish grin.

"We should sleep," I whispered. "Regroup in the morning. Solidify our plan."

A muscle jumped in Griff's jaw. His eyes held the twinkling stars as he nodded. "I'll bring coffee to your room in the morning." My stomach warmed at the promise and the yearning still written on his face. "Corinn, I think I'm going to dream about you tonight."

I laughed. "Let me know how that goes, will you?"

"Bet on it, lovely."

I wasn't sure how we were supposed to depart after tonight, so before I could linger on my elusive feelings surrounding Griff, I gave a genuine smile and turned toward First Residence.

CHAPTER 30

There was no thawing the icy pit inside me on Sunday morning. In a few minutes, there would only be a hundred candidates remaining. We were dwindling down, and instead of my confidence increasing with each week, I knew my chances of leaving only grew. I was the last Low in the entire competition, and that painted a pretty target on my back. I wasn't supposed to be here still. I was like a weed, the kind Grandma cropped and killed.

I'd noticed the tension in Accolade before, but it had increased tenfold since Friday night. This was no longer a ploy for me to escape who I was; it was the opportunity to leave Miota for greater horizons.

Facing eliminations was already bad enough, but doing it with the weight of Miota's liberty on my shoulders was nearly unbearable. What if I wasn't good enough to help the island? What if I didn't hold the strength to save those I loved?

I despised the familiarity of competing with others. My whole life, I'd poured my energy into proving myself. Though everything was different now, my circumstance seemed exactly the same. I was just a Low who wanted—*needed*—more.

I had to beat every other woman here for the crown. Then, I'd marry Griff, rule Miota, make decisions, command the Queen's Guard . . .

No. More like instigate new laws, coordinate boats to and from the supercontinent, and maintain order, despite the inevitable revolution. It left me swaying underneath The Gathering Hall's lights. If I wasn't firmly planted in my seat, I would've fallen onto my face by now.

Remi sat next to me, her mouth drawn in a taut line. Many candidates had been on edge since Holland died four days ago; granted, it *was* unsettling to know someone died in the building.

Murder pegged as asympton. Each time I remembered the truth, the ball in my stomach wound tighter.

Because of Holland's untimely death, I'd been placed in a three-way head-to-head competition against my partner from last week, Addison Maybee, and her new partner, a Middle-Tiered man from Yorkinson I didn't know. Either way, it didn't matter. Addison surely beat us both in the head-to-head vote.

Friday night's adventure with Griff had only caused more tension within me as we'd entered what candidates now called the blind weekend, which was the time between Friday and Sunday when our ranks disappeared. It left me with nothing to do but ruminate on the possibilities and hope I'd done enough to secure my spot into next week.

Their Majesties greeted us, and Julia gave a brief speech on behalf of Holland and her family in Cape. Cameramen feasted upon me since I'd been her last head-to-head partner, and their lenses surely captured all the subtleties in my facial expressions.

"As a reminder," Julia said, "pairings will happen immediately following eliminations, so please stay seated afterward." A light pause. "The first to leave us is Remi Hushe of Pointe."

I poured all my shock into keeping a neutral expression. The Middle-Tiered cook was going home.

"You're next, *Low*," she muttered, echoing my fear, before strutting out of the hall.

Her empty chair mocked me with Julia's every pause. Remi had fought for weeks on end, and it amounted to nothing. She was just a vacant seat, a name announced among everyone, marked as *not good enough*.

The cycle of name-calling was exhausting. Fear of hearing my name, followed by relief with someone else's name. Fear. Relief. Fear, relief . . .

"Elliot Stanton of Pointe."

I kept my gaze planted on the ground, unable to turn and look at the eighteen-year-old leaving in a cast. The air lightened once he was gone; I could finally shed my guilt surrounding him. I focused back on myself. Would Abner save me again if I landed in the bottom fifty?

I now knew he'd saved me because I was an essential piece in his plan to overthrow his wife. He'd saved me so he could properly use me.

Which was what I *still* didn't understand. Abner was the king, one of the most powerful people on the island. Why couldn't he free Miota on his own? Why did he need me? Why wait so long when people were suffering?

Julia finished announcing the eliminated candidates, and I wasn't among them.

Thank the moon. Griff and I had our fighting chance.

Julia explained the pairing rules. A list of candidates would appear on our panels, and we'd choose a partner. Mutual selections would be officially paired, and those remaining would be left to scramble for a partner until everyone had a match.

Cameramen combed through the crowd, ready to livestream the drama for citizens back home.

The first round began, and though I selected Griff's name from the list of remaining candidates, it did nothing to alleviate the pressure in my chest. Remi's empty chair taunted me, reminding me I could ultimately leave Accolade as nothing more than a vacant seat, a broken promise. A deficient key the king placed a poor bet on.

"Congratulations to the following pairs," Julia announced, reading from her panel. Her smooth voice hypnotized everyone in Miota.

But I now knew the cruelty of the Delldovas.

As pairs were announced, I realized the only audible reactions came from partnerships between candidates of different cities. I braced myself, mustering what strength I could, in anticipation of my name being called alongside Griff's.

I practically saw the news headlines in my mind's eye, ridiculing all candidates who paired with someone from outside their city. We were even sentenced to lose points weekly now, based solely on the fact that we'd paired with someone from *somewhere else*.

I still didn't understand why it was so bad to form relationships with candidates from other cities. No matter where we hailed from, we were all prisoners of the same crown.

Julia's voice regained my attention. "Corinn Januski of Pointe, and Griffith Howard of Salford."

It was official.

Though I was filled with relief, reality hit me like I'd slammed into the Fort. Griff and I *had* to win. If one of us slipped, we'd both fall. Abner's plan would be in shambles, and I'd go back to Pointe as an assured lifelong outcast, not only for my Tier, but for pairing with a Salfordian.

I'd live a half-life while other civilizations existed and thrived beyond Miota. I nearly gagged at the thought.

"Izzy Eddison and Salem Redding, both of Pointe." I smiled at the thought of Salem with Izzy, a nurse back home. I wondered how much longer Salem would last here; he was doing his best to get kicked out, yet because of his high status, he endured each new week.

"Addison Maybee and Killian Clerc, both of Salford."

I didn't know who Killian Clerc was, but I'd half expected Addison to pick Griff as a partner—and then fight for scraps once he'd rejected her.

More names were called, forcing candidates together until we were all paired off. Some pairs, however, were much happier than others.

Abner, my new mysterious ally, gave us protocol for the next week. "As a reminder, any couples paired from different cities will lose an automatic fifty points each week. There will no longer be weekly group competitions between cities, though solo and head-to-head competitions will remain as normal. Social hours here in The Gathering Hall will continue, and lecture days will become more demanding as we enter the final few weeks of Accolade."

I fortified my nerves as best I could. The competition would only increase from here. But I would *not* go home without a fight. There was too much at stake for Miota. Thoughts of Theo and Tellie whisked through me. They deserved better than being choked, stuffed into the bottom of a society that was nothing more than a star compared to the suns that were the supercontinents.

This victory wouldn't solely be mine, my family's, or even the Low Tier's. It would be all of Miota's. I couldn't wait to spite *Her Most Royal Majesty, Queen Julia Delldova*, who ruled an imprisoned landmass. Everyone born here deserved to know the truth.

There would no longer be group competitions, which gave me a sense of direction. I needed to focus on winning my head-to-head and solo competitions each week. Griff could continue teaching me history, and I'd have to branch out socially to gain head-to-head votes. I'd need to befriend Tops.

The terror of socializing with Tops turned my insides to liquid, potent with dread. But maybe, with Griff and Salem's help, it would be possible... maybe I'd be *enough* for once, successfully outrunning my status as a Low.

We were released from The Gathering Hall, gifted with an empty Sunday afternoon. Salem, smirking like an idiot, found me as we exited the building.

"Congratulations," he said with a quick whistle. "Pairing with Griff? I can't wait for you two to work together, realize you're in love, and then win Accolade—"

"Shut up, Salem." I bumped him with my shoulder. "You sound like a love-crazed lunatic."

He guffawed. "Sure. Just you wait. It's bound to happen."

I rolled my eyes. "So. Izzy Eddison, hmm? Do you two talk a lot?"

"More now than ever before. But I don't want to be here, and Izzy said she wouldn't marry anyone left in Accolade if her life depended on it, so we figured we'd pair up. Hopefully, between the both of us, *one* of us can land in the bottom fifty soon."

It was the exact opposite of what Griff and I were doing.

When I made it back to my room, I changed into a lightweight skirt that Lily gifted me weeks ago. I cherished the afternoon; our free time dwindled with each passing week. Julia and Abner inserted themselves further into our lives by the day, and the demands would continue increasing as we began tasting our victory in these final weeks.

All but two would be shattered by it. Ninety-eight candidates still had to leave, clearing the path for one lucky couple.

It *had* to be Griff and me—there was no other option. An island of people unknowingly depended on us. But if the queen learned what we planned to do first, she'd float our dead bodies into the ocean.

There was a firm knock on my door, and I figured it was Griff. Relief washed over me as I sprang from my bed, excited to see my *partner.* We were officially bonded, fighting as one.

But it wasn't Griff. My newest ally, the King of Miota, stood in my doorway, grinning. "Care to chat?"

CHAPTER 31

"Your Majesty." I was whipped to the time his wife appeared at my door unannounced. She'd come to question me, to figure out what I knew.

But why was Abner here? Had he come to strategize with me? Had he heard Griff and I went to Pointe?

Abner entered my room with nothing but a dim smile, though once he shut the door, his face hardened. "I hear you went to Bernie's," he said, lowering himself onto my bed.

I wrung my hands behind my back. "Did you talk to him, Your Majesty?"

"I did." He left it at that. He sized me up, his eyes of iron sharp enough to cut me, and in this moment, I wondered if he had the potential to be just as lethal as his wife. "So, you finally know you and I are a team, hmm?"

"Yes." Although, I wasn't sure I'd define this partnership as a *team*. I was a pawn, a tool, to do Abner's bidding. "Your Majesty, since you're here, I . . . have a question for you."

Abner nodded, a small flick of his head, still studying me with a look of unrefined stone.

"Why me?" I asked. "Why haven't you . . ." It wouldn't deliver well, and I braced myself as the words tumbled out. "Why didn't you or Cass do anything to free the island already?"

Abner sighed, sinking deeper into the mattress. "You have no idea what I've been through. I do all I *can*, but Julia actively looks for ploys against her. Communicating with my brother is hard enough—forget about revealing her biggest secrets to the island."

"Couldn't you just deliver an article about it?" I'd meant to be helpful, but it sounded accusatory. I averted my eyes. "That came out wrong."

"As easy as the *action* would be," Abner started, "the *consequences*—her retribution—would kill you. I learned that much early on, which is why I came up with the plan involving you and my son—now you and Griff. You're a Low, Corinn, and Julia would never expect you to know any of her secrets since you're generally supposed to be clueless. I'll tell you the rest of the plan after you win Accolade." He swallowed, not realizing the punch his words had delivered.

There were pieces of his plan I didn't know, fragments he wouldn't bring up until it was too late for me to refuse him, and those unknowns drew goosebumps across my arms.

It almost sounded like . . . Abner planned on using Griff and me to keep *himself* out of danger.

I kept my feet firmly set, though it did nothing to hide the quiver in my voice. "Are Griff and I safe in this plan of yours, Your Majesty?"

"Yes." Abner shifted on my bed. "As long as you don't give Julia reasons to suspect you know her secrets."

"What if she finds out on her own?"

"If she suspects anything, you'll probably end up like me." Abner gave me a measured look before gingerly unbuttoning his shirt, peeling it from his skin.

My hands flew to my mouth to mask my gasp as Abner

unwrapped the gauze from his upper back. Marred, yellow tissue amassed around his shoulders and down his back. His skin was made of hills and peaks, some blotches bone-white and others nearly the purple color of a bruise.

He didn't need to explain. This was Julia's torture he'd alluded to before. She'd *scalded* him.

"Your Majesty," I finally said. "You have necrotic tissue . . . Are you at least going to get a graft? You can't live like this—"

"I know, Corinn. Julia just recently caved when she realized how bad the injuries were. She's been bringing in a burn specialist from Pointe."

I perked. "Ingrid Walker?"

"That's the one. She's been debriefing me, or whatever."

I almost passed off a smile. "*Debriding* you?"

"Same thing." Abner shrugged.

I bit my lip at Abner's swollen skin, blemished beyond repair. Even with a specialist as skilled as Dr. Walker, Abner would be damaged. For life.

"This is . . . because you saved me at eliminations?" I dared to ask, needing confirmation.

Abner's lip grimly curved upward as he nodded. "For undermining her in front of the country. Don't worry about it, though; I'll survive. My wife wouldn't have enough fun in her life if she didn't have someone to torment."

"And if she accidentally kills you?"

"She won't." Abner released a scoff. "If she wanted me dead, I'd already be *dead*. She kills with poison every time. It's . . . efficient."

My blood ran cold. This woman, our queen, was *evil*. Cass's mother. The keeper of this island. She was nothing more than an illusion, a cruel trick of the eye. She didn't care for Miota and its prosperity; she only wanted to keep her dominion on this overgrown rock. She sacrificed her humanity for power, her compassion for control.

Abner sighed deeply and immediately winced at the expansion of his rib cage, rippling the skin on his back. "Okay, put the bandage back on me, doc. I was just trying to prove a point: Even if my wife doesn't kill you, she'll make you wish she would."

I had no response to that.

Abner cleared his throat. "I have this gel Dr. Walker's been using, so feel free to douse me with it."

I froze as my mind caught up to his words.

Me? Bandage him and care for his burns? I'd undergone proper schooling, sure, but didn't Abner know better? I was no doctor.

Abner blinked at my paralysis. "You *did* complete the medical track, right? Or is there another Corinn Januski I should know about?"

I lurched into action, noting his dry sense of humor that matched his brother's. Though my hands shook, and I didn't apply the antimicrobial gel evenly . . . I was *being a doctor.*

"This isn't why you came here, is it?" I asked, reaching to wave the bandage in front of Abner.

He gave a featherlight laugh. "I see why my son liked you."

I furrowed my brow and tried focusing further on applying the gel to his back. "No offense, Your Majesty, but I know the truth now. Cass was only following your orders to see me, so you don't have to act like that was real."

"Corinn, I think some part of it became real. Over time."

"It doesn't matter." I wrapped the gauze around Abner, starting just below his ribs. Simultaneously, I covered my internal turmoil caused by Cass's death. "Either way, he's gone."

Abner didn't speak until I finished wrapping him. "I suppose you've moved on, hmm?" he asked as he buttoned his shirt. "To Griff Howard?"

I stiffened. I didn't want to talk about boys with Abner, especially when his dead son was among the subjects in question.

Abner's inky eyes softened. "No matter, Corinn. I just came here to make sure you realize what you're getting yourself into. If you're going to play this game on my side, I can't have you *sneaking off to Pointe* in the middle of the night. From now on, you stay *here*, in Castle Circle. Understand?"

I agreed.

"You know about panels tracking your location," Abner mumbled, more to himself than to me. "They also keep tabs on articles you view, messages you send, when you're using which applications . . . so be wary."

A startling realization hit at the mention of panels, and I stumbled backward. "This whole time," I started. "I—every time I met Bernard and Cass in the greenhouse, I had my panel."

But Abner gave a small smile. "Yes, you did. But neither Cass nor Bernard had theirs. It all goes back to you being a Low. Julia sees Lows scattered around Pointe during normal working hours and thinks nothing of it because you're precisely that—*nothing*." The words didn't roll off my skin as easily as I wanted. "Besides, her trackers aren't precise enough to know if you're in an abandoned greenhouse or standing on the street outside of it. But making a move as drastic as leaving Castle Circle in the dead of night? That'll earn you a death sentence every time."

I didn't concede. "Salem had his panel, too."

"There was a reason Bernie didn't want him there. Luckily, Julia had more important matters to mull over than a child's location."

I willed my breathing to stay even.

"Anyway." Abner pursed his lips. "I came to see you because I wrote the head-to-head exam this week, and I'm giving you the answers. Who's your partner this week? My wife has been assigning the head-to-heads."

A bitter taste rose in my mouth; Julia's authority explained a lot about my past partner assignments. "Killian Clerc," I replied. "Blond, Salfordian, paired with Addison Maybee."

I'd already planned on asking Griff who Killian was based on sheer curiosity, since Addison had immediately paired with him. But now his name mattered to me. We were competitors this week.

"Ah." Abner shook his head. "Poor boy never should've made it this far—kind of a *dud*. I won't be sorry to see him go, though Addison's a nice girl . . ."

I ran my tongue across my teeth and plopped into my desk chair. "You have answers for me?" I prompted the king.

"Right." He bent his head over his panel, and we discussed each question until the answers came as naturally as breathing. It wasn't unlike when Bernard would quiz me in the greenhouse, ensuring I was prepared for each test I took throughout school. The brothers had the same disposition—they were impatient, yet fiercely determined, which left me begging for more time to think before I was demanded to answer a question.

"You're ready," Abner stated after our tutoring session. "You'll do great this week. You'll even see an old friend later—I'll keep that a surprise, though. He's talked a lot about you."

My stomach twisted in a knot, tightening with each passing second. "Who?"

No one in my life knew Abner except for Bernard, Griff, and Salem. Clearly, Abner didn't mean any of them. *An old friend . . .*

"You'll see, won't you?" Abner set his palms on his knees as he stood, towering over me. "Just think about it, Corinn. You can narrow it down."

"Your Majesty, please—"

"Until next time, Corinn. Stay safe." And then he was gone.

I was squashed between Griff and Pandora in a limo brimming with candidates. Some sat in others' laps, a few squatted on the floor, unable to retrieve a seat, and the rest of us were crammed together like the food my father canned in Pointe's packing center.

At least the drive was short. We reached the barracks housing the Queen's Guard to tour their facilities. With fifty Accolade couples and fifty guards, Their Majesties assigned each pair to a guard to escort us around.

The barracks was a dense brick building lying just outside the castle wall, in a different portion of the same field Griff and I had crawled through on our way to Pointe. The place was surrounded by a shining gate and slinky electrical wires, adorned as delicately as Addison Maybee's jewelry. The building seemed to turn the air gray, suffocating the life and energy from around it.

I couldn't believe city patrol members fought to claim a spot in the elite Queen's Guard when this place seemed so desolate.

Our limo sighed in relief as our driver, a butler, parked. We flooded out of the small compartment. When I stepped out of the car, Griff held a hand on my back, making my heart flutter.

We hadn't had much time together since our journey to Pointe. The game was speeding up—or maybe it only felt that way, with the amount of new information we had. While Accolade previously felt like a race I was being dragged through, forced to keep up, it was now a footrace between the remaining hundred candidates where I needed to win in order to keep *breathing*.

I needed a day with Griff to be as we once were. I missed having drinks on the patio, speaking silently in glances across The Gathering Hall, and hearing Lorenzo tell me I was Griff's *favorite subject.*

And maybe, in that theoretical future free time, I'd be able to sort my feelings for Griff Howard, categorizing them as necessary. Being partnered with him blurred the lines between what came from my heart and what came from our situation.

I slipped my hand into Griff's as everyone congregated outside the front door. His thumb stroked the dorsum of my hand, and I drew strength from his touch.

We could do this.

Their Majesties hadn't accompanied us, which left the atmosphere brighter than usual, without Julia's prying eyes. I guessed the guards were Julia's strength, so we wouldn't get away with anything illegal *here.*

The Queen's Guard marched out of the barracks in a loose formation, as if they couldn't help but stand in order even now. Each member—brawny and tall, with arms the size of my face and jawlines as sharp as knives—announced the couple they were ushering around.

A guard with pale skin and fiery red hair, slicked back in a bun, called Griff's name with mine. As we neared him, I noticed his rippling muscles and piercing black eyes that thickened my blood. Griff's hand grew heavier against mine, rendering himself my protection, and I silently thanked him for it.

"I'm Officer Wesley Ranke," the guard started with an expression that might as well have been carved from rock. "I will be doing your tour today." Wesley's eyes focused slightly past us, and his monotone voice hit me in the face.

"Nice to meet you," Griff offered, stiffening beside me.

Wesley didn't reply as he spun on a sharp heel and walked us inside.

The stuffy main hallway, dark and narrow, reeked of mold. I wrinkled my nose and ignored the impending headache as Wesley led us farther into the building. The wall's wood paneling weighed down the damp air, making the place feel cramped. Wesley took us to the end of the hallway and stopped at a large room filled with rows of beds.

"This is where we sleep." His voice was still cold and empty. "Men on one side, and women—"

"Officer Ranke." A shriller voice interrupted, drawing a shudder down my spine. Another guard, with pale blond curls spilling from his cap and gangly limbs, tapped furiously on an odd-shaped panel as he led another couple: Nelly, the maroon-haired girl from my residence hall, and her dark-skinned partner, Petyr. Nelly offered a *smile*—it was reserved, sure, but it was progress.

"Officer Ranke," the guard repeated, ceasing to type on his panel. He studied the redhead with . . . curiosity. "Officer Ranke."

Wesley blinked furiously.

"You have been reassigned to Nelly Porta and Petyr Vahla. I have been reassigned to Corinn Januski and Griffith Howard."

The voice . . . I'd heard it before. I held my breath, frozen, as the guard eyed me.

This was the guard who'd disposed of Holland's body.

Wesley, evidently pliable as mud, intercepted Nelly and Petyr. "Yes, Officer Reno."

Reno. That confirmed it.

The room spun.

Had Julia sent him to capture Griff and me? If Reno knew of our crimes, this man wouldn't let us waste another breath of air.

And the predatory look in his pale eyes told me he knew *exactly* what Griff and I were guilty of.

CHAPTER 32

"I'm Officer Maximillian Reno," he started as I mentally plotted the best escape route. I clamped tighter on Griff's hand. My partner knew something was wrong, though he didn't let it show in front of Reno. "But just call me Max. Let's begin in the washing room, shall we?"

Officer Reno wasn't as robotic in his speech patterns and movements as the rest of the guards were. It hardly helped his case, though, as I relived the moments following Holland's death.

"We'll stick with Wesley," I blurted, unsure of how to get out of this mess. Every second with Reno increased our danger. Wesley had dragged Nelly and Petyr into the next room, leaving Griff and me alone with the lethal guard.

Reno's lips stretched across his teeth into a forced smile. "What's the matter, Corinn?"

I shivered at his voice; the sound pulled me back in time to when he'd dragged Holland's lifeless body across The Gathering Hall. Fear scattered every rational thought; I could only deduce that Officer Reno was here to do the same to Griff and me now.

"Please," I begged, my voice a whisper. "Whatever you think we've done, we can explain. Just give us a chance."

Reno's expression darkened. "Come with me to the washing room." He glanced at his panel, tapping its screen. "I'll explain everything. But we have to go *now*." He jerked his head, motioning us to follow him.

I peeked at Griff, who was potent with confusion. He didn't know this was the man who killed Holland; how could he?

I had to save us.

"No," I told Officer Reno, biting my lip too late.

His face rippled with misunderstanding as his attention settled back onto me. "Corinn, don't be dumb. Do you *want* to die?"

"I don't." I faintly put weight through my hand wrapped in Griff's so he would know which direction I planned to run. Through the door, into the hallway, and probably out the main door or into another room. Either way, we *had* to run; we couldn't win a physical battle against a guard, even this scrawny one. "Which is why we'll be leaving now."

I let spontaneity rule as I darted out the bedroom door. While I dragged Griff initially, he soon realized what we were doing and kept pace with me, bolting in a zigzag pattern.

"Corinn!" Reno beckoned, his voice hardly reaching me in the humid hallway.

"This is bad," I hissed at Griff, whose face was a concoction of worry and incomprehension. When we turned a corner, I targeted the first door and whipped it open, which revealed a cramped closet containing nothing more than a half-full bucket of water and a mop. Those items alone took up half the space.

But it was too late to change the plan. I jumped into the closet, and Griff followed, shutting the door and submerging us in shadows.

The weight of our situation seeped into my skin. Ideally, we'd wait here until Reno became occupied with something other than killing us. But, more realistically, he'd find us in here. I'd trapped us.

Griff and I, pressed against each other in the constricted closet, fought to catch our breath. The space oozed with odors of dirty water and wet wood.

There weren't lights, but I didn't need to see Griff to feel his stilled energy and hesitancy. His hands found my waist, settling on the valley above my hips. "Corinn," he said roughly, his breath tickling my temple. "Who's the guard?"

I swallowed, ignoring the heat blossoming from where his fingertips grazed me, nursing the infiltrating chill from Reno's presence. "He's the one who killed Holland. I think, somehow, he knows about Pointe . . . what we did."

Griff's knuckles pressed harder into me, firmer than a moment ago, but still giving only a sliver of the pressure I wanted from him.

Why did Griff and I only end up this close in near-death situations? I wasn't sure if my rise in adrenaline was from the imminent doom or Griff's body next to mine.

He pulled me against his chest, where his heartbeat drummed a steady song. Even amid our pathetic situation, no thanks to me, I wanted *more* from Griff. More of his touch. More of his voice. It was so unfair to him.

"I made a promise to protect you before we went to Pointe," Griff murmured. "I haven't given up on that, and I never will."

I swallowed. "I'm sorry I couldn't protect *you*."

He laughed, his broad chest rocking against my cheekbone. "Don't speak so soon, Corinn. We're going to get out of this. I refuse to die in a closet next to a dirty mop."

I looked up, imagining I'd be staring at his lips if there was light in here. "You're confident," I said neutrally.

"I just have faith in us." His half-grin cut through the splinter of darkness between us.

I reached to hook my hands behind his neck. My fingers

skimmed his hairline, nearly plunging into his hair, though I thought better of it.

Griff let out a shaky breath. *"Lovely."* He swallowed, digging his flexed fingers harder against my sides. "Why is it that, when I'm with you, I feel most alive?"

My heart could've leapt from my throat and fluttered out of the dark closet. "Griff . . ." My voice delivered huskier than I'd meant. His touch beckoned for me, and I let myself give into it. In case this was all the time we'd ever have. Because if Reno found us . . .

I traced from the back of his neck to his earlobe, down his jaw that felt as hard and angled as I'd imagined. His trace of stubble nipped against my fingertips. "You do that to me, too," I whispered. "You make me see the world for more than what it is— I see what it *can* be." A world beyond the Fort. A world untethered from the Delldovas.

All my life, I'd wanted more. And here it was, right under my grasp. Griff was my key to leaving the Low Tier, freeing Miota, and *maybe* finding someone who wanted me for exactly who I already was.

When my fingers dared to roam to Griff's lips, his breath hitched against my skin before he planted light kisses on each digit, which did more than simply melt my core—it threatened to burn me, engulf me in flames.

I wanted those lips on *mine*.

While I'd thought of romance before, it was never something I allowed myself to dwell on for long. I might've married a Low-Tiered farmer if Pointe's population began declining and they needed more workers for the fields. And my daydreams for the past few years feebly embodied Cass, though I'd always shoved those thoughts away as soon as they arose.

But *this* . . . This was tangible, what was happening in this dim and dirty closet. Griff's lips tracing my hands, my quickened breaths filling the air . . .

Without thinking, I reached on my toes for Griff. To kiss him.

Before I felt his mouth—once he sensed what I was doing—he straightened, staying out of my reach.

His action, as trifling as putting steel in his spine, changed everything. It sliced the air between us, severing the tension in one quick snap, though the painful aftermath lingered.

I was a fool for thinking Griff would want to kiss *me*.

I tried swallowing the searing knot in my throat, but it was futile. While biting back simmering tears, I crossed my arms, fighting to keep my composure. I would not break down now.

"We need to get out of here," I said, hating how raw my voice was.

Griff set a hand on my shoulder, a knife in the dark. I wriggled away from his touch. He'd pulled me in just to cast me away. "*Lovely*. Let me explain—"

"Explain how to get out of this closet, I hope? Because that would be appreciated."

There was only silence. Stillness. And then, "Yes." The pity in his clipped tone was a slap to the face. "We're near the front door. We could just . . . make a run for it?"

"And go where?"

"Somewhere they can't find us."

I rolled my eyes, a wasted movement without Griff's ability to see it. "We're on an island. They'll find us wherever we go."

"Then we leave the island," he said.

"Griff, I'm being serious."

"So am I."

I chewed on the idea. Miota had an underground tunnel network, and based on the map I'd studied from Bernard's pile of books, there were covert entrances leading to the beach. But it didn't seem possible.

I couldn't think clearly with Griff's body crammed against mine. What were we going to do? We couldn't run, but we couldn't stay here, either. Was Reno truly going to kill us? Could we reason with him?

As Griff inhaled to speak, the door opened, and my heart heaved into my throat. Griff shielded my body with his, and the hall's light revealed the agony scrawled on his face.

"Gotten enough of each other yet?" a voice spat, low and gravelly.

I peeked around Griff's shoulder. Abner, the *king*, stood with Officer Reno, who looked ghastly as ever. While Reno was a snowstorm, silent and looming, Abner was a thunderstorm of pent-up rage. Why was the king here? Was Julia nearby?

Abner snarled at us. "You two. With me. *Now*."

I flicked my eyes to Griff, though I found him already staring at me, and I looked away. Humiliation gripped me as we navigated out of the closet.

Was Abner going to save us? I couldn't consider the options as Griff and I jogged to keep up with the two men.

We weaved through the mildew-smelling halls to the second floor, darker than the main level since it lacked windows. The tang of metal coated my nose; this floor was nothing but wood-paneled walls and heavy steel equipment I assumed was used for training.

Abner veered right and threw open a decrepit side door painted the same hue as a rotting leaf. A chill slapped me upon entering what appeared to be the washing room. Three archaic washing machines lined one wall, and rows of clotheslines were strung across the room's width. It was odd, seeing washing machines indoors; back home, our machine sat in our backyard. Theo did the family's laundry, though I often helped him with it, my standard peace offering following our fights.

"You killed Holland," I accused Reno in the safety of Abner's presence.

Reno *smiled*. "It worked, then. You were awake."

I didn't break eye contact, even though every cell in my body wanted to waver. "What?"

"At that group competition, I shot you with a short-acting tranquilizer. I wanted you to see what happened to Holland."

I stared, my mind spinning. "You *wanted* me to watch you drag Holland away after you killed her?"

The guard shrugged. "Not *that*. But I wanted you to know it wasn't asympton. Cass always said you were smart—I figured you'd use your brain if you knew Holland was actually murdered. You'd figure out there was something bigger going on."

Wait. *Cass?* It was like a shower of bullets as each bit of information flew at me with personal lethality. "You knew Cass?" I squawked, ignoring how every muscle in Griff's body twinged.

Reno's mouth gaped. "Do you not . . ." He set his jaw. "You don't recognize me, do you?"

Abner let out an exasperated sigh and rubbed his eyes with his palms. "Oh, *by the moon.*"

I searched the blond guard for any recognizable features. Was I supposed to know him? Was this my *friend* Abner promised?

"I was Cass's courtier," Reno mumbled, averting his gaze. "We've *met* before, you and I. At your Commencement."

I froze. The image lay across my mind: Cass, two guards, and his pale courtier, none other than this man in front of me now.

I doubled over, about to be sick.

Abner crossed his arms and paced alongside the clotheslines.

"Max is working with *me*. Clearly, there was a misunderstanding about how well you two knew each other."

A thousand excuses rose on my tongue. How should *I* have known this was Cass's courtier? I never expected a courtier to join the Queen's Guard, and I didn't speak directly to Max Reno at Commencement.

"Max listens to Julia to stay on her good side," Abner continued. "Speaking of my wife, you're lucky she's not here to see this—though, if she watches the feed closely, she *may* notice a ten-second cut in the footage . . ."

Griff and I exchanged confused glances from across the room. I hated how I still felt the ghost of his lips on my knuckles, still felt the bite of his rejection.

"What are you talking about?" Griff voiced our matching thoughts.

A haunted look possessed the king, chilling my skeleton. His eyes flicked to Max before focusing on me. "What did Bernard tell you of Miota's deal with the supercontinent? Technology for people?"

I gnawed at the inside of my lip. "He . . . briefly mentioned it."

"Red Fox," Abner started. "Her ally on the supercontinent. Every month, she sends them people, and in return, they send her tech and other supplies." He shuddered. "Red Fox's technology can brainwash you with a neural implant, and Julia controls the Queen's Guard that way. Red Fox also sends her surveillance cameras, trackers to embed in panels . . . Things to ensure Julia keeps her *peace and order.*"

Abner clapped Max on the shoulders as he passed the guard during one of his laps around the room. "Max Reno here is the single-most powerful person in Miota right now. At least, until the next shipment from Red Fox comes, delivering *his* implant."

Max gave Griff and me a sly grin. "I don't have a neural implant yet, so Julia can't control me. Julia trusts me, though, because we grew up together—I was one of her earliest friends. Plus, after practically raising Cass and then killing Holland last week, she's not worried about my betrayal. But my true allegiance is to Abner."

I clenched my jaw as the information came pouring in. "She trusts you, but she's still going to make you get the implant?"

"Better safe than sorry," Max said with a shrug, too calmly.

Griff's body tensed. "So, the guard members are all . . . brainwashed?"

Max nodded. "Thanks to the implants, Julia can suppress their ability to create independent thoughts. The Queen's Guard operates at her will alone."

I creased my brow. "How do the implants go in? Surgery?"

Abner slowed his pacing as he crossed his hands atop his head. "Yes. By Jameson Klemmins, full-time certified and licensed evil goblin, part-time surgeon—"

"Yeah," Max interrupted, throwing Abner an amused look. "There's only one doctor who knows about all this. Jameson Klemmins does the surgery, and once he puts the implants in, the guards aren't . . . *people* anymore."

My tongue thickened, unable to respond.

"What about our first guard?" Griff asked Max. "Will Julia know you took us from him?"

Max's brow quirked upward. "No. I cut the security camera's footage from the main level for about ten seconds. We were supposed to get up here, to the second floor, in that amount of time, but you hid in a closet instead." He flung a quick frown at me. "Luckily, that also kept you out of sight from the hall's cameras until I could safely cut the footage again. Abner's also working around the cameras since he's not supposed to be here."

Shame flowed through my bloodstream. I hadn't trusted Max initially, and by frantically deciding to run away, I'd nearly cost everyone in this room their lives.

"Fortunately for us," Max continued, "there's only the one camera downstairs—you don't really need surveillance when the guards' brains aren't their own. And as far as Wesley goes, Julia can only monitor his brain activity, which should read the same no matter who his assigned couple is."

I could've collapsed at Julia's cruelty. What she was doing was *so wrong*. Guards were husks of people, and nothing more.

"Max," I said as Griff moved to invade my personal space. "Aren't you worried about your implant?"

An unreadable expression claimed the guard's face. "No. I'm doing everything in my power *before* the surgery to ensure I've done my part. Before I'm no longer . . . myself."

Though I externally accepted the answer, I couldn't help but wonder how Max coped with knowing his brain would soon be fried, belonging solely to the queen.

"Max is braver than most," Abner offered. "And I'm helping him work through it."

Oh. I understood: Abner and Max were keeping secrets. It summoned the same angry flare that was present in Pointe, when I'd learned I was nothing more than a tool to be honed.

"If we're going to help you free the island, couldn't you at least tell us your plans?" I blurted. I didn't realize asking such a question had been a mistake until Abner's blazing face settled on me. He marched over, but Griff stepped between the king and me with clenched fists.

"Settle down, Howard," Abner said with a smirk. "Never thought I'd say *that* again." He crossed his arms and peered at me from around Griff. "I can't spend my life managing you. If you're going to win Accolade, you'll be in a constant game of deciphering the riddles I throw at you. If you can't handle not knowing every part of every plan, then this won't work after all."

I heard his threat clearly. *If* I should win. *If* I didn't ruin anything else.

Apparently, Griff caught on, too. "What do you mean, *if*?" he spat. "You're fighting for us, aren't you? That's what Bernard said."

Abner had almost a head of height on Griff, which he boasted as he slid his downward gaze to my partner. "I'll fight for you two unless you show me I've wasted my time. I'd *prefer* you win, but if you're going to be reckless, you can be replaced."

"We'll cooperate," I said to appease the king's relentless stare.

"Good. Because if you two are careless, if you get caught, my wife *will* kill you. That was exactly how it went with Charles. I tried to hide his missteps, but . . . in the end, Julia knew. Things didn't quite add up, and he suffered."

Beside me, Griff went taut at the mention of his father. On instinct, despite his earlier rejection, I slipped my hand into Griff's, and he held me like I was the only thing keeping him tethered to the present.

Abner sighed. "You two just need to focus on winning this stupid competition, so by this time next month, you'll be living in the castle, training to take over Miota. In the meantime, here's some advice: *don't go for the points*."

"Don't go for the points?" I echoed. "What does *that* mean?" I couldn't afford to fumble this odd command, not after Abner threatened to remove me from his plan if I became too reckless.

Abner frowned. "This is another test, Corinn. One *last* test, because I can't afford to show my cards to Julia. If you can't figure this one out, consider yourself on your own. As far as riddles and hints go, this one isn't nearly as vague as the ones you'll receive in the castle, should you win Accolade. Do *not* go for the points."

"Fine." I wouldn't go for the points. If I did, Abner wouldn't be my ally any longer, and I'd farm for life. In a world with supercontinents, I'd live my life on a plot of land, tilling the dirt of a man-made island. The thought made me want to rip my hair out.

I looked at Griff, who already watched me with an expression that told me he was reliving those moments in the closet.

Why did you stop? I wanted to ask. But it didn't matter. There were much bigger things to worry about than kissing a boy.

CHAPTER 33

As the week continued, I made friends, keeping my personal promise. I attended house dinners with a smile plastered to my face, hoping it would help me in the upcoming head-to-head vote. The only candidates left in First Residence were Nelly, Pandora, and Vivienne—all from Kendall—alongside Izzy Eddison and me from Pointe.

They were all Tops, which excluded me from certain conversations, but the girls had warmed up to me well enough. If we stuck to discussing Accolade, I held my own. Izzy even acted like my friend, though I knew it was Salem's doing since she was partnered with him.

While house dinners took mental fortitude, everything else took grit. During social hours, Addison and her partner Killian—my head-to-head—lingered nearby, no matter where I went, as if they had nothing better to do than torment me. My only sanctuary from them was on Pointe's lecture day, when we learned about the monarchy's legal system. I struggled to pay attention from inside the office building, where the gaping windows served as a distraction, displaying candidates walking Castle Circle in droves, plotting and scheming . . .

This week's lecturer was Vee So, Lorenzo's aunt from Salford's portion of Miota's executive council. I recalled Salem telling me Lorenzo's father *and* aunt were on the council.

Despite her thin frame, Vee commanded the room's attention. She had the same dark skin and hair as Lorenzo, though from my seat in the front row, I noticed floral stems threaded into her eyebrows, a unique ornamentation I hadn't expected from anyone related to Griff's best friend, one of the most relaxed people in Accolade.

"You've surely all heard of the Hold before," Vee said, her ruthless gaze combing through Pointe's audience as she paced the front of the room. "Correct?"

I nodded as a few Pointeans chimed in agreement, their thin voices echoing in the nearly empty room. Of the hundred candidates left, only fourteen were Pointean. I'd spent past weeks thinking these lecture days would be more bearable as the pool of candidates narrowed, but I now knew the opposite was true. Our city had reached the point where we saw each other not as allies, but as competition.

After all, only one couple would win Accolade.

"And how long are citizens kept in the Hold?" Vee grunted. "How about you, *Low?*"

I blinked, snapping my eyes to Lorenzo's aunt. *Low,* a name that could only mean *me*. A few snickers floated through the air. I tried not to fixate on Vee's stemmed eyebrows as I held her stare. "Um . . . a month?"

That sounded correct. The Hold was a confined space of cold stone, hidden underneath the castle grounds, infamous for keeping convicts in horrid conditions until their trials. Surely, criminals weren't held for more than a month before Their Majesties decided their fates.

"*Two* months," Vee corrected me with a flick of her head. "We know you won't be here for much longer, but in the meantime, at least *try* keeping up."

My stomach boiled. Next to me, Salem typed on his panel with increased speed. Within seconds, he'd sent me a message, threading together every colorful word possible to describe Vee's temperament. Admittedly, it made me feel a little better.

"I'll give you another chance," Vee said. At least there were less Pointeans than normal to witness my embarrassment. "What are the odds you make it *out* of the Hold, through your trial, and back to your city?"

I gulped. The mind-controlled Queen's Guard intercepted those who committed capital crimes and took them to the Hold. Criminals stayed locked in the underground prison until trials— which I now knew took place every *two* months. The Hold didn't have space to keep criminals locked up for life, so trials ended in either death or pardoning, of which the latter wasn't heard of.

"I don't know," I admitted.

"Anyone?" Vee opened the question.

Nolam, a Top-Tiered scribe, thrusted his hand upward. I'd never interacted with Nolam directly, but he made sure everyone in his vicinity knew he wanted to join Pointe's executive council at the next position opening.

"It's difficult to calculate an exact number," he answered. "But no one has survived their trial in over three years."

"Precisely." Vee clasped her hands behind her back, slowing her pace. "The odds of leaving the Hold are *low*. Which is why you all need to be aware of the laws and regulations at play. The future king or queen may be in this very room, and these decisions will be up to *you*."

Though Vee never looked at me, refusing to acknowledge that

my presence here meant I could rule the country, I inhaled her words, processing them as best I could.

Nolam spoke again, not bothering to raise his hand. "About one in five convicts don't even make it to their trial—they die from the Hold's conditions."

My skin pebbled. Next to me, Salem shook his head.

The disturbing facts must've percolated my mind because I received a perfect score on our exam. *Take that, Vee.* I'd have to ask Lorenzo if his aunt's behavior was usually so condescending.

That night, Their Majesties announced an event happening tomorrow morning. Griff messaged me, asking if I wanted to get dessert, but I declined. I needed to recuperate after listening to Vee all day. Besides, if I spent time with him, I wouldn't be able to ignore the throbbing in my chest still stemming from his inability to kiss me a few days ago.

I knew the pain surrounding Griff came from a place deep within me that had hardly been brushed before. But the Salfordian was quickly making a home in me, taking hold of my feelings and working his way into the crevices of my heart.

I couldn't face it tonight. My heart was so willing to give itself to him, and I couldn't dwell on the sting of his rejection.

While I was soaking in the bath that night, Salem messaged me, saying Griff sat on the sidewalk immediately outside First Residence. But it was too late to cave now; I was getting ready for bed. The seam in my chest only ripped apart further.

Somehow, amid Julia's overbearing rule and Abner's threats, nothing broke me the way Griff's denial did.

I shouldn't have tried kissing him. No matter what he felt for me, no matter the secret knowledge we shared, I hadn't been enough. Just as I'd *always known.*

That night, I dreamed of Tellie transforming into a worm and suffocating in the cornfields outside Pointe. My young cousin, who'd already lost so much, didn't deserve to live as a Low-Tiered farmer when there were prosperous worlds beyond Miota.

So when Lily entered my room Friday morning, I was still deflated, but I held a new sense of purpose. I should've mended matters with Griff last night, like Salem had urged, but I'd only thought of myself. Today, however, I *had* to right things with Griff. We were Miota's hope.

I walked with Izzy to The Gathering Hall, and we theorized what this morning's event would be since we'd already had the week's group competition. I hoped it would be the solo competition, which I desperately needed to do well in, as I remained right around the elimination threshold of fiftieth place.

The Gathering Hall was set with neat lines of chairs, which hardly took up a fraction of the space now, compared to when the original three hundred chairs ran across the floor.

Their Majesties occupied the dais, watching us file in. Abner stood angled toward Julia, keeping his burns shielded from her, and the queen clasped her hands together tightly—a habit Cass had possessed as well, often seen after a heated argument with Bernard.

Though Julia wore an effortless smile, I now saw her sharp canines for the daggers they were. I knew how poisonous she was. She disarmed herself with gauzy dresses and glistening jewels, hiding her true barbaric nature. It was so vile, so corrupt, trading *people* for supplies to torture her guards with—to split their craniums and plant devices in their brains, controlling their thoughts and actions. It now made sense why Wesley, our first guard, had been so absent.

He'd been erased.

Izzy sat next to me; with Remi gone, her surname was closest to mine. On my other side was Blaire Northe, a Top whose father was on Pointe's executive council. I thought back to Commencement, when her father had opened an umbrella on me. That day, the same day Cass died, seemed like something of another lifetime.

"We have a special morning planned," Julia started, giving a coy smile to the candidates and cameramen bleeding into the hall's shadows. "But first, we have a questionnaire. You will find it on your panels, and you may take it now. It is not a race nor a competition."

Abner's eyes flicked to me as the hall ruffled with movement. I navigated to the quiz on my panel, which was only one question: would I rather see two of my family members or gain five hundred points for the week?

Five hundred points. That would be enough to jump Killian, or really anyone, in the rankings.

The choice seemed easy. But as my thumb hovered around the option, I recalled Abner's words to me. *Don't go for the points.*

Surely, this was what he'd meant; Abner wanted me to see my family. Would I get to choose the two members? If so, I'd likely pick Theo and Tellie. My brother was a steady rock, always there for me, even amid our disagreements. And Tellie's spirit so often healed me, her laugh a medicine more potent than anything found in Pointe's hospital.

Would I have to go *home* to visit them? The thought of going back to the Low Tier was enough to wash out Abner's voice. Back to the weathered streets and alleys laced with clotheslines and malnourishment. Forced to live in a place wrought with disease, reminded of how unworthy I was, taunted by the very life I was trying my *hardest* to outrun—

500 points.

I clicked it on the instinct of self-preservation, and my

stomach plummeted to the ground. I hadn't *meant* to click the option for points . . . I was going to select the answer to see my family, as Abner had ordered.

Do not go for the points. *One last test . . . if you can't figure this one out, consider yourself on your own.*

Abner wouldn't trust me after this.

I cursed aloud, gaining a sideways glance from Izzy. "I accidentally clicked the wrong answer," I hissed.

The sun blared through the windows too brightly. The hall's air was strangely thick. Too many eyes were on me.

I couldn't *breathe*.

Maybe this hadn't been Abner's vague hint. Maybe this was unrelated, and I'd done the smart thing. I was saving myself, and wasn't that just as important as anything?

But I couldn't shake the feeling I'd doomed myself. I shot my hand in the air, ignoring the cameras panning toward me. A young butler came over, and I whispered to him. "I chose the wrong answer. Can you tell Their Majesties to reset my quiz?"

He shook his head. "Their Most Royal Majesties said there are no wrong answers. Pay more attention next time."

This was *bad*. No, it was much, *much* worse than bad. Abner wasn't going to fight for me anymore. He'd already saved me countless times—letting me stay when I'd been eliminated, teaching me all the quiz answers in my room, saving me when I'd run from Max in the barracks.

I was *doomed*. I'd be lucky to last another week, which was a real possibility due to my apathetic choice to receive five hundred points. But after this week, without training and help from the king, I'd become a farmer and return to my lowly status.

I was a rare shooting star, the kind that burned brightly before ultimately fading into the night, sinking into total darkness. I'd shone for a time, though all good things seemed to meet their bitter end, and my light was finally simmering out for good.

After another minute, Julia brought her microphone to her mouth. "Wonderful. I will now announce each candidate's choice." Her gaze landed on a camera, and I slumped in my seat, wishing I could shrink away. This was broadcasting to all of Miota; everyone would know I cared more about self-preservation than my own family. No wonder Abner hadn't wanted me to select the points.

I didn't deserve to be here. Who would want a queen as selfish as me? At every possible turn, I'd chosen myself.

Julia began with Cape, giving all twenty results. Of that number, eight chose the points over their families. Maybe I hadn't made a terrible decision after all; the points might've been what I needed to stay out of the bottom fifty.

In Kendall, almost everyone chose the points over their families. It still didn't help my nerves as Julia announced Pointe next. I'd done exactly what Abner told me *not* to.

Julia announced each name, and time crawled slower until she reached mine. I peeked at Abner, whose eyes already weighed on me.

"Corinn Januski. Five hundred points." Julia grinned.

Abner's lips bunched. He gave a swift shake of his head, and the hammer fell on my chest. He was done with me. The years of scheming with his son, the copious burns on his back, the torture he'd suffered from Julia on my behalf... he'd fight for me no longer.

The king refused to meet my eyes after that.

Salem chose to see his family, to no surprise. There could've been a third option on the quiz for one to drop out of Accolade entirely, and Salem would've selected it.

Salford came next. Killian Clerc was announced first, and he'd chosen his family. When Julia delivered Griff's choice two names later, my heart cracked. "Griffith Howard. Visit two family members." He'd followed Abner's orders. Maybe there would be a way for Griff to save me, to bring me out of this mess.

Because, after learning about the world beyond Miota, I couldn't return to the farming sector. I'd sooner sentence myself to the Hold in an attempt to end this shadow of a life quicker. There was *so much more* outside Miota, and Griff and I were supposed to deliver the island into that world.

Addison chose her family, and Lorenzo chose the points.

Once everyone's name had been announced, my point value jumped, catapulting my rank to fifteenth. For a fleeting moment, my apprehensions simmered away. Maybe I could somehow win without Abner's help. If I played a strong enough game, did I have a chance?

"We wanted to see where your priorities lie," Julia said. "If you chose your family, you are caring, and you would sacrifice yourself for those you love. Those are important qualities to possess in a ruler and leader.

"If you chose points, you are ambitious, and your commitment to the crown shows. However, you must be able to put the needs of others before yourself. For this reason, three hundred points will be deducted." I watched my rank drop to thirty-ninth place. "And for those who chose family, you have proven your ability to follow morals instead of glory and power. You will be *rewarded* three hundred points."

At that, Abner pinpointed me with his leaden eyes, and I heard his silent words clearly. *I told you so.*

I bit my lip and looked into my lap. Ultimately, those who'd selected seeing their family ended up one hundred points better off.

"And," Julia lulled, unfinished, "we have brought two family members here for everyone, whether you chose to see them or not. They know your decision, so I have no doubt they will . . . act accordingly."

The thought of my family assuming I'd rather do better in Accolade than see them sent a cord of ice-cold despair through my chest.

Family members flooded the hall in an excited string of gleaming smiles and bright chatter.

But I shut down. My family wouldn't want to see me, and Abner would no longer fight for me. I'd ruined myself.

CHAPTER 34

When Theo and Mom appeared in the crowd, I couldn't contain the bulge in my throat. I choked on a sob, thrilled to see them, even though I didn't deserve it. I'd rejected them, and they knew it.

Even so, when they spotted me in the crowd, they sped up. For a moment, I forgot about Accolade entirely. This felt like the pinch of time just before a storm, when warm winds blew in and lightning crackled in the distance. My family's scolding was imminent, though still at bay for now.

Theo wrapped his arms around me, squeezing until I couldn't breathe. He smelled of home, of soil and mildew. I didn't miss the Low Tier or farming sector, but I *did* miss my family.

Theo's arms were as gangly as I remembered, a result of living off one ration of food per meal. Mom was built similarly, barely more than a skeleton from leading a farming unit while living off mush.

"Missed you so much," Mom said with a grin, intercepting me from Theo. The hollows of her cheeks were more prominent than usual, casting shadows across her face. I felt the depressions between her ribs as I hugged her.

"I'm so sorry," I cried into Mom's shirt.

"How come?" She stroked my hair. "You've made it so far."

I sniffed. "I chose the points over you. I wasn't thinking, and I swear I didn't *mean* to do it, but . . . I still did."

Mom pulled away to look at me. I met her green eyes, a trait neither Theo nor I had inherited. "Don't apologize for wanting to win this. We've been watching you at home, and you're doing great."

Theo nodded, wrapping an arm around my shoulder. "You can win this, Corinn." I grinned at my brother, wiping the tears settling below my eyes. "Okay, how's Castle Circle?" he asked. "The competition? Your room? The food?"

"Griff Howard?" Mom chimed.

I gave a nervous laugh, an unsteady exhale. I couldn't tell the truth—*We're on a man-made rock, the queen is holding us hostage, and the king is no longer fighting for me to win Accolade as of five minutes ago!*—so I settled for, "It's hard sometimes."

Theo and Mom blinked, clearly waiting for elaboration.

"But . . . it's been fun. And Griff is a good friend."

"Just a friend?" Mom challenged, a glint in her eye. She set her hands on her hips. "Anyone can tell you have a crush on him."

My heart jolted. *Anyone* could tell?

Could Griff?

It took a few more seconds for me to digest how easily I'd accepted Mom's implication—I *did* like Griff. Entirely too much. And it was killing me.

"Mom," I gasped. "He's just my partner."

"Why pick someone to potentially marry if you don't *like* them?" Theo wondered.

My cheeks burned. "Because it's part of Accolade! We *had* to pick someone to pair with if we wanted to stay here."

"Then why not pick Salem?" Theo shrugged, smirking.

I sighed. "It just had to be Griff, okay?"

"What had to be me?" a voice rasped from over my shoulder. The mere sound of his low voice sent a warm shudder through me.

I spun to meet Griff with a towering woman and girl around Tellie's age. They all sported the same dark hair and deep olive skin, a common thread between many Salfordians.

"Corinn, meet my sister." He wrapped a quick arm around the young girl, who grinned brightly and waved. "And my mom."

I smiled up at Mrs. Howard, who loomed above us all, and I could've melted on the spot. My smile felt too forged. I didn't deserve her son; I was a Low, and I'd just opted to win points instead of see my family.

"It's nice to meet you," Mrs. Howard said, offering a quick wave. "We see a lot of you two on the projector, so it's nice to speak with you."

"Nice to meet you, too," I uttered, unsure of what else to say. I could tell she was only faking kindness for Griff's sake.

"I'm Jessalyn," Griff's sister said, rocking forward on her feet. "But everyone calls me Jess. Are you sure you want to marry Griff? His bedroom is always dirty, and he likes tomatoes . . ."

I crossed my arms, though I was thoroughly amused as I looked at my partner. "And here I was, believing you when you said you don't like food from Pointe."

"Tomatoes are the exception," Griff insisted, stepping closer to embrace me. "They're divine."

Jess made some noise equivalent to a choke. "*Disgusting!*" she squealed. "How am I related to someone who likes tomatoes?"

"They're in season right now," Mom added brightly. "My unit just picked a bunch last week. I'm Corinn's mother, by the way." Griff broke contact with me to shake Mom's hand.

I swallowed, wishing Mom's comment indicating our Low-Tiered status didn't bother me as much as it did.

"And this is Theo," I added. "My brother." Theo straightened his spine and shook Griff's hand.

Jess led all conversation after that, and thank the moon for it, because my family and Griff's had nothing in common. The awkward tension between everyone seared me. While so many Tops reunited around us, my family had no one. We weren't supposed to be here.

Lorenzo and two people who I assumed were his parents approached Griff's mother, and they broke into warm conversation laced with laughter and hugging. Mrs. Howard's face shone as she spoke with them, which confirmed my theory. She'd feigned her approval of me.

And why *would* she like a Low? My fate was tied to Griff's, and my odds of winning Accolade were stacked against me.

A path cleared toward us. I expected to see Their Majesties, but I found Addison leading two dark-haired figures—her parents, Salford's mayor and his wife—reeking of their own power. I'd seen Addison's father in passing each Friday night, when the executive council intruded on Accolade for their weekly meeting with Julia and Abner.

Watching Mrs. Maybee embrace Mrs. Howard put a boulder in my stomach. Griff's mother probably wished her son had paired with Addison instead.

Griff reached for my hand, crossing the emotional abyss between us. He didn't stop there as he pressed a kiss to my temple, surely leaving a flaming mark on my skin.

"Jess is a character," I breathed.

He squeezed my hand. "She's everything. She and Mom are all I have now, as far as immediate family goes."

I nodded, swallowing hard. "Well, I can tell you mean a lot to them, too."

"Who else do you have at home?" he wondered. "Besides Mom and Theo? I'm sorry for not asking weeks ago."

The fact he'd thought to ask at all filled my lungs with new air, and then shame blew it out. I'd never wondered about Griff's family before, aside from his father.

"My dad, grandma, and cousin Tellie. She'll do her career screening next year."

"Ah." Griff beamed. "Tellie and Jess are the same age, then. Maybe they'll be friends after Accolade."

"I hope so." My mood lightened temporarily, but it was weighed down by Addison and her mother stealing glances at me and laughing to themselves from a few feet away.

Griff's face morphed as he followed my gaze. He opened his mouth, but Mrs. Maybee spoke first.

"Griff, darling, you could do so much better than a Low." She spoke like the queen, in a silky tone to undermine her jagged words. "Addison could carry you to the finish line—"

"I don't want her," Griff swore. "Corinn's the best thing to ever happen to me."

Addison sneered, puffing her chest and lifting her chin, mirroring her mother. "Please, Griff. Her mother is a *farmer*."

"Don't bring my family into this," I snapped. Rage churned in me as I sidestepped from Griff to position myself between my family and the Salfordian Tops.

"A Low with a temper," Mrs. Maybee chided with a cluck of her tongue, eyeing me like prey.

Addison's face filled out with relief. "It's about *time* someone else saw it! A Low in Accolade's top hundred? Is everyone around here blind or just *stupid*—"

Griff curled his fingers into fists at his sides. "Ads, if you want to speak to my partner, you'll have to go through me first."

There it was. *Ads.* The name always summoned a physical reaction from my body as it reminded me of their history.

"*Partner,*" Mayor Maybee scoffed, adding to the conversation. His deep voice overpowered everyone else, snuffing out our kindling exchanges. "Not for much longer, hmm?"

Why not? Because he thought I'd get us sent home? But Addison and her mother shared a knowing look, and ice prickled down my neck, around my shoulders. What did they know?

I snuck a glance at Theo and Mom, who watched in horror. My heart clenched; they didn't deserve to witness this. I lugged my family away before tears welled over my eyelashes.

Theo called Addison's family a number of vulgar names once we'd mazed through hordes of families to one of The Gathering Hall's nooks, well out of their earshot. If I remembered correctly, this was where I'd been hit with a tranquilizing dart the day Holland died.

"Sorry about them," I mumbled, keeping my gaze cast downward. "I hate them. I hate Addison, and I hate *all of this.*"

I was being stifled into the Low Tier when all I wanted was *more.* More freedom, more life, more than what Miota could ever give. Even a family like the Maybees held virtually no power in the scheme of things. Because *Miota was nothing.* If I floundered in this life, on this man-made hunk of synthetic dirt, how would I ever taste true *freedom?* How would Griff and I liberate all these people?

Especially when Abner was no longer fighting for me to win. Maybe the king would still support Griff, and I'd stand a chance in Accolade because of my partner. But I also could have doomed us both by undermining Abner today.

"Tell us what's going on," Mom urged. I cocked my head toward her, reeling myself back to reality.

"You look like you're about to hyperventilate," Theo said as lines appeared between his brow. "Are you all right? These people here . . . they're terrible."

"Well, they're Tops."

Mom and Theo nodded, accepting the explanation.

"You can beat them," Mom said, keeping her voice hushed. "Seriously, Corinn. There aren't normal eliminations after this week. Their Majesties will likely judge character, and you have plenty more of that than these people."

By the moon. I'd forgotten. Sunday was the fifth and final routine elimination. The last two weeks hadn't been explained to us yet, but with fifty or fewer candidates left, we could assume rankings wouldn't matter much in Accolade's final days.

"You do," Theo agreed. "You've already made it far, Corinn."

His jarring similarity to Cass's promise at Commencement unleashed the sobs boiling beneath my skin. I covered my face, wishing to leave the hall, wishing to hide myself from the cameras scouring the crowds. Mom and Theo sandwiched me as I composed myself, tying myself tighter.

For Miota, and for myself. For freedom and my Tier. I couldn't leave now, after fighting for this long.

"Just keep being yourself," Theo said from behind me. "You're smart enough to make it through each point-based elimination, and once it comes down to a matter of Their Majesties' opinions? You'll win because of your kindness and determination."

I let Theo's message absorb into my skin, seep into my blood vessels. I didn't feel kind. Not when I'd left Elliot on the floor during our group competition weeks ago, and not when I'd nearly refused to pair with Griff out of fear for myself. Even *today,* I'd chosen points over my family.

But Theo also said I was determined, and he wasn't wrong

there. I was still outrunning myself, as I'd done my whole life. And for the first time ever, it had been *working*. Maybe, somehow, Abner would still save me with Griff. Our fates were tied; he couldn't separate us.

I grounded myself in my determination, thankful for my brother, who always knew what to say.

I could still win Accolade and escape what I was—I had to, because it was my only option to free Miota and myself. I couldn't go back to Pointe knowing there was an entire hidden world beyond the Fort, knowing everyone on this island was trapped, already corpses who just happened to have heartbeats. I needed to become Queen of Miota.

"Thanks, Theo."

"I mean it."

I grinned up at him, meeting his frosted eyes, their hue identical to mine. "I know."

CHAPTER 35

Their Majesties kept us busy all weekend. I never got the time I wanted with Griff before eliminations snuck up on me. Five weeks into this competition, my body still reacted the same each Sunday morning, a concoction of quickened heartbeats and shallow breaths.

My footsteps were hesitant on my walk with Izzy to The Gathering Hall. Though I'd spent time with every Top in hopes of gaining their favor against Killian in our head-to-head vote, I wasn't sure it was enough to save me. After all, he was partnered with Addison, an obvious favorite.

It was terrifying, knowing I'd fought to secure my place this week and it still might not have been enough. Knowing I could give my all and still be blatantly rejected.

I shook as I took my seat in the hall, unable to breathe steadily. Nausea settled in, and I was glad Lily hadn't forced me to eat more than a bran muffin this morning.

Those ranked fiftieth or lower would leave today, along with their partners. It wouldn't affect pairs where both partners ranked in the bottom fifty—they would've both left today, anyway. But if pairs transcended the threshold between the top and bottom fifty, *both* candidates would leave. It essentially guaranteed that no one was safe. If I was in the bottom fifty, Griff and I would both leave.

I leaned forward, past Blaire Northe, the candidate inserted between Salem and me alphabetically. "Tell me something good," I pleaded to my best friend.

"Griff won't stop looking at you," Salem replied, adjusting his glasses as he nudged his head toward Salford's section of chairs.

I followed Salem's gaze. Griff's face lit up when our eyes met, despite Addison jabbering two seats away from him.

"Okay, now reassure me about this elimination," I said.

Blaire huffed, studying her filed nails as she unsuccessfully smothered a smile.

"What, Blaire?" Salem propped his elbows on his thighs, unamused.

She snorted. "Nothing, really. Just . . . something my father said after Commencement this year." I braced myself. "When will you stop trying to be something you're not?"

My throat quivered, and I looked forward in an attempt to block out all sound. *I will stay here.*

But why would I? Why did I deserve it?

By the time Their Majesties commanded attention on stage, I was completely unraveled, the string of a threadbare sweater too tangled to be put back in its proper place.

Their Majesties both spoke, though their words sounded like they were coming from behind a layer of plastic, their timbre unable to fully reach my ears.

"As you know," Abner said into the microphone. "This week, we will eliminate the candidates ranked from fiftieth to one hundredth. You each chose a partner last week with the understanding your fates in Accolade would be tied together. For most pairings, *both* candidates are ranked in either the top or bottom fifty—the sign of a well-matched partnership. But for eighteen unlucky individuals, you will leave because your partners ranked in the bottom fifty."

The air among us was dense enough to slice. It was almost worse knowing the statistic beforehand. Eighteen people were about to leave, even though they'd done enough to secure themselves.

Julia began. "The first to leave today is Proper Ingol of Yorkinson, and by association, Kadin Vellum of Yorkinson. Kadin would have otherwise been safe today, placing in the top thirty."

Blaire let out a small noise next to me while others across the hall gasped.

We reached a spurt of names where both partners were in the bottom fifty and would've left either way. Then, "Petyr Vahla of Kendall, and by association, Nelly Porta of Kendall. Nelly would have otherwise been safe today, placing in the top ten."

Top ten. Nelly was leaving because Petyr had dragged her down with him; his failure was hers. I chanced glancing sideways at Kendall's portion of seats. Nelly's flushed face glowed, embodying rage and destruction, as she refused to move.

Julia cleared her throat in warning. The present guards tightened their arms on their waistbelts, ready to move at Julia's command. Now that I knew the truth of the Queen's Guard, I couldn't help but detect their blank stares and empty eyes. They were human puppets.

Nelly gave a frustrated grunt, making a few candidates wince, before storming out.

The list continued. I braced myself for my name, and therefore Griff's, but it never came. We'd *survived.*

I still held my breath, cautious to accept a preemptive truth. But then, from Julia, "Congratulations. You are the final thirty-two candidates."

It should've been the final fifty. But eighteen candidates left today because of their partners.

I opened the Accolade folder on my panel to see the remaining rankings, now public. I'd been forty-seventh, and Griff—

Eighth. I didn't know how eliminations would be conducted after today, but I already knew it was written in the stars: I would hold Griff back from his potential. He could accomplish so much more without me. Acid burned through me once I noticed Addison Maybee's name in first place. She was more powerful than I could ever dream of.

Salem sat in thirty-fourth place in the rankings. He'd actively tried to *leave*, and he was still positioned comfortably. Meanwhile, I'd fought with everything I was, and I'd held my place here by a fingernail.

This week, I needed to regain favor with Abner—it was the only way I'd stay here. The only way I'd escape Pointe, the Low Tier, Dr. Ova . . . the only way Griff and I could free Miota.

I was a ticking clock. And each passing second felt like a plummet to my inevitable destruction.

We were forced to eat lunch in our residence halls, a stale occasion with only Vivienne, Pandora, Izzy, and myself. Nelly's empty chair at the table's head, alongside the silence accompanying her absence, short-circuited my brain. The only sounds at lunch were the clanking of silverware and filling of water. I never thought I'd grow to miss Nelly's presence, but here I was, feeling sorry for the girl who'd left on her partner's account.

To keep from thinking about Accolade, I locked myself in my room and pored over the meager notes I'd taken under Pointe's greenhouse. I memorized the tunnel network and brushed over the trade deal with Red Fox: Miotan people for the supercontinent's technology.

I rifled through my memories, recalling anyone who'd disappeared without notice. Mom told stories of farmers who went missing in the fields . . . were *they* the ones sent?

A knock on my door made me jerk, and I bashed my knee against one of the desk's legs. I winced and shoved the notes back into the drawer they came from before gingerly opening my bedroom door.

It was Griff, which surprised me, especially when he looked equally shocked that I'd answered. We hadn't spoken since our families visited on Friday.

His apprehensions seemed to haunt him as he leaned against my doorframe. "Hey, lovely."

My heart kicked for only a moment. He nearly bowed into me, and it took every bit of willpower to stay planted firmly. This was *my* room, after all.

Griff's throat worked as he crossed his arms and withdrew. "Corinn, I can't do this anymore. I can't keep acting like this rift between us isn't *torturing* me. I haven't been sleeping well, knowing you're upset, and I need you like I need air, so . . . please. Let's talk, and let's make this right."

My heart stopped. Was he speaking as my Accolade partner or as my friend who'd discovered a new world with me? I hated how I overthought everything between us ever since that *stupid* almost-kiss in the barracks.

"Okay," I muttered. I mimicked him, crossing my arms while turning my feet to lead. Though Griff was close enough for me to make out his individual eyelashes, I wore the doorframe like a shield, trusting he wouldn't cross the barrier into my room. I swallowed. "Let's talk."

Griff's eyes roamed my face before catching on my lips. He wasn't touching me, had barely *said* anything, yet my body wanted him closer. But I wouldn't make that mistake again. I stayed in my spot, inches from his face, yet *technically* a room apart.

"Corinn." Griff tried capturing my gaze, but I wouldn't let him. If I looked into his eyes, I'd drown in them. And he wasn't going to win this game in *my* residence building. "Things . . . *changed* at the barracks. Was it Max Reno? Being Kier—Cass's—courtier?"

I blinked. Griff thought my doubts centered around Max Reno? While I was blindsided by Max's true allegiance to Abner, I hadn't thought about him much, except to scold myself for not trusting him on my own accord.

"It's not that," I admitted as I gathered every ounce of strength I possessed. I forced each word out. "I'm *scared*, Griff. Scared you're going to wake up and realize how much better you can do than *me*." Shame bubbled in my stomach, burned through my veins. "I've done so many things *wrong* already. I feel like . . . like I'm on borrowed time. So I thought if I left first, if I . . . shut you out . . . your rejection wouldn't hurt as bad."

Griff reached out a hand. It settled on my hip, and I had to pretend it didn't send lightning through my nervous system. "I'm not leaving you, Corinn. I'm here to win Accolade with you. And go to the supercontinent at your side. We'll have adventures, and while I'll be ecstatic to see the ocean and stars and skies, I'll just be thankful to do it all with *you*."

His words left my heart strung up, pinching in my chest beneath my too thick breath.

Because I wanted it, too. I wanted to win Accolade, carry out Abner's plan, and bask in freedom with Griff Howard.

And still, as profound as his confession was, he'd dodged me in that closet. Why did all my thoughts lately land on Griff's inability to kiss me?

"Do you *want* to kiss me?" I asked before my brain knew what my mouth was doing.

It sounded pathetic, but I couldn't take it back now. I waited for an answer, sentencing myself to Griff's mercies. Whether he knew it or not, he held the power to break me now.

A storm of emotions ran through his face, and I couldn't decipher any *one*. "What brings that up?" he finally said in a low, brittle voice. "You're reading my mind now, hm?"

I chewed on my cheek. "Reading your mind?"

Griff dipped his head, sending loose strands of hair across his brow. "I've wanted to kiss you for . . . a *while*. It first crossed my mind that night before the first elimination, when we talked about the stars, and I learned that you were like *me*."

My lips parted as I thought back to the night so early in Accolade it could have been a dream.

"But . . . the thought of kissing you took over my *entire mind* that night in the cornfield. We were so close to being caught and killed, and I didn't care, because I was with *you*." His voice trembled.

"In the barracks," I blurted. "Why . . . why didn't you . . . ?" He knew what I meant, surely. My heart battered, sending my pulse roaring through my head.

Griff offered a smile that sent a thousand butterflies to my intestines. "Oh. Because I like to think I'm a romantic. And I wasn't going to let our first kiss happen while hiding in a *musty closet*."

I released a light laugh. "I thought we were going to die in there."

"I knew we'd be fine," Griff said. "I wasn't lying when I said I always have faith in us. I didn't know how to say it then, but I wanted our kiss to be perfect, because I've never had a kiss *mean something* before, and you're *everything* . . ." He bumbled his words and raked a hand through his hair.

"Griff," I whispered.

His eyes fluttered shut at my voice before he inhaled and

centered his gaze back on me. He was going to crush me with the weight of his expression. "It seems selfish when I look back at it, not kissing you then. But don't be fooled, lovely. Every breath I take, every heartbeat... There isn't a part of me that doesn't belong to you."

Griff took my face to guide my mouth to his.

I stopped breathing. His lips were warm, *soft*—

The stairwell door clanked open, and Vivienne appeared, shrieking at the sight of us as she made her way to her room across from mine.

I tried jumping back from Griff, but he kept his grip firm on me, still lazily leaned against me in the doorway.

"By the moon, Corinn!" shouted Vivienne. "If you're going behind Addison Maybee's back, at least have the forethought to *close the door*." Vivienne scanned her panel to enter her room, and she slammed the door shut behind her.

I tensed in Griff's arms. Addison wasn't even here, and she somehow spoiled this moment. How did she manage that? *I* was Griff's partner, yet it didn't seem to matter.

"Corinn, I'm not with Addison."

"I know." I peered at the ground. "But you *were*. For most of your life, right?"

How does one erase so much history? How could Griff love someone for years to ultimately hate them? I let the question show on my face. *Tell me what happened.*

Griff nodded, letting his hands fall. There were only a few inches of space between us, but they felt like miles. "Our dads forced us together from way too young of an age. Dad had some ulterior motive, but I never quite learned what it was. I think he just wanted me to have a connection to the mayor. I thought I liked her, but looking back, it was hardly even attraction. I was pressured into it all, physically and mentally. I never loved Addison, and I'm not even sure she loved me, but she seemed to think I was her only option. She suffocated the life out of me, and I'd gone numb, and the day Dad died, I realized I couldn't do it any longer."

He flexed his hands, reliving the memories. "But when I broke things off with her, she didn't listen. She . . . tried acting like she owned me, like I was an *object* for her to play with. So I vowed to never say her name to her face again—in her family, where titles and names correlate with power, that's what it took for her to finally get the point."

Oh. "That's why you call her Ads," I ventured.

He nodded with a quick smile. "It was Lorenzo's idea. It worked; she hates it. Kind of spiteful sometimes, but . . . I don't know. She took so much from me."

I hooked my hands around his neck as my heart raced. "You deserve so much better than that, Griff." My statement shocked me; I never thought I'd speak of someone like Addison Maybee in such a way.

Griff looped his arms around my waist, pressing me against him as our lips hovered in the same air. "Well, I *did* find this girl from Pointe. You may know her, actually." When I smirked, Griff's mouth parted. "My whole heart belongs to her. It has for a while, really. Pretty much since we crashed that first night of Accolade."

I held my breath deep in my chest. "The night *you* crashed into *me,* you mean."

"Semantics," he murmured, walking into my room, guiding me as I stepped backward.

I laughed, glancing behind me to ensure I wouldn't fall. "What're you doing?"

Griff shut my door behind him, letting me go for a quick moment. "I just realized Vivienne was right about *one* thing. We should probably close the door."

CHAPTER 36

I hardly registered the click of the knob's automatic lock before Griff pressed me against the door. His lips left a fiery trail from my temple down to the hollow of my neck, drawing a gasp from me.

"You're so *lovely*," he whispered against my skin.

I laughed, unable to take the desire crawling up my arms and down my legs. "Is this a romantic enough spot for you to kiss me properly?" I teased. "Because I think you need to—"

Griff's mouth covered mine fervently, catching me by surprise. I stilled in his arms as my head buzzed wildly. I didn't have another kiss to compare this to, save our transient exchange before Vivienne interrupted, but it surpassed anything I could've conjured up in my mind.

My shock morphed into something bolder, richer, and I welcomed his unyielding lips as he pressed closer, practically melding into me against the door.

I hadn't expected his mouth, his tongue, to be so *soft*. All I knew in this moment was Griff Howard—his hands, lacing through my hair and pressing the small of my back; his lips, committing my mouth to memory; his tongue, wandering gently yet deliberately, as if he'd practiced this in his head.

I untethered my restraint between hasty breaths, letting my hands roam up Griff's broad shoulders before plunging into his hair.

"Corinn," he spoke on my lips before moving back to my jaw, dotting kisses on my skin like the constellations he'd told me about. "This is pretty much all I've been thinking about since that night in the cornfield. You owned me before then, but that was the night I realized it."

I exhaled. "I wanted to kiss you so bad that night," I whispered.

"Then we have some time to make up for, don't we?" He walked us to my room's velvet couch, his lips never leaving me once, drawn to me like I was his center of gravity.

In school, I'd learned that being alive was about having a pulse and established airway. But right now, I didn't think I could survive without this dark-haired boy filling my vision and clogging my taste buds.

I'd found someone who believed in me, someone who shared pieces of my soul. Someone who wanted a better, freer Miota. And now I knew he wanted me in return.

I wasn't sure how long we stayed there before thunder grumbled outside, drawing us out of our own tempest. I peered out my window to find oncoming gray clouds peppering the sky.

"I think I could do this for the rest of my life," Griff said.

I ran my fingers down his arms and traced his fingertips. "Then it's a good thing we're partners."

His eyes darkened beneath their cloak of thick lashes. "In two weeks, we'll be celebrating our victory."

"Ours and Miota's," I agreed, shivering. Something about Griff's presence made me believe we could *still* win Accolade. We'd free the island. We'd retaliate on Julia and her forefathers. "Although . . ." I remembered my situation, and it threatened to deflate my mood. My chances of winning Accolade were as bleak as the looming storm. "Abner isn't fighting for me anymore."

Griff ran a thumb along my bottom lip, catapulting my pulse. "You don't need anyone fighting for you, except for *you*. You're stronger than you think, Corinn."

I tried to shield myself from his infiltrating words, all lies. If I was strong enough on my own, I wouldn't have needed Abner to save me after being eliminated weeks ago. I wouldn't need to keep anyone's favor or rely on others to carry me through the remaining weeks.

On my own, I was a Low, unable to help *myself*, let alone the entirety of Miota.

Griff's face softened, and he offered a roguish smile. Somehow, he'd sensed my remorse. "But if you ever need it, you have my support. Always. No matter what, I'm fighting for you."

Good. My partner was fighting for me, and maybe Abner was still fighting for him. "That helps," I admitted. "Thank you." A few seconds passed in silence where Griff and I lay on our sides, facing each other. Griff skimmed my arm with idle fingers, and I basked in the warmth and bliss of his touch. "I *do* need to win Abner back, though."

"I still can't believe he stopped fighting for you," Griff mumbled, his breath tickling me. "After spending the last four years trying to get you on the throne, you think he'd have some grace. It seems like a lot of work on his part, supposedly all for nothing now."

If that didn't describe me, I wasn't sure what did. *A lot of work, all for nothing.*

"I'm pretty sure Bernard chose me first," I said. "When I was young. So maybe Abner never cared about me as much as his brother did." I shifted on the couch as thunder rolled beyond the Fort. "Either way, as far as *grace* goes, Abner's given plenty. He saved me from being eliminated on a live broadcast, told me how to win a solo competition, gave me history quiz answers, and covered our tracks when I ran away from Max." There were also his burns; he'd been scalded for me. He'd fought for me since before I knew his motives, and now he was done. I'd taken the king's help for granted.

"Lovely. Look at me." Griff's voice was too gentle, too merciful. And it undid me. Tears stung my eyes, and I couldn't bring myself to face him. "Corinn?" When would he learn I wasn't *good enough*? Rain pattered against my windows. The world succumbed to a storm, just as I was about to. "Please let me in," he mumbled, planting whispers of kisses on my forehead.

"I don't deserve you." *There.* I said it.

Griff's face went taut. "What makes you think that?"

My pupils burned as I strained to stay grounded in his dark eyes, as deep as the sky he watched at night. "I don't know if I can *change*, Griff. If I can become something better. I'm still a Low, I've been carried through Accolade so far, and I don't think I can hold on much longer. Especially without Abner."

Griff shifted even closer to me. We lay face-to-face on our sides, breathing the same air. His radiating body heat enveloped me. "You like the moon, right? You told me that our first week here?"

I huffed. "Yeah. I thought of it as a friend."

Griff beamed at that, catching me off guard. "That's fitting, because your eyes are the color of moonlight." He pressed a quick kiss to my lips. "Anyway," he murmured, "what was I saying? You distract me too easily."

"Griff Howard, ever the flirt."

He laughed, his thumb grazing my shoulder. "Only for you, lovely." He cleared his throat. "I was *going* to say that the moon changes, just like people do. Did you know that when the moon fills up with light, it's called waxing, and when its light is leaving, it's called waning? That's what Dad's book told me, at least." He glimpsed downward, sending twines of dark hair across his forehead.

I latched on to the forbidden knowledge. Thunder rumbled above us.

"People are also made of dark and light. Sometimes, one overpowers the other. But when the darkness gets bad, I remind myself that *waning* is only a phase. The light will return."

I swallowed the lump in my throat, digesting Griff's words. Could I be a waxing moon, growing brighter with each night? "How do you *know* the light will come back?" I asked.

Because I wasn't sure my light would prevail. I was caught in the same cycle as the moon: trying to be something more, only to return to darkness, to nothing.

But Griff answered simply, as if there was no other explanation. "The light is already there, waiting. You just have to learn to let it in."

☽ ☽ ☽ ○ ☾ ☾ ☾

The storm came and went by morning, though the sun stayed hidden behind a veil of clouds. Similarly, though I'd slept through the night and gotten ready for Their Majesties' last-minute garden party, my thoughts were still stuck on Griff's lips and the warmth of his touch buzzing beneath my skin.

I blinked away the glistening visions as I sat crammed in one of the limos hurtling toward the castle. My vehicle contained the remaining candidates from the first three residence halls, which unfortunately included Addison. She eyed me the entire ride with eyes that danced in a gloat.

I bit back anger not because of Addison's current intimidation tactic, but because of how terribly she'd treated Griff for years. She didn't deserve the pedestal I'd placed her on.

The limo's windows darkened when we entered the castle grounds, as they had the first night of Accolade, inhibiting our view. The strain in the vehicle spiked once the limo lurched to a stop, leaving us at one of the castle's many covered verandas.

The patio exploded in a labyrinth of pink roses, yellow daisies, and sky-blue delphiniums. Lush, trimmed topiary lined the perimeter, and intricate garlands hung from a pergola.

We approached the decorated patio, and I couldn't shake how exposed I felt among the few dozen candidates left. There was nowhere left to hide—no weaker competitors to shield myself with, no buffer for the next elimination.

My eyes wandered to Griff, and he already eyed me from where he stood with Lorenzo. But before I could approach the pair, Salem materialized next to me. "How's this for a garden party?" he asked, shoving his shirtsleeves up to his shoulders, an unrefined choice which I knew would leave Mrs. Redding's face as red as her hair once she saw it on a projector back home.

"It's great," I answered with a grin, "as long as your definition of a garden is very loose." In Pointe, the word *garden* was synonymous with earthworms, jumbled weeds, and dirt-caked fingernails. *This* was just outdoor elegance.

Of course, the *real* royal gardens were elsewhere, likely hidden behind the tall foliage and evergreen underbrush in the distance. I recalled the map of the tunnel network and knew there were two entrances from the royal gardens. Julia wouldn't risk sending us so close to her secrets.

Their Majesties waited for us under the patio's awning, and we all drifted toward them, staying within the limits set by the mind-controlled Queen's Guard.

I found Max across the balcony, looking straight ahead with the same blank visage, blending in perfectly with the other guards. Had his surgery already happened? Or was he still acting the part to keep Julia's trust? Abner's words from the barracks played in my mind: Max was currently the most powerful person in Miota. As long as he stayed in Julia's favor *and* maintained his free will, he played both sides.

Still, I supposed, Julia won, even now. Because Julia would kill him for stepping out of line. Max proved his false loyalty to the queen by killing Holland. My stomach tightened, churning too quickly. Holland had died for something so trivial—a ploy for Max to earn Julia's trust for a few short-lived weeks. In the end, he'd undergo the neural implant surgery, and Julia would gain another puppet.

Bernard had described war as a deadly game. The moment Holland died, Accolade turned into exactly that—a war in which neither royal was innocent.

A hand settled on my waist from behind me. *Griff.* The sun seemed to peek from behind the clouds.

Griff planted a kiss on my hairline, prompting Salem to wiggle his brow at me. I rolled my eyes in return, but a sloppy grin still claimed my mouth.

"We'll talk to Abner after this," Griff whispered, his breath tickling my ear.

I nodded. We'd find Abner and convince him to continue fighting for me. I held firm to Theo's words from last week, my brother's wise reminder. I was determined; I could win the king's favor.

"Good morning, candidates," Julia started. A breeze floated through the air, threading through her perfectly curled hair. "Welcome to the final two weeks of Accolade. We have many events planned for the upcoming weeks, so we hope you are adequately prepared." Her eyes flicked across the candidate pool, hitching on Addison before continuing.

Dread trickled down my body. The queen and Addison had shared a silent exchange. I *knew* it; Julia had the same scheming wink in her eye that Abner had with me.

Back when I was in his favor.

"There are no more rankings," Julia continued, her voice as level as the smooth stone balcony we stood atop. "You are the final thirty-two candidates, and you have shown distinction among the original three hundred. However, you must *now* seek favor with me and the king, independent of points and competitions."

Her words landed in the crevices of my brain. I truly *would* need Abner's support to continue in Accolade. I'd also need to gain Julia's approval, and I doubted she wanted a Low on the throne.

As if sensing my unease, Griff slipped his hand into mine. I tried steeling my nerves, tried reminding myself of waxing moons. *Dig deep and find strength*, Bernard would tell me now.

"As you already know," Julia said, "your partner in Accolade is the *only* person you can win with. All but one pair will go home within the next fourteen days."

The queen dissected the crowd, ensuring she had everyone's attention—each candidate and each cameraman dotting the patio's border.

"My husband and I feel as though not every pairing is of equal merit, which causes a predicament on our end. How can we choose the two best candidates when they are in different pairings? It has been an oversight on our part."

Griff's thumb, brushing my hand, stilled. I kept my breath in my lungs, unsure of where this was going. Nothing moved on the balcony, save the sporadic sway of leaves and buzz of insects.

Julia's voice cut through the silence as easily as a scalpel blade.

"Therefore, we have gathered you here not only for a garden party, but to choose new partners as seen fit."

What?

The balcony broke into motion, a mix of fear from some and relief from others. Through it all, as my ears rang, I looked at Addison. I only saw her profile, but her mouth drew upward, and she kept her gaze tethered to the queen.

They were *allies*. They planned this.

What had Addison's mother said last week? Something about how Griff wouldn't be my partner for much longer?

Had this been the plan all along?

"Using last week's rankings as a basis for the sequence, you will each be given the opportunity to select a new partner. This way, our strongest candidates—those who ranked highest last week— will be given the chance to claim a partner of equal worth. Once a candidate chooses a partner, they will be unavailable to *anyone else*."

Griff cursed and clutched me tighter, refusing to let me go. While I was a mess of a battering heartbeat and spiraling thoughts, Griff was steady as the Fort, unwilling to move for anyone or anything. He wouldn't let me go.

Which meant he also knew *exactly* where this was going.

"Our first-place candidate last week was Addison Maybee of Salford, so she will now select a new partner, if she would like."

I dissociated from the veranda. I didn't need to watch anything else or hear another word. Griff and I knew, as we forged our hands in an unrelenting grip, we were being torn apart.

Still, when Addison spoke, my ears couldn't tune out her velvety voice, dripping with victory. "I select Griff Howard as my new partner."

CHAPTER 37

My thoughts were made of thick jam, my body of wet cement. I expected to wake up any moment in my bed, lips still burning from kissing Griff.

But I knew this was real as warm bile climbed up my throat. My knees wobbled, threatening to give out under me.

Julia's eyes slitted toward Griff, unrelenting. She showed no sign of backing out of this twisted rule.

Griff was now paired with Addison.

He kept me in an iron grip, refusing to let me go as Addison sauntered over with a predatorial glint in her eye. Instinctively, I glanced at Abner, but he refused to meet my gaze.

"Corinn, he's *my* partner now," Addison whispered, her voice singing.

My blood boiled.

"No," Griff said, laying a fortifying arm around my waist. "Ads, please don't do this. *Please—*"

"It's already done." She feigned a smile as sweet as the surrounding flora, though her widened eyes gave a vicious glow.

When I looked at Griff, his face was as red as the cherry

tomatoes Grandma prized from our shack's garden. "*No.*" His voice was a bristled plea. "No, Ads. Please. *No.*" Each coarse syllable cracked my heart.

"Stop making a *fool* of yourself," Addison said, gritting her teeth as a rouge appeared on her cheekbones. "We're finally back together."

Griff ignored her, keeping his arms around me. It was all I could do to keep my tears from falling as they amassed, blurring my vision with a bite.

I couldn't comprehend the rest of the patio until I heard my name from Salem's level voice.

". . . Corinn Januski as my new partner."

I let out a shudder. Why Salem? He didn't want to win Accolade.

I channeled my emotions—confusion, fear, anger—into staying straight, stiffening my spine, and rolling my shoulders back. I wouldn't show my weakness here, in Their Majesties' home. With a thinned Accolade crowd, it wasn't easy to hide; we were all on display.

Salem gave me a measured look as he approached, clearly sensing my simmering temper. I stood in Griff's arms, leeching strength from him.

I added to my plan with each new pairing.

Lorenzo and Selleca paired together. *I'll speak to Abner as soon as possible.*

Natalya Lil chose Christopher Kingsley, an older man who wasn't her previous partner, and they stole the cameras' attention. *I'll use Salem's status to help me get to Abner.*

Pandora stayed with her long-time boyfriend. *I will convince the king to pair me back with Griff for the sake of Miota's freedom.*

Once we were all paired, Their Majesties advised us to use the garden party to learn about our new partners.

Griff's spine bowed as he kissed me. The embrace was too quick, though I didn't think there'd come a time when Griff's mouth didn't feel like it was meant to be savored.

Salem intercepted me from Griff with a half-hearted smile. Why did Salem choose *me* as his partner? Why not Izzy, like before? She wanted to leave Accolade, same as Salem.

Meanwhile, I needed to *win;* I didn't have another option.

Their Majesties made rounds visiting the new pairs, and a cold knot tangled in my stomach when they approached Addison and Griff. Julia spoke sweetly with them, and Abner shared a jovial laugh with Addison. Even Griff managed a grin.

Only *I'd* endangered Abner's plans—the king was still fighting for Griff.

And why shouldn't he? Griff could live out his father's legacy. He was liked by both Julia and Abner. He was a Top and could still free Miota from his new partnership.

And I wasn't sure where that left *me*. Because I couldn't have made it this far in Accolade, come *so close* to tasting true freedom, just to be tucked away on a plot of land as a farmer.

"Hey," Salem said, snapping my thoughts. "I thought you'd be happy I chose you."

I swallowed, attempting to ground myself in Salem's freckled face. "I just *really* needed to win with Griff."

Before Salem could respond, Their Majesties appeared in front of us, and we bowed deeply.

"Congratulations, you two," Julia cooed. "You must be so proud of yourselves."

Though she stared at us, she fiddled with something in her dress pocket.

A sharp odor filled the air for only a mere moment, and I was slammed back in time to the asympton lab. That smell—

"Thank you, Your Most Royal Majesty," Salem replied as I lost my voice entirely. I nearly bowed *again* to mask the sure flush of my face and goosebumps on my skin, out of place amid the humid weather. I didn't want to explain my odd hallucination of smelling poison.

I pinned my eyes to Abner as we spoke, though it was to no avail. He still refused to look at me, and I wanted to scream at him. He'd *given up* on me. The rejection stung, but I was just as frustrated with the now confirmed implication: Abner only found my worth in following his commands.

He'd willingly sacrificed himself when I played my part as a naïve Low, but now, I was too dangerous to take chances on.

"Is everything all right, Corinn?" Julia asked sweetly. *Expectant.*

I blinked, focusing my gaze on her. Her green eyes and gaunt face embodied so much of Cass, it startled me every time. "Yes, Your Majesty. Your garden is beautiful." Cass always said his mother liked flattery; would this distract her?

"Thank you." She gave another staged smile and slid her hand out of her pocket. "We will leave you two to celebrate. It is wonderful that you two, such good friends, are paired together now. Friends are a wonderful asset in life. They will be there to . . . lend a hand, or *tend to your burns.*"

My body went ice cold as fear licked up my spine, lathering my scalp. My lungs deflated on the words' impact, stealing my breath entirely.

She knows. Julia knew I'd worked with Abner. As every organ in my body screamed for me to retreat, I stood my ground and maintained eye contact with the queen, letting my irises glow the color of the hottest type of fire. I refused to fold.

Julia knew I'd nursed the king, but she didn't know everything. If she did, Griff and I would already be dead for committing treason.

I was still safe. For now.

"I give my special congratulations to *you*." Julia directed each word at me in a deliberate lilt, a sharpening of a blade. "A Low-Tiered girl, now competing among the best in the country. But let me warn you, Corinn, from one strong-minded woman to another: keep your eyes and ears sharp. You do not *know* what you are getting yourself into."

I bowed to keep from quivering in Julia's face. When I looked up, Their Majesties had moved on.

"Why did you choose me?" I asked Salem the moment we entered my room after the garden party.

Anger churned within me—because of Abner's abandonment, Addison's victory, Griff's separation from me, and Julia's ominous threat—and Salem was the unfortunate person present to receive the brunt of it. I hurled my shoes at my bed, across the room, and relished the sound of them bouncing off the mattress and onto the floor.

"Why?" I raked a hand on my scalp. "You don't want to win Accolade!"

His blue-green eyes livened behind his glasses. "But you do." His words were just as pointed as mine, and I couldn't blame him for it. "You want to *win*, Corinn, and I can help you do that."

I froze, holding Salem to his spot by the couch—where Griff had kissed me, where we'd lost track of time . . .

"You're going to win Accolade with me?" I drawled, outrage pooling in my chest. "We're going to get *married*?"

"No!" Salem tilted his head. "By the moon, Corinn, I thought you'd be *happy* I did this! No one else in this competition would look out for you."

"Griff would—"

"And he's not an option right now." Salem set his hands on his hips as his expression challenged mine. "Look, I want to help you win Accolade *with* Griff, but that won't happen if you keep acting like I did something wrong!" He plopped onto my couch. "We need to work together and think of a plan."

I blinked. Admittedly, Salem *was* a good second choice. He knew what life I'd go back to if I didn't win Accolade. And no one else here—aside from Griff—would fight for me the way Salem would. "Sorry," I muttered. "Okay. I already have a plan, but it all centers around winning Abner's support back. If I can't regain his favor, we might as well—"

"Wait." Salem whipped his head to me, skewing his glasses. "Win *back* the king's support? What do you mean?"

My voice hitched in my throat. "Nothing." But Salem looked on in disbelief. "Just that Abner was fighting for me and Griff. But now he's only fighting for Griff, so we need to convince him *I'm* better than Addison."

Such an answer didn't give away any illegal information. Though, admittedly, I often wondered how Salem would take finding out the truth. I wanted to tell him about the supercontinent with every fiber in my body, but doing that would only endanger him.

"You had a deal with the king, and you didn't tell me?" While Salem used a light tone, I saw past his mask. We never lied or kept secrets.

Attempting to deflect Salem's question, I stalked toward my bed and picked up my shoes from where they'd landed. "There's nothing to tell." But my words delivered too breathlessly, and Salem's posture slumped.

"Fine. Keep your secrets. It's not like I won't figure them

out." He wasn't wrong; Salem knew how to study me like I was merely an article of medical text. But I couldn't let him learn anything, for his own safety.

I shrugged, playing his game. "I'd like to see you try."

The statement seemed to appease him. He rolled his eyes and stood, holding out his arms in stubborn defeat. "Come here."

I walked into his hug, and it turned into a contest of who could squeeze the other harder, which undeniably lightened the air between us.

"Corinn," Salem started, his chin moving atop my head. He'd towered over me for as long as we'd been friends. "You don't need to hide things from me. I'm your best friend."

"My *very* best friend," I mused, grinning.

"And don't you forget it when you're living large in the castle," he replied. "Queen of Miota, married to Griff—"

"*Love-crazed lunatic,*" I grumbled. "And you're getting ahead of yourself. Right now, we just need to focus on regaining Abner's support."

"Right. Whatever you say."

Luckily, Salem soon gave up on prying for information, and he left. Though I sighed with relief, my invasive thoughts quickly swooped in. In past weeks, I'd either study history or grovel to the Tops in First Residence. But now, the only thing left to do was win Abner back.

Everything I was depended on it.

CHAPTER 38

We spent most of our hours in The Gathering Hall learning about the monarchy's legal duties and implications. Trials were approaching for prisoners inside the Hold—which I now knew occurred every *two* months, thanks to Lorenzo's aunt. There were enough people in the Hold for each Accolade couple to prepare for a trial, which we'd run beside Their Majesties next week, the final week of Accolade. It would be the pinnacle of applying the information we'd learned so far.

Natalya Lil mentioned that some candidates were wasting their efforts since an elimination lay between now and the trials; some couples could spend all week planning for a trial just to leave before getting to apply the skills. Despite the fact, everyone prepped with grit, determined to survive the next elimination.

Tables sparsely speckled The Gathering Hall during social hours, giving each pair the privacy to discuss their assigned trial. Salem and I brushed shoulders while reading about Silas Hart of Yorkinson, who attempted to steal food from the Common for his young daughter.

While stealing food was a crime that would land someone in

the Hold every time, it seemed harsh when the Lows—the majority of each city's population—were barely given enough food to survive. I'd seen the effects of malnutrition too many times to count. Citizens turned feral, they became a sickly yellow, and their eyes bulged too far from their skulls.

It brought angry tears to my eyes, thinking about how no one would go hungry if we were taken to the supercontinent, the land of abundant resources.

I found Abner across the hall, speaking to Griff and Addison. His garbled voice recoiled off the floor, though I couldn't decode a word he said. I inhaled sharply as Griff's gaze met mine, weighted even from this distance.

Abner said something to Addison, making her laugh and wrap her arms around Griff. I wanted to gag at the sight, even with Griff's evident struggle to escape her hold.

"Yoo-hoo," Salem muttered, tapping our tabletop. "Did you hear anything I just said?" Salem slid his panel toward me, showing me the details highlighted in Silas's report.

I gave him nothing more than a quick glance. Dread flowed through my stomach as Julia waltzed to join her husband and the couple. Julia spoke to Addison. Abner schemed with Griff. They all laughed. And my heart split.

I knew it was selfish to think of myself when people like Silas Hart were sentenced to die for attempting to feed their starved families. But Griff was supposed to win with *me*. *I* wanted to liberate Miota. I wanted to help lead the island into a better world.

The harsh realization came slowly over the next hour. Griff winning Accolade with another Top would be the best way to ensure *real* change. Because who would ever listen to a Low? I didn't hold enough power to free Miota without help. Griff and Addison together, though . . .

They were going to win. How could I ask Abner for resumed support when Griff and Addison were the better options for the island? Their voices held more weight than mine ever could, and if they managed to get Addison's father on their side, they stood a real chance against Julia.

It was all for the best.

It was in Miota's best interest for me to leave Accolade. To go home and join the farmers, to live out my Low-Tiered life and leave tasks like freeing the island to more qualified, worthy people.

The air in the room thinned, leaving me gasping. Salem spoke, but I couldn't hear him over the ringing in my ears.

I was going to be eliminated, and I *didn't want to be.*

I needed to leave the hall. The world dimmed as I fled to the restroom. I staggered as best I could, trying not to tip over completely. As I passed candidates deep in strategic conversation, their eyes snagged on me, only making my chest ache more.

When I made it to the restroom, I shut the door, happy to lock myself away. I couldn't face my revelation—couldn't face anything—in front of others. I wasn't sure how much time passed before there was a small rap on the door. After examining my face in the mirror and ensuring my eyes weren't blotchy, I left the room for the next person in line.

I swallowed and held my head upward as I paced back to Salem. The weight of others' attentions pressed into my shoulders and against my back, restricting my lungs. When I chanced looking at Griff, he eyed me with concern. Next to him, Addison scowled.

At the safety of our table, I leaned toward Salem, who'd put his head down in my absence. "This is useless," I started in a whisper. My legs shook restlessly, and I picked at my nails, ripping off the white ends. "We won't win Accolade—you don't want to be here, and I'm a stupid *Low*. There's no reason why we shouldn't march home right now."

Salem turned his head, still lying on the table, to face me. "You wouldn't have made it this far if you didn't have a shot."

"I've been *carried* to this point," I countered. "By Abner. Who, all of a sudden, *hates me*. There are candidates out there who'll do better things for Miota. I—we can't win, Salem. We can't *do this*."

I was going home.

I was going to be a farmer and likely double over one day, dying from hunger or the diseases that ransacked the fields. Or maybe I'd get split open on the monorail, meeting my end quickly.

My heart rate doubled, as if making up for the lost time it too foresaw.

"Corinn." Salem droned my name, teasing out the syllables. "Breathe. You're okay."

I tried listening to him, but I couldn't. Not with the cacophonous taunts flooding my every breath, every thought, every cell in my body.

You're going home. You're finally getting what you deserve.

"You're a fighter," Salem said as a tear slid down my cheek. "You didn't come *this far* to give up on yourself, did you?"

"I'm not giving up," I said, sniffling. "I'm just being realistic." There were better people in the candidate pool to free Miota. Abner realized it last week, after I'd caused him so much trouble. And now I realized it, too.

Salem gave me an incredulous look. "You're giving up. I won't let you get us sent home."

The corner of my mouth twitched. "Because you aren't itching to leave this place."

"Don't let the cameras hear you say that," he said with a facetious smirk. "If Mom finds out I'm still trying to leave, I can't imagine the scene she'd cause."

"We'd hear her crying from here."

"Her voice *does* carry," he agreed.

We shared a smile, though fear crept back in too quickly, like an old friend returning home. I was going to leave Accolade. After making it this far, after discovering Julia's secrets and risking my life for something *more*, I was going home.

I didn't know what to do. I didn't *want* Addison to win Accolade with Griff, but she seemed like a powerful option. Abner was likely hoping to use her to his advantage.

Time slowed, then stopped completely.

This wasn't about *power* with Abner; it was about manipulation. If Abner cared about how much influence someone held, he never would've picked me to carry out his plan in the first place. He only wanted someone to manipulate, someone to do his dirty work and keep the blood off his hands.

Maybe I could still prove myself. If I showed Abner that I could still do his bidding, if I skirted around Julia with stealth and ease, would it give me an edge over Addison?

"I know what to do," I said in a hush. "Sneak into the castle. Find Abner and bargain with him to pair Griff with me. Do whatever the king asks." Abner valued his life, always doing what he needed to evade the end of his noose. If I threatened to spill his secrets to Julia, would he cooperate with me? Something told me he would.

"Corinn, no." Salem sat up as horror filled his face. "Absolutely *not*. That's a sure way to die."

I kept his gaze. "What would you rather me do, then? I need to speak with the king, and . . ." I dropped my voice so low, Salem had to read my lips. "This is the only way."

"No, it's not! Talk to *Griff*. He's still your ally. That man looks at you the same way you look at the stars. He still wants to help you, and if you can't see it, you're blind."

I sat with Salem's words as I stared at Silas's background information, unable to comprehend a word of it. I eventually sighed and studied the rest of the hall. I spied Max Reno standing at attention with the other guards, and that was when the idea formed.

Max held Abner's ear. Maybe sneaking into the castle *was* taking it too far. But Max Reno lived in the barracks; I knew where its single surveillance camera lay, and the building wasn't actively watched by Julia thanks to everyone in the place being mind-controlled. If I went in the middle of the night, I could avoid the sleeping guards and find Max, who still had his fleeting autonomy.

Determination. I clung to Theo's descriptor of me. I'd make it in and out of the barracks undetected, because the alternative— becoming a farmer—was unthinkable.

I spent the rest of the day planning how and when I'd get to the barracks. I planned to speak with Max and do whatever the guard ordered on Abner's behalf, therefore regaining the king's favor and trust. Abner needed to be reminded *I* was the key to freeing Miota.

It was my only option, and while it posed risks, I knew it was possible. My light was waning, but *this* would bring it back. Griff and I had left Castle Circle before, making it to another city and back unscathed. This would be no different.

I would play Abner's game of manipulation once more, and this time, I planned to *win*.

I sent my last message of the evening to Salem, letting him know I was taking his advice to meet with Griff. That way, Salem wouldn't worry if his messages went unanswered; he would just assume I was with my old partner.

I never imagined this week involving sneaking around my best friend, but Salem had become increasingly curious about my relationship with the king. Tonight, it would be best if he thought I was with Griff.

Because I was going to the barracks. I'd spent the week dropping hints to Max Reno of my visit, and he'd caught on quickly. Each time I mentioned it, his face paled before he gave an almost imperceptible nod.

"Do you . . . *know* Anzalone's plan?" he'd asked yesterday with a look of terror coating his face.

Anzalone? I hadn't recognized the name and told him as much. Max then told me I was in over my head and needed to be careful. While I appreciated his concern, I knew what I was doing. Griff and I had gone to Pointe and back, and this was no different.

Some part of me screamed for sneaking out of Castle Circle without Griff, but I couldn't bring myself to let him know what I was planning. It would only endanger him, and he didn't need me weighing him down. He still maintained Abner's support, and it needed to stay that way. Still, his father's pocket watch and flashlight could've helped me tonight.

I spent the evening strengthening my nerves, knowing I'd never make it to the barracks and back if I carried apprehensions.

I planned the route in my head. First, I'd go to the greenhouse down the street and take a few pots to stand on in order to scale Castle Circle's fence independently. I'd then crawl through the surrounding grassy plain, toward the barracks.

I'd get into the building using a ground-level window I remembered from our tour that led into a small bathing room, just outside the large bedroom where guards slept. Without daylight, I'd get into the bedroom without being seen by the hallway's lone camera. I'd find Max, and he'd tell me how to regain Abner's support.

I only hoped my theory was correct, that Abner cared more about manipulation than power. If this was based on worthiness, it would all prove pointless, and I'd become a farmer.

But I believed my idea. Abner didn't want a shining model on the throne; he wanted a cunning thief capable of killing not just a queen, but a dynasty. If I could prove to Abner that I was most worthy of such a job, I knew he'd help me once more.

You're an idiot, Corinn, a malicious internal voice responded to my plan. *You'll never make it alive.*

I slammed the voice away. This was my only choice if I was to stay out of the Low Tier and save Miota.

Time passed too slowly. Minutes felt like hours, and the hours like days, each pocket of time its own small eternity. I paced my room and listened to the reruns of *Accolade Times* that played into the night, never granting projectors a moment of rest these days. I let myself overthink the gossip—it was better than the alternative of fixating on the barracks.

I froze at the sound of Griff's voice. My eyes snapped to the projector. His face simultaneously calmed me and put a weight on my chest. He was my true partner. I'd kissed those lips, run my hands through his hair, felt the muscles beneath his skin.

I trudged toward the projector and increased its volume using the control panel embedded on its side.

"I always want to obey Their Most Royal Majesties' wishes," Griff started to the cameraman recording him. This was from earlier today, made apparent by the sun shining on his face. "They know best, after all. However, it wasn't *their* choice to pair me with Addison, but her own. And given our history, I'm not sure she had our best interests in mind."

Their history. I recalled Griff telling me what he'd endured with Addison in the past. Was she torturing him similarly now?

"Who would *you* have chosen as your new partner if you'd been in first place last week?" the cameraman asked.

Griff furrowed his brow. "I wouldn't have chosen anyone new. I've wanted to win Accolade with Corinn this whole time. She's been the best thing to ever happen to me."

My heart galloped. *Oh, Griff . . .* I missed him more than words could say. We'd hardly been given a moment to speak since we'd been separated, always busy with Their Majesties' commands. Maybe it was purposeful, a ruse to keep us from scheming.

"Even though she's a Low? And you're now partnered with the descendent of multiple Salfordian mayors?"

I stiffened, wondering how Griff would respond to the facts, preparing to be sliced by his words.

"Has it ever occurred to you," Griff started, his face hardening, "that people are a lot more than their Tier—"

The broadcast ended abruptly, flickering to an earlier livestream of our hours in The Gathering Hall. Salem and I mulled over Silas's case, and from across the room, Griff watched *me*.

The interview infiltrated me, landing in my bones and softening my spirits I'd spent so long bracing. What would Griff think about my plan to scheme with Max tonight?

It didn't matter what Griff thought. It *couldn't* matter. *I* was the person meant to free Miota from the start, back when Cass was alive. If I became a farmer now, I'd never be able to help the island. My family, who worked their hands to the bone and bodies to their breaking point, deserved to know a life outside the Fort.

I turned my projector off, ready to get this over with. A slick rush of fear blanketed me, but I moved despite it. I stuffed pillows under my sheets to give the appearance of a sleeping silhouette, and I slipped my panel into my nightstand so I wouldn't be tracked.

It was just after midnight, long past the weekly Friday night executive council meeting with Their Majesties. If all went according to plan, I'd find Max within the hour and make it back here by two.

My body buzzed as I traipsed down the stairwell and through First Residence's gilded lobby. I inhaled deeply as I stepped into the night. Moonlight bathed me, so I slinked into the shadows cast by each building's awning.

"How was your talk with Griff?" a voice materialized behind me.

I jumped, whirling toward Salem, who leaned against my residence building with one foot propped on the stone exterior. He'd been *waiting*. After he drank in my dark outfit and braided hair, his eyes flickered northward, toward the gate I planned to scale.

He knew I was leaving Castle Circle.

CHAPTER 39

"What are you *doing?*" I hissed as my anxiety spiked. I wasn't supposed to be seen by anyone, but *especially* not Salem. "You need to go to bed."

"I plan to," Salem said, nudging his glasses up his nose. "Once you do." He peeled himself from First Residence's exterior wall.

I searched his face, at a loss for what to do. I simply repeated my order. "Please, Salem. Go to bed."

His teeth glinted in the moon's light as he grinned. "I'm going wherever you go."

I couldn't turn back now; I needed to do this. It was already Friday night, which only left me with Saturday to show Abner I was the best fit for his gambit against his wife. If I didn't do that, Salem and I would go home first thing Sunday morning.

I resumed my quick pace and headed toward the greenhouse. *Pots,* I reminded myself, then added, *and get rid of Salem.*

But he stayed on my heels. "Corinn." He didn't need to elaborate; I heard his unspoken question, a repeat of what he'd initially asked about my talk with Griff.

"It was great," I said dismissively, not even throwing a glance over my shoulder. "We've worked a few things out."

"That's funny," Salem started, breaking into an uneven jog to keep up, "because *I* talked to Griff, and he said he hasn't heard from you since you two separated as partners."

I stopped, scuffing my shoes on the diamond-encrusted sidewalk. Salem rammed into me, his chest thudding against the back of my skull.

"You . . . talked to Griff?"

He lidded his eyes toward me and crossed his arms. "*I* know how to communicate."

I ran my tongue over my teeth. "Care to *communicate*, then, why you were outside First Residence in the middle of the night?"

"Really?" Salem almost laughed, a glimpse of sun among the night sky. "Your message screamed 'Don't talk to me because I won't answer. Probably because I'm busy with my stupid plan.'"

I opened my mouth and shut it. "What'd Griff say?" I changed the subject. "When you talked to him?"

"That he misses you. And that you're *waxing,* whatever that means. Does he think you have hairy legs?"

I scrunched my nose and broke a smile. "No. It's . . . not that." I was a waxing moon. I was discovering my light, glowing brighter with each passing night. A warmth ignited in my chest, as it always did when I thought about Griff.

I stepped onward. Salem followed.

"Why are you out here?" he finally asked, reaching the crux of this whole encounter. But the dread in his voice indicated he already knew the answer.

"Gardening," I answered sarcastically as we approached the greenhouse. There was no sense hiding the truth now. Salem's presence wouldn't stop me from saving myself, saving *Miota.*

I pried the greenhouse door open, entering the space dotted with soft, sporadic lantern light. I grabbed the first pot I saw, filled with scattered sprouts, bright green against the dark soil. Gingerly, I worked at the dirt, sliding the entanglement of roots and buds out of the pot. I'd probably need three or four total, I guessed.

As I started on another pot, Salem hunched over next to me, mirroring my movements.

I groaned. There was *no time* for this. "What are you doing now?"

He glared at me. "Helping you."

"No." I froze, ready to scream at him. Was he delaying me on purpose? "Stop it! Can't you just go to bed?" My voice rose in pitch.

Salem chucked the hunk of dirt to the side and jutted the now empty clay pot toward me. "I'm up to whatever you are."

I laughed, though there was nothing humorous about Salem's actions. "You're a pain in the ass, Salem. You're not coming with me."

"You're welcome to try and stop me." Amusement laced his challenge.

I gnashed my teeth as a sure flush claimed my face. "Salem, get *out of here*. You're not doing this."

"Then stop me from coming."

It was no use. Salem would beat me in a physical fight, and his stubborn nature rivaled mine. I instead threw it back at him. "Stop me from *going*."

"How?" Salem grabbed another planter. "The only way you wouldn't go is if I locked you in my room. And I couldn't live with myself if I did that."

I stilled. It spoke of his character. Because I knew if I had the physical advantage, I wouldn't hesitate to use it against Salem.

Selfish . . . you're so selfish. That same incessant voice was back.

Salem and I were at a stalemate. The only way I would get to the barracks tonight would be to bring him with me.

"You can't risk yourself for this," I muttered, my spirits dipping lower. I already knew how tenuous the odds of successfully making this trip were, and with an added member, they became even worse. "I won't let you."

"We can do this all night," Salem said. "If I can't stop you, then I want to join you. You'll need someone to work with if you're actually going to sneak into the castle."

I studied Salem, and no part of him hinted at deceit. He truly would endanger himself for *me*. "Well, I'm not going to the castle anymore," I admitted. "I'm going to the barracks. One of the guards is working with Abner, and I'm going to talk to him." I extended my knees to stand, hauling the pots in my arms as I left the greenhouse. Salem, my annoying shadow, followed.

"That's better. But I still don't think you should go—"

"Salem, if you're not going to physically stop me, there's nothing you can do about it." I scanned Castle Circle for onlookers and luckily found no one. We hiked behind the greenhouse, to the fence surrounding the lane. "But *you* should turn back."

If it wasn't so late in the week, I'd wait and sneak around Salem another time. But this was my *only* chance.

"I'm your partner," Salem said. As if that were a reasonable justification for following me.

I threw him a vexed look before eyeing the iron fence, the black metal wet with summer dew. This would be harder than I thought.

I stacked the pots, though it only gave me an extra foot or so of height. My spirits deflated, but I still wiped the fence's horizontal bar, preparing to scale the structure as I shook out my limbs. With my lack of upper body strength, this required assistance, but I wouldn't involve Salem.

"Go to bed," I said once more, glancing behind me, where

Salem watched with worry lining his face. "I'll be back before sunrise."

I couldn't bring myself to bid him a true goodbye—such an act seemed too permanent, like I was marching into my demise. So I reached for the fence's horizontal shaft and used the stack of clay pots to jump upward. Hopefully, once I was outside the fence, Salem would realize this was more trouble than it was worth, and he'd leave me.

I didn't have the strength to pull my weight over the fence, but an external force propelled me upward. Through my mind's panic, I hitched a leg over the tops of the spokes and rolled in one quick motion, keeping my grip on the top bar. Gravity brought my body back toward the ground, and I landed outside Castle Circle.

I turned to ward off Salem once more before starting the crawl through the field, but I found him perched atop the fence.

"Salem!" I hissed, my blood running cold. He struggled to hold on to the top bar while simultaneously dropping his body back to the earth. In a breath's time, he crumpled to the ground.

Salem was outside Castle Circle. It cleaved all my courage. If anything happened to him . . .

I bit back tears and pressed my tongue against the roof of my mouth. "Turn around *now*. Why are you doing this?"

He collected his glasses from where they'd landed on his descent. "I knew you'd do this—you're too stubborn for your own good. And if anything happened to you, and I hadn't tried to stop or help you. . ." He shook his head. "I couldn't have lived with that."

Time seemed to halt. Because that was how I felt *now*.

I couldn't risk bringing Salem with me. But I couldn't abandon this trip.

"Leave your panel here." I gave him a brazen expression and

dropped to my stomach. Damp fingers of grass tickled my skin. "Just know that I hate this. And you're being an idiot."

Salem huffed, hardly hesitating before dropping his panel and crouching onto the ground. "Insinuating *you're* the real idiot—"

"Salem, I *have* to do this! You don't!" I began crawling.

"Why?" Salem demanded. "Because you don't think we'll win Accolade? And that means going home, where Dr. Ova is ready to demote you?"

I ignored him. Did Salem find me so self-centered? This was about more than my demotion; it was about freeing Miota. Wasn't it?

Admittedly, my fate as a farmer terrified me. Would I be so willing to undergo this trip tonight if my life in the Low Tier didn't depend on it? I couldn't say.

I chewed on the thoughts as we made our way across the blank field. After what felt like at least ten minutes of crawling, I realized we needed to get closer to the castle grounds' wall than I'd planned. I broke a sweat, due to both the humid air and my stewing. If the guards stationed at the wall found us, we couldn't hide in this flat scape of land.

If we *were* discovered out here, our best shot at surviving would be to run for a tunnel entrance. I'd studied my hand-drawn map of the underground tunnel network enough to know there was an entrance near the gate into the castle grounds.

That was when it hit, thinking of gates and fences. I was an *idiot* for forgetting about the electric fence surrounding the barracks. It would fry any trespasser; we'd never make it into the home of the Queen's Guard . . .

Turn back now.

Logic pounced, clearing my vision and gripping my mind. My blind determination had led me into a rash plan. This wasn't anything like when I went to Pointe with Griff. He'd had a concrete strategy, a map with directions, and a specific goal. He'd thought through the path and possibilities. *This,* here and now, was nothing more than my pathetic attempt to save myself.

This was death disguised as hope.

"We're turning around," I chanced whispering into blades of grass.

I craned my neck against the dirt to see Salem, barely visible in the moon's light. His eyes were pinched shut, and his face distorted with fear.

I had done this to him. To us.

Salem's eyes fluttered open, and he gave a curt nod.

I couldn't breathe as we turned around, likely moving too loudly in the lawn. Each shift of my elbow made the grass rustle, and we were *too close* to the castle wall, to the guards. I winced as my pulse accelerated past the threshold of what I thought was humanly possible.

Then came the monotonous *voices.* Which meant guards lingered nearby.

My heart thrummed as I dropped flush to the ground, willing myself to melt into the dirt. I couldn't tell how far away the voices were, but it wouldn't matter, as long as we were in this blank field. We were at the mercy of empty space, nothing but cropped grass. As soon as a guard member's panel shined on us, we'd be revealed, as good as dead.

I trembled. Even my jaw quivered and teeth chattered. I tried to make it stop, worried it was creating too much noise.

We were condemned to move at the pace of a sprouting plant while every cell in me screamed to *run, run, run* back to Castle Circle, glittering in the distance.

We successfully turned around, with the castle grounds and

barracks now at our backs. *Slow. Steady.* We could do this. But my thoughts were not slow; my body was not steady.

Especially once the barrel of light landed on us.

"Stop!" a guard called.

I exploded into motion, lugging Salem off the ground, screaming for him to follow me. We were too far from Castle Circle to make it back without a bullet to the skull. There was only one place close enough to provide sanctuary now.

A weapon fired. Salem wailed. The world reeled, and I fought to see straight. To *run* straight. Salem became heavier behind me as I dragged him along.

Toward the castle wall's front gate. To the underground tunnel entrance. This was our best option at survival.

Another weapon resonated. I didn't know how many guards chased us from sporadic points along the wall, and I couldn't waste time looking to find out.

One guard stood at the front gate, and she burst into action at the sight of us. Her brain activity, controlled and monitored by Julia, surely alerted the queen of people's presence outside her home.

Salem crumbled as more rounds fired, but I didn't stop running. We were *so close.*

"Come on!" I cried, hauling Salem. He doubled over, holding his shoulder, bumbling on his legs.

Had he been . . .?

No. Just the possibility tore a gash in my chest. Salem was *fine.*

Panel lights bounced around us, which I used to scan the ground for a chink in the dirt. According to my memory of the map I'd studied in my free time, we now stood atop a tunnel entrance.

I looked for any sort of handle but couldn't find one. More rounds fired. These bullets differed from the tranquilizing pellets used in group competitions; these were lethal, made to kill anyone who committed treason.

"Please," I whimpered, jumping on the ground with feral determination—because that was a trait that helped me *so much*. Hair stuck to my face where tears caked my cheeks.

We were going to *die*.

The ground groaned. I crashed to my feet, ready to pry open a door.

But the ground caved from under us. I pulled Salem close, ignoring the sticky warmth spreading across his shoulder. My heart suspended in my chest as we fell into darkness.

CHAPTER 40

I lay on the cool floor, unable to breathe, unable to see or think. My lungs screamed for air, and I struggled to inhale.

Would the guards follow us down here? Did I truly trust myself to navigate us through these tunnels, especially in the dark? Now that I'd abandoned my plan, where were we supposed to go?

And then came the most torturous question of all. Had Salem been shot?

My throat burned as the shock wore off. I gulped air into my lungs at the expense of my seemingly corrosive trachea.

I probed for my best friend, reaching outward with fanned fingers in shaking, sweeping motions. "Salem?"

He grunted, sounding a few feet away. My insides churned. I took a few measured breaths and crawled toward his voice, feeling a cool, smooth material beneath my palms. Was this tunnel made of metal? If so, it was vastly different from the one in Pointe composed of soft earth.

As I crawled, harsh lights flickered on. I winced.

And every thought flew from me. I visualized Salem's perpetual grimace and the deep scarlet oozing from his shoulder, pooling on the floor.

My stomach hitched. *"Salem."* I hovered over his body, searching for the wound. My head swam as I assessed him.

You know what to do. You went to school for this.

But I wasn't a real doctor; everyone knew it. My hands shook as I rolled Salem onto his side. "Can you hear me?" My voice cracked as I spoke. *"Salem.* Can you hear me?"

"Yeah," he croaked, bringing a palm to his outer arm. Blood coated his shirt, making the material stick to his skin. I rolled his sleeve up as best I could, given my shaking hands and the slick layer of gore.

Airway. Breathing. Circulation. All three were evidently intact. *Thank the moon.* I studied the wound, though I couldn't subside the quaking of my hands.

The bullet hadn't entered his arm, but it grazed him, leaving a fleshy opening. I hadn't been trained in how to treat bullet wounds since firearms were rare, only held by field patrol and the Queen's Guard. I racked my mind for standard care protocol, but all rationale simmered away at the sight of Salem's steaming blood. My best friend.

I did this to him.

"Where are we?" he uttered.

"A tunnel. Underground. Were you hit anywhere besides your arm?"

Why couldn't I remember a damn thing from school? I'd spent six years learning medicine, and none of it stuck when it mattered most.

Because you're a Low. You're not a real doctor.

And here Salem was, paying the price.

I applied unsteady pressure to his arm. The blood wasn't gushing, but it was constant enough to dribble on the metallic floor.

I was right; this tunnel wasn't anything like the one in Pointe.

We were encased entirely in smooth steel, glinting under fluorescent bulbs. I'd only seen motion-sensing lights a handful of times, but I figured that was what these were. The small section of tunnel that Salem and I occupied was illuminated, and the light reached out in either direction until succumbing to shadows. We'd been dropped in the middle of a path, left with no sense of direction.

I didn't know where to go from here.

"Salem, are you all right?"

He held my gaze like a lifeline. "I've been better," he admitted. The knot in his throat quivered. "You knew about this place."

It wasn't a question.

I grimaced. "Let's just worry about getting you help." He needed a doctor immediately. The nearest one would be in the castle's hospital wing. Cass used to speak about the lone doctor who practiced medicine for his family.

I wondered if it was the same doctor who performed guards' surgeries and obeyed Julia's cruel commands. It didn't matter, really, since he was the only person who could treat Salem.

"Rate your pain," I blurted as I helped him sit up.

He couldn't put weight through his right arm. As he raised his head, he choked, dry heaving before standing. "Eight?" He stayed hunched over, even after rising to his feet.

I chewed on my cheek. *Nice going,* I chided myself. *How's that information going to help?*

"Just an eight?" Blood dripped onto the floor, slapping the ground of the unbearably quiet tunnel. I couldn't stop reeling—this was *Salem* in front of me, bleeding out. My best friend's life was in my hands, and I couldn't have asked for anything worse.

Salem's unreadable eyes tracked me as he attempted rising to his full height. "Maybe a seven, if you tell me where we are."

I huffed, though relief evaporated from me. If his sense of

humor was still intact, he was doing better than I thought. "I'll tell you everything once I know you're fine."

I didn't know if I was lying. Salem had been caught with me outside the castle gates, and now we were in the tunnels. Wasn't he already as good as dead, whether I told him the truth about Miota or not?

Salem glared at me, blinking quickly. "Use my shirt to make a tourniquet, and then tell me *exactly* where we are and what's going on."

A tourniquet—of *course*. My mind was too slow, too scattered, and Salem was suffering because of it. Maybe Lows weren't meant to be doctors after all.

Salem lifted his left arm easily, though he gagged on a few screams as I maneuvered his right arm out of its sleeve. I gritted my teeth, blinking away tears at the sight of him in pain—pain *I* caused. We wouldn't be here if I hadn't left Castle Circle.

I tied Salem's shirt around the top aspect of his arm and used his glasses to help twist my knot tighter. Once the blood stopped, I tied it off. Tourniquets stayed on for two hours at most—at least I remembered that much—so we now had a timer.

I guessed which way would lead to the castle, praying to every star in the sky for accurate guidance, hoping it wasn't a huge mistake to search for the royal doctor.

At least Salem's glasses were tied to his arm instead of seated on the bridge of his nose. It meant he couldn't watch the tears stream down my face.

Because I knew what he didn't. This tunnel was only delaying our inevitable punishment. I'd doomed us; I was delivering us to die. It was the only possibility I foresaw, our inevitable fate strewn out, an invisible string guiding my premonitions.

We walked down the tunnel. Section after section of lights

flickered on, creating a buzz as we ventured farther. I nearly gave myself a headache trying to envision my map of the tunnels from memory. I'd only paid attention to the entrances and exits, not the paths themselves.

Another shortcoming of mine. Another reason this plan was cursed from the start. Another mar on my conscience, a knife's slash within my chest.

Salem heaved. "The tourniquet was only half the deal. You have to tell me how you know about this tunnel."

I bit my lip, which wobbled automatically. "Um." My voice refused to stay level. I halted in my tracks and vomited. My limbs rattled as the shock worked through me. Though I knew the mechanism, I couldn't stop my body from reacting to it.

We were going to die.

Salem rested his unaffected arm on my back. The person who'd been shot was comforting *me*.

I let my stomach work out its contractions before I spoke. Another section of lights blinked on once we resumed walking. I chose my words carefully, slowly. "This tunnel system is one of the monarchy's secrets. It lets you travel underground—it's how Cass made it to the greenhouse in Pointe."

Salem took it well, mulling over the words in his head, though I hadn't told him the worst part yet. I now had to tell him we were going to die because of *me*. There was no way out of this.

"There's . . . a world *outside* Miota. Bigger than anything imaginable. There's a huge land mass called the supercontinent, and there are people and resources there. They're not *trapped*. Griff and I were supposed to free the island and take everyone there. Now, I guess Griff will do it with Addison."

Salem remained silent.

We walked deeper into the tunnel. Another section of automatic lights flickered on.

Another.

Another.

I finally dared to speak again. "Salem—"

"No." His word had the energy of the bullet that wounded him. "You're . . . *no.* That's not true, Corinn! We're all the world has."

"I couldn't make this up," I whispered, once again crying in the safety of Salem's impaired vision. "It's why . . . why there're so many rules." My stomach lurched. "And it's why, once we're found, we'll probably be put in the Hold, best case-scenario." Salem didn't reply. "I'm sorry." But no apology could fix this.

More silence. Salem winced and glanced at his tourniquet, which I knew he couldn't visualize well without his glasses. Guilt consumed me whole. I never should've left Castle Circle, especially with Salem.

In the mesh of sheer panic coursing through me, I thought of Griff. What would he think when he heard Salem and I were in the Hold—or worse, dead?

I stopped short as more lights blinked on with a hum.

A *door.* Metal and bulky. But as quickly as my heart soared, it slammed back into my thoracic cavity. This door was our deliverance.

Maybe we could run away and escape Julia's grasp. Maybe we could go to the supercontinent.

Except, I knew we couldn't, even if it were somehow possible. Salem was in agony, and he needed help. I swallowed the stubborn lump in my throat that urged for self-preservation. No matter what was to come, I'd suffer through it and find aid. *For Salem.*

"There's a door," I said, slicing through my best friend's stewing temper. His anger chipped away at any seedling of worthiness I had. "I don't know where it leads, but we should be ready—"

"To do what?" he interrupted. *"Die?"*

I flinched. Acrid shame and bitter dread devoured me. "Salem, I'm *sorry.*" My tone delivered too defensively. "I should've given you more warning."

"It's not that," Salem said, coughing with each breath. "I knew leaving Castle Circle was illegal. But whether I came wouldn't have made a difference. Right? *Nothing* would've stopped you from doing this." He threw me a brazen expression, to which I only swallowed, loud enough for him to hear. "*That's* the problem. You're so dead set on making sure you're worth something to the people who don't even matter in the end."

"Tell me, then," I spat, unable to control myself. "*Who* matters more than the king?" I needed Abner's approval to win Accolade and become someone worthy of saving Miota.

"Your friends and family!" he shouted, spitting bile after his outburst. I stabilized his shoulder as he guarded it. All thoughts escaped me as a shudder ran through his body. "People like Griff. And me. *We* could help you figure this out. You didn't need to get *killed* to p-prove—" He choked further, and panic lay its cold grip on my skin.

My fault. My fault . . .

"You're dizzy," I charged. Salem didn't deny it, which was as good as any confirmation. I didn't care what was behind the door; I needed to get Salem out of here and into the care of a real doctor.

I hitched the latch and leaned my weight fully into the door as it creaked open with a shrill scrape of metal hinges.

I stopped short as every bit of air was robbed from me. "By the moon . . ."

We were no longer in a tunnel. The moon shone high above, illuminating the night. Warm, salty air whipped my face. A fizzing sound advanced and retreated nearby in a hypnotic roar, a thrumming pulse that tugged at my heart.

Though I couldn't see anything in the darkness, I knew where we were.

"Salem. We're on the *beach*. We're . . . outside the Fort."

"Outside?" His voice was too thin. "How?"

I studied the door, flush against our island's looming wall. "The tunnel cuts through the Fort. We must be on lower ground now." I spun to Salem, unable to make out anything but his silhouette in the inky night. "I . . . I don't know where to go from here. But you need help, and *quick*."

Salem nodded. Or maybe I only imagined it.

Even given the circumstance, being on the beach woke something deep within my soul, a fragment I hadn't known was there before. The beach called to it—to *me*. I held fast to its beckon, a taut thread leading into the ocean and beyond.

The supercontinent. Another world. *That* was what I wanted.

As I wandered across the shifty ground with Salem, I inhaled the tangy, salt-speckled wind, letting it settle on my tongue and in my lungs. I wanted to bottle it up and bask in its sharp promise of freedom.

A beam of light darted around us, and I froze. Time stretched to a stop as I nearly became sick in the loose dirt.

"Help," Salem breathed, lurching away from me with a staggering gait. "They can help." In the darkness, on the shifting ground, I lost sense of where he was, and my fear spiked. Anyone on this beach from Miota—*or elsewhere*—would have reason to kill us on sight.

We wouldn't survive tonight. We'd never see the sun again.

"Salem!" I shouted. "Salem, *stop*! You're going to get us—" *Killed*. But this wasn't his fault. The second we left Castle Circle, the blame became mine. Salem's blood stained *my* hands.

I pushed onward, blubbering nonsense into the dark, as Salem shouted for help.

The thick beam of light fixed on him long enough for me to watch him fly backward as a projectile hit him.

"*Salem!*" I collapsed. Limbs shaking, I crawled toward his body, determined to reach him. Determined to save him.

A frothy wave shoved me onto my stomach. The ocean's icy temperature struck my lungs, leaving me breathless, and pungent water filled my mouth. I swallowed the stuff and gagged.

Salem! Salem!

The dirt here differed from Pointe's. This substance clung to my teeth, and I couldn't scrape the kernels away with my tongue. I couldn't do *anything,* tethered between land and ocean.

Was Salem dead? Was I? Were we on the beach to float out to sea and reunite with all Miotans who'd passed on?

"Corinn?" a nasally voice hummed.

I released a sob. "Is Salem—"

Hasty fingers crammed something into my mouth and forced my jaw shut.

I searched for the muddled voice. I wanted to find it. I *needed* to find it—find Salem.

Salem. Salem, Salem . . .

But I was too far gone.

CHAPTER 41

JULIA

My temper could have boiled the water quicker than the hot plate I stared down. Seething anger curled in my chest before churning toward my stomach and singeing down to my fingertips.

I could not *wait* for Corinn and Salem to endure my questions. Jameson Klemmins said the two candidates were already broken, which meant this would be simple enough: if they did not answer my questions, they would be scalded. And in their states, they would not bear boiling water for long.

I rapped my nails on the wooden counter, craving to hear the kettle whistle as my patience grew thin. Although, if a stray maid or butler came to this kitchen right now—one of their only permitted locations—it would look like nothing more than a scene of peace: a queen brewing her bedtime tea.

Perhaps in another life, where Josiah was the king and I was simply his unimportant younger sister, I could live a life with such tranquility. But fate was cruel, and Josiah was dead. I was the only person left who could secure the empire my forefathers had fought so hard to create.

It made me livid. I had sustained countless miscarriages, the death of my only son, and the burden of selecting his replacement. And now, two candidates had escaped the Fort, an impossibility.

How was I to survive this?

"You were made to rule," Father told me, giving my chin a quick squeeze. "You're the strongest Delldova."

"The people wanted Josiah." I hid my face in my hands. "I wanted him! I want my brother back!"

"I don't care what the people want," Father snipped. The gravity in his voice crawled across my skin. "They need you."

"Do you even feel bad?" I whispered, knowing that asking him such a question would be the bravest thing I would ever do. But I needed to know.

Did he mourn the son he murdered?

Father tugged my hair and ripped my face from the safety of my palms. My heart kicked against my ribs, but I knew he would not harm me. I was Miota's only heir now. I met Father's eyes, cold and tumultuous as the ocean at night. "I did what I had to do," he spat through clenched teeth. "With the job we have, remorse isn't something we have the luxury of considering. We do what needs to be done, and that's all that matters. Do you understand?"

I nodded, biting back more tears. My scalp stung from Father's grip on my hair. "Yes, Your Majesty."

Father let me go with a shove. "Trust me, Jules. It's better this way."

Father had been so wrong. Nothing about this was *better.*

I stole a glance at myself in a large cooking pot's reflective metal, and Father's lethal green eyes and dark features stared back. The same cruelty that destroyed him now lived within me.

Everyone in the castle knew Josiah was the nice one. But a benevolent Delldova could never wear the crown.

The kettle whistled, and I nearly jumped. *Finally.* I grabbed it and exited the kitchen.

I refrained from running and kept a slow, steady pace down the servants' corridor and up the stairwell to the main floor.

While the basement and second level of my home were finished with cold, wood flooring, the ground floor displayed blood-red carpeting in every square inch. Josiah had often complained about the moldy smell it gave off, but Father said the deep crimson signified life and death, both of which were necessary for the continuation of our dynasty.

Focus, Jules, Father sang, losing his patience inside my head. Though his presence was strictly confined to my mental space ever since his premature death, he still haunted my every move.

"If you fail us . . ." he had said in his final days. "Your people will kill you. Keep your control on them, Jules. If you don't, I'll see you soon."

Was Father's warning coming to fruition? Corinn Januski and Salem Redding had left the Fort. I did not understand how they could do such a thing and live to tell the tale, especially when *Max Reno* had been the one to discover them.

Max had been preparing the docks for the oncoming ship from Red Fox. When he found the candidates, he should have killed them and thrown their bodies into the foamy ocean. It was the law, and Max had blatantly ignored it. Maybe I had underestimated my friend's loyalties after all these years . . .

I devised a plan for Max as I walked down the hall. He would sit in a cell in the Hold until his implant arrived from Red Fox. Once he underwent the surgery, his mind would belong to *me*, and it would be impossible for him to disobey whatever I force-fed him.

If Max was not so useful, I would simply kill him now. But he conducted foreign relations with Red Fox, and he was one of the select few Miotans who knew my family's secrets. I could not lose him entirely and undergo the toil of replacing him. Frankly, I did not want anyone else on this entire rock doing his job.

I used my panel to summon four guard members, tasking them with detaining Max Reno and placing him in the Hold.

Red Fox's technology was, admittedly, genius. The electrodes placed in the guards' heads made it so they could not think for themselves. I filled their empty minds with commands and concurrently activated what Dr. Klemmins called the limbic system, which made the guards fear for their survival. Their brains and actions were mine to mold.

I slipped my panel back into my pocket and approached the medical wing. *Now you can help me,* I thought, summoning Father. He was better at this sort of thing.

I'm here, Jules, he purred, filtering into my thoughts, my shoulders, my demeanor. I embraced him and entered the white room.

Even with Father's strength, I sucked in a small breath. I hated this place, reeking of chemicals and buzzing under the lights' fluorescence.

Beneath layers of white blankets, in their own beds, Corinn and Salem lay still, hooked up to a machine monitoring their vitals.

Father snarled. The castle's medical resources were being used on *criminals.*

I set the kettle on the floor and watched the candidates. Corinn's heart rate seemed steady, though Salem's fluctuated drastically, racing before nearly slowing to a halt.

I was no doctor, but I would not count on Salem's survival. I needed to channel my torturous questions toward Corinn, then.

Why not poison them now? Father asked. *Be done with them.*

It was enticing enough to make my mouth water. I rolled the sealed vial in my palm.

But I could not give in *now.* Since they were here, alive, I needed to know *how* they left my fortress. The brain activity of the guards stationed outside the castle's gate had spiked for only a minute before diminishing; they had clearly witnessed the Pointeans before ultimately returning to their vegetated baseline state.

Had Corinn and Salem found a tunnel and disappeared in front of my guards? How did the candidates throttle the guards' need to kill them? Was this going to be an offense repeated by others, or had this been an astronomical fluke?

Was my reign going to end as brutally as Father warned?

Get a hold of yourself, Father groaned. *You are the* queen.

I straightened my stance. I would end these criminals; they would not end me.

Jameson Klemmins barged into the room, his face ridden with panic. The doctor's receding hair, dark as night, stuck straight up. "My queen." His spine bent, yielding to my presence. The surge of power revived me. "I'm *so sorry* for what's been done—"

"You are treating them," I interrupted.

The doctor paled, accentuating the blue in his eyes. "Max Reno said you *wanted* me to treat them. So you could question them properly."

I threaded my fingers together while training my face to stay motionless. *Do not move a muscle* . . . "Red Fox's next shipment will have Max Reno's implant. He will need his surgery immediately. How are *they*?" I shifted my attention to the candidates. Max was in the Hold; he was a problem for tomorrow.

Jameson skirted around Salem's bed. "Redding's lost a lot of blood, Your Majesty. He's sustained multiple gunshot wounds . . . he's in critical condition." His eyes flitted to Corinn. "Januski's consciousness appeared to be altered. She was experiencing an episode of psychosis. I've sedated her for now—figured you'd want to deal with her in your own way."

"When will they wake up?" I asked.

"Any moment." Jameson strolled toward Corinn's bed. He fumbled with a machine that displayed numbers and bore bags of fluid. "I'll adjust her meds as needed. You just tell me when to wake them."

On instinct, I brushed the vial of purple poison in my pocket, drawing strength from it. Father always said the deadliest person in the room was the most powerful. Between my vial and kettle of boiling water, *I* held that title.

I lifted my chin. "Do it now."

Jameson dipped his head in submission.

Slowly, Corinn stirred, as if the doctor was breathing life into her. Salem's waking was not so graceful. He coughed on a sob, which triggered Corinn. She shot up in her bed, and I raised the kettle, locking eyes with her.

Father feasted upon her, imagining the numerous ways to make her cry alongside her friend.

"Hello, Corinn," I started, keeping my throat heavy and low, willing my voice into a confectionary tone.

Her eyes widened. "What did you—"

"*No,*" I snapped, sharpening my stare. "You can make this easy or difficult. Truly, it is up to you."

She glanced at her friend, pain distorting her face at his agitated state. "Salem!" she whimpered.

"Josiah!" I cried, reaching for my brother's body. His bloodied, inside-out body.

"Jules," Father growled, pinning me back. "Let. Him. Go."

I blinked away the memory, still visceral enough to make me retch. The smell of his organs splayed outside his corpse—

"Corinn." I said her name for my own sake, to ground myself in the current task. The girl's eyes stayed glued to Salem. "Corinn, tell me what you remember."

At last, her glazed eyes bounced toward me. She wiped away the blonde locks plastered to her face, then she cleared her throat. "Your Majesty, what happened was an accident. I swear."

I tilted my head and stood. "Really? That would make the pair of you the first Miotans to accidentally leave the Fort. What an *accomplishment*."

The girl swallowed. "I know the law, Your Majesty. Yet, here we are, alive. Is it because you know this was all a mistake?"

"It was not!" I shouted. If it had truly been an accident, then the Fort was not impenetrable after all. And that was a possibility I could not muster. "This was purposeful, Corinn. You will either answer my questions, or you will find out how *hot* the water in this kettle is."

Fear slipped through the cracks of her brave façade. After all, she had seen Abner's burns from this same method. If she would not talk, I would mutilate her flesh in an identical manner.

Salem groaned. Corinn looked at him, but he was not my concern; I was not confident he would make it out of this room.

I floated to Corinn's bed, standing at her footboard. "What led you two to the beach?"

The girl stared with a challenging glow. "We fell."

I waited a moment, swirling the kettle by its arching handle. "Care to *elaborate*?"

She swallowed. "We fell into a tunnel. On accident."

I pictured a map of the tunnel network. Not a single entrance lay in Castle Circle. They had jumped the fence. "Where was this tunnel entrance?"

"It's . . . difficult to remember, Your Majesty—"

I dipped the kettle, letting scalding water spill onto the tangle of sheets covering her legs. Through the layers, she flinched, letting out a cry.

"Please," she bellowed, fumbling with her elbow. She was . . . attempting to remove her needles. To *flee*. But her fumbling hands were too clumsy; she was stuck to the bed.

"How did you get to the tunnel?" I raised my voice. "Where did you enter from?"

"I didn't mean any harm, Your Majesty." Her voice wavered in time with her bottom lip. "None of this was supposed to happen."

"Which part was not supposed to happen, hmm? Intentionally leaving Castle Circle, or me finding out about it?"

When she did not immediately answer, Father overtook me. I ripped the sheets from Corinn's bed and exposed her legs, as white as moonlight, before emptying the kettle.

Her screams flooded my ears as I locked my conscious thoughts behind a metal cage. Father threw the key.

For the dynasty, he assured me.

Yes. For the dynasty. I ignored Corinn's thrashing and kicking. Scarlet now marked the sheets near the crook of her arm, and I knew her IV had been dislodged.

Salem erupted at Corinn's voice before ebbing away into stillness. Jameson compensated his medication amounts, pulling the boy back under.

"Will you cooperate now?" I asked Corinn over her shrieking. *"How did you know where to find a tunnel entrance?"*

"It . . . w-was an . . . accident!" she sobbed.

Jameson adjusted her IV and chained her arm to the bed with some sort of thick restraint. Though Corinn fought against it, she was no match for the doctor.

"Stop lying to me," I hissed at her before pouring again. Substantially.

Her wailing persisted, laced with ragged screams. She writhed in bed, chained to her spot as I ruined her legs beyond recognition, until she was marred in copious blotches of brightening pinks and reds.

I did not feel pity. I could not feel *anything* when Father ruled me.

Her noises continued long after I leveled the kettle. Jameson peered at Corinn's monitor with bunched lips. "She's going into shock," he informed me. "Blood pressure is dropping. It's not uncommon, due to the heat and the pain . . ." His eyes flickered to the kettle in my hands. "You probably won't get much out of her in the meantime, Your Majesty."

You're a delightful little monster, Father chuckled, admiring Corinn's maimed legs.

Because of you, I replied, holding my tongue between my teeth and examining the girl. "Is she . . . okay?"

Corinn's eyes rolled back, and she swam in and out of the room. I did not want her incapacitated. Perhaps Max *had* done me a favor; I needed to know how she left the Fort. It was my greatest mystery. How did a *Low* escape?

"Yes. I'll sedate her for now and give morphine for pain. Should . . . do you want her burns treated now, Your Majesty? They really should be covered."

I tapped my foot within the safety of my floor-length skirt. "No. I am not done with her yet."

Jameson's brow twitched, but he bowed and crossed his arms.

My gaze volleyed between Corinn and Salem. Salem and Corinn. An anomaly, really: a friendship transcending Tiers. It was unheard of. Society was supposed to be stagnant. It was why cities remained divided, why Tiers dictated ways of life.

Your people will kill you. Keep your control on them, Jules. If you don't, I'll see you soon.

Father's ultimate message to me now echoed within my storm of thoughts. It had been his farewell to me, a last warning from when he existed outside of my head instead of within it.

Keep your control on them.

Letting the son of an executive council member befriend a Low was *not* keeping control.

"We really only need one of them to answer my questions," I told Jameson. The words tumbled from my lips without thought . . . but there was no stopping them now. I met his blue eyes. "You may dispose of Salem Redding however you wish."

His lip curled upward. "Your Majesty, if you will lend me your ear, I have an idea."

PART FOUR

"While the ratios and frequencies of this trade are able to change upon annual review, the fundamental exchange will remain: MIOTA will provide viable, working-aged people while Red Fox will provide standard technology and necessary supplies."

—*The Royal Codex, Section 1, Para. 2: Trade Rules*

CHAPTER 42

I was on fire.

My heart rate quickened, and each time I tried moving, searing pain shot up my legs. The sensation of being scorched alive kept me tied to my place in bed. Sobs escaped me as fire pressed against my skin and bones, leaving the pain with nowhere to go but up my throat in a cry.

Where was I? I gathered all my strength into opening my eyes.

The Low Tier's color surrounded me—white ceiling, white walls, white sheets.

This was a hospital, though not Pointe's, judging by this place's more refined ceilings. Besides, I was in Castle Circle. I couldn't have been in Pointe. Last I remembered—

Oh.

The memories crashed into me, squeezing the air from my chest. I swore someone ripped the flesh off my legs at that very moment, though no one stood near me anymore.

The queen was gone. She'd glowed with fury, with *delight*, as she'd poured the kettle's boiling water on me.

I lifted my head to peer at my legs, raw and ragged. Tears rolled down my face.

I couldn't register my legs as my own. Someone else's limbs stuck out from under the plain, oversized shirt I wore. Deep red splotches muddled the swollen, sickly skin, and blisters peppered me in glistening clusters.

In the bed beside me, Salem lay still.

All. My. Fault. My heart clenched. As soon as I'd realized he wasn't going to stray from my side, I shouldn't have left Castle Circle. For *any* reason.

I remembered the bullet grazing his deltoid in the field outside the castle grounds, before we fell into the tunnel, but he'd also been shot on the beach.

My stomach dropped thinking about the ocean, the waves, the freedom. We'd found it, Salem and I, and we were going to die for it.

I strained to see Salem's vitals monitor and immediately wished I hadn't. He was bradycardic by twenty beats and hypotensive, confirming my fear. He'd lost too much blood.

"Salem," I croaked, my voice barely above a whisper. The effort of speaking sent searing pain down my legs, burning all over again.

He shifted in bed, favoring his left side. I couldn't visualize his wounds with his body underneath sheets and knitted blankets. He turned, and his bright eyes clashed with mine.

"Salem," I sobbed, my throat burning. When I reached out my hand, trying to minimize all distance between us, I realized I was detained—tied to my bed's rail. "Salem, I'm *so sorry.*"

He tried reaching toward me with his right arm, but he couldn't. He guarded his shoulder, keeping it tucked at his side.

Each time I thought I could master my swells of guilt, a new wave came, knocking me to the ground. It was like my short-lived time on the beach, when a fresh surge of water had throttled me every few seconds.

"Corinn," he whispered, his eyes fluttering closed again. "I'm okay."

"Oh?" I struggled to breathe.

He coughed. "It's only that so many people went through the trouble of shooting me . . . I figure it would be rude if I didn't suffer . . . at least a *little*."

"*Salem.*" I glared at him, though I couldn't turn my body to face him properly, and he couldn't keep his eyes open long enough to see me. "All your readings are low. Your heart—"

"I feel fine, Corinn." The ghost of laughter filled the fraction of his visage visible to me. "It's probably just the sedative. I'm hanging on."

I bit my lip as flames of unease settled in the corners of my vision. "Just *hanging on?*"

"By a thread. A *strong* thread. I won't pull on it."

"You better not," I shot. Tears blurred the ceiling above me. "I don't know how to sew."

Salem's low laugh filled the dry air, a sound that only chipped away at my heart further, lodging grief and despair where light used to be.

"Salem, this is all my fault." My body spasmed as fear settled in, the emotion icy cold, yet useless in alleviating my burning legs.

"Hey, you can't put this all on yourself," he said.

"Yes, I can." As soon as I'd jumped the fence, this became my fault. I wanted to prove my worth, but I wasn't *good enough* to save myself or Miota. And now Salem and I were going to die for it.

I didn't want to die. Not like this.

I only wondered what Their Majesties would tell the other candidates. What would Griff think of me? He'd said I was the best thing to ever happen to him. Would he still think that after learning I'd gotten Salem and myself killed?

"Trials are coming up," Salem said. "Next week. I'm sure we'll get one. Why else would we be receiving treatment right now? There's no point if they just planned on killing us."

His words lit a beacon of hope in me, as his presence always did. While I was Griff's moonlight, Salem was my sun, a steadfast presence promising brightness and warmth.

Besides, Abner had once told me Julia would poison someone if she wanted them dead. Right now, she *wanted* something from us. And whatever it was, it was saving our lives.

It slammed into me, and even though it was nontangible, my legs pulsed all the same. All her questions earlier . . . Julia had no idea how we'd left the Fort. It was our hold over her.

She wouldn't kill us until she got what she wanted.

All I needed to do was endure her methods of torture and hope to the stars she never grew too impatient.

Maybe there was a *tiny* seedling of hope after all.

"Thank you, Salem," I said.

A dark-haired man, lanky and wearing a white coat, entered the room with a sadistic smile. "I knew I heard you two. Conspiring, are you?"

I couldn't remember if this was the doctor from before, when Julia had scalded me. I tried my luck. "Can you look at Salem's vitals?"

The man smiled, though nothing but cold flames burned within him. "Not right now." He waltzed to my vitals monitor and adjusted the dosages of medication running through my IV. "How are your legs? I'll administer some painkillers . . ."

Before he'd finished his sentence, the world faded, morphing into an abstract scape.

These were no painkillers.

I couldn't move my lips to protest. After time yawned into oblivion, my vision went black.

Echoed voices rang, melding together in my mind. I tried grasping individual words but couldn't.

The fire pent inside my legs persisted, pushing against my skin. The weight of the room's air on me was *too much*.

Julia materialized at the foot of my bed as my eyes gradually opened. The sight of her jolted my heart. *Please, no. Not again.* But her sinister smile told me begging would prove futile.

"I am so glad one of you survived the night. Who would I question if you were *both* dead?"

Too slow. Everything moved too slow.

What was she talking about? Salem was next to me. I held my breath and peered at my best friend.

He was . . . still.

His vitals monitor was shut off.

Salem lay in the bed. Asleep.

"What—" I gagged as my flaming throat caught on itself. "What do you mean?"

I glanced at Salem again. Sleeping.

"Wake him up," I told Julia as my head inflated three sizes.

She cocked her head and gave a knowing smile. "How can I wake someone who no longer has a pulse?"

Her words slammed into me like a pile of bricks.

Body quaking, tears flooding my eyes, I watched Salem's sternum. For movement, for *anything*.

I waited.

And waited.

"I said *wake him up!*" The room spun.

Julia said nothing. Salem did nothing. I thought of *nothing*.

"Salem," I called. "Salem, can you hear me?" I ignored how my voice cracked. How the screaming charred my lungs.

Ice settled into my bones at the rate autumn changed to winter. My legs trembled, though the raw pain was outweighed by this new torture of waiting for Salem's next breath.

He *would* breathe again.

He had to.

I lost all sense of time as I stared. Waiting. Salem's blond hair brushed his forehead, nearly falling into his eyes. His face was naked without his glasses. His mouth didn't possess its usual curve, his omnipresent promise of a smile.

"Salem." My voice was louder this time. Rougher. My chilled bones throbbed from inside me. My jaw shook. "Salem. Wake. Up."

I waited.

"Now."

But he didn't move. His chest didn't move. His eyes didn't flit open.

The room twirled, Salem at its center. He was the room's gravity. *My* gravity.

I couldn't breathe without him. Salem Redding comprised the best parts of me.

He couldn't be *gone*. He was still *here*. Next to me. He'd come back for me. He'd wake up. For me.

Somewhere, voices lashed out. I couldn't reach them from within this internal torture.

Each second of denial built in my chest, increasing the pressure inside me. He just needed to wake up, and it would all dissipate.

But time raced onward. And Salem did not.

The rigid cord inside me, strung too tight, snapped.

He's gone.

Salem is gone. Because of me.

My heart shattered the same way glass broke: into a hundred tiny pieces, invisible shards impossible to put back together.

I killed him. I did this to him.

"Salem." Each sob unleashed a new one, worse than the last. Not Salem. Please.

Not my best friend. I was *nothing* without him.

This pain—a deep, visceral ache—was worse than any burn Julia could unleash. I was missing a piece of myself, a vital organ.

Salem was as necessary as the air I breathed.

I couldn't live a day without hearing his voice. Touching his skin. Seeing his smile.

He suffocated my thoughts. My head was so full of *Salem.* Scruffy hair. Smart eyes. Thick glasses. Slender fingers. A spray of freckles across his cheeks. Firm hugs. Playful nudges on the shoulder. Bubbling laughter. A fountain of hope. He believed in me when no one else could—when even *I* gave up on myself.

I thought reflecting on his essence would bring him back. But he stayed there. Lying in bed, chest unmoving, fingers curled, lips slightly parted.

I screamed. The effort it took induced gagging, and I vomited on the floor as even my stomach rioted. Bile dribbled from my mouth as I leaned over the edge of the bed.

"I didn't get to say goodbye!" I broke. My body and soul ruptured, now cleaved into mismatched pieces that didn't fit together without him.

I need my best friend.

I welcomed the pain radiating through my legs—a pain caused by something *other* than Salem was a comfort. By the moon, I nearly begged the queen to dump more scalding water on me and rescue me from this agony. My legs cooked, feeling like nothing more than charred ash, as if they were succumbing to the same fate as the bodies I'd burned in the asympton lab.

Salem always kept me from spiraling too far into despair. How could I carry on without him? How could I stop the pain when he was its source?

I killed my best friend. I *destroyed* him, and I couldn't save him.

I was not whole. My heart pierced gashes into my lungs with every wheezing breath I took. Tears spilt onto my sheets. The fire from my legs spread mercilessly, threatening to consume me whole. Threatening to burn me alive.

I hoped it did.

What was I without Salem? He was my reason for having the shred of hope that I was worth *something*. He was my solace. My support. My reason to smile.

Now he was just dead.

As I fell apart, I wondered how I'd ever breathe without feeling like I was inhaling a million steel shards.

Julia watched from the foot of the bed, reeking of . . . *poison*. The same kind from Pointe's asympton lab. *Please use it*, I tried saying. *Let me follow him*.

Salem had said it himself: *I'm going wherever you go*. That was how our friendship worked—how we had *always worked*.

When I peered at the queen, I saw no remorse on her face. She was cool and calculating, a model figure, unaffected by emotions. She'd retreated into her mind and was planning her next move.

The next move. I thought she wasn't going to kill us. I thought we'd get a trial. Clearly, I was wrong.

"When d-did it happen?" I asked, sniffling. I kept biting through the pain to look at Salem's motionless body, somehow still trying to convince myself he was alive. Despite the unreadable vitals monitor. Despite the stillness of his chest. Salem always embodied hope; maybe he had one miracle left in him.

I knew that was irrational, but *this wasn't fair.* Salem left while I'd been knocked out from the sedative the tall doctor had forced into my bloodstream.

I hadn't gotten to say goodbye.

Salem had told me once himself, on a hospital rotation last year, that death was rarely fair. If he could see himself now and speak those words out of existence, then maybe he'd still be here.

Except, this wasn't some ironic twist of fate; this was *my fault.* Here I was, burned but alive, while Salem's heart had stopped beating.

"It was hard to say." Julia motioned to the tall doctor. "Everything slowed to a gradual stop. Dr. Klemmins tried to save him, but . . ."

She had no reason to finish the sentence; I knew what she'd say. It might've been the queen's first mercy toward me, saving my ears from hearing what my body refused to accept.

My stomach twisted when I looked toward the doctor, the infamous Jameson Klemmins. He'd forced a sedative down my line. He'd deprived me of my final words to Salem.

What *had* my last words been? I couldn't remember.

Julia shifted her stance as I broke apart in front of her. "I can't get information from her when she's like this," she muttered to Jameson Klemmins, like I wasn't even in the room. "Make it stop."

Yes. Please. Make it stop.

But some fraction of my mind snagged on her words. She *did* need information from us—*me.*

"I can't use medicine to make her speak, Your Majesty," Klemmins replied flatly.

Julia, a watery blob through my glassy eyes, studied me. "Tell me how you left the Fort," she demanded.

"It was an accident."

"Quit lying!" Julia paced across the room and returned with—

Red dots clouded my vision as she scorched my legs with water from her kettle. My skin *screamed*, slowly peeling off muscle and bone and sinew alike. Each pour of the kettle was a shower of needles raining down on me, a saw carving off my flesh layer by layer, radiating, radiating, *radiating* . . .

In another room, someone screamed. I flailed in the bed, unable to escape the torture. While I thought this would dampen the pain of having Salem stolen from me, it only accentuated it, lighting every aspect of my mind and body ablaze.

Oh . . . *I* was the one screaming.

I couldn't tell when she stopped; I only looked up, and Julia had retreated, leaving me with my spoiled and swollen limbs.

I sensed Dr. Klemmins's presence behind me, fumbling with my medicine again. There was no sense fighting it now. I was better off unconscious, if not dead. I should've born Salem's fate; it belonged to *me*.

I was nothing. If I hadn't already known it, there wouldn't have been a doubt in my mind now. I'd killed my best friend. I knew that Griff and Abner, once my allies, would now avoid me at all costs, too terrified to associate with someone as selfish and reckless as me.

I should've stayed in the Low Tier and never applied to Accolade. I should've held my tongue in the asympton lab as Dr. Ova sliced cadavers. I should've incinerated the bodies and mopped the floors and emptied the trash, detached from what my Tier meant. Then Salem would be alive, and I'd be good for what I was worth.

The world faded as I delighted in thinking of a life as peaceful as rotting to death in the Low Tier.

"Pulse is stabilized," Dr. Klemmins said. "So she's under."

Under? No, I could still hear. And I still felt my burnt legs and cracked heart.

Julia hmphed. Their voices faded slowly. "I thought getting rid of Redding would make her talk."

"She may yet, Your Majesty. On a more pressing note, those for tonight's shipment are ready. There weren't a ton of bodies for the city's labs this time around. Reeves upping our quota is taking its toll."

I second-guessed if I was still awake; these words were senseless. Bodies for the city's labs? What quota, and who was Reeves?

Julia spoke. "Yes, Reeves is going to suck our population at this rate . . . After Accolade, I will have to make the announcement. Only *one* body will be permitted for each city's asympton lab—the rest are off to Red Fox. If there is backlash, I will need you to write an article about asympton's increasing danger."

"Wonderful thinking, Your Majesty." Klemmins's voice was a blur now as the sedative dragged me down, down, down.

One body per city? The rest were . . . off to Red Fox?

Why would Klemmins falsify an article about asympton?

Surely, it didn't mean . . .

I fought to stay alert, but the drugs smothered me, working through my veins. I steeled my thoughts, hoping I remembered them when I woke up.

"What of Januski?" Dr. Klemmins asked, a distant, hollow sound.

I strained to stay above unconsciousness as Julia answered. She was the last garbled voice I heard before I *truly* went under.

"She awaits her trial. Put her in the Hold."

CHAPTER 43

When I woke, I opened my eyes, and it was still dark. My legs ached underneath their persistent fire. A chill laced the air, stale and foreboding.

My memory trickled back, as if knowing I couldn't tolerate it all at once.

Was this the Hold? I recalled the exchange between Julia and Klemmins before I'd gone under. This dark, callous place was surely the infamous underground death trap made for storing criminals until bimonthly trials.

Of which I was among the criminals now.

But their conversation had held more weight than deciding my fate. They'd . . . mentioned asympton.

Julia decreasing the number of bodies sent to the asympton labs. Klemmins faking an article about the disease's increasing danger.

Why would they lie about such a thing? Because Reeves—whoever that was—upped a quota?

Klemmins said there weren't tons of bodies for the city's labs. Julia suggested sending one body per month to each city.

The rest are off to Red Fox.

Julia's ally on the supercontinent. The other half of Miota's trade deal: technology for Julia in exchange for *viable* people. It meant that . . . those who died from asympton . . . weren't actually *dead.*

I sucked in a breath as the Hold shrank around me, squeezing my burns and lungs and throat . . .

Asympton *wasn't real.* It was safe to assume those claimed by the disease were the ones Julia chose to send to Red Fox as part of the trade.

And the select bodies sent to the labs for autopsy were . . . what? Killed off to stage a fake disease? I wasn't sure. Regardless, this was the pinnacle of the monarchy's heaping secrets.

Everyone knew those who died of asympton were floated to sea. But now, I saw through the veil. Those who died were taken to the beach—a place inaccessible to the public—and floated off Miota by guards, who were Julia's mind-controlled minions.

An incurable, asymptomatic disease. It wasn't *real.*

I was a fool.

There wasn't a national medical emergency; there was only a covert trading of people for goods. As if lives could honestly be exchanged for technology—tech that I knew Julia used for her own malicious needs. She was a bigger monster than I'd ever thought. She ruled the island and kept us wrangled within the Fort and city walls all for self-preservation.

Ever since I met Cass four years ago, I'd always wondered why he cherished his time away from the castle when he had everything he'd ever wanted within those gilded gates.

But he had to survive in Julia's arena. He had to live in her cage.

Just as we all did. And it was not living.

While my asympton theory was plausible, it still begged questions. How did people drop dead from a feigned disease? What was the pathogen I easily recognized as the asympton bacterium, found in every infected body?

The questions tortured me until I couldn't take it. I shifted on what I assumed was a bed. The vinyl mattress didn't have sheets, which left my skin frigid. Though my arms shivered and teeth chattered, my legs stung, radiating with an internal fire. As much as I strained my eyes to see anything, it was futile.

The Hold held Miota's slew of prisoners. Were they contained elsewhere, in their own darkness, or were they with me?

The unknowns swept in new fears, a prickling feeling at the base of my skull.

"Hello?" I said and immediately clapped a hand over my mouth. How *stupid* was I? What if the other prisoners could locate me now?

A low rumble filled the darkness. Panic crippled me, locking up every joint and muscle in my body.

"The new girl's awake," a low voice rasped. I judged it to be at least a room's length away.

"Where are you?" My voice wavered as I spoke, and I cringed. If anyone here could sense fear, they'd know I dripped with it. My hands grew slick with sweat, and my heartbeat was palpable against my sternum.

"The *Hold*, darling," the man deadpanned.

The fire burning in my legs transported up to my stomach. "I gathered *that*. How is this place . . . laid out?"

"Wondering if we could come in your cell and eat you up?" the voice teased. "Don't worry. We're all locked in our own cells. Can't have us ripping at each other's throats to end our misery early, can we? You're lucky, coming down here so close to trials. You might remember the taste of sunlight by the time this is all over."

The *taste?* I didn't question him. We were, after all, completely swathed in grim darkness.

"Beautiful imagery, Silas," spoke another voice, a man with a higher intonation. His sarcastic tone undermined any sweet intent.

Every emotion churning inside me suspended in my chest. "Silas?" I blurted. "Hart?"

"What's it to you?" the first man charged. "You're not a Yorkie."

Yorkie? From Yorkinson, I assumed.

"No, I . . ." Butterflies filled me. How did he know that? "I'm a candidate in Accolade—or, I *was* . . ." I didn't know what I was anymore. I was in limbo, poised between life and death, citizen and criminal, freedom and confinement. "Anyway, my partner and I were assigned to do your trial with Their Majesties." Not that I'd get that luxury anymore.

And then I remembered what my subconscious had tried *so hard* to forget. Salem was dead. Recalling his lifeless body set me aflame as cries rose in my throat.

I whimpered. The pathetic sound resounded through the Hold, but I didn't care. Salem was gone. And he'd never come back. And it was because of *me.*

In the dark, I broke all over again. I kept ripping out the makeshift sutures in my heart, my lousy attempts at convincing myself this wasn't real. Somehow, Salem was still alive, and we'd be granted a trial, and we'd go free.

But Salem was dead, and before long, I would be, too.

Mending my broken heart was impossible, no matter how I tried stitching it up. After all, I wasn't a surgeon; I wasn't even a doctor. I was a researcher for a fabricated disease. I was somehow the *most* useless person in the Low Tier.

Why was I even trying to fight Julia anymore? It would've

been easier on everyone if I just gave her what she wanted. I was a hollow shell: seemingly of substance at first glance, but reducing myself to emptiness, nothingness, with a single crack.

Julia would only prove that when she killed me.

"What's Accolade?" Silas asked.

The question pulled me from my internal storm. I searched for Silas, seeing if I'd adjusted to the total darkness, but my eyes remained useless. Just like every other part of me.

"Accolade?" I said. "It's a competition to pick the new king and queen."

"King? Did the boy refuse ruling or something?"

My mind moved at the pace of a sprouting seed. The boy? Refusing to rule?

Oh. Two months ago . . . was the beginning of May, not long after my eighteenth birthday. Cass was still alive then. Anyone who'd been in here for nearly the full two months *wouldn't* know what was happening.

"Cass died," I squawked. In some sick regard, it felt *nice* to think about a death that wasn't Salem's. "Er, the prince. Kierran. So there's a tournament to rule Miota, and I was in it. We all lived in Castle Circle and competed against each other."

"Sounds like a Top's idea of fun," Silas spat.

Another criminal laughed. "Silas, I tried telling you about it when I came down here, but you wouldn't listen."

"I don't care what happens up there anymore," Silas replied, mumbling his next words. "We're never going to be part of that world again."

The words sobered the Hold, stilling the air.

Soon, we'd face our trials, and there was nothing we could do to save ourselves. Fate was no longer on our side or in our hands.

Not that our lives were ever owned by us. No matter what

Tier or city we hailed from, we were prisoners of the same monarchy. We were essentially in a glorified holding cell, for Julia to pick off and send people to the supercontinent for her tech. We didn't have even a glimpse of freedom. It was all an elaborate façade.

Even Accolade. Silas was right; the competition was a gaudy form of entertainment. Every projector in Miota was clogged with ten hours of live competition footage per day and even more content from reruns, which played long into the night. Countless articles were published regarding unimportant matters, like theories of who would win and comparisons between girls' dresses.

Though Abner introduced the idea of Accolade, its production and logistics belonged to Julia. The competition forced Miotans to obsess over candidates' partners and points and rankings, all while she looked for someone to rule *exactly like her*. She didn't want someone of grit to win; she wanted someone made of clay and dirt, easy to mold.

Someone like Addison.

Accolade appeared to be a dramatic competition for finding love and vying for power, but it was much deeper than that. It distracted everyone from the fact that, for the first time in Miotan history, the Delldova line had ended. Julia had *failed*, and she was putting on a show before anyone realized how monumental this was.

Accolade was nothing more than the queen's device.

My legs zinged as I shifted again on the mattress. I needed to see light before the darkness swallowed me whole. I tried envisioning Griff—sharp angles, chocolate hair always slightly askew, and eyes deep enough to swallow me whole. What had he said about the moon and its light?

It was difficult to take his words to heart when darkness

shrouded me. No light could reach me now; it was too late for that. I had nothing left to do but suffer through my burns, mourn my best friend, and wait for my death.

Growing up, I kept track of time by counting each year of school. During Accolade, I tracked time by tallying each passing week. But ever since I ruined everything by leaving Castle Circle, there'd been no reliable way to measure time. My only possibility now was tracking the periods between our meals, though we were brought food at seemingly inconsistent rates. I didn't know if I should've attributed it to my lack of keeping time or the fact that we probably weren't fed regularly on purpose.

Time wasn't my biggest problem down here. Salem's ghost, stamped on my heart, was my constant. There was nothing to do in this cell but dwell on all my past shortcomings.

I thought about the day Bernard first offered to train me to match with medicine. I'd been at the hospital with Mom and Theo, and I wouldn't stop talking about how I wanted to save someone. Bernard mistook it for selflessness and bravery, but he hadn't realized I'd only wanted to do something important, something worthy of approval.

My actions of self-preservation only started there. When Cass first appeared in the industrial greenhouse four years ago, I might've bragged about it, breaking my promise not to tell anyone, if I hadn't desperately wanted to keep Cass to myself.

And then there was Elliot's broken arm. The fact I'd used Griff in the beginning to help me win competitions. My choice to earn points instead of seeing my family. Every step of Accolade, I'd been so wrapped up with myself, even after we'd learned about the supercontinent, after I could've stayed safe in Abner's plan.

I'd paid a price because of my actions, sure. But more than that, *Salem* had reaped the consequences. He'd befriended me, trusted me, followed me . . .

Again, the seams in my chest burst, sending fragments everywhere. My lungs, my diaphragm, my esophagus . . .

A few meals ago, Silas told me he'd heard enough of my crying and sniffling to last him a lifetime. I hadn't cared, since there was nothing he could do to stop me, and it was the only way to ease the guilt I carried.

With each passing meal, it became easier to bear weight on my legs. I trudged across my cell to cope with my nervous energy, keeping my hands in front of me to prevent running into the cell's metal bars or knocking over the bucket for toileting.

My lower extremities could only handle around ten steps before they seethed and threatened to cave underneath me. I'd probed through the darkness what I assumed was *yesterday*, and I'd learned that this cell, somewhere around a ten-foot box, only held the vinyl mattress and bucket.

I plummeted toward insanity the longer I stayed here, wondering if my eyes were opened or closed, wondering if I'd gone blind. A few times, when I'd met my wits' end, I'd prodded my eyes just to *know* if my eyelids were working.

As time passed—in either minutes or hours, I couldn't tell—I realized I was meant for this place and its darkness. I'd spent so long trying to outrun myself and miraculously escape the Low Tier, but I now accepted it as my only real home. I never belonged anywhere but chained to the bottom of society. No one like *me* possessed the power or strength to free Miota from Julia.

Maybe if I'd managed to escape the Low Tier, I could've saved Salem, Miota, my family . . . and all these people with me now, sentenced to die for petty crimes.

I sniffed.

"By the moon!" Silas yelled. "Will you *shut up*, Corinn? Max warned us you'd talk, but he should've mentioned the *crying*."

I crumpled my brow, even with no one to witness it. "Max? Max Reno?" An unfamiliar surge ran through me, and the emotion seemed too . . . light.

The light is already there, waiting, Griff's voice caressed me.

"Does he bring food down here?" I asked. I didn't know who brought our ration of food; I was always too focused on their beams of light, the only reprieve from the darkness.

Silas snorted. "No, he was in your cell. They released him, and you came down here before the next meal. Max said you'd be down here, as long as all went to plan."

Ice slinked through my intestines. "Silas, *tell me* you're lying."

"Do I sound like a liar?"

The hope—the light—blossomed. Max had been down here, and he knew I'd follow. There was a plan.

The only question was *which* plan. Was he referring to Julia's scheme, which entailed letting me rot down here before questioning me one final time at my trial? Or was Max referencing another plan? Was Abner secretly fighting for me still?

"You should've told me that the minute I got down here," I said. "What else did he say?"

Silas hmphed. "He just said to keep your eyes peeled, and he hasn't changed that much."

Helpful, I thought with a bite at Max's vague advice, though I still chimed my thanks to Silas for feeding me vital information.

I sat back on my bed to steady my spinning mind. Max had been down here, imprisoned. But why? And where was he now?

He'd known I was going to visit him Friday night. And he was still looking out for me now, even with everything I'd done wrong.

Who matters, I'd asked Salem, *if not the king?*

Friends and family. That had been his answer.

People like Salem Redding, my best friend, despite our Tier disparity. Like Max, who was still concerned with my whereabouts. Like Griff—my heart ached—who once convinced me I could win Accolade without help from anyone. People like Mom, Theo, and the rest of my family, who were proud of me simply for being *me.*

My friends and family saw me as enough for exactly who I was. They knew my worth. And, slowly, I could come to learn it, too.

I lifted my chin. An inferno the size of a molecular cluster relit inside me. It was the spark most people regarded as my stubborn nature, and it was the twin flame to Griff's *difficulty.* Though I now saw our commonality for what it truly was.

Determination.

I'd been fighting to win Accolade, but that wasn't the *true* victory. Success would come from ruining Julia's reign and freeing Miota.

I wouldn't win Accolade. I'd destroyed myself. I'd be lucky if Julia let me *live*; I could forget about winning a competition never meant for someone of my status.

But everyone on the island was still trapped; we were *all* doomed under Julia's reign. And these people deserved the truth. They deserved a better life. My family, Griff, and even Dr. Ova, who was unknowingly fighting a battle she was predestined to lose.

No, I couldn't win Accolade, but I could still help liberate Miota, once and for all. I summoned my tenacity. Even if Abner wouldn't fight for me, I would fight for *him.* Too many people depended on it.

I nearly bent over in fear, ready to put my head between my spoiled legs to keep from passing out. *You're so stupid,* a small voice said. But what was I supposed to do? Spend my remaining limited days sitting and moping in an underground cell?

I would not go down like this, accepting my death.

I'd been fleeing from my scant fate since Bernard gave me hope of leaving the Low Tier ten years ago. And I was *tired* of running. It was time to face what I was and summon what I had left to offer—for this island and the people I loved on it.

I swallowed my selfishness, which now bled into my cowardice. Maybe they were one and the same. The emotions fought to regain dominance, but I couldn't let them. I clung to Max's words like a lifeline.

There was a plan. I was in the Hold for a reason. If Max was still fighting while staring down his implantation surgery, I could do the same while facing a trial. I couldn't sit back and accept death while so many Miotans suffered. I was going to *fight*.

I let the airy feeling fill me, clear out my bloodstream, and reset my head.

I found it, I wanted to tell Griff. *I found the light.*

It was already there, just as Griff had vowed. The light was waiting.

And I was going to let it in.

CHAPTER 44

I faked misery when guards came with food—they were *guards*. It was like the stars were on my side. Guards meant a direct link to Julia.

I wailed, giving my best impression of someone on the verge of death. With a pang, I remembered I *was*.

"My legs," I moaned to the guard who shoved food and water into my cell, through the lattice of metal bars containing me. "Tell Her Majesty. I'm Corinn Januski, and m-my leg..." I gasped, forcing a cough. My throat caught on its own abrasive texture, and I gagged, spitting on the ground.

The guard shone his beam into my face, blinding me. I drank in the light.

"My burns are infected," I said with a greater force. This was my only shot at getting out of this cell before my trial. "I'm going to *die* if they're not treated."

If the guard comprehended my words, his face didn't show it.

"They'll let you die down here," Silas told me long after the guard had left, a sentence delivered in darkness.

"I know." But I was the exception. I possessed knowledge

Julia needed, and until she extracted it, the queen would keep me alive.

While I didn't share that fact with Silas, my point was proven when Dr. Klemmins ventured into the Hold what I guessed to be a few hours later, escorted by a guard.

It worked. A rush of power rolled through me. I was going back above ground. But neither man on the other side of the light beam seemed motivated to open my cell.

"You're infected?" droned Klemmins, unconvinced. "Show me."

I motioned to my legs, wincing. I filled my lungs with air and held the breath before blowing it out slowly. I could do this; I knew what I was talking about. In this moment, I couldn't be a Low; I had to be a trained doctor.

For Miota.

It was like I *just now* realized what my journey to Pointe with Griff had really encompassed. I'd been so worried about winning Accolade for myself, I'd forgotten the ultimate goal. This wasn't about becoming a queen; it was about *ending* one. I set my internal sights on Julia and her crown.

"There's a biofilm," I started, shoving one of the more gruesome blisters on my leg into Klemmins's small cylinder of light. "I'm sweating, but I also have chills, and I think fever's setting in." Dr. Klemmins's face wrinkled slightly. "My burns were never covered, let alone *treated*, and now I'm lying in my own filth. Think of the bacteria down here!"

I only hoped my speech and disfigured legs were convincing enough. My burns were left to heal in open air; how could I *not* attract infection from a medical standpoint?

Dr. Klemmins narrowed his eyes at me. He produced a thermometer from his pressed coat and shoved his hand through the metal grates of my cell, swishing the probe against my temple before I could stop him.

He read my temperature and gave an amused noise. I held my breath as he turned to the guard. Klemmins knew the truth; he knew I was faking. How did I honestly expect to convince the royal doctor—

"Get her to the hospital wing," Klemmins ordered.

The guard obeyed with a blank stare.

My eyelids flew back. I was . . . being released. It *worked*. With a chill, I realized this likely meant I truly had a fever, which indicated a real infection. At least I'd get treatment now.

Maybe Griff was right. Maybe I possessed the internal power and strength to carry myself after all. Maybe I was comprised not of how high I could climb in society, but of how steadily I could rise to my feet.

With each breath, I allowed more light in, washing away the cobwebs of self-pity and despair that had engulfed me recently.

Inmates shouted in protest as the guard unlocked my cell. He entered and forced something small into my mouth. The pill washed away the single plume of light, though I had confidence that when I woke, I'd be in the castle.

The hospital wing was unchanged, still made of white walls and drowning in the scent of aseptic alcohol, though its air was entirely different.

Salem was gone. Without his presence, as crucial as oxygen, I didn't know how to function. It was like all my cells had splintered, and they needed to relearn how to live what was left of this partial life.

I was pulled from my thoughts when I landed on a face that made my stomach lurch. He sat across the room, studying me with pensive eyes. His guard attire was crisp, keeping his posture tall, and he donned a bulky hat, the most obnoxious part of his uniform.

"Max." I propped myself up in bed. Too many questions ran through my head. Every nerve ending inside me hummed as I anticipated why he was here.

His lip curled upward. "They knocked you out good, huh?"

"I've been sedated enough the past few days to last a lifetime."

Max leaned forward, setting his elbows on his knees, as his smirk melted into a frown. "Okay, Corinn, I'm not sure how much time we have. Their Majesties are in a meeting, and I've disabled the cameras in here for now. But neither of them knows I'm in the castle, so let's get to it: we're in trouble."

"We?"

"You, for leaving the Fort. Julia knows it wasn't an accident. And me, for saving you two *on* the beach."

My mouth parted. I hardly remembered the beach—all my memories had been groggy since that night—but I recalled a voice uttering my name. Max was there? Had *he* shot Salem?

I swallowed the rising lump in my throat. No matter who delivered the life-threatening blow to Salem, he'd only been endangered because of *me*. I might as well have fired the weapon myself.

"Is that why you were in the Hold? Because you saved us?" When Max nodded slightly, I folded my brow. "But . . . then she let you *out*."

Something like amusement claimed Max's features. "Did she? I'm avoiding her for a reason, you know."

I inhaled to reply, but Max pressed on.

"I promise to explain everything later, but right now, I need you to listen to me if you're going to survive your trial. You're only alive because Julia wants answers from you. The second she discovers how you left the Fort—or decides it's all more trouble than it's worth—you're as good as dead."

Right. Reality set in, resonating in my legs, irritating my crusted, oozing skin. If Miota's queen had her way, I knew my life was a waning moon.

"But . . . you're helping me," I ventured. "That's what Silas Hart told me in the Hold. Is it because you knew I was coming to see you in the barracks on Friday?"

"*What?*" Max stood from his seat. "You . . . thought I was at the *barracks* that night?" He paced the room, walking small laps by the foot of my bed.

"Yes. Where else would you be?" He had easily intercepted all my hints from previously in the week. "You *knew* I was going to meet you there!"

He only paced faster.

I blinked at the pale man crumbling in front of me. He was keeping secrets, just as Abner once had. *No.* I couldn't play this cryptic game again. Not when I was nothing more than a tool in it.

If Max wasn't in the barracks Friday night, my plan never would've worked. I'd doomed Salem and myself from the start. Max was on the beach; he'd said as much. Had he expected *me* on the beach that night? Was this all tied to Anzalone's plan, whoever that was?

"Tell me what's going on," I finally said, hardening my voice. "Silas Hart said I'd end up in the Hold if all went *to plan.*"

Max whirled toward me, bearing frantic eyes. "If you knew there was a plan with you *in* the Hold, why'd you scheme your way out? Would've been a lot easier to talk to you if you were still down there. I'm risking my *life* to be here right now."

The question slammed into me, halting my every thought. Only my innate instinct to survive had spurred my desire to escape the Hold. I hadn't thought about it complicating Max's plan; all notions had been fixed inward. I'd only worried about myself.

"I'm sorry." It was the best answer I could give. "Why are you doing it? Risking your life for me?" *I never asked you to.* But I kept that to myself, figuring it wouldn't help anything.

Max gathered himself and sat on the bed that once belonged to Salem. The pressed sheets, drawn up too tightly, made it seem as though the bed had never been occupied before. My heart pinched, and I bit my tongue to keep from screaming at Max to move.

"Okay, look." The guard tipped his nose upward, holding my stare. "Julia wants you dead for obvious reasons. And Abner doesn't exactly care what happens to you anymore—he doesn't think he can control you, so you dying is about the only way he can guarantee you won't spill all his secrets to his wife."

Rage darkened my vision. While I knew Abner wasn't fighting for me to win Accolade, I didn't think he'd stoop so low as to want me *dead.* "Why would I tell Julia anything?" I choked out. "I *want* him to free the island!"

Max shrugged, letting sympathy fill the hollows of his face. "He thinks there's a chance you'll say whatever you need to get out of Julia's torture." His eyes found my legs. "He's just being paranoid. I've tried changing his mind, but I can't. Which is where *my* plan comes in."

"And whoever Anzalone is?"

Max's shoulders tensed, and he didn't answer. I took it as confirmation. "You were supposed to be in the Hold. Because from *there,* you go . . . to . . ." He nodded slowly, attempting to coax an answer from me.

"Die?" I guessed. It wasn't wrong.

He rolled his eyes, leering. "I was looking for 'your trial.' Because from there, you're deemed guilty, and how do you die?" I opened my mouth, but Max waved a dismissive hand. "It's rhetorical, Corinn. Just think about it."

I worked it out mentally. During our lecture with Lorenzo's aunt, I'd learned that criminals deemed guilty at their trials were sedated. Guards then transported the unconscious convicts to the beach—it was easier and cleaner to slay the bodies beside the ocean than from within the castle.

If I was deemed guilty, I'd be sedated and taken outside the Fort—outside Julia's domain.

"Will *you* be on the beach?" I wondered. If Max operated around Their Majesties on the day of trials, like he currently was . . .

I recalled the day we'd toured the barracks, when Max overrode Wesley's neural controls and prevailed over Julia for an ounce of time. If he could do the same on the beach, following my trial, Max could save my life.

He gave a sober nod, a quick downward flick of his head. "This'll require some effort, though, okay?" It would. I'd have to plead guilty to the queen—and *survive* it. "No matter what happens, no matter what you see, I need you to *trust me*, okay? I'm here to help you—help Miota. Can you do that?"

I drank in the implications of agreeing to Max's request. No more thinking of myself first; no more acting on my impulses of self-preservation. Max was willing to help me survive.

Besides, this was my only option.

"Yes." My accord sealed my deliverance, though whether it was to a fate of Julia's fiery destruction or my own star-flecked splendor, I didn't yet know. The heavens seemed to brush over my shoulders, weighing the options alongside me.

I swallowed the plan again, finding its steps too fibrous yet too elusive all at once. I'd plead guilty. Go to the beach. Max would save me. From there . . .

A seedling of an idea formed. "Can you take me back to Pointe?" Max grimaced at the suggestion. I bunched my bed's fitted sheet in my palm, wringing out my nervous energy. "Once we're on the beach? Take me to Pointe, and I'll stay in the tunnel where Griff and I met Bernard. Julia doesn't know about its existence."

"How feasible is it, though?" countered Max, biting his lip and leaning back on the bed—*Salem's* bed.

"My grandma is good at sneaking food from our greenhouse, especially this late in the summer. Executive operatives get lazier. My family can bring me food." Max didn't budge. "It would only be until Griff and I can start a rally against the crown."

Max didn't speak for too many heartbeats. Then, "Fine. But you'll be on your own in Pointe. I won't be able to help you survive."

I nodded, clinging to his concurrence. "Thank you." I paused. "How *is* Griff?" I spoke delicately, not wanting to be burned by Max's answer. What did Griff make of all this? Did he regret telling the news he wanted *me* over Addison?

Max tilted his head. "He's . . . as good as he can be. I haven't spoken to him personally, but when the cameras aren't around, you can tell he's a wreck. Only nine couples remain, so I think Castle Circle is getting lonely—and cutthroat. This upcoming Sunday, Accolade ends." He broke eye contact. "Abner says it'll be Griff and Addison."

My eyes fluttered shut. Knowing I'd lost Griff was a new ache, piling on top of the heartbreak for Salem. It was odd, mourning someone who was still alive. Though Griff and I were from different cities and opposite Tiers, we were parallel spirits, forged from the same stars. His heart mirrored mine.

"Is there any way for me to see him?" I didn't bother masking how raw my voice became. "If he wants to see *me*, that is. He needs to know the plan for my trial."

The logical part of me knew Max could easily relay the information to Griff himself. But every cell in my body wanted to see Griff *so badly*. I wanted to touch his skin, feel his breath, taste his lips.

"He'd give anything to see you again," Max answered softly, indulging me. "But there's no getting you out of here, so I'd have to get Griff *into* the castle. It'd have to happen in the middle of the night, and I might need Abner's help with it."

"Abner knows you're not in the Hold, then?"

"Yeah. We're a team, remember?"

I gnashed my teeth at the elusive explanation. "I remember," I assured Max. It was difficult to forget: the guard and king working together, conspiring against a queen to extinguish her dynasty. The monarchy was fractured and poised against itself, and Miota's citizens had no idea.

"Abner would be pretty pissed at me, though, for bringing *his* Accolade candidate here," the guard finished. "If Julia catches Griff, I can't imagine she'd let him live—forget handing him a *crown*."

"Is it possible, though?" I said. "To get Griff in here? To work around Julia?"

Max swallowed, fixing his gaze on a distant spot. "Yes."

"Then . . . blame everything on me. Tell Abner I forced your hand. Say whatever you want against me, as long as you get Griff here. Would that work?"

"I think so." He stood, once again pacing at the foot of my bed. "But Abner would never forgive you."

"I don't care." I startled myself with how much I *meant* it. It didn't matter what Abner thought of me. I had no reason to prove myself to a man who held no interest in my survival. The king and I were no longer aligned. Max could tell Abner whatever he wanted if it meant I'd get to see Griff again.

I didn't need the king's approval; I didn't need *anyone's* approval. Those who knew me already believed in me and witnessed my light.

I stifled my sob. It was exactly what Salem tried telling me.

Max slowed his steps to a halt, though his mind still worked behind his eyes. "Then . . . it'll happen tonight. Julia will be busy prepping for trials, so I can cut the camera feed in here without her noticing. I don't know how much time I can guarantee you two, but at least you'll get to see him one last time, before . . ."

"All madness breaks loose?" I offered drily.

"Exactly." Max's lips split into a smile. "Tonight, Januski. Until then, stay put."

I breathed a sigh of relief. The guard tipped his cap before spinning on his heel to slink out the door.

CHAPTER 45

Nothing else mattered after that. Julia visited the hospital wing, and when I refused to answer her questions, she warned me that her patience would end at my trial tomorrow.

Tomorrow. I would attempt cheating death tomorrow.

In the meantime, she persisted with her current approach of pouring boiling water on me. I *screamed*, breathing fire. Heat built, my vision darkened, and pain seared my limbs. Steaming, steaming, *steaming* . . .

No one occupied the room; I must've passed out. My radiating legs still pulsed, and tears stung my eyes.

I only needed to endure this today. My trial was tomorrow, and I'd have to tell Julia some twisted version of the truth, incriminating myself. To deem myself guilty and place my fate in the hands of Max Reno.

Miota's executive council attended trials. Could I sway some of them against Julia? But facing the council also meant facing Mrs. Redding, and I wasn't sure how I'd look at her without shattering. Her eyes and nose and lanky figure were *Salem's*. Salem, who'd never again grace Miota with his life and laughter.

Dr. Klemmins came periodically throughout the day, pumping my IV with medications in a likely attempt to keep me strapped in bed, unable to move or think. But I found reprieve in the groggy state; it took the edge off my pain, enough to at least dull the throbbing in my limbs.

He also lathered a cool gel onto my burns before bandaging each leg. Though I knew this meant Julia was finally finished scalding me, I found it hard to be relieved. She was moving onto worse means of torture, should I not cooperate.

Abner never visited, but his absence didn't surprise me. Everything he did was out of selfishness, and while I initially thought the trait made him unpredictable, I now knew it made him more straightforward than ever. Since Julia viewed me as a criminal worthy of death, Abner wouldn't risk associating with me.

The room's single clock, mounted to the wall above my bed, became my closest companion. I craned my neck to peer at it every so often. Before long, checking every half hour turned into checking every handful of minutes.

At an hour before midnight, my stomach churned, stress skittering within me. What time was Griff coming tonight? Without a panel or way to communicate, how would I know if he couldn't make it?

A siren interrupted my questions. A few breaths later, the power crackled before the room turned over to darkness.

The only immediate sound was my heartbeat. I lay still, unsure of what to do.

Was this Max's way of disabling the cameras—by turning off *all* power? And why was a siren blaring?

Without a window, this room was nearly as dark as the Hold. But as time crept forward at a painstaking rate, I waved my hand in front of my face and swore I saw blurred movement.

A shrill clinking sound came from the hall, and my blood went cold. Muttering bled through the door until the metal knob clattered onto the tile floor. Abner entered, holding a flickering candle. Flanking him was Griff—

The entire world washed away.

"Corinn." His voice was warmer than sunlight and sweeter than any rich delicacy the castle could offer.

Everything about Griff was priceless.

He rushed to my bedside, throwing his arms around me. I absorbed his breath, hot on my skin, and it was like I could finally *breathe* again.

He mumbled against my neck, whispering soft condolences and saccharine promises and my name all in the same breath, making up for lost time.

"Happy?" Abner groaned, scratching his head. "Bernard made a grave mistake choosing you, Corinn Januski. I guess it's good my son is dead, if only so *you* don't become the next queen."

I recoiled at the statement—out of shock, not regret. Out of anger on Cass's behalf.

Abner could say and think whatever he liked regarding *me*; I had Griff at my side, and that was what mattered.

Griff whirled toward Abner, and the king's free hand flew into the air, claiming innocence. His candle's flame flickered at the movement. "I'm *done,* Howard. Just had to get that off my chest." Abner focused on me, and fury burned on his face. "You have about an hour. Max let a few prisoners out of the Hold, which sent the castle into an automatic lockdown and power outage. Most of the castle's locks need electricity to open, so a lot of people are stuck where they are. Julia will be in the bedroom corridor until she can get her guards to wrangle the criminals back into the Hold and turn the power back on."

This drew my attention, even with Griff's steadfast presence. "Max let prisoners out of the Hold? Julia doesn't know *he* did it, right?"

"Of course not. Max wouldn't endanger himself just for this stupid ordeal of yours." Abner threw me another hostile expression, ensuring I sensed how brittle his patience was. "I'll be back for my Accolade winner soon."

The king stalked to the broken door, slamming it behind him, leaving Griff and me alone.

"I missed you so much," Griff breathed, pressing his lips to mine, a sweet surprise in the darkness. My senses lit up, forgetting all about the king's temper. "Are you all right? You're hurt, aren't you? Abner said you were."

I swallowed once, hard, and nodded before remembering he couldn't see the motion. "Yeah. Julia . . . has been burning my legs. With boiling water."

"*No.*" Griff's voice was a low, lethal rumble. He brushed my shoulder, careful not to entwine his arms with my IV and catheter lines. "I'll kill her. If she does *anything* to you—"

"*Griff.*" I set a stabilizing hand on his side. We didn't have time to waste. "Can you lay with me?"

He inhaled sharply. "Will I . . . hurt you?"

"No." I scooted to one side of the mattress. "You won't." My voice was thick, and I knew Griff sensed my emotions because he didn't argue. He fiddled with . . . "Are you taking your shoes off?"

"*Yes.* I have manners, you know." He crawled, rigid as metal, atop the white sheets.

I laughed. "So *Top-Tiered.*"

"Guilty as charged." He poked my side lightheartedly, then retracted. "Sorry. Did that hurt?"

"No. It's only my legs."

"All right." Griff shifted onto his side and draped an arm across my stomach, holding me as best he could.

The last time we'd delighted in each other's touch was in my room, in the wake of a storm. Back when Salem was alive, and I was paired with Griff, and Julia didn't want to kill me. After that day, Addison had taken Griff, and . . . everything went so *wrong*.

I sniffed, wiping my nose with my free arm.

Griff's head lifted. "Corinn." His thumb caressed my cheekbones, swiping at my tears. "Tell me everything."

I confided in him, in this finite fraction of time gifted to us.

"Things were going so well," I said, my voice scratching my raw throat. "You and I were paired, we were going to win together, Salem was here—" I broke into a sob. The shaking of my body sent blazing waves through my legs.

"He was the best of us," Griff said after a few minutes of letting me weather the emotions. "Julia announced it was asympton, but I'm willing to guess that was just a cover."

"It's my fault," I cried. "I d-did it. It's my f-fault."

I killed my best friend. *By the moon.* I killed him, I *killed him*—

"Lovely, look at me." Griff shifted so he lay next to me on his stomach, propping himself on his elbows. If only there was light in here . . . I needed the weight of his eyes. "I don't know what happened, but I know it *wasn't your fault.*"

"It *was*." I squeezed my eyes shut. And I told Griff everything, trying to keep my voice level.

I explained all of it. How I planned on sneaking into the barracks to meet Max. How Salem found me, and I let him come. How we were caught. How Salem looked in that hospital bed, pale and unmoving and so helpless.

Griff's thumb grazed the angle of my jaw. "Salem knew what he was getting into—"

"I never told him how dangerous it was," I croaked. "I didn't warn him of the guards' implants or the supercontinent . . ."

"No one is safe outside the walls," Griff insisted. "Everyone in Miota knows that. Maybe he didn't have all the information you and I do, but Salem knew what he was doing. *You* were worth the risk."

I hated this. Salem never should have risked his life for *me*. I'd give anything to bring him back. I couldn't live on this island, knowing Salem wasn't here walking on the same earth as me. Knowing he was a floating corpse, left to decompose in the ocean.

I almost vomited on Griff. "I'm not worth it," I said, my voice a thin screech. My attempts to remain calm were utterly failing as my head spun. "I'm not . . . I'm not—"

"Corinn." Griff's velvety voice enveloped me. "Listen to my voice, lovely. *Listen*," he drawled out the last word. "You're going to be all right. You are *not* the reason Salem is gone. Trust me, I've been there. I blamed myself for what happened to my dad for . . . entirely too long."

His father. How had I forgotten? "I'm so sorry," I managed to get out. "I—by the moon, Griff . . ."

He pressed a kiss to my jaw. "Don't apologize. For anything."

I sipped a breath, coaching my lungs to steady themselves. "How do you live with it?"

Griff blew out a breath before bowing his head. "It's not easy. It's been three years since Dad died, and it can still creep up on me. I wonder . . . what if I'd been strong enough to stop the guards, or what if I hadn't pestered him with so many illegal questions in the first place . . ." He sniffed. "But Dad made his own choices, just as Salem did. We'll live on, Corinn, because we have to. We can still find comfort in all the good this life has to offer."

I stilled at his sentiment. We lived on, not because we wanted to, but because we *had* to. Life wouldn't stop and wait for me to catch up. I'd have to learn to carry the added weight of Salem's memory.

"Besides," Griff said when I offered no response, "you can still feel the pull, can't you? The invisible tug on your heart when you think of him?"

"The grief?" I asked.

"The grief, the love, all of it. It's your connection to Salem, and it's still *real*. It's your proof that he isn't gone for good—some intangible part of him still exists. Not even *death* can ruin your friendship, and I find that kind of comforting."

I wiped under my eyes. "When I asked Max to get you here, I wasn't expecting you to make me cry the whole time."

Griff laughed lightly. "Not my intention. I just wanted to make sure you're doing all right first. I know we don't have long, and an hour isn't anywhere *near* enough time when I want an eternity with you . . ."

My insides fluttered. "You're one with words, Griff Howard."

"I'm just telling you the truth." He paused. "Do you think Julia will let you go? Is there any . . . *hope* for us?"

My heart squeezed. "I don't know. Sounds like you and Addison are winning Accolade, and I'm going on trial tomorrow, so . . ." I couldn't imagine a scenario where I'd end up with Griff—at least, not before he and Abner freed Miota.

"I'll refuse the crown," Griff said, his breath tickling my neck, "and go back to Salford. You'll be ruled innocent at your trial, and you'll go back to Pointe. We can . . . meet in the fields." His tone grew flat, unconvincing.

He'd reached the same conclusion I had. He needed to win Accolade for Miota's sake. And there was no way Julia would let me survive my trial.

But Max and I had a scheme, and Griff needed to know it.

"There's a plan," I whispered in the dark. Threads of hope, of light, swirled in my brain. "Tomorrow, at my trial, I'm going to plead guilty. I'm going to let Julia kill me."

CHAPTER

46

"What?" Griff released a shaky exhale. "Corinn, please. You can't—"

"Hear me out. I won't actually *die*." A heartbeat. "Hopefully."

"I never want to tell you what to do, but *please* think about what you're saying."

"She'll only *think* I'm dying. She's sentenced me to a trial. Think about it: what happens after I'm declared guilty?"

From where he lay, Griff's heart flitted wildly against my ribs. "You're sedated. Taken to the beach, killed, and thrown into the ocean. Keeps the castle *clean*." Sarcasm dripped off him.

I smiled and weaved a hand into Griff's tousled locks. He melted into the touch. "I've talked it out with Max. They'll put me under, and Max'll be on the beach. We've seen him work around the other guards before—he did it during our barracks tour. He'll take me to the tunnel in Pointe, and I'll stay there until we—*you*—can show Julia's true identity to the island."

But Griff didn't budge. "And if she kills you before the trial's over?"

"She can't. Trial laws."

"Bullshit." He sat up. And though he was right next to me, he felt a city away. "Lovely, I'm sorry, but Julia doesn't care about *trial laws* with you. You left the Fort—she wants you *dead*. She won't let you spill her secrets to her council during your trial and then send you off for someone else to kill. She'll do it herself, just like she did with Dad."

Griff's words punctured my skin, letting a chill settle into my bones. I wanted to brush him off, tell him he was being paranoid, but I couldn't. He was *right*.

Salem was gone because of my lack of tactical planning. My flimsy strategies had cost my best friend everything. I couldn't make the same mistake now.

Thank the moon for Griff Howard.

I shuddered, choking on this newfound reality. My trial would not be an interrogation; it would be an extermination.

Julia's going to kill me.

"What should I do?" I barely got the question out.

"Let's think through our options." My heart surged at Griff's phrasing: *our* options, like I was an integral part of him. "You have to plead guilty. Best case, she sedates you, and Max gets you back home."

That scenario was my best chance at helping Miota. From the safety of Pointe, deemed dead by the island, I could work with Bernard to conspire against the queen. We'd fight Julia from beyond her immediate domain while Griff and Abner worked from inside it.

"Other options?" Griff continued. "Julia or a guard shoots you during the trial."

"Maybe," I conceded. "But I doubt it." Abner's haunting voice resonated inside me. *If she wanted me dead, I'd already be dead.* I knew the queen killed with poison.

Julia had smelled of poison more than once before: the day we chose new partners on the castle veranda, and just days ago when I was in this room alongside Salem.

I voiced it to Griff, ruling in the possibility of being poisoned.

"You don't think a guard would shoot you?" Griff confirmed.

"In front of the executive council? I doubt it."

"Hmm. I wish *you* could bring a weapon, just in case. Do you have any . . . guns? Knives?"

His question percolated, and I gasped, *finally* realizing exactly where we were. The *hospital wing*. This was what I knew best. I'd gone to school and trained for this. And, with the cameras currently disabled, this was my only chance to gather supplies.

Victory—my waxing light—settled in my chest.

"I can do better than guns and knives. But you'll have to grab everything for me." I was still strapped to my lines, unable to leave the bed. "What do you know about scalpels, chemicals, and needles?"

Without a clock, I couldn't tell how long it took Griff to rifle through the cabinets. He'd found a pocket light early on—used for eye exams, I told him—so locating the items I'd asked for came quickly after that.

Griff relayed materials to me until I had everything secured under my shirt and in the waistband of my shorts. In the morning, before going to my trial, I'd only have to slip the needles into my pockets from where they currently sat, just under my mattress.

While Griff collected each item, I told him what it would be used for and in which possibilities I'd have to use it. We continued until we'd exhausted every plausible option.

I was prepared for my trial.

"You're a walking weapon," Griff laughed lightly as he wound his way back to the bed, where I sat up against my pillow.

I rolled my eyes, smiling.

"Don't worry, lovely. It suits you." His eyes stayed fixed on me as he sat on the bed with cautious movements. *This* was painful in its own way—wanting to be wrapped in Griff's touch, knowing I couldn't with the state of my legs.

"Let me look at you," I said, offering my palm to take the pocket light from Griff. After he left tonight, I wasn't sure the next time I'd see him. For all I knew, we wouldn't see each other again until the supercontinent was revealed and Miota was a changed world.

Griff gave me the light, and I cupped its beam in my hand, creating a soft glow to visualize his features. He sat with his legs hanging off the side of the bed, twisting his torso so he faced me.

It hadn't quite been a week since I'd seen him, yet he seemed *different*—heavier, weighted. Like he was silently carrying a world on his back, forced to bear it alone. He and I were similar in that way.

He collected stubble on his jaw, giving him a rough look, too wild for Castle Circle. His hair was disheveled, and he wore bags under his eyes like a crescent moon donning shadows.

I realized how strong my pull toward him was, tying my wandering soul to his. Griff was light. Freedom. Safety. And right now, he was *mine*.

"I don't want you to leave me," I whispered as I leaned forward to trace his jaw with my empty hand. I lingered, moving slowly, hoping it would somehow stretch out time itself. Because once Abner came and took Griff, he'd be gone. And it killed me not knowing how long I'd go without seeing his face, hearing his voice.

"No matter what happens," Griff said, his mouth moving under my touch, "I'll never stop wishing for you. On every star in the sky." He collected my hand to kiss the skin of each knuckle. Each peck sent a rush of adrenaline through me.

Then he slipped off the bed, kneeling at its side, and coaxed me to the edge. My legs hung off the mattress on either side of him. "Does this hurt you?" he murmured, eyes roaming my face for any sign of distress. He tilted his face toward me, like I was his beacon of moonlight.

"No." I trembled. "It's just my shins, really. A *few* spots above the knees, but . . . I'm good here."

Griff laced a hand through my hair. *"Good."* He brought his lips to mine and kissed me, moving with a slow and intentional grace.

I sighed against his mouth, and he drank in my breath. Griff wrapped his other arm around me and pressed my torso against his.

"Let me know," he said between kisses, "if anything hurts you."

"Okay," I breathed against his open mouth. I tangled my fingers in his hair, keeping his mouth steady against mine.

Griff's hand traced down my back, slowly roaming from my shoulder blades to the bend in my hips.

The supplies! a voice of reason echoed through me. I was kissing Griff while stockpiling vials and syringes and scalpels—all donning caps and covers, but still.

But Griff seemed to remember the medical supplies I was ridden with as he kissed me with revered caution. His hands, though deliberate, were delicate. He placed pressure only in the exact spots he intended, on the curves of my spine and slope of my waist.

I lost myself in Griff, not sure how anything in life could measure up to *this*. He was a child of the moon, a product of the cosmos, tasting like mint and stardust alike. He mumbled my name—*Corinn, lovely*—against my mouth and neck and hollow above my clavicle. I let out a rattling breath each time his lips departed from my skin. The electricity between us, rivaling that of the island's underground battery stores, could've brought the castle back to life.

Griff's voice washed over me. "Twenty years on this island, and every moment before I met you was . . ." He inhaled, planting more kisses below my ear. "Never *enough*."

I gave a husky laugh. My pulse skipped underneath Griff's lips. "Is this more of that poetic talk you promised me?"

"No, it's just the truth."

Nothing could smother my stupid grin. "Just kiss me."

His lips grew fervent. I lost all sense of time and space, and the greater part of me hoped he'd forced me out of reality and created a new space only for *us*. While his lips were fierce, his hands were tender, and his tongue was soft.

My legs were on fire, but so was every other part of me. I'd fallen victim to Griff's inferno, though his fire brought relief, not torture.

It was freeing and untamed. It was everything I'd ever wanted.

If the castle had power, my vitals monitor would be beeping wildly. My heart thumped against not only my rib cage, but against Griff's. Gingerly, he laid me onto my back and aligned himself on top of me—

I let out a sharp cry. Pain radiated wildly up my left leg.

"Lovely." Griff flew to his feet and examined my legs with the pocket light. "Are you all right?"

"I'm fine. I just bumped my shin." Underneath my bandages, it was like someone had ripped off my skin and poked at my fleshy leg with a stick. But I gritted my teeth, hoping it masked my pain.

"What can I do?" he asked, scanning the room.

I shook my head and shifted in bed. "Nothing, it's . . ." I seethed as I moved my legs. "It's fine, I promise. I survived the Hold; I'll be fine now."

Griff's eyes kept me glued to my spot. "Don't downplay this, Corinn. Are you all right?"

I swallowed. "I will be. Seriously. I'm learning to live with it."

A muscle jumped in Griff's cheek, obvious even in the dim light. He sat back on the bed, drawing near. The mattress dipped under his weight. "I don't think you understand how much I want to *hurt* Julia for doing this to you."

I smiled. "Well, please don't. *One* of us needs to stay on her good side, and I'm pretty much out of that picture." I sighed. "The sooner we expose the supercontinent, the sooner we can be together."

Griff nodded, drawing gentle circles on my shoulder. "Do you remember when I said you'd make a great queen? I take it back. You're too *good* for this place; this island doesn't deserve you." Was Griff purposefully targeting my internal thoughts, attempting to crush them all? "But they'll need a leader to take them to the supercontinent, and I can't wait to do that with you."

"I hope it happens soon," I said. "Where should we meet after tomorrow?" I almost broke at the thought. Griff and I would have to meet in secret, sacrificing our lives each time we met, just as Abner and Bernard did.

"Until I know exactly how Abner sneaks around, I'll probably have to keep my guard up. Julia's kept Addison and me busy lately."

I paused. "I'll tell Max to find you tomorrow, after he takes me to Pointe, so you know I made it home. After that, we'll probably have to recruit Abner's help with communication."

"That'll work." Griff's mouth bowed upward. "Though Max doesn't quite have the same effect that *you* do on me."

I tried quirking an eyebrow and failed. My heart tore in two; Salem could lift one eyebrow perfectly.

"And what effect is *that*, Mr. Howard?"

He lingered over where I lay, placing his arms on either side of my head, and dipped himself to speak against my neck, which sent a chill through me. "I think you know what, *Ms. Januski.*"

The door ruptured open, and a male voice shouted as a beam of light flooded the room.

"I expected as much," the king groaned, "but nothing quite prepares you for the sight of others' affection." Abner looked on with apathetic eyes. "Time to go. Power's turning back on in five."

CHAPTER 47

It was still a punch to the gut. I knew we only had a finite amount of time together, yet this was *agonizing*. We hadn't had enough. I needed one more minute, one more second. One more touch, one more kiss.

"We've got to go *now*," Abner reiterated. It took practice not to snap at him or break down entirely. I didn't want to live without Griff.

Griff steadied his gaze on me. "Be careful tomorrow, all right? I'll see you *soon*."

When he kissed me, it enveloped both a conclusion *and* a beginning. The Delldovas' reign was ending in mere days, and it would come with a procession into a new society.

"I'm leaving," Abner said, spinning on his heel.

I didn't need a mirror to know I wore a face of panic. I *had* to survive my trial tomorrow. For Miota, for Griff, for my future . . .

"Hey. I love you." Griff was set with anxiety, though filled out with hope. "You can do this. You can do *anything*, Corinn."

I nodded. My lungs betrayed me, unwilling to inflate and let me speak. I halfway sat with my mouth open as Griff stalked across the room, each step an obvious effort.

"I love you, too," I whimpered as he slipped through the crack of the door.

Did he hear? I hoped so.

I was on my own now.

I should've slept after that, but it was impossible. My future teetered, and I couldn't say for certain which way I'd fall. I was prepared to fight and weather any possibility, but I still lay awake, wondering what I could've done differently.

In Accolade. In life.

With Salem.

My current place—going on trial tomorrow—was the sum of all my actions. The stars led me this far; surely, they wouldn't fail me now.

Miota needed to be free of Julia Delldova. We were prisoners, and the Fort was our holding cell.

Tomorrow *needed* to work. I just had to evade death and make it home, because I knew everything afterward would work. Griff and Addison would win Accolade, and while the thought sliced at me, I wore the armor of assurance.

Griff was *mine*.

Griff would have immediate access to the crown. I'd have Bernard's ear. Abner would once again become my ally, no matter how he felt about it. Together—Griff, Bernard, Abner, and I—we could take down Julia. We owed it to everyone stuck on this man-made rock.

After tossing and turning for who knew how long, I fixed my syringes with the appropriate needles from under my sheets so Julia wouldn't know what I was doing if she watched through the room's camera, once again recording me, thanks to the castle's restored power. I kept the needles capped to evade pricking myself.

I peeked at the clock above me. I wasn't sure when trials

started, but I hoped mine came soon. I needed to know my outcome. Would I have a life trajectory past today?

By six, I grew impatient and dove under my blanket to down the vial Griff retrieved for me last night. If everything went according to plan, this substance would save my life.

Just before seven, Klemmins entered the room with Wesley, the burly, redheaded guard, and—

Max Reno.

Max was *here*. My insides went slick. He was supposed to be navigating around Julia, not escorting me *to* her.

Something had gone wrong—*very* wrong.

The two guards stared blankly at the wall while Klemmins targeted me. "Ready?" the doctor asked with a feral look in his eye. He approached to discontinue my IV.

I gulped. My body shook violently as I held out my arm. Klemmins detached me from the bed. Summoned me toward my trial.

I held my breath as I fumbled with my catheter, determined to remove the line myself. If Klemmins touched my clothes, he'd realize how many supplies I'd tucked against my skin.

Once I was free of lines, I stood, hoping to the moon and stars that the needles and scalpels tucked against me didn't clank to the floor.

The supplies stayed flush against my stomach.

"Let's go." Klemmins grinned. "I wish you the very best with what little time you have left."

Ice rinsed my bloodstream. What if Griff and I hadn't thought of every possibility? What if Julia still found a way to exploit what I knew and kill me for it? Max's plan was already collapsing in front of my face—he wasn't supposed to be here.

My vision blurred as we stepped into the hallway. My legs

were still tender, seething under my body's weight, but now that I was moving, I realized how stiff the joints were. My thighs quivered, the muscles already showing signs of atrophy.

I couldn't control my bumbling movements, as if my flesh had forgotten its connection to my brain. If I wasn't careful, a stray scalpel would rattle to the floor and reveal my stockpile of medical weapons.

But I couldn't stop *shaking*. I was walking to my death.

Max gripped one arm and Wesley the other. Each step I took felt like my undoing, one stitch at a time.

I was going to combust. My muscles rattled faster as we turned off the castle's main cavity of ruby carpet and onto an ashen, stone hallway, generously inset with windows.

Outside. I hadn't seen it in so long. The last time I saw sunlight would've been my last day in Castle Circle, the day Salem and I snuck out.

That would've also been the last light Salem saw. And he'd never see the sun's golden rays again.

Tears itched my face, but with my arms in a hold, I couldn't wipe them away.

Nerves ricocheted off every organ in my body. This was it. This was the time to fight for my *life*. Griff was out of my reach, Abner was no longer an ally, Julia wanted me dead, and Max . . . I couldn't count on him.

I was alone, solely holding the power to save myself.

Why are you here? I silently screamed at Max, hoping he miraculously heard my thoughts. Of course, it proved unsuccessful.

The courtroom sat at the end of the hall, behind two oak doors. My head inflated as we approached. I braced myself to face Their Majesties and the executive council, ready to judge me accordingly.

If nothing else, I'd get Julia's secrets out to her council. That would be a victory for Miota. No matter what else happened.

But the thought hardly eased me. I didn't want to die.

Klemmins opened the door to the courtroom, and cold air knocked into me. Our shuffling footsteps echoed on the floor as the guards ushered me inside.

Floor-to-ceiling windows bathed the entire space in bronze light. Long, unoccupied tables, which I assumed were for the council, lined one side of the room. I savored the silence while it lasted.

"Good morning." I recognized the queen's voice.

I whipped around and found Julia in a navy dress—the color of her country, her prison. She flaunted a dazzling smile, and my already dry mouth turned to cotton.

"Welcome to your trial, Corinn. Let us begin."

I blinked, noting the empty tables. Not even Abner was here yet. "Your Majesty, what about the executive council—"

"They are not coming," she replied. "You may stand in the middle of the room."

The council . . . wasn't coming. The council *always* came to trials. But they wouldn't be at mine.

Okay. *Breathe, Corinn.* Max's plan was still in play . . .

Or was it? Julia clearly knew he was no longer in the Hold. Had she let him out? How was Max going to escape this courtroom to save me on the beach after this?

I took my place in the center of the floor, standing on stone sculpted into the shape of a crown, which mocked me. *You belong to the monarchy. Your life always did, and today is no different.*

Julia sat at one of the spacious wooden tables, with Max and Wesley on either side of her. We were the only four in the room, since Klemmins left, and it was more daunting than having a pile of

Tops judging me. I tried shooting Max a discreet look of my internal panic, but he refused to meet my gaze.

"Are you looking at my guard?" Julia asked, amused. Her smile was genuine. "I know you and Max get along well. In fact, that was why I brought him here today—to show off his new personality. I thought it might entertain you."

My knees went numb. "What? Your Majesty, we aren't—"

"Max Reno," Julia called, still looking at me. "Turn around."

The guard obeyed, turning his back to us in mechanical movements.

I didn't know how to keep a straight face. Because Max Reno had a crusted incision trailing the length of his skull. His head had been shaved clean to his scalp.

He'd undergone his surgery. He was no longer a free man. Julia was inside his head at all times.

Which meant his plan was no longer valid; he couldn't save me.

The world darkened as I deduced what this meant. I was trapped in a room with two armed guards, whose minds were not their own, and the country's poisonous, wicked queen herself.

I was going to die.

CHAPTER 48

How I stood my ground, I didn't know. I should've collapsed, or maybe stuck one of my stowed scalpels into my flesh to save myself the torture of dying at Julia's hand. But somehow, amid my racing thoughts, I stood tall.

When was Max's surgery? How did Julia know I'd worked with him? Did she realize I knew of the cranial implants, then?

And where was the stupid executive council when I needed them?

I thought I'd known every possibility; I thought I'd read Julia completely. But who was *I* to compete with a queen?

I couldn't have outsmarted her. Fighting to change myself had been for nothing. Only Griff could save Miota now.

Julia laughed, of all things. It shook her shoulders and scrunched her face into a sneer. Though the sound was joyful, its venom crawled up my spine, where it collected at the base of my skull.

"You look petrified," she finally said.

I tried swallowing, but I couldn't. Not when the queen's emerald eyes fastened on me like I was nothing more than her prey.

"Yes," I admitted. My voice didn't bounce off the stone ground; I hadn't spoken loud enough.

"Then you must know this is the end." Julia lifted her chin as she studied me. "My rules are very simple: answer my questions or die."

I clasped my hands behind my back to hide how terribly they shook. "And if you don't like my answers?"

The trace of a smile left her face. "I control everything in this courtroom, Corinn. You are only alive right now because I have made it so. When you are no longer useful, you will die."

I chewed on my cheek and rolled over her stipulations. Once, twice.

How could I have forgotten? She still needed something from me. If I could evade giving concrete answers, maybe I could stall long enough to think of an escape plan.

Was it too risky to attack Julia outright?

"And what if I answer all your questions?" I asked.

Julia spoke with confidence. "I suppose there is only one way to know for certain—if you manage to survive that long."

A taunt. My arms and legs turned to water, and even my teeth chattered. There was no way out of this.

Without Max, I was truly alone. The best I could do was stall. So I nodded. *Ask away*.

Julia propped her elbows on the table. "How, *exactly*, did you make it to the tunnel entrance?"

My tongue felt like a pile of dirt. "We ran into it by accident, Your Majesty. We were on the grass, and the ground gave out from underneath us." The heat in my scorched throat was a relief against the deep fear ensnaring my bones.

Julia cocked her head. "Wonderful. And please tell me *why* you were in front of the castle's wall in the first place."

I'd been near the castle to find Max at the barracks and win back Abner's trust, but I couldn't say that. Max was *gone,* which meant the king was the only hope left—the only person who could help Griff free Miota.

Abner. Griff. Theo, Mom, Dad, Tellie, Grandma. All of Miota. I needed to help them. Every Miotan deserved better.

The thought was enough to sharpen my spirits. This was *not* the time to back down into submission, where Julia desperately wanted me. To her, I was a pesky Low-Tiered girl.

Yes, I *was* Low-Tiered. It was the status that had thrown me into the career of asympton research.

How could you forget, *Corinn Januski?* I recalled the concoction I slipped down my throat earlier. *It* was my protection, my savior.

Fibers of hope churned within me as I lifted my chin and rolled my shoulders back. I would weave my *own* future, starting today. I'd no longer hide in the shadows of what others thought I should be; I'd instead expand to what *I knew* I was capable of— someone able to help Miota, exactly as I was.

I was a Low. I was an asympton researcher. And I was going to throttle Julia's monarchy. I still had a few surprises in me, and they were going to save my life.

I would fight for myself. For Miota. And that was enough.

"I left Castle Circle with Salem." Strength returned to my voice. "I . . . wanted to see the castle. I never meant any harm."

Though it was a lie, a ragged note claimed my voice at the mention of Salem. I should've done things so differently for him. He'd still be here, if not for my selfishness.

"You risked your life," Julia said coolly, "to *see* the castle? You have been to it before. Why go in the middle of the night?"

She raised a rational point. I couldn't evade her questions like this; I needed to be *valuable.* It was the only way to prolong my life.

Julia wanted precious information from me, so I decided to throw her some, saying what first came to mind.

"I knew Cass."

Julia's jaw slackened, and even from my distance, I saw the ghosts flooding her vision. I'd seen that look in Pointe's hospital, just before one met death.

But more than Julia's shock, I noticed the thick fear in Max's eyes—eyes that should've been empty, a prisoner to his mind's trespasser.

I must've been imagining his terror.

"You . . . *knew* Cass?" Each syllable was an effort for her.

As I opened my mouth to answer—*Yes, I did*—Max flicked his head, a quick shake, while glaring at me with unrelenting heed. A warning.

"No," I said without thinking, my tongue deciding to listen to Max Reno. *What is happening?* "No, I didn't know him. I wanted to see if that would change anything, though."

Max's stature relaxed.

Was . . . was Max still sentient? Had Julia's talons truly penetrated his mind, or was he . . . still *here*?

I had to be delusional. I only *hoped* for Max's independence because we could then carry out our original escape plan.

But I saw the incision. Max's mind belonged to the queen.

"Yet you know my son's most intimate name." Julia tapped on the desk while her other hand plunged into her dress.

The poison. I'd smelled it before—the same toxic chemical we used in the asympton lab to clean after bodies were burned. It was in her pocket, and I needed it.

I nodded. "His Majesty said it once. I figured it was a nickname since his middle name was Cassius."

Julia frowned. "I do not believe you."

Next to her, Max tensed all over again.

I couldn't study the guard without Julia growing suspicious. So I darted my eyes between Julia and her guards, not letting my gaze linger on Max for more than a second.

"Your Most Royal Majesty," I said through an exhale. "Please. I *didn't* know your son. How could I have?"

Max slowly . . . *slowly* . . . nodded. Approving.

He was . . . free. Julia didn't control him.

"Is your plan still in place?" I asked, contriving every shard of self-control to stay on *Julia*. In my periphery, Max nodded again.

He understood my question. He was free. Yesterday, Max had said to trust him, no matter what. I could do that; I had to. I was going to save myself from Julia's grasp, and I'd trust Max to carry out the rest.

I continued speaking before Julia noticed my pause. "Do you truly plan to kill me, no matter what? Can I do *anything* to help my case, Your Majesty?"

Max is fine. He's here. He's going to help.

My odds of survival rose drastically.

"If you do not become useful *very quickly*," Julia gritted, "my guards will put bullets in your body." She tapped on her panel, and the guards raised their guns, pointing them at my chest. Max's gun lifted only slightly after Wesley's. "One in your head and one in your chest. How does that sound?"

The room turned red at the sight of Wesley's barrel staring me down. Even Max's weapon pinned on me made my knees wobble. He'd killed for Julia before, but he surely wouldn't do so now . . .

"Wait," I uttered. My heart seemed loud enough for the trio to hear across the stone room. "Please, Your Majesty. I have so much to tell you."

"I suggest you start talking, then," she snipped. "My patience is wearing *quite* thin."

Griff had been right. Julia wouldn't let me out of her sight until I was dead. She wouldn't sedate me here; she wanted to kill me herself and witness my demise.

I was going to let her.

I needed the poison from her dress's pocket; it was my only shot at survival now. Max could still get me out of here. His plan was still in play.

I just had to trust him. I could do that; I *had* to do that.

Julia wanted me to speak. Become useful.

It was now or never. I took the chance, saying what I knew would affect Julia most. If this didn't work . . .

If it didn't work, I wouldn't know, because I'd be dead within the minute.

Still, I didn't stutter when I spoke. "I know about the supercontinent and your deal with Red Fox. And I'll tell you why."

Max's gun wavered.

Julia turned inhuman. The monstrosities boiling within her poured onto her face in an expression brewed of rage and anguish. Her lips ripped apart in a snarl as she comprehended what I'd said.

While her mind was distracted, I wished to every single phase of the moon for my triumph. And I solidified my bravery. And I braced myself for the pain this would unleash on my legs.

And I hurtled toward the queen.

CHAPTER

49

My body severed its connection with my brain as I escaped all sense of logic. A single thought lived inside me, dictating my every move.

Go for her pockets.

Julia's eyes widened, and she stood from her seat as I neared.

My legs *screamed*. The inflamed skin couldn't take the quick movements and strong pressure.

But I *had* to do it. I had no choice—every other option had been exhausted. Obtaining her vial of poison was the only way to make it out of her court alive.

My eyes snagged on Julia's panel sitting idly on the table in front of her, and I outstretched an arm, pushing her device away. It flew a few feet from me, landing sharply on the stone floor. Wesley and Max still traced my actions with their guns, though they didn't shoot at me. Julia hadn't given them the command.

The queen turned on me with fire in her eyes. "What did you do?" She jumped toward her panel, and I took the opportunity to fling myself onto her, determined to get in her pockets. She proved stronger than I'd imagined, able to maneuver her body and enclose her arms around mine, pinning me into stillness from behind.

Her positioning gave her the human body's strength advantage—the muscles she used to hold me were stronger than the muscles I needed to break free. My vision already swam from the stress on my lower limbs.

So stop trying.

The meek thought slinked down to my arms. I was wasting energy in a lost battle.

I twisted one arm from Julia's clutches by slipping it down my body until I could bend my elbow. I fumbled to find Julia's pockets, feeling the vial weighing on her skirts.

"Shoot her!" Julia screamed at her guards. Though she couldn't mechanically control them without her panel, their minds still bent to her commands.

Or, rather, *Wesley's* did.

But neither guard shot as Julia and I struggled.

"Shoot her!" the queen repeated. "What is *wrong* with you?

"You're within the target area." Wesley's monotonous tone chilled me. "We can't guarantee your safety—"

Stay near her, I noted.

"I do not care!" Julia leaned her weight into me, forcing my hands to tuck into my sides. It ripped my empty grasp from Julia's pocket. *No!* I hadn't gripped the vial hard enough.

Once Julia realized what I was targeting, she shoved me. I tripped, falling on the stone floor. My legs *seared*. Lesser pain bloomed on my palms, and I knew I'd broken the skin. I was in no shape to continue.

But I was still alive, so I would fight. I couldn't separate from Julia. I needed her in the line of fire, *and* I needed her vial.

I stormed her again.

"Shoot—"

Too late. I toppled us both to the ground. My head pounded as my visual field darkened.

I screamed. Agony pulsed at my upper thigh. Sharp, cutting, *slicing*. A scalpel, once covered and strapped underneath the leg of my shorts, had come undone. Its blade carved into me before the medical weapon clattered to the ground.

A thin, red stream whittled its way down my leg, staining the bandages wrapped around my shins. I fell to my knees, still crying out. Julia sprang to her feet, standing at my head, and released her command once more. *"Shoot. Her. Now."*

A gun reverberated.

I lay on the stone floor. A bloody scream came from beside me. Was *I* screaming? Was I dead?

No. *Julia* cried out, collapsed on the floor.

The guards froze, falling silent. I chanced taking my eyes off them to observe the queen.

She'd been shot in the foot, an inch from my head.

This was a miracle, and those only came once in a lifetime. Maybe the stars were watching over me after all.

"W-what did I d-do?" Wesley shook, dropping his gun with an unsettling *crack*, and he stared at his unsteady hands. His own wailing rivaled Julia's irregular screams from where she writhed on the floor, kicking her foot in the air.

"Call for Klemmins!" the queen screamed.

I ignored the surrounding scene, ridden with damage and panic, and summoned my strength, channeling it into the task at hand. I sat up, blinking away the stars speckling my vision. Julia and Wesley—my two enemies in the room—were distracted by the repercussions of the guard's unfortunate aim. I stood, refusing to crumble, and pursued the screaming guard.

I bristled, breathing through gritted teeth. I could barely walk, and the sheer amount of pain surrounding me threatened to rob me of consciousness. My vision's perimeter went black. Red. Purple.

But I couldn't let it beat me. Not *now*. I was so close.

Hands shaking, I produced one of the armed syringes from the waistband of my shorts. When I neared Wesley, who still looked upon Julia with terror, I uncapped the needle and stuck his neck, since his uniform covered every other inch of his skin. A thick scarlet drop swelled at his neck, and within the next handful of seconds, he crumpled into a limp pile on the floor.

Julia still thrashed on the ground, and Max stood still as stone. It was Max and me against Julia, and those odds almost filled me with relief.

Almost.

I still had to die in front of the queen for this to work.

"Your Majesty," Max said. "Officer Ranke was aiming for the girl, and—"

"Max Reno!" the queen demanded, choking on spit. "Call for Klemmins *now*."

Max kept an unnervingly straight face as he picked up Julia's cracked panel, evidently still functioning.

Or it was a trick to stall for time.

This is your one chance, my determination sang from within me, summoning me to rise to the task at hand.

It was time to stage my death.

Even though I'd planned this, the moment slammed into me harder than expected. What if I'd miscalculated everything? What if someone other than Max dragged my body away once I was unconscious? What if Julia's vial contained a similar poison to that in Pointe's asympton lab, but this was something stronger, deadlier?

What if this truly killed me?

But this was my *single* opportunity.

I held my family's faces close in my mind. Even if my plan didn't work today, Griff would save them. He'd save *all* of Miota; I had faith in him.

I strode to Julia, who still screamed. My legs—blistered, bleeding, and raw—felt like how Julia sounded. Though I shook, I blew out a breath and plunged into her skirt's pocket, knowing exactly where the vial was this time.

Julia scratched at me with her fingernails, rupturing the skin on my forearms. My head swelled as the superficial pain added to all other agony.

As soon as I secured the vial, I clenched it and put a few feet of distance between us. "I am *done* with this," I spat, though my voice quaked. "I'm going to *keep* my secrets."

Please let this be right. Please, please, please . . .

My throat shut tight, rebelling against what I had to do. If I'd misjudged this step, I'd die for it. But I looked at Max, who wore a face of reassurance from where he watched behind the queen, and I knew this was the only way.

I was not done fighting Julia for good—only for today.

Before I could covertly turn to stick myself with needles, the oak doors burst open, and Klemmins appeared. Fear and confusion fought to control his expression as he surveyed the scene: Julia and me facing off, Max silently watching on, and Wesley lying unconscious.

Through my blotched vision, I witnessed Klemmins rush to Julia's side. He assessed her state, and with their attention turned away from me, I seized the fleeting moment to stick myself with the two needles still stuffed in my clothes. I eyed the vein on my forearm and injected them.

I worked against time as the sedative pounced onto me,

summoning the sensation I'd grown accustomed to in the last few days. I wouldn't feel anything from the other medication, but I knew it would slow my heart to a near stop. I only hoped it wouldn't cease my heart entirely after mixing with the sedative.

Max gave a knowing grin as I threw the syringes. Already, the tranquilizing effects slammed on my eyelids. I grappled with the fact I *had* to drink the poison before I went under. It gave me only about a five-second window, starting *now*.

My determination gave a final kick. It was time to be brave.

"Your Majesty," Max shouted, which set Julia's sights back on me. Even Klemmins watched from where he crouched beside Julia's foot. "She's going to—"

"No!" Julia shrieked.

Thank you, Max, thank you . . .

I raised the vial of poison clenched in my rigid fingers, and everything went numb—from fear or the sedative, I didn't know.

What if this wasn't right? What if I was making a huge mistake? I'd made so many wrong moves before. Was this just the last error in the string of my life?

No time to wonder. I'd find out . . . or I wouldn't.

"I'm done," I declared, my tongue barely working to produce any more sound. I locked eyes with the queen and wrung out every bit of power my arms could muster, aiming my last conscious movements toward bringing the vial to my lips.

This isn't right.

The smell was corrosive enough to make me vomit, nearly knocking me to my knees and spilling the poison. But I forced myself to drink. To swallow.

And once I did, the world combusted.

CHAPTER 50

Water rushed in my ears. Then receded.

My legs crumbled as I tried to move them. But I was stuck to my spot on the . . . ground?

Everything was dark. I fought to open my eyes, but I stayed blind, bound to darkness.

My heart recoiled in my chest. Where was I? I grazed the ground with my fingertips, and soft grains of dirt clumped in my palms. It was the loosest earth I'd ever felt, vastly different from the compact stuff Grandma preferred for our greenhouse.

"Corinn?" a voice called. "You're back. We've got to move. Open your eyes."

I pried my eyelids open with my fingers and found Max hovered above me.

"Get up," he said, taking hold of my arm in what felt like an ensnarement. "Come on, princess."

I flinched at the name. *"Princess?"* I was still groggy; was I hearing things?

Max's eyes danced. "That's what Cass called you. Since you were supposed to marry him and all. It started out facetious, but the name sort of stuck."

My skin crawled. "Well, don't call me that."

His throat bobbed as his mouth twitched upward. He was choking on a laugh. "I won't. This is goodbye." He leaned back, but his grip on me didn't relent.

Without Max in my vision's forefront, I noticed the cloudless blue yawning above me. The Fort rose, stretching upward to meet the sky. I sat up, ignoring the sting gnawing on my legs.

And my jaw hung. I knew this place. I'd been here once before with Salem, though it had been dark then.

We were on the beach.

I should've known from the salt on my tongue.

Glittering waves crashed against the shore. My eyes drifted outward, spanning the length of the ocean until it turned into blue sky on the horizon.

The horizon!

I felt it again—that deep, internal calling, waking a dormant shard of my soul. The feeling that there was something *more* out there. This was only the cusp of freedom.

I laughed. The sound swelled before drowning in the sea breeze—just as the waves ebbed and flowed, as the moon waxed and waned. The world was made of ethereal clockwork beyond Julia's reach.

My spirits diminished when I saw a large vessel in the water. Waves lapped against the rusting seacraft, partially submerged in the ocean.

I shuddered, remembering how cold the water had been that night with Salem. "What's that?" I pointed with my free hand.

"A boat," Max answered matter-of-factly. As if that explained *everything.* "Julia thinks you're dead, by the way."

My eyelids flew back as Max helped me stand on the shifting ground. "She does? The plan—it all worked, then?"

"It all worked," he confirmed in an echo, setting a hand on my shoulder as he led me along the beach.

The plan *worked,* and I had my asympton partners to thank for it. They'd told me about the synthetic chemical that coated the entire gastrointestinal tract upon consumption, making it impossible for any substance to penetrate the linings of the mouth, esophagus, and stomach. It created a temporary holding vessel, leaving one's body unaffected by their stomach's contents. Which reminded me . . .

I plunged my fingers into my mouth and retched purple bile, expelling the poison. Max leaned to avoid it, still keeping a protective hand on me.

"You could've faced the other way," he grumbled.

"Sorry." I spat into the dirt too many times to count as my stomach spasmed.

The remedy would slowly degrade over the next few days, which would cause dry mouth and fitful nausea. Eating and drinking would also prove pointless until the chemical layer decomposed further, but I was alive, and that was what mattered.

I'd see Griff again, and I'd see my family *soon*. My soul sang.

Once I finished heaving, Max guided me along the beach. We walked parallel to the Fort, toward whichever one of its doors led to Pointe.

"What about Julia's foot?" I wondered. "And how are you here? Did you actually have surgery?"

Each question elicited another.

Max grinned. "Julia's fine. She *will* be, anyway. The bullet hardly nicked her. She also told everyone she killed you in the courtroom—which is fine, since you're deemed dead either way."

I nodded. "As long as you tell Griff I'm alive." Griff knew I'd be announced dead and it would be fake, but I knew he'd still worry until Max delivered the news.

A pang thrummed through me when I thought about my family receiving word of my death, but I'd see them in the next few hours. The tunnel spanning the distance between here and Pointe would likely take an hour or so to walk, so I'd be home before sundown.

"Yeah, I'll tell him," Max said. "And to answer your other question, I *did* have surgery—quite a few days ago, actually. I was never sneaking around Julia; she let me out of the Hold so I could have the procedure, and after that, she believed she controlled me."

Anger flared in my chest. "So you lied to me—"

"I had to. I needed your fear in that courtroom to be real. Julia needed to see you hopeless—needed to know you didn't have some secret way out."

I rolled my eyes, though his explanation made sense.

"I have the same implant as every other guard; the only difference is mine's a sham. Its output is still hooked up to Julia's monitoring system, so everything *seems* normal on her end. She thinks I'm asleep in the barracks right now. And the input is similar, so I can still know what she wants me to do. I'll only have a delayed reaction, since everything is voluntary for me. But that should be the only hiccup to work around."

"Your implant is . . . *fake*? Did Klemmins tamper with it?"

"No one tampered with anything." Max veered slightly in his path. In my periphery, he gave me a sidelong glance. "It never worked in the first place. Red Fox sent Julia an implant that only *mimics* real signals—because some people there don't *want* me in Julia's control." His tone suggested there was more to the story.

"Why not?" I played his game, probing.

We descended the sloped shore, Max's hand still encircling my arm. He was taking us away from the Fort, toward the water. I blinked.

"*Max.* Why not?" I tried keeping my voice level, but dread prickled my scalp when he didn't answer.

Max was keeping secrets. And on Miota, every secret carried power.

Still, my dripping trepidation didn't turn into gushing *fear* until Max's hold on my arm tightened. His fingers dug into my skin, and no matter how I twisted, he kept me confined. With time, and against my every morsel of strength, he forced my arms behind my back, my wrists into metal chains.

I was trapped.

He walked me toward the boat as I fought, but I was no match. The vessel released a tangy stink into the air, causing my already upset stomach to curdle even further.

"Things are . . . more *complicated* than you know," Max said.

I shouted for him to let me go, looking for anyone to save me from the guard, but the beach was empty. I was such a *fool.* Had I unknowingly played into my demise?

Max was no different from anyone else. I was an instrument to him, just as Griff and I had been to Abner, and just as every citizen was to Julia.

Did human lives mean *anything* to anyone on this wretched piece of rock?

Two men, appearing around my age, emerged from the boat's top hatch and jumped into the shallow waves. They approached, disregarding my pitiful attempts to untether my wrists and wriggle from Max's hold.

"Max Reno?" the blond one asked.

Max nodded, shoving me toward the stranger made of bulky muscle and sharp angles. I tripped, falling into his arms.

"She'll need it intravenously," Max said. "Orally won't work right now."

What was *happening?*

"Let me go!" I shouted, attempting to kick my captor.

He didn't budge, standing as firm as the Fort as I flailed against him. He even had the nerve to *laugh*. "He was right," the man said with an amused lilt. "You have spirit."

"*Who* was right?" I choked out, still hopelessly wriggling.

The two men shared an unreadable glance with Max, who finally faced me again. "Corinn, you'll be safe with them, okay? We'll see you again—Miota will—as long as all goes to plan."

"What are you *talking* about?" Were either of these men Anzalone? Was this Max's intended result from the start?

Max swallowed. "They'll tell you everything soon. I promise." He spun on his heel and left.

He *left* me.

"*Max!*" I cried after him. "*Max Reno!*"

The dark-haired one—a mere *teenager*, I realized—tried holding my gaze with an expression I knew well from eighteen years in the Low Tier. He was pitying me.

My eyes traveled to his hand, where he held a hypodermic needle filled with rosy liquid. I screamed. Kicked. Tried biting. But I was no match for these men.

The needle pierced my neck, a concentrated sting. I kept fighting, even after I saw the blinding stars.

Until they faded. And I fell into the abyss.

CHAPTER 51

GRIFF

Piping hot water tumbled from the showerhead, sending thick clouds of steam through the bathroom. I took my time, using the scalding water as a distraction from reality.

Corinn was announced dead earlier today. I only hoped that meant her plan worked, that she'd faked her death and was safely in Pointe's tunnel network.

I held my breath deep in my chest each time my brain tried spinning out of control, which was a calming trick Lorenzo had taught me when Dad died.

Breathing in and out with measured holds. It was all I could resort to right now, because I didn't know if Corinn was *all right* . . .

I couldn't fixate on the possibility that she was truly gone. The idea alone carved through every layer of my flesh, stripping me to nothing.

She was everything. She made me feel *alive*, a sensation I'd chased since the day Dad died.

Everything I'd wanted in life, I found in Corinn. In the two short months of Accolade, she'd grown to take up so much space in my heart, she could've claimed it as her own. She was the one the stars made for me, the soul to match mine, as Dad would've put it.

The shower grew cold, a sign I'd stayed in for too long. I couldn't bring myself to care, though, when I didn't know for certain if Corinn was alive. I stopped the water and toweled off.

A harsh knock on my bedroom door ripped my thoughts back to reality. I gave a prolonged eye roll, wanting to deal with *anyone* but Addison right now. She was a frequent visitor, even with my best efforts to keep her away.

Our unfortunate partnership in Accolade meant we spent more time with each other than I'd ever wanted. We'd already been together all day, between preparing for our trial and conducting it. Our case had involved a woman from Cape who'd been on the streets after curfew.

The act was so trivial, and Julia had sent her to die for it. It hadn't mattered what anyone else in the room thought—not that the executive council held any real power in that courtroom. It was clear from the start they were only there for appearances. Most council members hadn't even paid attention. How had Dad treated these trials when he was alive and on Salford's portion of the council?

It was all so wicked, yet it was how life on Miota had always been: stay in line *exactly* as Julia wanted, or die for straying from the law. Her kingdom lived in black and white.

The knocking resumed, quicker and louder. I let out a groan and slipped into dark clothes before padding across the bathroom, leaving toe-shaped imprints on the floor behind me.

The bedroom air was a cold slap to the face. I didn't adjust in the time it took me to cross the room. I peered into the hallway, combing my brain for an excuse to make Addison leave.

But I faced Max Reno instead, and my stomach lurched into my mouth.

Corinn.

I whisked the door open. "Is she alive? Is she okay—"

"*Shh.*" Max widened his eyes and rushed into my room. By the time I shut the door, he was already pacing frantic laps, trying to speed up time itself.

"Is she all right?" I asked again.

Max met my eyes, stopping in his tracks. "Do you swear to win Accolade with Addison, no matter what?"

Terror knocked into me, and I leaned against my bed as my legs gave out. "*Where is she?*"

"It was Julia," Max insisted, raising his hands in innocence. "Not me."

"What was?" My throat went dry as timber catching fire. "*Is Corinn alive?*"

Max clamped his mouth shut, keeping his gaze trained on me. And then, "No. She's not."

I stopped breathing. Waited for Max to laugh and claim he was lying. And then I'd strangle him for joking about a life as precious as Corinn's.

But Max said nothing. His visage remained the same. Fearful. Contrite. Somber.

My stomach roiled. "*What?*" I must've heard Max wrong. Misunderstood him. "Corinn is *alive.* She's in the tunnels." I paused. "*You* helped her escape!" It was accusatory, and Max caught my tone, cocking his head.

It was the truth, though. If anything happened to Corinn, it was Max's fault.

"Julia killed Corinn during her trial," he said as levelly as possible. "I tried to save her, and I couldn't."

My lungs deflated, robbed of all air. This was not real. "You tried to save her," I growled, clenching my fists. Trying to contain this *rage*. "And you *couldn't*."

Max swallowed. "I'm sorry."

I laughed as tears fled my eyes. A storm boiled in my chest, and it would soon beg for escape.

Corinn. *Dead.*

"You're sure?" I knew it was a stupid question. But I still *hoped*.

I choked on that hope, blinding myself with the starlight I wished on each night. For Corinn.

I *always* wished for Corinn.

"Yes." Max was a whisper in the wind, a hazy shadow.

I bellowed.

Covered my face in my hands.

Raked my fingers through my hair.

Paced. Back and forth, forth and back.

Back and forth. Forth and back.

"Griff."

I raised my eyes to Max, who stood like a stone figure by my desk. He didn't watch me with pity, but guilt. *Good,* I thought. He *knew* his shortcoming, then. He'd been in the room with Corinn. He'd promised her safety. And he'd *failed* her.

I should've known better. I should've tried escaping with her last night during the power outage. Could she have made it out in her injured state? Could we have snuck around Julia's minions of guards?

I wasn't sure it would've worked, but maybe I should've *tried*. Because I *knew* this story, and it always ended the same: someone threatened Julia's rule, and she killed them.

I was *done* with it.

"Griff . . ." Max tried again, his voice a warning. "You and I are on the same side. We both want to free Miota. Don't lose sight of that."

Yes. Right. We were on the same side. Only, it didn't feel that way when Max had *been there* when Corinn died. He'd watched it happen and did *nothing* to stop it.

I kept my jaw taut to keep from crumbling further. Held my thumbs in my fists. Bottled my breath deep in my lungs. "Right," I rasped. "Until you get your implant. Then you'll be on Julia's side."

"I already *have* my implant." He removed his cap, revealing his shaved head and scar running the length of his skull. I stared, unable to process the implication. "It's fake. I'm on *your* side. You'll accept the crown, and you'll win Accolade with Addison. You have to, Griff, to free the island."

Right. The island's freedom. That was still the mission, even now. "I wouldn't give up the crown for anything," I forced myself to say, simmering into silence, hardly audible.

Max crossed his arms. "And you still have to play nice. With Julia. You can mourn Corinn in moderation, but if you take an ounce of it out on Julia—or pretend Corinn wasn't the one in the wrong—you're out. She won't hand you a crown."

Pretend Corinn wasn't in the wrong. That would be impossible.

I'd dreamt for weeks of winning Accolade with Corinn. The sound of our names being called alongside each other. The thrill of freeing Miota together. Spending my life with her, no matter what it brought.

I was always supposed to win Accolade; I'd wanted it more than anything. For Dad. But it wasn't supposed to happen like *this.* An irate blaze brewed under my skin, growing with each passing second.

"We can still navigate around Julia," Max pressed me. It took every effort not to scream at him to leave. "You just need to get through this week. Accept the crown. Mourn Corinn, sure, but still let Julia know you think she did the right thing—"

"She didn't!" I shouted, pulling my hair as I spun toward Max. "She *didn't* do the right thing! She killed Corinn! *By the moon*—" I gagged, ready to run to the toilet if necessary, but nothing came up my throat. Even my body was in denial.

"I know," Max sympathized. But his sorrow wasn't enough. Nothing would be enough unless he could rip apart the seams of time, going back to when Corinn was alive so he could save her. "Trust me. I *know*, Griff. Julia's the enemy here. We just need to appease her through the transition."

I squeezed my eyes shut. "Transition?"

"Of power." Max paused. "Until Julia gives her power to you and Addison, we're still walking on glass. She can do whatever she wants."

"She'll *always* do whatever she wants, whether she's the technical queen or not." I kicked my bedframe, needing an outlet for the eddying grief. Grief and *fury*—at Julia, Abner, Max. "Which means we need to take her down as soon as possible." *And be done with this.* I stared off, trying to keep my clutches on reality.

No amount of deep breathing would help.

"And we *will*," Max said. "Don't worry. Miota will sink." His eyes finally glowed with the same vengeance as mine, and his steel gaze forced me to control my rampant emotions.

I knew what I needed to do. I needed to blindside Julia, and that would only happen if I played her game. I hadn't given her a reason to suspect I knew anything Dad did, and I couldn't do so now. Not *yet*.

I'd accept her offer for the crown, and then I'd make her *pay* for killing Dad and Corinn.

I couldn't wait to bring her crashing to the ground. I couldn't wait to set her island on fire.

I'd play my part and become a puppet. *For now.*

Because once I held power, nothing could stop me from making Julia taste her own cruel, bitter poison.

And nothing could stop me from making her burn.

EPILOGUE

CORINN

Clear broth swam in the bowl in front of me. It wasn't appetizing, but I didn't care—I'd eat anything. I took another measured sip, careful not to swallow too quickly and upset the nausea already sitting like a rock in my stomach.

As I drank the bowl's liquid, I worked to remember how I got into this dim, musty room. Aside from the sporadic memories of the world swaying at an odd rhythm, the last thing I remembered was Max leaving me. Those two men sedating me.

I'd already tried leaving this bed, but plastic bonds encircling my ankles secured me to the frame. The shackles didn't chafe my burns, though. In fact, my legs sported fresh bandages.

This room, though messy and strewn with random belongings, gave no indication of where I was. My curiosity lashed out at the windowless, cream-colored walls and oak furniture littered with worn clothing and small trinkets.

My spoon thudded against the bottom of the porcelain bowl.

On cue, the room's plain door swung open, and a woman

entered, the same one who'd brought the first bowl of broth. Her curly, multicolored hair—blue and green and pink—sharply contrasted her close-fitting jumpsuit, dark as night. Her boots clomped against the floor as she extended another bowl toward me. Coils of steam rose from the dish.

"Keep eating," she urged. The single lamp in the room drew ominous shadows across her cheeks as she bared teeth. *A smile.*

"Thanks," I groaned, accepting the bowl. Pain seethed through my throat; I hadn't spoken since . . .

How long ago was I screaming at Max, begging him not to leave me?

I sipped the broth. It was hotter than the first bowl, and it scorched my throat as it traveled down my esophagus.

"Can I get you anything else, Corinn?" She spoke with an odd inflection, sharpening her vowels. But I brushed off the distraction and jumped at the question's opportunity.

"Who are you, and where am I?" I coughed. "And how do you know my name? What happened to me?"

Those questions barely scratched the surface. I buzzed, recalling all that had happened leading up to Max's betrayal.

It *had* been a betrayal, right?

The woman's brown eyes, set deep in her skull, crinkled. "I'm Lorella Anzalone, part of the leadership here in Red Fox."

My throat went bone dry. "Red Fox—as in, that's where we are?"

She nodded, giving a close-lipped smile. As if confirming my location in the world would comfort me.

My insides contorted. We were on the *supercontinent.*

"You're Anzalone," I realized aloud, causing Lorella's brow to lift. "You know Max Reno." Max had mentioned Anzalone's plan—this woman's plan. "And you . . . wanted to get me here?"

She blushed, leaning against the tall dresser. As she put her weight on the furniture, the spray of finger-sized figurines atop it rattled. "It wasn't *just* me. But, yes, our goal was to get you here."

And here I was. The supercontinent.

Did my family think I was dead? Did Griff? After the beach disaster, I didn't think I could count on Max telling Griff I was alive. What game was Max playing? I grabbed the insulated cup of water from the nearby nightstand and took small sips.

"Take me back," I said without thinking.

Lorella laughed lightly. "Back where? To that *island?*"

"Yes." I was supposed to help Griff free Miota. We had a *plan.* I'd survived my trial; it was supposed to be easy after that. But an ocean now lay between Griff and me. My heart squeezed. "We need to help them! Julia's—"

"We know, Corinn; we know everything. It's *you* who needs to be caught up." She threw me a pointed look from across the room. "Which'll happen once you finish eating. You need to regain your energy first."

I bit back a sneer. How was I supposed to trust these strangers? They'd kidnapped me. *With Max's help*, I remembered. "So . . . Max is working with Red Fox, then."

Lorella bit her lip. "He's working with *me* and my team, not with Red Fox."

I couldn't stifle my eye roll. I was so *tired* of cryptic answers. Wherever I went, everyone seemed to have a set of secrets; they were proving to be a valuable commodity. "Your team?" I asked, letting the disdain drip from my tone.

"Yes." Lorella shifted her weight. "A few of them are here now, actually, if you want to meet them."

"I'm not in the mood to meet people," I grumbled.

But Lorella laughed and headed for the door. "That's what you say *now.* Wait here." She closed the door behind her.

Because I have so much of a choice! I internally retorted, eyeing the bonds keeping me strapped to the bed.

In Lorella's absence, I scanned the room further, looking for a way to escape. There were two doors—the one Lorella had entered and left through, and a second one leading into a bathroom.

I had to go back to Miota. How was I supposed to help Griff from *here?* It was torture, knowing he was alive yet *so far* from me.

I'd wanted to be on the supercontinent more than anything; I'd wanted to taste freedom. But I'd wanted it with *Griff.* With my family. Miota wasn't free, and maybe my heart had stayed planted on the man-made island because I didn't feel untethered from it at all.

Lorella slipped back into the room. "Okay, I can't keep him out any longer—this *has* been his room."

My jaw worked to stay shut, and I gave Lorella another extravagant eye roll.

But then the visitor—this room's inhabitant—skirted in.

And everything froze. All the time in the world collapsed into this single moment.

This was a hallucination . . . or I was delusional.

Because *Cass*, the Prince of Miota, stood at the door with his hands jammed in his pockets, wearing a sheepish grin. "Corinn. You made it."

END OF BOOK ONE

THANK YOU FOR READING!

To my dear reader, thank you for taking a chance on this story and these characters. I hope you found magic in these pages.

As a self-published author, each and every review helps this book reach new readers. Please consider leaving a written review on Amazon, Goodreads, or social media.

And if you'd like to be the first to receive news on the remaining books in this trilogy, subscribe to my newsletter.

Thank you!

ACKNOWLEDGMENTS

Fourteen-year-old Brittany is in awe right now. I've written stories my whole life, but I never expected to be here, writing acknowledgments for an actual, *published* book. My gratitude is overflowing.

Thank you to my family, who has witnessed me write way too many stories but always supported me and my dreams. Thank you for encouraging me to keep going, even when it got hard. And thank you for raising me to have faith and trust in God.

Thank you to my husband, my best friend who supported this endeavor whole-heartedly from the get-go. You offered words of wisdom, a shoulder to cry on, a platform to celebrate and laugh with, and, yes, financial support.

Thank you to my amazing beta readers, who quite literally turned this story upside-down in the BEST way possible. This book wouldn't be a fraction of what it is today without your insights, help, and support. To Kiara, Alli, Marcella, R.J., Kimberly, Meredith, Teresa, Aly, Ashley, Julie, Sydney, Autumn, Michelle, Marissa, and my mom—you all deserve an abundance of credit for this book.

Thank you to my editor, Silvia Curry, and my proofreader,

Angela Knotts Morse. You two were not only incredible people to work with, but you hyped me up when I needed it most. You helped shape this story into its best and final version.

Thank you to my cover designer, Maria Spada, and my cartographer, Rachael Ward. You both outdid yourselves and created amazing art that really helped bring my book to life.

Thank you to my Instagram family! I remember starting up my writer account in November 2022 with no idea of what to expect. The support you've given me is unreal, and I cherish each and every one of you. Thank you for being my friend.

Lastly, I want to thank *you*, my dear reader. I know your list of books to read is long, and time is fleeting, so the fact that you took the time to read this story gives me chills. Corinn has learned a lot, but her story is far from over (sorry about that cliffhanger!), and I hope you found bits of yourself in her. Because you, too, can do anything you put your mind to. Thank you for trusting me to tell you a story; I hope I did it justice.

ABOUT THE AUTHOR

Brittany is a medical student by day, author/bookworm by night. She loves nothing more than curling up with a cup of coffee and a good book. Brittany loves going on walks, trying out new restaurants, and visiting all her local bookstores. She lives in the Midwest U.S. with her husband and two cats.

Brittany is active on Instagram daily, where she talks about publishing logistics, the books she's reading, and her love for fictional characters.